Niv Kaplan was born in Kibbutz Ayelet HaShahar in Northern Israel in 1959. After high school, Niv served three years in an IDF special-forces reconnaissance outfit and took an active part in forming the IDF's Alpine unit which he served in reserve duty. Niv received his BSc degree in Business Administration (Marketing) from Cal State University Northridge (CSUN) in 1992, spending nearly ten years in New York and Los Angeles. Niv has worked for 30 years in the Aerospace Industry and has written seven books so far, four of which have been published: *Disappearance*, *Tracks*, *Sea Raid*, and *Kibbutz, Unplugged*. Three books will be published soon by Austin Macauley: *The Hijacking*, *Whiteboy*, and *Sleepers*.

Dedicated to my grandchildren, Abigail, Aloni, Lianne, and Sofia.

Niv Kaplan

SLEEPERS

AUSTIN MACAULEY PUBLISHERS®

LONDON * CAMBRIDGE * NEW YORK * SHARJAH

A CIP catalogue record for this title is available from the British Library.

ISBN 9781035887644 (Paperback)
ISBN 9781035887651 (ePub e-book)

www.austinmacauley.com

First Published 2025
Austin Macauley Publishers Ltd®
1 Canada Square
Canary Wharf
London
E14 5AA

Prologue

July, 2018

The man drove his 2017 Model Rover to town, parked it in an underground garage, took the elevator two floors up to a small shopping center, and came out in front of a large church that stood out in the town square.

The sun peered between the clouds, illuminating the shop windows around the square, as small streams of water ran among the cobblestones from the summer shower. He waited a while, remaining at the entrance to the shopping center, watching the square carefully. Several people in light jackets passed in front of him, swaying on the slippery cobblestones. He waited a few more minutes, making sure he was not being followed, then lowered his gaze and headed for the church.

The church was mostly empty. A few people sat in the front rows, busy dealing with the Lord. No one paid any attention to him. He stood a while, adjusting to the darkness, as faint light illuminated the altar from several elongated rectangular windows at the sides of the tall structure, then took a seat at the very last row.

He felt around the seat next to him and found what he was looking for.

In the back of the seat, underneath, its metal strut had a slit with a small envelope jammed into it, which he carefully pulled free and quickly put in his pocket. He sat there a few more minutes just to make sure no one was watching, then got up quietly, left the church, went back to the garage, and drove out of town toward the prison.

When he reached the parking lot outside the fenced structure, he opened the brown envelope, took out a magnetic identity card, studied it a while, then walked to the gate, flashed it at the security guard, and was buzzed into the inner courtyard.

He teetered along the slippery walkway and finally entered a two-story white building with blue windowsills and headed for the visitor's window, where he showed the identity card again, signed his name in the visitor's log, was frisked, then went through a metal detector and was buzzed in.

Inside was cold and still, and the echo of their footsteps could be heard as he and his escort walked along the dimly lit corridor until they reached a barred door, which clicked open, and they entered a chamber with a glass partition on one side and two locked doors on the other. His escort produced a key to one of the doors, and he was let into a small room with two chairs and an empty table in between.

He removed his jacket and sat down to wait. It was time. He had gotten the signal.

In fifteen years at the Home Office, he had become a team leader, then a section leader, and now he is deputy chief. He received his Bachelor of Arts degree in Politics and International relations in 1996 from Westminster University in London, worked in Bristol for the Ministry of Defense procurement office for five years, and then went on to get his master's degree in International Relations and Security at Westminster, graduating with honors in 2003, joining the Border Force law enforcement command within the Home Office, dealing with smugglers and immigration enforcement.

No one suspected a thing.

He had cleared the government's rigorous security measures with ease. There was no reason to suspect him. He spoke fluent English with the right accent, had a British ID, a British name, a London residence, and above all, he had the right features: he was tall, had smooth white skin, black hair, and blue eyes.

When the prisoner came in a few minutes later, for a split second it seemed to him as if he was looking at himself in the mirror. Aside from the orange overalls, the prisoner looked like his twin brother. He was just as tall, with graying raven-black hair, blue eyes, white skin, thin lips, and a crooked nose, just like his. Even his creased forehead and wrinkles around his eyes seemed the same.

The man got up to shake the prisoner's hand, and they eyed one another curiously for a few seconds before they sat down.

"I am Agent Frost," the man said, "head of the special task force…"

"I know who you are," the prisoner interrupted in English with a slight accent. "No need for the introduction."

"That's good," the man said, studying the prisoner. "Six months from now, you will be moved to a different prison with better conditions."

The prisoner bowed his head.

"A week before you move, one of my men will visit you with all the details," the man informed him. "Meanwhile, if you keep behaving in the manner you have been behaving, we'll make sure and give your poems to a publisher like you've asked."

"That is mighty generous of you, Agent Frost," the prisoner said. "Have you had a chance to read any?"

"Yes, I've read a few, and I liked them, especially the one you named *Cause and Effect*."

"Yes, that one I take special pride in," the prisoner said, his accent becoming more noticeable. "I guess we have learned our lesson."

"You certainly have," the man said and got up from his chair. The prisoner stood up, and they shook hands, eyeing one another one last time, before the man called the guard and left the visitor's chamber, leaving the prisoner with a smile on his face.

Part One

Chapter One

The long-tail boat rattled and hummed as it cut across the mirror-like waters of the Andaman Sea.

Frosty stood at the bow, staring over the wooden boat's elongated front, which curved toward the cloudless sky. The Thai captain stood at the back, manning the engine with its long tail rod protruding into the water, pushing the boat along.

The seaman had a rugged appearance, his skin sun-stricken and windswept from being out at sea under the scorching sun every day. He wore a blue, red, and white ribbon around his head, matching the Thai flag; a similar ribbon danced at the bow of the boat, tied to its wooden nose.

Frosty's partner, Jemma Stone, stood next to him, her long red hair pulled into a ponytail, keeping it from blowing in the wind. They were posing as newlyweds embarking on their honeymoon after a wild wedding night in one of London's posh hotels. She was on his team, trained at MI5 in counterintelligence, and was chosen for the job by Harry Fleming himself. She was an inch shorter than Frosty, with a well-conditioned body and broad shoulders; she carried herself like a ballerina, erect, with the aura of a princess. Her high cheekbones and nose were sprinkled with freckles. Her lips were pressed together as she concentrated on their approach, glancing sideways at Frosty from time to time, smiling and occasionally kissing him on the lips, as newlyweds should.

She was ex-military intelligence, turned spook, once she completed her mandatory officer's service of four years. Harry Fleming had employed her in Saudi Arabia on several operations, where she proved to be cool under fire.

The boat passed by immense verdant cliffs protruding out of the water as it maneuvered toward a sheltered cove.

The pier appeared as the boat turned a bend along a natural gorge created by the surrounding cliffs, covered by tropical vegetation and palm trees. The captain steered the boat alongside a row of similar long-tail boats moored side by side along the pier.

Frosty took both backpacks, and he and Jemma hopped from their boat, across two more boats, before reaching solid ground. They climbed a flight of concrete steps and came out onto the pier.

The taxi was a pickup truck; the driver was dressed in a khaki outfit and was smiling broadly when Frosty gave him the directions he had been given to the resort, nodding his head knowingly as he threw the backpacks into the back and opened the door for them to climb in.

The ride cost 800 Baht, a mere 15 £.

It was a paved road at first, quite narrow as it weaved its way among small shops and houses nestled among the lush tropical scenery. Scooters swished by to and fro, passing them with three and even four people piled on one small bike—entire families, it seemed to Frosty. He thanked god for the air-conditioned cabin; the air outside was unbearably hot and humid.

They turned onto a dirt road and started climbing into a lush jungle, bumping over ruts and holes.

Frosty could see cabins, raised above the ground on wooden logs, scattered in the woods, and waterfalls gushing down a mountain further ahead. The sun almost completely disappeared overhead behind large ferns and leaves as the taxi pushed further into the jungle. Several kilometers ahead, past a series of steep inclines and drops, the beach revealed itself in all its glory as the bumpy road ended and they entered the resort.

Two Thai men greeted them and offered to take their backpacks, but they both declined and followed the men along a paved walkway that wound among more palm trees and lush vegetation, with a man-made waterfall and a small pond dotted with closed lotus flowers, to the reception area, which was an open hut with a high wooden roof. Several comfortable-looking sofas with low glass tables decorated the waiting area, where they were offered a seat and a cold, sweet drink that tasted like iced tea.

A woman dressed in a traditional purple outfit came by with the paperwork, kneeling in front of Frosty, smiling politely, her eyes slanting, her nose flattened between her ample cheeks and round face, explaining the various packages that were available, then showing him where to sign.

A few minutes later, they were escorted to their room on the far side of the lotus pond. It was a lovely, air-conditioned room with large windows on all sides, a shower that was part of the balcony outside, and a king-size bed fitted with a white net overhead.

They settled in. Frosty unpacked, took a shower, shaved, put on his swimming trunks, and waited while Jemma did the same. Then they went out to explore the premises, their white skin glistening under the bright sun.

He wondered if their man was really there.

They had been briefed and re-briefed, shown several photos of the same man, computer generated. Different looks: with a beard, without one; with a mustache; bald; with long hair; with sunglasses and without.

He was known as Maximilian Kruger, the product of a heinous scheme conceived by a group called "Sons of Jihad," which kidnapped babies from Western countries, brought them up in Lebanon, brainwashed and trained them, then sent them back to spy and do damage in their native countries.

Frosty and Jemma were part of a task force assembled not long after the "Sons of Jihad" scheme was discovered when its main compound in Beirut was infiltrated and destroyed by British, Israeli, and US forces.

The operation had remained entirely classified. No official report ever came out, but rumors circulated, and various details of the terrorist scheme were uncovered.

Frosty was a unit leader at MI6, working in Afghanistan, when he was rushed to Whitehall for an urgent meeting. They were briefed by Group Captain Harry Fleming himself, an ex-Tornado fighter pilot turned intelligence, who was among the few who had been involved in the original operation.

Israeli Commandos had freed three kids, age eleven, from homes in Beirut where Muslim families had been raising them—and not a minute too soon, as it was later learned that at age fourteen they were to be separated from one another as each trained for his or her specific mission.

But the joint operation in Beirut was only partially successful; the British SAS and US Navy Seals ran into trouble at the "Sons of Jihad" compound and had to fight their way out, losing several good men in the process.

They managed to destroy the compound but did not learn the exact details of the overall scheme: how many kids were kidnapped and trained? Their whereabouts at the time? How many were already sent away, and to where?

The Lebanese families hosting the kids knew very little, but investigators did learn a few things from two captives about the money trail, which revealed the financing pattern of the operation but did not lead to anyone's location.

A meticulous, top-priority international investigation had been launched by the US, the UK, Israel, and other NATO countries to try to uncover any active agents or sleeper agents ready to strike.

Group Captain Fleming, reporting directly to the defense minister, assembled a team of MI6 and MI5 personnel whose sole purpose was to flush out any such agents in the UK, collaborating with similar teams from the US, Israel and other European countries.

Adrian Frost, or Frosty, as he was known to all, in part due to his family name but mostly due to his cool demeanor under pressure, joined the SAS in 1987, roughly two years before the Russians retreated from Afghanistan. He served eight years, mostly in that region, before he was offered a job in Intelligence. Then he moved to MI6, became an operative, and was sent back to Afghanistan to keep an eye on the Taliban. He participated in various covert operations in the region before becoming a team leader. One such operation involved escorting a Taliban snitch, who had revealed some of the methods used by the regime of Islamic fundamentalists to keep the general population in line with their anti-modern ideology. Escorted from his house in Kabul, around roadblocks and random inspections, across the border to Pakistan, the snitch received refugee status in Islamabad, then was whisked away to the UK for further interrogation. The operation would have gone belly up if not for Frosty keeping a cool head. While making a wide berth around Jalalabad, they ran into a Taliban patrol, and rather than flee, or hide their captive, he decided on the spur of the moment to let the captive speak for the group, explaining to the Taliban commander that it was he who was guiding a group of journalists—the usual subterfuge—to various abandoned Russian strongholds.

Frosty was of average height, 5 foot 10 inches tall and average weight, with a wide build. He had a rugged, battle-worn face with a scar that ran from under his right ear toward the middle of his jaw, a reminder of grenade shrapnel he took while in the SAS, encountering an ambush on the border between Iraq and Kuwait in the weeks following Iraq's assault into Kuwait. He had sharp features, a straight nose over a newly grown mustache and wind-chapped lips, but his most distinct feature was his clear blue eyes, sunken under a long forehead etched with lines. His hair was fair, grown well past military length to give him a touristy look, and he walked with the movements of a cat, sleek and silent.

Frosty and Jemma first explored the greenish, elliptically shaped pool, with a small island in its middle, lush with tropical growth. One side of the pool had an opening toward the beach, while the other was a wooden deck with folding easy chairs, several people sprawled on them, sunbathing. None of them resembled their man, Max Kruger.

They continued toward the beach. A tropical bar was busy, with waiters in traditional Thai uniforms walking to and fro with cocktails and other drinks for the guests sprawled along the white, sandy beach with its green, clear waters and coconut trees providing some shade.

Walking about, they were startled by a loud popping sound and, looking up, saw a man high up on a palm tree cutting down branches and coconuts, all of which hit the ground with a bang.

They took towels from a bin marked "fresh towels," spotted two available easy chairs, and settled in them, scanning to their left and right but not identifying anyone even remotely resembling the person they were seeking.

Jemma signaled a waiter, who came over bowing with the palms of his hands clamped together. She ordered two Singha beers and settled on the chair, raising her hands behind her head, and exposing her smooth white underarms. She smiled at him, then remembered something and fished in her bag for suntan lotion, which she had him spread over her back and shoulders.

Then she did the same for him and whispered in his ear, "Don't forget we're married..." She was smiling.

He kissed her on the lips but kept his eyes wandering, watching for any reaction from bathers nearby. No one seemed to take an interest.

An hour later, they took a stroll around the resort, noting the two dining areas; one offered a Thai menu, the other European food. Further along from the dining huts was an activity center with scooters, ATVs and kayaks for rent. A fit-looking attendant wearing an Adidas sports outfit pointed out to them in a laminated notebook the various activities available, including rock climbing, scuba diving, and boat rides to nearby islands.

A short distance from the activity center, a few long-tail boats and speedboats anchored to a small pier stood rocking on the small waves.

Jemma walked out to the wooden pier and then to its end, looking out at the tall cliffs that enclosed the resort's secluded beach. She could see the entire resort from that angle, noticing the living quarters almost completely hidden from view within the vegetation behind the sandy white beach. She waved to Frosty and called him over. He approached reluctantly. When he reached her, she hugged and kissed him on the lips again.

"Relax and enjoy…" she whispered to him, but he remained rigid.

"I just hope we didn't come all this way for nothing…" he muttered.

"It won't be the first time…" she said.

They walked back to the dining hut and ordered a Thai lunch with a vegetarian egg roll, cashew nut chicken, egg noodles, and steamed rice.

Jemma ordered a banana shake and Frosty another beer. The man did not appear.

Chapter Two

They spent another hour on the beach, then went back to their room to shower and rest. Happy hour was at six at the beach bar, where they ordered two cocktails for the price of one. They sat there as the sun descended, and it got dark.

At the dinner buffet, Frosty found himself standing next to him.

He was waiting at the buffet for the chef to prepare his stir-fried vegetables when the man walked up and stood by his side. He was suddenly there with a plate full of vegetables, waiting his turn.

Frosty kept his eyes on the chef, but his pulse began racing. He turned his head and nodded to the man, taking a closer look as the chef emptied the contents of his steaming wok onto Frosty's plate. He walked away, stopping at a row of silver-topped containers; he opened each one, looking to see what was there: fried rice, sweet and sour pork, chicken curry, fried shrimp and noodles. He added some fried rice to his plate, then walked to a row of fruit platters and chose a few small pieces of watermelon, all the while keeping the man in sight.

The man was dressed in a blue silk shirt, gray designer shorts and brown moccasins. His black hair was cut short, and he had a mustache. On first observation, he looked like the man, but Frosty studied him carefully from the corner of his eye, looking to make sure. He was skinny and quite tall, his shoulders angling down, and he looked agile.

A woman came by, and the man gave her his plate, which she took over to a table not far from where Jemma was sitting.

Frosty noticed Jemma giving him a meaningful look, following the woman with her gaze. She apparently had noticed their target as well.

The woman was quite attractive, wearing a white blouse and a colorful sari that touched the sand. She had black hair done up in a bun and piercing black eyes.

She did not smile and seemed to be checking her flanks as well, her eyes roaming the dining hut.

The man picked out a few more food items on two different plates and walked across the sand to join his partner, who was nibbling at her food.

Frosty joined Jemma, taking a seat with a line of sight to their man, who was leaning over the table talking quietly to the woman as if trying to pacify her.

Frosty leaned over as if to kiss Jemma, whispering to her, "What do you think?"

Jemma smiled at him, kissed him, and whispered back, "It's got to be him…"

They began eating slowly, trying to camouflage their interest in the couple a few tables over.

A small hostess came by to inquire if everything was OK and to ask if they needed anything. They declined gracefully and kept watching.

All around them, guests were moving about, getting up for more food and drinks, getting new plates of goodies to eat. The air was hot and humid, and Frosty was thankful for the small fan attached to the shed's wooden frame above his head.

An hour later, the couple finally left. Jemma had positioned herself in advance at a dark corner toward the living quarters as soon as the couple had ordered two espressos and asked for the bill. Frosty remained at the table.

"Room 219," she informed him when they met in their room.

"OK. We take turns," he said. "We cannot let them out of our sights!"

"You take the first shift," he suggested. "Wake me when you've had enough."

"We can see their room from our balcony, I think," Jemma said and walked out through the shower.

Frosty followed her.

"It's right across… there, you see? There's their entrance."

Between the curtains, he got a glimpse of the man walking about in a hut below theirs, toward the beach and across a paved walkway that led from the lower row of huts to theirs.

Frosty and Jemma's hut was 318. "Lucky break for us," he marveled.

"I'll keep an eye on them. You get some sleep," Jemma said.

Frosty nodded and walked back into the air-conditioned room, leaving Jemma outside in the dark, sitting on a small swing on the balcony.

She woke him up at two in the morning with nothing to report.

At eight, he woke her up and left to follow the suspects, both of whom carried a backpack to the dining area, where they sat down to have breakfast.

He quickly ran back to the room. He and Jemma both filled their backpacks with essential items: wallets, hats and several bottles of water, and left their room.

Jemma went to the activity center, where she planned to rent a scooter bike just in case, while Frosty kept an eye on the dining hut.

A half hour later, the couple got up, walked toward the pier, and stood waiting as several other guests made their way to the pier and joined them, waiting to board a boat.

"Where's that boat off to?" Jemma nonchalantly asked the attendant, who sat behind a small wooden desk filling out forms for her rental scooter bike.

"To the main village," he said smiling.

"And can I rent a bike there?" she asked, all the while watching developments on the pier.

"Of course," he said. "One hundred and fifty baht, but it will cost you three hundred to take the boat."

"I think we will do that…" she said, urgently looking at the people filing onto the long-tail boat, Frosty looking at her expectantly from afar.

"No problem," the man said and whipped out a different form, which Jemma quickly signed, paid cash, and hurried toward the pier, where the last of the travelers had already boarded the boat.

To their relief, the attendant came rushing past them, signaling the two boat drivers, who were ready to push off from the pier, to wait.

They jumped in, ignoring curious looks, and settled at a vacant area at the front of the boat, looking forward as the boat took off, leaving a white wake in its path.

It was a gamble, which drew attention to them, but they could not afford to lose sight of their targets. They did not dare look back and busied themselves taking photos of the magnificent views of their island and adjacent ones with their small Canon camera.

It took twenty minutes to reach the pier at the main village, and as they filed out, they noticed their suspects approaching a scooter bike rental shop. Jemma identified a second shop across the street and headed over, Frosty in tow, keeping an eye out.

The shop sold everything from food to clothes to diving gear. Jemma pointed to a blue bike among a row of bikes that stood outside the shop, took out 150 baht, and was about to pay when Frosty whispered to her, "Better take two, just in case."

They bought a map of the island, put their helmets on, mounted their bikes, and waited to see what the couple was doing.

It was not long before the two took off on a single bike, the man in front, the woman clinging to him, and headed south toward the village center.

Frosty led the way, with Jemma right behind, keeping a fair distance from their prey, who so far seemed oblivious of their followers.

The narrow asphalt road wound among the lush tropical vegetation, with patches of sandy beaches popping into view every now and then, as Jemma and Frosty followed their targets.

They entered a small village as the road reached the shoreline. On one side were palm trees lazily dancing in the breeze, shading the white sand where a few massage huts were spread along the beach with signs and prices; here and there, bathers could be seen swimming or catching some sun. On the other side, they passed by a gas station, several bungalows offering accommodations, and a few food and clothing stores.

The couple on the bike in front of them seemed unaware of the surroundings as they sped along past the village and made a surprise turn onto a dirt road that wound up into hilly terrain covered by rainforest.

Frosty stopped at the turnoff and did not pursue, watching the bike disappear among the trees.

Jemma stopped next to him. They looked at one another. Frosty surveyed the dirt road leading into the trees and the main asphalt road that led from the village ahead of them.

"Let's park the bikes further along near the beach there," he finally said, pointing to a tract of beach not far away.

"Then we should explore the dirt road on foot."

Jemma looked at him from beneath her helmet. "It could be a long walk…" she pointed out.

"What choice do we have?" Frosty questioned. "If we ride in there, they'll hear us a mile away."

"You're probably right," Jemma said. "But we could be in for a long, hot march."

They parked their bikes next to a small hut facing the beach, offering ice cream, beer and tropical drinks. A heavyset Thai woman sat on an old swinging sofa, smiling at them.

"Want a drink?" she said in halting English. "Thai massage, oil massage, scuba diving?"

"No thanks," Jemma said, "Maybe later after we swim."

They left their bikes by the hut, each taking their backpack, and headed for the beach. They walked on the sand along a deserted beach for a few hundred meters, making sure the Thai woman had lost interest, then cut across to the main road, crossed it and headed back along the tree line toward the dirt road the couple had taken into the rain forest.

They tried walking next to the road, but it was difficult to penetrate the jungle with its huge palm leaves, tall trees, and ferns, so they decided to use the road cautiously.

They veered to the dirt road and walked along its path, ready to jump into the bushes if anyone approached.

The weather was stifling, and they were sweating profusely. It became a little easier when they reached a grove of gum trees with several elevated huts on stilts among rows of trees, but soon it was jungle again.

The trail reached a little creek and followed its path. Frosty and Jemma sprayed some water on themselves from their water bottles to cool off and continued. Two hours into their trek, they heard a vehicle coming in their direction and took cover in the bush.

It was the scooter bike with the man they were after and his partner, on their way back. The scooter followed the trail along the creek and disappeared among the trees.

"We continue," Frosty said. "We'll never catch them anyway, so we may as well try to find out where they went."

They made a few stops along the creek to drink water and recuperate from the blistering heat; two hours later, the trail abruptly ended. Exhausted from the demanding trek, they took refuge underneath some large palm leaves in the tropical bush and surveyed a clearing, where four elevated huts stood facing one another, two on each side. A white Toyota pickup, smeared with mud, was parked next to an ATV and two scooter bikes, and they could see some laundry hanging on a rope stretched between the huts, but no people.

From their vantage point in the bushes, they watched for any activity. Frosty took out the Cannon, attached a magnifying lens, and they waited.

An hour later, two Thai men came out of one of the huts, boarded the ATV, and took off along the trail back toward the main road and the village. Frosty had their photos.

Two more men came out, and Frosty clicked his camera, taking several photos in quick succession. They were not Thai. Both were dressed in army fatigues and had dark black hair—one with a mustache and the other with a beard. They stood next to the pickup and were deep in conversation. After a few minutes, the bearded one walked over to one of the huts and knocked on the door. He stood waiting until a group of three men and a woman appeared and descended the stairs to join their two comrades. None of them looked Thai. The woman had long black hair and was also dressed in army fatigues, as were the rest of them.

Two were bald with beards, and the odd man out was relatively tall, with long brown hair, sunglasses and a somewhat suave European look.

Frosty had their faces photographed within seconds.

He looked over at Jemma, who was watching closely. Seeing these foreign characters in military fatigues in the middle of the Thai bush was odd, but not surprising, considering who they were after. They tried to pick up the language, but they were too far away to make out any words being spoken.

One of the bearded men went over to the pickup and took out a medium-sized trolley from the cabin. He laid it on the ground, and the group gathered around to inspect it. It took a while, but when they finally pulled it out, both Jemma and Frosty skipped a heartbeat, for what they saw looked like a bomb mechanism of some sort—sticks of dynamite wrapped around a detonating device.

The two bald, bearded men took hold of the bomb, and the group made its way beyond the huts, disappearing into the bushes. A few minutes later, they were hurrying back, taking refuge behind one of the huts as a muffled explosion rocked the surroundings.

Frosty and Jemma looked at one another urgently.

"We better get back," he said to her, and she nodded in agreement.

They watched the group return to the huts, then they backtracked along the creek. It took them almost four hours to get back to their bikes; by then, it was close to dark. The Thai lady was still there, rocking on her sofa as they mounted their scooter bikes and rode away.

When they got back to the pier, they learned that the last boat back to their resort had left an hour earlier. Exhausted from their long day, they decided to rent a bungalow in the village and spend the night.

Chapter Three

They kept the bikes and rode back to the village to seek accommodations, finding an available bungalow with air conditioning not far from the turnoff to the dirt road they had spent their day trekking.

They bought a few items to make sandwiches at a nearby food store and hurried to their room. Frosty downloaded the photos from the digital camera to a secure file on the militarized laptop computer he had in his backpack, marking it urgent and including a short report to MI6 headquarters in London.

Jemma prepared the sandwiches—cheese and tomatoes—and they ate hungrily. She then took her clothes off and disappeared into the shower, wearing only her bathing suit. When she came out, she spread out on the bed in a tiny slip and bra and looked at Frosty expectantly.

"They got the file," he informed her. "They are checking it now."

"We need backup," she said.

"Let's wait and see what they find out. I am sure they won't take this lightly," he said, then went into the shower. When he came out, she was asleep, her arms over her head, the covers thrown to the side. He crawled in next to her and was asleep within minutes.

At two in the morning, they both woke up as the laptop came to life.

"The backup team is on its way," they read. "ETA 24 hours. Do not go near! Keep tabs from a distance. One identified suspect."

A photo of the European-looking man appeared alongside several identical photos with and without sunglasses.

"Gustav Hoch, a former East German Arms dealer…" The rest were unidentified.

Jemma and Frosty looked at one another.

"We better get there bright and early," Jemma said, and Frosty nodded.

They slept until five, got up, packed their backpacks, and headed for their bikes. They reached the turnoff and parked as close to it as they could, hiding their bikes behind some bushes by the side of the road. They split up, Jemma covering the main road from the south and Frosty the approach route from the north.

They did not have to wait long. At six-thirty, the Toyota pickup truck emerged from the dirt road, spraying dust as it turned onto the main road north toward the village. Frosty, who was closer to the hidden bikes, jumped on his first and took off after the speeding pickup.

It drove past the sleepy village and turned east toward the water along the narrow street, heading for the pier, where it stopped and parked facing it.

Frosty stopped several storefronts behind, taking refuge behind a rack with coconuts swinging from it, Jemma joining him a minute later.

They stood watching the truck, which showed signs of life only when the rattily long-tail boat from their resort approached. One of the bald guys stepped out, holding a trolley similar to the one they had seen being taken out of the truck with a bomb the day before.

He stood there waiting as the travelers from the resort began filing out of the boat. The man, carrying a duffel bag on one shoulder, and his woman partner, dragging a trolley of her own, came out last, looked around, and proceeded toward where the bald man had stood. He had left the trolley next to a deserted gift shop and jumped back in the truck.

The man walked by nonchalantly, grabbed the trolley by its handle as if it was his own, and the two of them backtracked toward the pier, where a group of travelers waited, apparently for another boat.

"We need to find out what they're waiting for," Frosty whispered to Jemma. "Wait here," he said and began to move. But she pulled him by the arm and motioned for him to stay put. She put on a headcover—a piece of cloth she grabbed hanging on a rack in front of a gift shop next to the coconuts—and walked toward the pier.

Trying not to make eye contact with her targets, she approached a small group of backpackers who were sitting on the concrete smoking and inquired as to their destination.

It was Krabi Airport.

They were waiting for a ferry that would take them to the mainland and, from there, a bus to the airport. She hurried back to Frosty.

"We have fifteen minutes to decide!" she said, delivering the grim news.

"Assuming they do not intend to blow up the ferry," Frosty said.

27

"We need to get on it regardless!" Jemma insisted. "We'll inform the Thai police at the airport."

They left their bikes behind the coconut rack with 300 baht under the seat to pay for the extra day and followed the crowd as it boarded a small speedboat, keeping as far away as possible from their targets, who boarded first and took seats at the front of the boat. Having no prepaid tickets, they stuffed a wad of bills in the skipper's hand, saying they needed to get to the mainland urgently, and he allowed them through.

Jemma, her head covered, sat opposite Frosty, who managed to snatch a baseball-type hat from the front of the gift shop, leaving a 50-baht note on the deserted counter for the hat and the scarf Jemma had grabbed before. The trolley nestled between the two suspects as if it were ordinary luggage. The engines came to life, and the speedboat moved away from the pier and sped away.

The sun had only just begun to lift over the horizon, illuminating the Krabi cliffs in the distance and the mirror-like surface of the Andaman Sea. Frosty watched the trolley from the corner of his eye, imagining what it contained and what it could do to the boat and its human cargo if there was a bomb in it and it detonated.

He looked at Jemma, who was carefully watching from beneath her scarf. The couple at the front seemed oblivious, talking and taking photos of the scenery as the boat powered ahead.

They reached a crowded pier on the mainland and boarded a blue bus, which had a sign in English declaring its destination as the airport. The couple boarded the bus with their two trolleys and duffel bag and walked to the back, while Frosty and Jemma remained at the front.

It was an hour before they could see signs to the airport. By then, both agents were exhausted from keeping themselves in check while fighting the urge to end the nightmare right there and then. The closer they got to the airport, the more crowded the roads became; in Krabi, they even encountered a traffic jam.

The bus finally stopped at the terminal, a long one-story building that served both arrivals and departures. They got off the bus and entered the departure hall in front of their suspects. There was only one flight that morning, Thai Air to Bangkok. The couple behind them approached the check-in line and got in the queue.

Frosty and Jemma found a coffee stand by the arrivals entrance, ordered coffee and stood watching the check-in line as a Thai Air Boeing 737 jet appeared. They watched it through the large windows that had a view of the airfield, approaching its gate, and stopping.

The check-in line moved slowly.

Frosty looked around for police presence. A lone policeman sat on a stool by the Customs Office. "Keep watch," he said to Jemma, nodding toward the policeman, "I'll call in the troops."

He walked over to the policeman, took out his British Government employee ID card—used only in extreme emergencies—introduced himself, and asked to see the officer in charge. The Thai policeman barely understood what he was being asked. He looked him over, confused, and asked in lame English the reason Frosty wanted to see his boss.

"I have reason to believe someone is attempting to load a bomb onto this plane," he said, pointing to the jet that had just arrived.

The policeman looked dumbfounded. "A bomb?" he repeated.

Frosty nodded, trying to keep from exclaiming, looking back at the check-in line, and seeing the suspects inching closer to the counter. "I need to see your boss now!" He whispered.

The policeman was at a loss. He looked at the ID card in Frosty's hand, trying to make up his mind when a second policeman appeared. He called him over urgently, speaking Thai, showing him the ID card.

The second policeman took one look at the card and took off behind a concrete partition barred by a steel door that opened when he passed a magnetic card through a decoder, which looked quite out of place in the terminal's bamboo structure.

Jemma was watching closely as passengers from the incoming flight started filing into the arrivals hall; their suspects were by now at the counter, checking in the two trolleys and duffel bag in their possession and taking their boarding passes.

The officer in charge appeared with several policemen in tow just as the couple turned to leave the counter. It took a split second before they realized what was going on, but by then, it was too late.

Then all hell broke loose.

Frosty hurried across to block the terminal exit, pointing the couple out to the officer. The two froze for a second, then tried to flee toward the arrivals hall among the incoming passengers. The passengers stopped in their tracks, confused by the sudden shouting as the police spread around the terminal, zeroing in on their suspects. Then, as police personnel drew their weapons and lunged toward the fleeing couple, the crowd dispersed in all directions, running for the exits along the terminal walls and ducking behind any objects that provided cover.

The couple pushed their way through the panicked crowd, aiming for the open corridor that led to the airplane, but the policemen ran them down, cornering them near the gateway. They threw them down on the floor and cuffed them as passengers, trying to escape the scene, fought their way out of the narrow terminal exits.

Chapter Four

Old Harry Fleming himself walked through the large glass doors of the Royal Meridian Hotel in Bangkok into the posh lobby, the Thai attendant bowing and holding the glass doors open for him. His thin, fair hair was parted to one side; his weariness stretched his thin gray skin over his cheekbones, but his blue eyes were focused and intense. He was dressed casually in gray slacks and a white, short-sleeved shirt, carrying a brown briefcase and a trolley not too different from the one that had been used to hold the bomb that was intended to decimate the Thai Air jet in Krabi.

Frosty and Jemma greeted him and led the way to the elevator, which took them to the executive lounge on the 39th floor, where they settled into a corner sofa and ordered drinks.

"They'll allow us to interrogate them," he began without preamble, "but they will try them here. They'll probably get a death sentence."

Frosty and Jemma watched him as he took a sip from his Singha beer.

"They'll give us a few days while they prepare the paperwork for the indictment, but that is all. There is a media frenzy surrounding the event, and they want to make an example."

"So, when do we get to see them?" Jemma asked.

"Tomorrow, bright and early," Fleming said. "An embassy car will take us there. Do I have a room here? It's been a long trip."

Jemma handed him a card key. "Room 3408," she said, "with full use of this lounge, and there's a pool with a bar outside these doors," she said, pointing to where they had entered. "There's also a gym with a great view on the floor below."

Fleming looked exhausted. He had flown all night direct from Heathrow, had met Jemma and Frosty at the Bangkok Airport for a quick brief, then had gone straight to police headquarters to try to talk the Thais into letting him have the prisoners - a request he was almost certain would fall on deaf ears.

31

"Right, then," he said, gulping down the rest of his beer. "I'll be off. Meet you two for dinner at seven?"

They both nodded and got up as he took his leave.

*****

The police interrogation unit in Bangkok was a large concrete building in the Sukhumvit district not far from the hotel, but it took almost an hour to get there with the morning traffic.

Several TV crews were milling about the entrance as the black embassy car parked among a row of police cars, the driver remaining behind the wheel as they were escorted inside the building to the holding cells.

It was a sight Jemma would never forget.

The prisoners were jammed into their cells by the hundreds. Drug traffickers, thieves, sex offenders, and murderers all sat crammed on the concrete floors behind steel bars, awaiting their day in court. It reeked of sweat and bodily secretions.

They were led into an office of sorts, a secluded area with a table and a few chairs, and were asked to wait.

The two prisoners were brought in heavily chained. They looked nothing like the happy-go-lucky couple at the resort. The man had a black eye and was bleeding from the mouth. The woman's face was ashen, and her eyes were swollen. They were still in their own clothes that, by now, barely hung on their bodies. The chains were attached to their feet and arms as they shuffled along.

The Thai interrogator was barking orders that the prisoners could not understand, so he had his uniformed subordinates drag them by the chains and push them to the floor, nodding at Harry that he could begin.

"I have absolutely no authority here," Fleming began, addressing the two on the floor, "but I can assure you that if you cooperate, we will try to extradite you to England, where you will be treated with a little more dignity."

The two prisoners looked at him as if he had just landed from Mars.

"Do you belong to the 'Sons of Jihad' organization?" He finally asked, taking the direct, no-bullshit route, after seeing that his opening statement, which was a bald-faced lie, did not induce any reply.

The prisoners straightened their gaze at him a little but did not speak.

"I think we should interrogate them separately," he said to the Thai officer in the room. "This will not yield any results."

The officer nodded. "Which of them do you want first?" he asked.

"I'd like Jemma here to interrogate the lady while we deal with him," he said, pointing at the man on the floor.

The officer barked some orders, and the woman was lifted by her chains and dragged out of the room to an adjacent holding cell. Jemma followed.

"We know you were raised in Beirut and trained as a spy," Fleming continued when the others were gone. "What is your name?"

The man looked up at him and blurted out something that sounded like German.

Both Fleming and Frosty understood.

"Calling us 'American puppets' won't get you out of here," Fleming said, surprising the man.

"Nothing will," the man said, sounding desperate. "They will kill me!"

"Who sent you to blow up the plane?" The man remained silent.

"Is your name Kruger?" Fleming asked, just to be certain. "It said so in your passport."

There was a momentary flash in the man's eyes, but it died instantly.

"Did you know you were kidnapped as a baby?"

The man looked confused.

"You were taken from your family by force from Germany and raised in Beirut. You are not Lebanese. Where do you live now?"

"I come from Munich," the man whispered, causing Frosty to jerk forward in surprise, never expecting to hear a thing from the terrorist.

Fleming kept his cool.

"Then that is where you were taken from," he said. "They returned you to where you were born."

The prisoner looked around the room, cringing at his Thai captors, who stood threateningly by.

"Will you get me out of here?" he said in English with a heavy German accent.

"I will try, but only if you answer my first question: Do you belong to the 'Sons of Jihad' organization?"

The prisoner appeared to be contemplating the odds as he looked around at his captors like a frightened dog, avoiding eye contact with the officer in charge.

Then he nodded.

*****

"We need to see the Prime Minister," Fleming was saying to the ambassador when they convened in his office a few hours later.

"This guy could be the key to an entire network we've been after for over two years. We must get him away from here so we can interrogate him properly."

"That'll be a very tough task, if not impossible," the ambassador noted.

"He's worth a lot more alive than dead," Fleming pointed out.

"The Thais are an extremely patient lot, but when their patience runs out, they tend to hold a grudge and can become very cruel," the ambassador explained. "I would not put high odds on getting him out of here, but I'll ask for an urgent interview."

For the next hour, Fleming briefed the ambassador on "Sons of Jihad" and their atrocious scheme of kidnapping babies from Western countries, brainwashing them, and training them to go back to their native countries to cause harm.

"An affiliate group spent ten years tracking a kid who was kidnapped from LA when he was a year old, when, by incredible coincidence, they uncovered the scheme, which no one knew about. We tracked down the headquarters to Beirut and raided the place. They put up a fight, and the place was destroyed before we could get our hands on the list of agents, we believed had already been deployed. We have been after them ever since, and this guy is the first live body we have managed to find."

The ambassador nodded his head heavily. Fleming continued.

"If this guy talks, which I believe he will, we could bring down the entire network. The Thais have been beating him senseless ever since they caught him, and by now he'll do anything to get away from them," Fleming reasoned, pressing his point.

"What about the woman?" The ambassador asked.

"Both their passports had their genuine identities," Fleming informed him. "The woman's name is Taahirah Darwish. She admitted to Jemma that she was from Beirut, but not much else. Apparently, the women at the holding unit are treated a little less brutally, and she opted to hold out, but I am not sure she expects her partner to bail out on her. She's expendable. Let them make an example out of her."

*****

A week later, Max Kruger was escorted to a British Airways flight to Heathrow by an entourage of Thai police personnel, who handcuffed him to a middle seat in the back of the plane and handed over the paperwork to Frosty and Jemma, who flanked him on both sides, with a second team of two armed undercover agents sitting nearby.

The flight took twelve hours. Kruger slept most of the way, too exhausted even to relieve himself after his treatment at the Bangkok holding cells.

At Heathrow Terminal 4, he was whisked away by an armored police vehicle to MI6 headquarters in Central London.

And so began a race against the clock, or so they thought…

Chapter Five

Jemma and Frosty listened intently as the prisoner told his story. Maximilian (or Max) Kruger could not recall the early days, but he remembered an intense childhood from about the age of four in a suburb of Beirut. Growing up, he and his buddies always had to be on alert for air raids, random shootings and sirens, sometimes spending weeks in shelters or hidden away in their parents' houses. He never really understood why he had to travel all the way to the center of Beirut for school, considering all the hazards involved with traveling in such a battle-riddled city, but he never really questioned studying about guns and bombs, since that was part of their everyday reality.

Back then, he was called Kareem, and he had two older sisters, who went to a school near their home.

He vividly recalled when he was separated from his family at age fourteen and sent to Damascus, Syria, where he joined a "Freedom Fighters" training camp; there, he received his indoctrination into the world of clandestine operations.

Two years later, they sent him to a private school in Munich, where he completed high school, then went on to the Technical University of Munich, or TU München, to study aerospace engineering. He was accepted to the Deutsche Aerospace AG, the DASA Eurofighter program when he completed his degree.

During his time in Munich, he lived in both the high school and university dorms but was supported by a German Muslim family, who provided him with money every month.

By the time he had reached Munich, at the age of 16, he was a thoroughly independent person, who knew what his mission was. He spoke fluent German, and he had German citizenship; his task was to assimilate into German society, attain a position in their ambitious new fighter aircraft program, and await instructions.

Kruger was a tall, six-foot-one inch specimen, with raven-black hair, silky white skin and blue eyes. His nose was somewhat long and crooked, from a kick he had suffered in hand-to-hand combat training, and his lips were pale and thin.

He never questioned his Arab origins, even though he could see significant differences in his appearance compared to most of his fellow trainees in Syria. But it never occurred to him that he was anyone other than the son of Ismail Talal, a sergeant in the Lebanese police, though he had not seen him since he was fourteen.

When the "Sons of Jihad" headquarters was destroyed, Kruger had already been working at DASA for two years as an aerospace engineer, specializing in wing structure. He saw the report on television and recognized the area, and though the reports never specified who or what was attacked, he knew immediately that it had been the place where he went to school as a boy.

Soon after, he began receiving instructions.

The modus operandi had changed. Things got more urgent. They needed to take action. He was chosen to carry out the Thai jet assault in coordination with Malaysian-backed Muslims in South Thailand, who wanted independence and were eager to make an example. He wondered why they had chosen him, having become well-established at his post, but he never questioned his orders, as plans were never shared with him. He was a loyal servant, albeit a dangerous one.

Kruger described in detail their mode of operation, their contact structure, their payment schedules and the sequence of events that got him to the island in South Thailand and finally to Krabi Airport. What he did not know was where his fellow students from Beirut were. That was the best-kept secret in the organization, and since their time together, he had not heard or seen any one of them.

He was part of a group of six children who were taught at the "Sons of Jihad" Beirut headquarters and separated at the age of fourteen. He remembered them. There were four boys and two girls. He had no idea they were foreign like himself, and he knew them only by their Arab names, which he divulged. They all lived close to one another and were driven to school together, so he knew each other's families too. But that would not prove much use, since they were all sent away at age fourteen.

Furthermore, he did not know who his controllers were; he received messages at remote locations in the form of notes stuck in bottles or cans, after finding chalk signs on walls that alerted him where to look. At that time, the organization was adamant about avoiding any form of cellular communication or electronic media to convey information, a policy they adhered to today, though not always strictly followed.

The Krabi Airport affair was his first and only "wet" mission. Before that, he had participated in several trial actions designed to test his responsiveness.

His collaborators at the island had not been caught, and he did not know who they were. The two bomb experts, who prepared and tested the altitude-sensitive bombs, arranging them in the suitcase that was given to him, were Malaysian; that he concluded by himself. The rest were unknown to him, including Gustav Hoch, the arms dealer who most likely supplied the hardware.

It was the first operation launched by "Sons of Jihad," and Thailand was chosen for its lax security measures, but it was unclear why an asset such as Max Kruger was sacrificed. Speculation ran wild, but when the dust finally settled, most experts agreed that the organization must have had very limited available personnel, namely those six Kruger had mentioned and possibly only a few more they had managed to unleash before the assault on their headquarters left them in ruins.

They had something to prove after they were discovered and attacked with whatever means they had in their arsenal. Of course, they did not expect to be caught, but it was an obvious risk for an asset such as Kruger, who had already infiltrated the European Aerospace industry.

It remained a big question of why they had chosen to take the risk, but it was difficult to speculate since their overall intentions were still unknown.

An urgent directive went out to all the defense industries in Europe and the US to begin taking measures to flush out suspect employees and investigate them, but that would take some time, and counterintelligence agencies wanted quick results.

It was not by complete chance that Kruger was spotted two weeks before he reached the island. The special task force led by Group Captain Fleming and his counterparts, David Kessler from the Israeli Mossad and Colonel Doug Collins of the CIA, had put out international feelers and alerts at border crossings, and Kruger was the first one caught in that net. It was an algorithm of names of all missing children from Europe and the US reported over 20 years, which failed to produce until Kruger presented his passport in Frankfurt on his way to Bangkok.

Fleming was notified immediately and decided to let him go through, intending to pick up his trail when he reached Thailand. He alerted his MI6 agents in Thailand, who picked up the suspect's trail at Don Mueang airport in Bangkok and followed him to a nearby hotel, where he remained for almost a week before heading south to the islands.

It was then that Frosty and Jemma were called in and briefed. For a few thousand baht, the agents in Bangkok had gotten hold of Kruger's itinerary, which they got from a travel agent he visited while in Bangkok, which included his destination and the duration of his stay.

Fleming had reported this remarkable breakthrough to his colleagues but insisted on using his resources without the assistance of other agencies in order to minimize the mission's exposure.

He and his team received accolades for thwarting the attack and saving innocent passengers, but for a very long time, Fleming could not help but feel discomfited, wondering whether Kruger was sacrificed for a reason, for something a great deal more terrifying that lay ahead.

As agreed when he was transferred from Thai hands to British jurisdiction, Kruger pleaded guilty to the attempted bombing and terrorist activity, was sentenced in the UK under heavy secrecy, media coverage banned by a special court order, and locked up for life at a maximum-security prison on the coast, near Blackpool, where he would be visited by an array of spooks for many years to come.

Part Two

Chapter Six

Monday, January 21, 2019

Frosty sat in his office in Whitehall, staring at a set of reports that had just landed on his desk, consumed by what he was seeing. The first was from Malmo, Sweden. An undercover agent was reporting unrest in and around a certain mosque.

"Calls for 'Jihad' were heard as followers exited the mosque," the agent wrote in his brief.

The second report was from London, and it was alarmingly identical. "You coming to lunch?" Jemma asked, poking her head through his door.

Frosty cast a disturbed look in her direction, and she immediately stepped in, knowing all too well what his looks meant.

"What's the matter?" She inquired worriedly.

"It's these reports that keep popping up," he said.

"Which? The mosques…?" she inquired.

Frosty nodded.

He had taken over the task force from Group Captain Harry Fleming several years before; she had been his deputy throughout. They had been part of several task forces that had evolved within the British security services for twenty years but essentially had one goal: to try to track down a handful of sleeper agents who were considered a dire threat to their government and other friendly governments, and so far, they had made little progress.

She knew Frosty well and had been a loyal confidant ever since they had prevented the Thai Air bombing in Krabi in the spring of '99. That had been their first mission together, and they had been together professionally since.

The original task force, which was now one among several in the Task Force Bureau (TFB), had been formed by Group Captain Fleming soon after the assault on the "Sons of Jihad" compound in Beirut in 1996 and the release of Sammy Baker Jr. and two other abducted kids.

Sammy Baker Jr. had been abducted from his home in Los Angeles in 1985 when he was a year old by a terrorist organization that was discovered ten years later. The organization was known as "Sons of Jihad," and it had been formed and sponsored by the Arab League of Nations and several infamous terrorist organizations. Sammy's mother, Michelle, was raped and murdered during the abduction.

When Sammy was found and rescued, he had been in the hands of extreme Muslims in Beirut for ten years. Sammy's father, Sam Baker, had formed an organization called "The Center for Missing Children" after his son's disappearance; its purpose was to assist parents around the globe in locating their missing children. Sam and his crew of specialized agents, with assistance from law enforcement agencies and an array of clandestine organizations, had discovered that Sammy Jr. was part of a heinous scheme to raise kidnapped babies as Muslims in Beirut, train them, and send them back to their native lands to spy and inflict terror.

A secret operation was launched against the organization by elite forces from the UK, US, and Israel, with assistance from Sam's group, to eliminate the threat and find the missing children. They managed to rescue Sammy and two other children and destroy the organization's headquarters in Beirut but failed to rescue other children who were known to have been there; and worse, they failed to learn the organization's plans and the location of agents already in place.

The task force had been part of MI6, collaborating with parallel task forces from allied countries, until the TFB was formed. The Task Force Bureau, with agents tracking threats domestically and abroad, had changed after the 9/11 disaster, becoming a separate entity under MI5, focusing mostly on domestic threats, reporting both to the Home Office, the Foreign Office and the deputy minister for Homeland Security. To further distinguish it from the more traditional security services, the TFB was given a secure location in Whitehall on Northumberland Avenue rather than space at Vauxhall Cross.

After the Thai Air episode, they thought they had a good start on dismantling the organization, having caught a live agent, Max Kruger, in the act, but their hopes quickly diminished as it became clear that Kruger was isolated from his counterparts and unable to provide information pertaining to other agents.

Kruger, together with Rafik Ammad, who was caught shortly before the famous raid in Beirut in 1996, and who had been responsible for raising capital to finance the organization, his wife Nyla, an assistant to "Sons of Jihad" head of recruiting, one Abu Yusuf, and the three children released from captivity all those years ago, were ample confirmation that "Sons of Jihad" had partially succeeded in their scheme. It was assumed they had managed to unleash several agents, as they had unleashed Kruger, and that those agents were lying low somewhere, waiting to strike.

The Ammad family was living under false identities in Israel, having received asylum for cooperating during the Beirut raid and after. However, like Kruger, they had no knowledge of the number of operatives deployed or their whereabouts. The agents had been isolated from one another in such a way that it was impossible for one to expose any of the others, and aside from having a vague idea as to the number of agents that were sent, with the exception of Kruger, the task force had been unable to track any one of them.

Frosty's task force, which initially numbered ten full-time people, was reduced in size over the years but still used many other assets and resources available at TFB, cooperating with an American CIA task force double the size, and several smaller Italian, German, Swedish, French and Israeli task forces, all dedicated to thwarting this looming threat.

In the waning Fleming days, as Jemma often called them, it was agreed that those sleeper agents must have been waiting dormant for their orders and would move only when ready to achieve their ultimate goal, which no one dared guess at. But the destruction of the Twin Towers in New York City on September 11, 2001, intensified exponentially the need to be vigilant.

"They've been at it for years," Jemma said, leaning on his desk.

"Yes, but it's intensifying," Frosty said, "and it's spreading. Last week I got a similar report from Venice, for Christ's sake!"

"Now that's a place we should definitely look into," she said, smiling at him mischievously.

"I might just send you there…" he said, smiling back. "I am sure Jake would tag along."

Jemma laughed. Her husband, Jake Hammond, a solicitor by trade, kept complaining to Frosty that he could never accompany his wife on any of her trips to the exotic places she frequented, such as Cairo, Jerusalem, the UAE, Riyadh or Amman. Of course, he was being sarcastic, since he never had any desire to leave his posh London office for any of those places, even when Jemma suggested a genuine vacation.

"Right, and Cindy would just jump at the chance…" she mocked, knowing Frosty's wife, a Google Analyst at Frost & Sullivan, who worked from home, was just as disinclined to travel abroad and leave her kids behind with the grandparents.

Frosty smiled in agreement. "Cafeteria?" he finally asked.

"Might as well," Jemma said and turned for the door when it burst open, and three policemen entered.

"Adrian Frost?" one of them addressed Frosty, who stood up behind his desk. "That'll be me."

"Come with us, please," their leader, a police sergeant, ordered.

"What's happened? What's the matter?" Jemma heard herself asking but realized the three policemen were completely focused on her boss.

"Can you tell me what this is all about?" Frosty questioned, grabbing his jacket from the back of his chair as he came around his desk.

"Just come with us, please," the sergeant insisted, and they all hurried out the door, leaving Jemma frozen to her spot.

They rushed through the corridors and down several flights of stairs before exiting the building at a side door on Northumberland Avenue, where a black Jaguar waited for them, its doors open.

"In you go…" the sergeant said, holding the door. Frosty climbed into the back seat, where he came face to face with Air Vice Marshal Alan Reed, the chief of his organization.

"There has been an assassination attempt on George Tompkins!" Reed said without preamble as the car screeched off, two police motorcycles leading the way with sirens.

Frosty looked dumbfounded. "What… how…?" he began.

"His car exploded when he came out of a meeting at the Ritz. He was not in it but is badly hurt. His assistant is injured as well, and his driver," Reed reported despondently.

"Car bomb?" Frosty asked, numb with shock.

"Not sure," Reed said. "Anything's possible… It might have been a damn missile for all we know."

Frosty knew George Tompkins quite well. He was the deputy minister for the Home Office responsible for the specialist protection branch (SO1) and had responsibility for Homeland Security operations. In fact, Tompkins was one of the people who had recommended Frosty to replace Fleming as head of their task force when Fleming retired.

"We're off to St. Thomas' Hospital," Reed was saying. "Let's hope he hangs on…"

"Let me call Jemma," Frosty suggested. "Send her to the scene…"

"You'll do no such thing!" Reed said harshly. "We've got half the police force already there, MI5 and all the rest…"

"Right, but shouldn't we get a firsthand look?" Frosty questioned, surprised by how adamant Reed was.

Reed gazed at him but did not offer an explanation.

The Jaguar whisked across Westminster Bridge and turned right at Lambeth Palace Road, coming to the entrance of the emergency ward.

It was mayhem, full of law enforcement vehicles, doctors in white coats, nurses, policemen, and already a few reporters, all crowding the area. Their driver tried to get through, but it wasn't until they got out of the Jaguar and physically pushed their way in that they managed to slip through, with help from the officers who knew AVM Reed.

They reached the ward but could not get in to see Tompkins, who was being treated by a cadre of doctors from various disciplines. He was finally taken away to the operating room, where his surgery would take five hours.

Frosty managed to call Jemma on his cell phone as he slipped away to the men's room, while Reed was busy avoiding the horde of reporters that had gotten the word and were now searching for scoops.

"Get over there and find out what's going on!" he instructed her.

"How's Tompkins doing?" Jemma asked, worried.

"He's in surgery now and will be for a while. Reed wants me to wait around, so take anyone who's at the office and go take a look at the scene, but make sure you report back only to me…"

"Why is that?" She asked, surprised. He had never asked her to do such a thing.

"Something's up," he said. "I wanted to send you there earlier, but Reed wouldn't hear of it. Gave some lame excuse about too many departments being involved…"

"OK, Frost, cheer up, I'll take care of it," she said to him and hung up.

Frosty smiled, concluded his business, washed his hands and checked the bathroom to make sure he had not been overheard before he went back to the emergency ward.

Family members and government officials started showing up, and by the time the surgery was over, the waiting rooms outside intensive care were full.

It was after midnight that AVM Reed and Frosty were called in.

Compared with the mayhem outside, the hush of the room was a welcome relief. The array of monitors and electronic life-preserving equipment hummed quietly, and Frosty was surprised to see Tompkins staring at them as they approached the bed in the dim light.

The deputy minister raised a weak hand, indicating with his fingers that they should lean in close.

"It's time…" he whispered, barely audible. "Kruger… he knows…" He swallowed. "The man said… they have taken over…"

Tompkins was making rasping sounds, struggling for breath. Suddenly, the monitors went off. A cacophony of beeps erupted. A nurse rushed in, followed by several doctors, who began to check the patient. The line indicator on the heart monitor went flat, and the two visitors were rushed out of the room.

Minutes later, the lead physician came out to deliver the news. George Tompkins was dead.

Chapter Seven

Tuesday, January 22, 2019

The maximum-security prison near Blackpool loomed dark and threatening as Frosty approached the parking area outside its gates. The rain did not let up as he put on his coat, opened his umbrella, and ran to the gate.

He was admitted through an electronic sliding gate, left his umbrella and coat, along with his mobile phone and gun at the visitors' window, and was led through a succession of steel gates to a secluded chamber, where he met Max Kruger for the first time in over 15 years.

He had visited Kruger in that very same chamber several times after the Twin Tower disaster of September 11, hoping to make a connection and assist the CIA in the investigation, but Kruger could not provide any useful information. In 1996, it had been established that the "Sons of Jihad" organization was at least partially funded by Al Qaida; preceding the raid on the compound in Beirut, Ahmed Abu Salah, a Lebanese arms dealer, was hijacked from his Beirut home and interrogated by the Israelis; he provided the information. But Kruger, who had already been sent back to Munich by then, had no knowledge of Al Qaida's involvement and could shed no light on the 9/11 investigation.

Since then, Frosty had not visited him. Others did, and there were a few times when he thought about it but decided it was not worth the effort. He was convinced Kruger had given them all he knew and was therefore surprised at Tompkins' last words asking him to go see Kruger at once.

Kruger wore the traditional orange prison uniform. He had aged well, Frosty noticed. His raven-black hair and eyebrows had hints of gray in them, his forehead was creased, and the skin around his eyes showed some wrinkles, but apart from that, he looked healthy and fit.

Frosty instructed the two guards to uncuff the prisoner, then motioned for them to leave them alone.

"I presume you know why I am here," Frosty stated as soon as the guards stepped out of the room.

"No, not really," Kruger replied, the German accent still present.

"George Tompkins was shot and killed yesterday," Frosty informed him.

"Well, yeah, everyone's heard that," Kruger said dismissively.

"Before he died, he instructed me to come see you," Frosty divulged. "Said something like: 'It's time' and that 'you would know'."

Kruger looked at him quizzically.

"Was there a call sign or a signal for the day you would be expected to take action? A day of final reckoning of sorts?" Frosty inquired, not expecting an answer.

Kruger kept staring at him as if in a daze. "I don't know of any, but maybe you do?" he finally said.

"Me?" Frosty said, surprised. "How would I know?"

"Well, you've been at it for twenty years. Maybe you've learned something?"

"Are you playing with me, or are you trying to tell me something?" Frosty asked a little impatiently.

Kruger sat back, smiling, a far cry from the frightened prisoner at the Bangkok police interrogation unit. Frosty had kept abreast of his progress at the prison; strangely, he had thrived. He had received a PhD in English Literature and was teaching inmates at the prison school, as well as publishing poems.

Kruger kept smiling as they stared at one another for a long moment before his stare became drawn and he turned his gaze toward the looking-glass window. Suddenly, Kruger stuffed his hand into the pocket of his prison overalls, dug something out, stuffed it into his mouth, and swallowed. Frosty was a split second too late to stop him.

Frosty cried out for help. The guards came rushing in and tried to assist Frosty in getting the pill out of Kruger's throat, but realized they were too late as foam and saliva began to drip out of the prisoner's mouth.

Kruger was dead in seconds.

The prison alarm went off, and the prison doctor rushed in, only to confirm Kruger's death.

Frosty and the two guards were escorted to the prison commandant's office, where they gave statements and were dismissed.

Back in his car, before leaving the prison grounds, Frosty called Jemma to let her know what had happened. After filling her in, he began driving. Two hours later, as he was on the M1 near Sheffield, she called him back.

"I am at Embankment Station," she said, sounding anxious and out of breath. "Had to leave the office to call you!"

"What is the matter?" he asked. "You sound upset."

"There's a welcoming party waiting for you."

He was suddenly very alert. "What on earth for?"

"I'm not sure, but Reed came storming in with a group of people who are now busy ravaging your office."

"What? Are they mad?" He called out, swerved to the side of the freeway, and stopped.

"Asked me for your computer password…"

"Are you serious? I hope you didn't give it to them."

"I said I didn't know it."

"Good girl."

"He threatened to accuse me of breach of Her Majesty's national security if I don't give him the password."

She sounded close to tears.

"Breach of national security?" Frosty repeated her words. "This is preposterous! What the hell…" He did not complete the sentence as she cut him off.

"It has to do with Kruger's death. They think you killed him."

"Who said that?" he demanded.

"I overheard them talking. They had an argument inside your office, and Dixon was saying you gave him the pill."

"Ross Dixon? Was he there too? How would he know anything?"

"Yes! He came with Reed, along with a red-headed guy I don't know, and Harriet."

"That bitch!" Frosty swore.

"They said you either gave him the pill or stuffed it down his throat… that there's a video…"

"Listen to me, Jemma," Frosty commanded, feeling a slight panic taking a grip. "I did no such thing! The man had the pill in his pants. I tried to stop him! The chamber video has to show it!"

There was a moment of silence as Jemma let his words sink in.

"Why are they saying it, Frosty?" she finally asked, sounding hoarse. "It has to be a misunderstanding."

"They said you ordered the guards to uncuff him."

"Yeah, so?"

"It's against policy."

Frosty's mind had been reeling since he left the prison, replaying the interview in his mind, wondering how Kruger got hold of a cyanide pill and why he chose to use it in his presence. He thought back to the previous day. Why was he asked by the dying Tompkins to go to the prison? Why was George Tompkins assassinated? And why was Reed reluctant to allow his people to visit the crime scene?

Reed had insisted he leave immediately for the prison, so he had driven all night directly from the hospital, using Reed's Jaguar. The only call he made was to tell Cindy not to wait up.

"Tell me what you found yesterday at the Ritz," he said to Jemma after a pause, moving the Jag back onto the motorway. The wind was wailing outside, causing the rain to hit the windshield head-on as he carefully merged with the traffic, looking for an exit where he could stop and think more clearly.

"The investigation has just begun, obviously, but it seems a bomb exploded near or underneath Tompkins' car as he approached it, killing his driver and his secretary, who were in the car. There was one other bystander who was killed and several wounded, including two motorcycle policemen who were escorting the minister."

"And no one saw anything? Not even the policemen?"

"I didn't talk to them since they were rushed to the hospital as well. But MI5 sealed off the area in a hurry and were interviewing witnesses."

"Did you talk to anyone?"

"I had Taylor and Edwards with me, and we were allowed on the scene. It was chaotic. There were glass and metal parts everywhere. Tompkins' car was ripped to shreds, and they were still collecting body parts…"

"But did you hear anything?"

"The witnesses were mostly hysterical. I listened in on a few of the MI5 and police interviews. No one said anything useful, but Taylor said he heard one of the hotel parking attendants mention that he was spared because he was fetching the car for the bystander who was killed, who had come out of the hotel just ahead of Tompkins. I put it all in the report this morning."

"Did you send this report to anyone?" Frosty asked hastily.

"No, not yet… I was going to send it…" Jemma was saying, but Frosty was impatient.

"Send it urgently to me but to no one else! Can you do that?"

"Sure, I've got it almost ready."

"Good girl," Frosty was saying, his mind still in turmoil.

"OK, I'll go back to the office," Jemma said. "But what are you going to do?"

"I need to think this through." Frosty said "I haven't slept in ages, and I can't think straight. I'll stop somewhere for a bite and a bit of a rest. Keep your phone close by. I'll call you when I've figured out what to do. If Reed gives you any trouble, tell him you have no idea where I am."

"OK, boss. Take good care. I'll wait for your call," she said and clicked off.

Frosty called Cindy, letting her know he would be home late, then exited the M1 at Nottingham, took the A52 across the River Trent to Nottingham City Airport, where he left the Jag in the main parking lot and rented an Avis Toyota Corolla, using cash.

The rain had finally let up, but it was gray and cold.

He continued east on the A52 to Grantham, where he found a roadside motel with a coffee shop. He rented a room for the night, had an early dinner, and headed for bed.

Chapter Eight

Jemma could not fall asleep. She tossed and turned and finally decided to get up and make herself a cup of tea. Jake was basically comatose, as usual, bundled under the bed covers as she turned on the bed lamp and got up, slipping into her cashmere robe, a present from Jake for her 40th birthday.

Out of habit, she stopped in front of the mirror to examine herself. In the dim bedroom light and without makeup, she noticed the light wrinkles forming on the skin around her eyes, as well as a little swelling under her eyes, which Jake actually liked. Her hair was all mussed, and she smoothed it to look less crazed. Her lips, she noticed, were still quite full, but the skin on her neck was beginning to crease a bit too.

She opened the robe to look at her breasts, realizing that after giving birth to two boys and breastfeeding, they too were beginning to sag.

Covering herself to avoid freezing, she went to the kitchen on the ground floor, switched on the kettle, took a mug from the cupboard, added a spoonful of sugar, and chose a green tea bag, which she dropped into the mug.

She then looked in at the boys. Colin was thirteen, and Ian was ten. Both had been born in St. Thomas' Hospital near Jemma's workplace. She and Jake had met in 2002 when she was taking courses to complete her International Relations degree at the London School of Economics and Political Science, where Jake was studying law. They met at the Plaza Café at John Watkins Plaza one afternoon when Jake had offered her a place at his table, seeing her searching for a seat.

She could not tell him much about her work at the Home Office, but he told her all about his family law practice and his plans for the future. He was dressed in a university jacket and a matching scarf and had brown curly hair and a genuine smile. She was attracted to him instantly, and apparently, the feeling was mutual; they ended up missing their next lecture. A week later, he invited her to

"Phantom of the Opera," which she was only too happy to see for the third time, and afterward, they had a late dinner in SoHo.

They began seeing each other on a regular basis, meeting for coffee at school and going out on the town; the relationship bloomed, and they became a couple.

Jacob Hammond was, like her, a native Londoner who grew up in London's West End and never really left the area. His father, George, established Hammond's Law back in the 1970s, a small but well-respected law firm on Marylebone Street in London, which Jake was well on his way to taking over now that his dad was close to retiring.

It was two years before Jake proposed. They married in October 2005, and a year later, Colin was born.

She looked in on Ian, who seemed to be dreaming, moving his head slightly from side to side, his brown curls spread on the pillow. Colin, in an adjacent room, had his face turned to the door but was covered up to his forehead like his dad, his black hair protruding from beneath the blanket.

It was freezing cold, so Jemma turned the main heater up a bit, adjusting the thermostat, before she went back to the kitchen to drink her tea.

She thought about what had happened that afternoon.

She had gone back to the office and sat at her desk, completing the report and sending it to Frosty, who had responded quickly by email that he had received it.

Reed and his entourage were gone from Frosty's office by then, leaving it locked. Andy Taylor came in an hour later, looking surprised to see her.

"Where have you been?" he asked. "Everyone's been looking for you."

"I was out to lunch and came back here an hour ago," she said innocently.

"Well, get yourself down to Reed's office on the double. He is dying to see you," Taylor said in a sarcastic tone.

"I can't say I feel the same," she said under her breath as she shut off her computer, took her coat and purse, and left, giving Taylor an accusing stare, as if it was his fault she had to answer Reed.

"Where have you been?" Reed fumed at her as she entered his office.

"I had lunch at Costa Coffee at Embankment, then went back to my office. Why?"

"Have you been talking to Frosty?" he asked accusingly.

"No, sir," she lied, looking him straight in the eyes.

"Did he contact you?" he asked again as if her first lie did not register.

"No, he did not," she lied again.

Reed looked at her thoughtfully. He had brown eyes and gray, almost white, hair, combed impeccably to one side. His skin was white with a few light brown blotches beginning to show on his cheeks and on the back of his hands. He wore a dark suit with a fashionable gray tie and sat erect in his seat behind a large oak desk.

"Why, then, did you disappear when you clearly knew something had gone wrong with your boss and I specifically asked you for his password?"

"Once again, sir, with all due respect, I do not have his password, and you did not involve me or any one of us in the matter, though I am very worried, and I would like to know what's going on."

"Who told you to go to the Ritz yesterday?"

"Frosty did," she said. "He called me from the hospital. Is there anything wrong?" A look of dismay crossed Reed's face, but he kept the thought to himself.

"Can you tell me what you learned there?" he finally asked.

"I was writing the report when Taylor came by to say you were looking for me."

"I'd like it today!" he demanded.

"You'll have it first thing, as soon as I get it done," she promised.

There was a moment of awkward silence. Reed seemed to be deliberating with himself.

"Listen," he finally said. "Frosty is in some trouble. It's got to do with the assassination and Kruger, who died yesterday while meeting with him. I don't have all the details yet, but I was told to bring him in for questioning. It's a serious matter, so don't involve yourself until we get to the bottom of this. If he contacts you, tell him to come in urgently. Is that understood?"

"Sir," Jemma said, choosing her words carefully, "I've worked with him for over twenty years. If there's something seriously wrong, I'd like to know about it so I can assist…"

"Assist us or him?" Reed cut her off.

"Since when has this become a conflict between Frosty and the organization? He's worked here for as long as I have."

"Sometimes tough questions have to be asked, especially when a particular task force has not brought in any results in over 20 years…"

"But, sir, he has not worked on his own. Everything he has done was always above board and sanctioned by the higher-ups," she reproached.

"Let's just leave it at that," Reed said. "When he comes in, we'll figure it out. Your job right now is to make sure he shows up."

In the afternoon, Reed called a meeting to inform the staff of what had happened. Whitehall was buzzing with rumors as the activity level increased twofold. The corridors and meeting rooms filled with people trying to get a handle on what was being described in the media as an intelligence collapse.

Not a word was mentioned on Frosty's situation, though his absence was more than obvious.

*****

Jemma poured hot water into the mug and stirred the sugar.

She had called Frosty on her way home, informing him of her discussion with Reed and everything else that had happened. He had refused to tell her where he was or what he was planning to do, arguing that it was for her own good in case things got ugly.

An hour later, he called her home landline from a cell phone number she did not recognize. He asked her to get a disposable cell phone so they could speak freely until Signal Intelligence, which was most likely monitoring their cell phones, tracked the new cell phones down.

It was already too late in the day for her to get a new phone, so she agreed to do it first thing in the morning.

She sat at the kitchen table sipping her tea, trying to make sense of the day's events.

This was obviously a huge misunderstanding, she thought, which should be cleared up once Frosty came in, yet he seemed to be taking drastic measures to avoid confronting the issue.

Did he know something she didn't? Did he have something to hide? Were Reed's concerns legit? She could not fathom it. Frosty had always been a straight shooter, always making sure everyone was briefed and up to date. To her knowledge, there was never an instance when he had operated on his own, without authority. And it wasn't only their task force that had so far come up empty. None of the others, including the Americans, who had far greater resources, had come up with any significant breakthrough, so what had suddenly changed to put her boss in such a predicament?

Shockingly, George Tompkins, Head of SO1, has been assassinated, along with three others, and Kruger had seemingly taken his own life. What did these events have to do with one another?

She thought of the report she had sent Frosty and the one she had later sent Reed. They were identical, but their recipients received them separately, and there was no one else copied.

There were things she could do, such as finding out the identity of the bystander who was killed or why the dying Tompkins had asked Frosty to go see Kruger.

Then she recalled Reed's reluctance to allow their team on site and wondered if she would be allowed to do anything at all.

She decided she had to trust Frosty's instincts and cooperate with him until things were cleared up. She felt it was her only recourse since Frosty was the only one who had been honest with her. Reed had not been as forthcoming; he had kept things from her that she had known about from Frosty.

She finished her tea, put the mug in the sink, and went back to bed, falling asleep content with her resolve, at least for the moment.

Chapter Nine

Wednesday, January 23, 2019

Cynthia Cunningham-Frost was an American from New York City who had met Frosty during one of his semi-annual visits to Manhattan to confer with his American and worldwide counterparts.

The foremost reason these conferences took place in New York was the involvement of a clandestine organization called "The Center for Missing Children," which had been the first to discover the "Sons of Jihad" scheme and was instrumental in finding their location in Beirut.

Sam Baker, whose son Sammy Jr. was one of several children kidnapped in 1985 and before, by the terrorist organization, and released from captivity in 1996 along with two others, had since been meeting with the various task forces on a regular basis; he and his crew were privy to any new developments. His son and the two other children released, were by then insulated from any involvement in the matter but initially, according to Fleming, they were a major source of information as to the methods used by the "Sons of Jihad" to train their captives; additionally, they helped identify a few of their captors and the other children who were there with them and had yet to be found.

Every six months or so, delegates from the various task forces of the different countries responsible for tracking "Sons of Jihad" would meet in New York for a few days to exchange information and brainstorm on how to proceed.

Cynthia, or Cindy, had been working as a Google analyst for the State Department and was assigned to the American task force to assist with online information when Frosty met her at a conference at the FBI offices downtown, just before Christmas 2003. Though she was an assistant, Frosty noticed her colleagues consulting with her on almost every issue, and she stood out with her blond hair and blue eyes, remnants of her Swedish ancestors who settled in Long Island in the 19th century.

Her face was thin with a snub nose and high cheekbones, with bright red lipstick on her full lips, and she seemed to always be smiling, in stark contrast to the usual gloomy faces around the conference table. When they would go for breaks, he would find himself milling around her group, watching the men trying to impress her, and she, typically dressed in a business outfit that combined a fashionable blouse, a short skirt, and high heels, showing off her gorgeous legs, would politely laugh at their jokes but every now and then would throw him a glance and smile shyly.

He finally worked up the courage to ask her to lunch one day, and then to dinner at the hotel where he was staying, and they ended up spending most of their free time together during the conference; before long, they were making trips across the Atlantic for weekends.

Frosty proposed a year later. It took some convincing, but eventually, Cindy succumbed to his relentless courting and married him in a private event near Washington Square in the Village, Jemma and Jake were among the few friends invited from the UK, and after some debate, Cindy and Frosty settled in London.

Their eldest daughter, Gabrielle or Gabi, was born in January 2006. Zoe was born two years later.

In London, Cindy had initially found a few independent contract jobs as an information analyst for a number of research organizations until she landed a steady job with Frost & Sullivan's UK subsidiary, which allowed her to work from home.

*****

She was woken at midnight from a fitful sleep on the living room sofa as the home phone rang, realizing that Frosty was, for the second straight night, absent from home.

The caller was her husband.

"Hi, dear," he said. "Hope I didn't wake you."

"Where are you?" she demanded. "I've been worried sick!"

"Sorry, I got caught up in something and I need your help," he said matter-of-factly.

Cindy was no stranger to clandestine work and was well aware of her husband's dealings, but Frosty had never been away from home without a proper explanation.

"Not before you tell me what's wrong," she insisted.

There was a brief silence on the other end of the line, and she heard him groan before he spoke again.

"I need you to get a different mobile phone before I can tell you."

"What!?" she erupted. "Are you kidding me?"

"Unfortunately, I am not," he said. "But meanwhile, I need you to…"

"Frosty," she cut him off, "I need to know what is going on! You haven't been home in two days, and you are acting peculiar. The girls are asking about you and I don't know what to say; plus, I'm worried too."

"Listen, Cin, I cannot talk because we may be monitored. We need to end this conversation as quickly as possible. I'll explain it all as soon as I can talk to you without the threat of being listened to. Get a phone and call the number on the screen as soon as you get it. Meanwhile, I need you to find out who visited Max Kruger in prison in the last few years."

"Max Kruger? The Max Kruger who…"

"Yes, Cin!" Frosty said, a little exasperated. "Him! I need to know who he met lately."

"But…" she stuttered.

"No buts, just do it and call me in the morning," he said and hung up, leaving her puzzled and frustrated.

She, of course, knew all about Kruger from the time she had been working for the State Department; she had been assisting the US task force responsible for tracking the untraceable "Sons of Jihad" sleeper agents, who allegedly had infiltrated key government and industry positions and were assumed to be waiting for a signal to strike.

Kruger had been the only one of them to be caught, and that had happened twenty years ago.

She quickly turned on her computer screen and instantly found out Kruger had died in prison the day before.

******

Reuben Santana was born in Manchester to an English mother and a Brazilian father. Sheila and Jose Santana, Reuben's parents, had met in Rio in 1980, when Sheila, a language major, was there on an exchange program from Manchester University, studying Portuguese. She met Jose on the beach at

Ipanema playing volleyball. They fell in love, and he came to Manchester for a visit a few months later when the delivery company he worked for laid him off. The visit was a long one. He found a job in a moving company in Manchester; they married and had Reuben. When Reuben was three, Jose decided to go back to find a job in Rio and send Sheila and the boy to join him when he had enough money.

That never happened.

He kept promising to bring them over but could never make enough money to stick to his word, and eventually, he and Sheila separated, though they never divorced. Reuben was raised by his mother and never saw his father, who kept in touch from afar but never visited.

When Reuben was twelve, they moved to London when Sheila got a job as a librarian in Camden. When he completed high school at eighteen, Reuben flew to Rio to spend time with his father. Upon arriving, he found that he had two sisters from a woman, Claudia, who lived with his father. He spent two weeks in their home in Rio, then flew back to London and joined the police force.

Reuben was a large man by any standards, six foot four inches tall and extremely wide. He completed his cadet training with honors, spent two years on patrol in some of London's mean streets, and then applied for motorcycle training.

He had done VIP escort duty many times before he was asked to escort Deputy Minister Tompkins to a meeting at the Ritz, and while waiting for Tompkins, a bomb had exploded, killing Tompkins and three others, wounding Officer Santana in the shoulder and head as he was climbing onto his motorcycle to clear the way.

His motorcycle and helmet saved his life, his helmet taking the brunt of the shrapnel, which still managed to penetrate and cut his scalp. He took more shrapnel in the shoulder, breaking his collarbone but doing little damage to his arteries.

He was treated in St. Thomas' Hospital together with his partner, Evan Wilson, who had been hit in the stomach. Santana's surgery was relatively short, and after two hours, he was in recovery, the shrapnel out of his body. His partner joined him a few hours later, losing his spleen and part of his colon, but relatively sound and alert.

As he lay in bed in the internal ward, his second night at the hospital, his shoulder and head bandaged and quite sore, he tried to replay the day's events in his mind. Something had caught his attention just before the explosion, but he could not recall it clearly. They had checked the car when the deputy minister left his office at Whitehall. They rode in front of the car the few streets to the Ritz without incident. Tompkins entered the hotel alone, leaving his secretary in the car, which was unusual but nothing to worry about. He was waiting with Officer Wilson near the bikes on the steps of the hotel when…

There was nothing out of place that he could recall; no one approaching the car as far as he could tell. He remembered noticing the secretary next to the driver, talking on her phone… Some pedestrians walking about… It was windy and there was some drizzle… Then Tompkins walked out, and Reuben turned to look in his direction…

It must have been at that moment…

Then he remembered: a bicycle rider. Partially obscured from his view by the minister approaching the car. There was definitely a bicycle rider on the other side of the car when…

Santana tried to think, but the moment was so brief he could not recreate it in his mind. But the image stuck. The rider seemed just a dark shadow.

Santana was 36 and still single. He liked the single life too much to settle down. He had olive skin, dark curly hair, and a well-proportioned face with a permanent half-smile, which made people, especially women, feel at ease around him despite his size and build.

On his motorcycle, with a helmet and uniform on, he was quite intimidating.

His mother and his current girlfriend, Camilla Parades, a Brazilian, had both cried on the phone when he told them what had happened but had yet to visit him, due to a standing order—which Santana thought very strange—that he was to have no visitors for the duration of his hospital stay.

His superiors had been in, and so had several internal police investigators, but none of his mates were allowed to visit, and there was a permanent guard outside his door.

He felt miserable about Tompkins getting killed, feeling he had failed in his duty. It was his job to keep him safe.

Suddenly, another thought entered his mind: "Where, for the love of god, was the SO1 detachment?"

There were always Special Protection agents around Tompkins. He had known a few of them. Not always the same guys, but they were always there.

So where were they this time? They were not in the car with Tompkins, and he could not recall them showing up in a car of their own as they normally did.

Maybe the deputy minister asked to go it alone, but why would he do that? And it wasn't his call anyway, Santana knew that much.

He looked at Wilson in the bed across from his. He seemed to be sleeping. The poor fellow was being given some heavy drugs, Santana knew, having watched them put morphine into his IV a few hours earlier.

He needed to relieve himself and stepped carefully off the bed in the dark, reaching for a chair next to his bed to steady himself. He walked unsteadily to the door and opened it, expecting to see the guard, but the guard was not there. It was the first time Santana had attempted to walk by himself, so he stood a moment, making sure he could reach the bathroom, which was just across the corridor. He stepped forward, reaching for the bathroom door with his good hand, opened the door, and stepped in.

As he was shutting the door, he happened to glance toward the nurses' bay, which was dimly lit at the end of the corridor, when he saw a sight that made the blood in his veins turn to ice.

Two dark figures stepped into the light. He saw the nurse on duty stand up, then get thrust back forcefully, disappearing under the counter as one of the figures, pointing a gun at her, shot—though all Santana heard was the familiar click of a gun with a silencer.

Then they were coming his way.

He shut the bathroom door quickly and locked it, leaving the light off, watching the corridor through a tiny window in the door, able to see the entrance to his room.

The two figures swiftly entered his room across the corridor and were back out in less than ten seconds, guns in their hands, looking left and right. They wore dark coveralls and dark hoods; he could not see their faces. One of them stepped to the bathroom door and tried it. Santana moved away from the door window and held his breath. He heard them shuffling near the door, speaking in soft voices, but could not make out what they were saying.

He knew he was totally vulnerable in his condition, and with no firearm, he was no match for them if they decided to break open the door, but to his surprise and relief, they moved away. He risked a peek through the window again and caught a glimpse of a dark figure exiting the room next to his.

He remained in the bathroom for several minutes, not knowing when it was safe to leave, wishing he had his phone with him, but it was in his room.

He peeked through the small window again, seeing no one. He waited three minutes more before unlocking the door silently and glancing down the hall to both sides.

It was empty and deathly quiet.

He crossed to his room and stepped in, expecting to be shot, but it did not come.

He looked around in the dark. Wilson was still in his bed. He moved toward his own bed, bent over with difficulty, and fished in his bag for his phone, found it, turned it on, and went over to Wilson, using the screen light to look at his partner.

Wilson's pillow was soaked with blood. Santana checked for a pulse. Wilson was dead.

He shivered, feeling faint, but forced himself to the room entrance again and looked around in both directions. It was still empty and quiet. He hobbled to the nurses' bay. The duty nurse was sprawled on the floor in a pool of blood.

He had to get out of there.

He looked around, seeing an office door open, and stepped in, locking the door, leaving the lights off.

He looked at his phone, unable to decide who to call.

His mind raced. Confusion blended with fear. Why were they targeted? Who could he trust now? Where was the guard who had been posted outside their door?

He thought of Evan Wilson, his partner and mate. Gone! Shot in his sleep.

He remained locked in the office for a few more minutes, unable to decide what to do. Finally, he called the only person he knew he could trust.

He called his mother.

Chapter Ten

Frosty caught the report on the BBC morning news on his television set in his motel room.

It was sketchy, to say the least, but he got the gist of it, and what he saw, he did not like.

He was beginning to wonder if he acted too severely, too prematurely, and was considering returning to the office and facing an inquiry from Reed and whoever else was there waiting for him when he caught the report.

A policeman, wounded in the blast that killed Deputy Minister Tompkins, shot and killed in his hospital bed; a second officer, apparently his partner, wounded in the blast as well, gone missing.

Cindy called a few minutes later from a mobile phone she had purchased. He told her all that had happened and his concerns as to the general scheme of things, which had now grown into a full-fledged conspiracy theory.

"I had to ditch Reed's car, which is most likely monitored, and rent a car for cash," he divulged.

"You're right to do that," she agreed. "Something definitely does not look right."

"Did you find out who visited Kruger lately?" he asked eagerly.

"He had a couple of visits from our US counterparts in the last year and one from the Italians. I recognized the names. Then he had two visits from people from here. A person by the name of Andy White visited just a week ago. I checked him out, and it turns out he is, or was, one of Tompkins's aides." She stopped and took a breath.

"The second person to visit him about six months ago, according to the visitors' manual at the prison, which I managed to hack into, was you, darling."

She said it in a casual, slightly teasing way, but it had a large question mark attached to it.

Frosty went silent for a brief moment, digesting the revelation before he came back to life.

"I haven't seen him in fifteen years," he finally said. "This must be a mistake, Cindy."

She did not reply immediately, choosing her words carefully. "Then somebody must have forged your signature."

"It had my signature?" he asked with genuine surprise.

"Next to your name and TFB ID number in print."

"This is unbelievable," he said. "Are you sure?"

"I should recognize your signature by now, shouldn't I, darling?" she said in her teasing, yet skeptical tone again.

"Listen, Cin," he commanded, "this has to be a forgery of some kind. I have not been to see Kruger since before we were married, until yesterday, but let's deal with this later. Tell me who this Andy White is?"

"Special Reconnaissance Regiment, sergeant, forty, fought in Iraq and Afghanistan; was involved in an ugly incident with his lieutenant in 2005," she read to him from a military court summary she had found on the net.

"He was leading a convoy of British troops in the Sangin valley in Southern Afghanistan when his vehicle was struck by an IED, and they got pinned down by Taliban fire. White claimed the lieutenant had ordered his troops to retreat, leaving him on his own in a ditch by the stricken vehicle. A military court ruled against him, and he was transferred to a NATO intelligence unit in Kandahar."

Frosty was listening intently.

"Majored in Political Science; Left the Military to join the Foreign Office in 2011; did a three-year stint in Tel Aviv at the British embassy before returning home and becoming a consultant of sorts to the Home Secretary Office on Homeland Security matters," she continued, switching to his personal file in a classified government site she had access to.

"So, what exactly does he do?"

"His job is, or was, to advise both Tompkins and Nigel Scott on Homeland Security matters," she said matter-of-factly.

"Wow, you've done your job!" he said, sounding impressed. "So, what would you say White's real job is?"

"I would dare say he consults SO1 and the Home Secretary's Office on matters that are best left unspoken," she said seriously.

"He does the dirty work," Frosty said.

"Quite possibly, yes," she said seriously.

There was an awkward silence suddenly, as if the line went dead.

"Cin, you there?"

"The girls are asking about you," she said.

"How are they doing?" he asked.

"They're OK, I guess," she muttered, "missing their dad."

"Give them a big hug and a kiss from me, will you? This'll all be over soon, I hope."

"Frost, are you telling me everything?" she asked.

"Everything except where I am currently at."

She did not reply.

"Look, Cin, it's better you don't know where I am…"

"I understand that," she concurred. "What I don't understand is what exactly you are involved in. I mean, Tompkins is killed, and you go into hiding? You should be the one investigating this, not running away."

"I told you everything I know," Frosty admitted. "Jemma should be calling me soon to clarify things, but I have an uneasy feeling I am involved in something that's way out of my league."

He sighed. "This concocted visit I supposedly made to see Kruger and now a report that one of Tompkins' police escorts was murdered in the hospital spells real trouble."

"OK," she suddenly said, "Do what you have to for the moment, but I want you back here tonight, you hear?"

"I'll try darling," he said. "And can you check for me these two police officers…"

"I'll do my best," she said. "Just make sure you stay safe. Love you," she said and hung up before he could reply.

He sat on his bed, blind to the TV for a while, thinking hard until Jemma called from an unidentified phone, a half hour later.

"Where are you?" she asked the second she heard his voice.

"Better you don't know that," he said.

"What's going on?"

"Total chaos!" she complained. "Hear about the hospital?"

"Saw it on TV. What in god's name is going on, Jemma?" Frosty asked again in frustration.

"No one's talking. Reed's at the hospital dealing with that mess. Nigel Scott has called a press conference after meeting with the PM, and we are all expected at Trevor Bishop's conference room in one hour."

"Sounds creepy," Frosty mused. "Did you talk to anyone today? Find out anything?"

"There are rumors circling around, but I can't tell what's real and what's not. We'll probably know more after the meeting with Bishop."

"I read your report, thanks," he said.

"Who's the bystander that was killed?"

"They have not released his name yet," she said.

"And they'll probably take their time," he said. "Can you find out who this guy was?"

"I can try," she said. "What about you? You going to stay in hiding long?"

"This thing is gaining momentum," he said. "The hospital attack is surely part of it, and so was my visit to Kruger. Something major is transpiring, and I am afraid that I am being set up on account of this."

"Why you?" she asked simply, and for the first time, he stopped to think about it.

"I would guess it must have something to do with our task force. Otherwise, I don't know."

"So what do we do?"

"Let's talk after your meeting with Bishop," he suggested. "Maybe you'll learn something useful."

"He will most likely ask about you," she pointed out.

"Well, you don't know where I am, do you?" he joked.

"No, I do not," she agreed. "I'll call you soon." She hung up.

****

Trevor Bishop was MI5's Director General. He was average height, thin, with a wad of straight black hair adorning a large head, slit clear eyes, a pointy nose and thin lips; dressed immaculately in a black suit and blue tie over a white shirt.

He was a political appointee of the Home Secretary, Nigel Scott, with very limited counter-espionage field experience at MI5, which he joined straight out of college, where he majored in economics. He left the service after a few years to get a Master of Economics degree and switched to procurement, where he climbed the ladder quite quickly to become an assistant to Undersecretary Scott, who was then head of Procurement for Defense.

Their paths remained joined ever since.

To his credit, Bishop acknowledged his lack of field experience and allowed his deputies, among them TFB chief AVM Reed, to handle most operational matters while he advanced his career networking at cocktail parties and social clubs with the government elite.

He stood at the head of the long conference table adjacent to his office at Vauxhall Cross, waiting for the murmurs of discussion to dissipate, coughed and addressed his subordinates.

He gave a brief overview of the sequence of dreadful events that occurred over the previous forty-eight hours, which have sent shockwaves all over the globe, and continued with partial findings from the initial investigation of MI5 and the police.

Nothing was conclusive, but it was quite apparent Lord Tompkins, his driver and assistant, along with a bystander, died from an explosion of a bomb underneath or close to the minister's car.

He went on to address the policeman's murder at the hospital, which was even a bigger twist—one that TFB chief, AVM Reed, was handling personally.

Finally, he disclosed to his people the truth, as he called it, about long-time prison inmate Max Kruger, who died in an interrogation cell under questionable circumstances that were under investigation as well. He did not elaborate further for the moment but sent a quick stare at Jemma, who cringed in her seat.

"Where is your boss?" he suddenly asked nonchalantly, looking at her inquisitively.

"I don't know," she replied instantly, maybe too quickly.

"Well, he should be here when such turmoil is going on, don't you think?" Everyone stared at her, but she kept her mouth shut.

"Yeah, where is Frosty?" someone asked.

"Can I ask a question?" Jemma blurted.

"You certainly may," Bishop said.

"Why aren't we involved?"

"Why, yes, you are," Bishop said in mild surprise. "Reed is out there right now with some people."

"But why were we not involved in the car bomb investigation?"

"Because that's a job for the internal people, not the TFB."

"Yes, but in an event of such magnitude, don't you think we could help?"

"You were sent to interview Kruger, let me remind you," Bishop stated. "And look how that turned out," he said accusingly.

The ambiance in the room turned tense. They were all aware of the raid on Frosty's office the previous morning after he was sent to interview Kruger by request from the dying Minister Tompkins, Kruger's death during their meeting, and Frosty's mysterious absence since.

Bishop coughed again, then addressed the room.

"I've been asked by Sir Nigel, after his meeting with the PM this morning, to deliver some grave news, which we need to address and not a minute too soon."

Forty pairs of eyes focused on the principal counterintelligence agent in Her Majesty's Kingdom, head of one of the most effective secret service agencies in the world, who looked directly at Jemma when he said his piece.

"There are serious indications we have a mole within our midst."

The air went heavy in the conference room as people looked at one another. Not all TFB personnel were field agents. There were several computer experts, hackers to be precise, technical support people, and a few secretaries. But all had cleared a rigorous security clearance procedure with personal background checks, interviews with security experts, and lie detector tests every single year, not to mention the field agents who had all been thoroughly trained and were expected to refresh their acquired skills on a regular basis at their various training facilities across England.

If there was a remote possibility for anyone at the agency to pose a security threat of any kind, it would surely have been detected, and yet, there it was, out in the open: a mole in their midst with definite insinuation to a senior and well-respected figure—a task force leader.

Adrian Frost.

Bishop did not utter it, but it was there for the taking, and suddenly people were looking at Jemma.

"Is Frosty suspected?" she asked out loud, her voice wavering, betraying her.

"Reed's car was found in a parking lot in Nottingham City Airport," Bishop informed them. "He rented a car and is hiding somewhere or used it as a diversion and flew somewhere under a false passport. You will figure it out when we find him. Now get to work," he said and stepped into his office, leaving his crowd in limbo.

AVM Reed appeared out of nowhere at the head of the conference table and began to hand out assignments.

Chapter Eleven

Thursday, January 24, 2019

The church service took place at St. Paul's Cathedral.

All the ministers were there to give a final farewell to the late George Tompkins, together with colleagues and associates, leading government officials, and Tompkins' family: his wife, Enid; his three children; and four grandchildren.

Sir Martin Webster, the Prime Minister, took the stand immediately after the Prince of Wales. He was a tall man, who at that moment looked older than his fifty-six years, with a businesslike haircut, a face creased with worry lines, penetrating blue eyes and a nervous demeanor.

One by one, the grieving entourage stepped up to the pedestal to say some final words. Sir Nigel Scott was the last before the vicar said the closing prayer.

George Tompkins was laid to rest at Kensal Green Cemetery near his home in Chelsea. AVM Alan Reed stood with Trevor Bishop and Nigel Scott by the long line of black cars at the cemetery's exit.

"Any word on our man Frosty?" Home Secretary Scott inquired.

"Not yet," Reed said, looking sheepish.

"We've got several teams out looking for him," Bishop added.

"Oh, I know that," Scott said somewhat impatiently.

"But is there any progress? The PM is getting nervous."

Bishop looked at Reed, who shuffled his feet but did not add anything.

A black Rolls Royce limousine, driving slowly along the narrow path, careful not to hit the line of cars, stopped by them.

Prime Minister Webster lowered the car window.

"Just the lads I was looking for," he said in a jovial tone, which caused the three men to stare in surprise. "Why don't you join me?" he said, and the car door opened.

Reed hesitated but was motioned in, and the three sat, facing the Prime Minister and the deputy to the late George Tompkins, Ross Dixon. Dixon, in effect, ran the specialist protection branch SO1, providing protection for the Prime Minister, the royal family, government ministers, ambassadors, visiting dignitaries and other high-profile citizens who were deemed to be under possible assassination or terrorist threats.

Dixon, speaking quietly on his mobile phone, was in his late forties. He had an athletic appearance he seemed to go to great lengths to maintain; he was quite tall, his knees sticking up above everyone else's, had a black receding hairline above a high forehead, blue eyes under heavy black eyebrows, a crooked nose and thin lips. His skin was unusually white, and he wore a black suit appropriate for the occasion.

PM Webster gave him a look, and Dixon shut down his phone, smiling apologetically.

"Gentlemen," the PM said without preamble, "I am going to nominate Dixon here to replace Tompkins." He said, stopping to watch their reactions, then continued. "This is to go into effect immediately but will only become official when we get approval from the House of Commons."

If they were surprised, they did not show it.

Granted, Ross Dixon was an up-and-coming figure in their line of work but nominating him as head of SO1 with responsibilities for Homeland Security at his relatively young age seemed a bit premature, unwise, even.

"I know a few people who would apply for such a job, sir," Minister Scott said carefully.

"Yes, Nigel, I know a few myself, but I haven't got time to deal with a full-fledged search right now," the PM said exasperatedly. "These are grave times, and we have to act quickly."

"I can do the job, sir," Reed said.

The PM looked at him. "I cannot replace you at a moment's notice, Alan. You have a job just as critical at the Task Force Bureau, if not more," the PM said, "and besides, you and Bishop work well together, and if Dixon here joins your team, I believe you all can do a splendid job."

There was a moment of silence in the car; the soft hum of the engine could be heard as they crossed Hyde Park behind the police motorcycles, which were clearing the traffic ahead.

AVM Reed looked disappointed but did not voice his opinion.

"So, you've made up your mind, sir," Scott stated matter-of-factly. "Have you notified the cabinet?"

"All in good time," the PM said. "But I first needed to run it by you before I announced it to the ministers. I'll talk with George Atkins to get the SIS perspective as well before I announce it, but I think he will go along."

"I'll appreciate your cooperation," Dixon spoke for the first time.

Sir Nigel and Bishop nodded their chins uncomfortably at him but refrained from verbally acknowledging his request. Reed looked out the car window.

"So, while we are here, can you update me on what's been happening?" the PM asked, sitting back in his seat.

All three looked at Dixon, not sure if he was cleared to know.

"That's all right, gents," the PM eased their concern. "Dixon is well-versed in what's been happening up until now."

"And how would he know that?" Nigel Scott asked, looking suspiciously at Dixon.

"Because I briefed him!" Webster said reproachfully.

There was an awkward silence in the car before Bishop obliged.

"We have yet to find Agent Frost," he began. "Reed here is handling it, and we hope to have results very soon."

The PM was nodding but did not comment.

"We are looking at several scenarios for the Tompkins assassination, as well as the hit on the police officer in the hospital. Tompkins and the three others were killed by a bomb that exploded under his car when he came out of the Ritz. We are investigating whether it was there already or thrown there when Tompkins came out."

"What about the prisoner who died? Any leads on that?"

"We'll know more when we find Agent Frost, but the cause of death is a cyanide pill he swallowed."

"And the second policeman who disappeared?" asked Dixon.

Bishop looked at him for a long moment before answering. "We're looking into that as well," he answered dryly. "He's wounded, so he could not have gone far."

"Listen, lads," the PM said. "I am getting lots of heat on all this from the opposition and from my people as well. I need results quickly or all of us will be out of a job."

They all nodded in unison.

"I've heard nothing new here," Webster continued. "And I need to be able to provide a few explanations and show some progress when I address the House tomorrow, not to mention the press and foreign leaders who keep pestering me."

"We'll get you results, sir," Dixon said, and they all looked at the PM with apprehension.

A few minutes later, they reached 10 Downing Street. Scott accompanied the PM to a scheduled cabinet meeting, leaving Bishop and Reed with Dixon in the car.

"Dixon, old chap," Bishop said in a jolly, if insincere, tone as they were driven to Whitehall across the street. "Can you point us to the people who escorted your boss to the Ritz on Thursday? We can't seem to find any of you who were there."

Dixon looked perplexed for a moment, then nodded.

Chapter Twelve

Frosty drove his rented Corolla toward London, avoiding the motorways, taking small back roads, careful to avoid any patrol cars.

Jemma had informed him of the latest developments and what had been implied in the meeting with Bishop.

He was now a wanted man, accused of treason. A mole, they had said!

A sense of panic washed over him at first. Cindy and the girls! What would happen to his family now? They might also accuse Cindy, whose occupation was well-known to them. It took him a while to accept this new reality and to acknowledge to himself that he now had to prove his innocence. But first, he had to find out why he was being framed.

He knew he was taking an immense risk going back into the lion's den, but he figured London was the only place he could get some answers. Cindy would be waiting for him at a coffee shop in Covent Garden, where they could get lost in the crowds, and there were a few people he needed to see before he could decide what to do.

Andy White, the SO1 special liaison to the Homeland Security Office, was one of the people he needed to see if he could get near him. Reuben Santana, the police officer who was targeted along with his partner in the hospital and disappeared, was another. Jemma had given him the name.

And he needed to see Jemma! Talk to her face-to-face and figure out what was happening. He knew she was under immense pressure and most likely extensive scrutiny by now, being his closest ally for so many years. He had ordered her to cease all contact with him until the matter was resolved but planned to approach her in secret without her knowledge so she could not be accused of collaborating with him if he got caught.

He reached Chesham at midday, left his car parked on the street, and entered the Tube. He took the Bakerloo Line to King's Cross, changed to the Piccadilly Line, and exited at Covent Garden.

In the train, he sat at the far end of the compartment, his back to the partition by the door to the next car, bowing his head slightly and watching carefully.

At King's Cross, he noticed several police foot patrols but nothing out of the ordinary.

Covent Garden was packed full of people, despite the freezing, cloudy weather and irritating drizzle, which was the primary reason he had chosen it for the rendezvous with his wife. He inched his way among the crowd, focusing on the cafe where they had agreed to meet.

He saw her from afar. She was seated outside at a corner table with another woman, who he had instructed she bring along. He watched her for a moment. Her straight blond hair fluttered in the wind, exposing her delicate features. He missed her: her soft skin, her large brown eyes, her freckled nose and sweet red lips.

The two women were busy in conversation at the noisy café, sitting underneath some glass panels, keeping out of the drizzle.

He stood a while, studying his flanks. If there was a guaranteed way to track him down, tailing his wife would be a primary recourse, so he had suggested she bring along a friend. He just had to hope her new mobile phone was not tapped yet.

He called her, saw her answer her phone, and instructed her to wait ten minutes, then go to the bathroom by a row of clothing stores across the open square from where she was sitting and choose the stall on the right.

He kept looking around, hoping to identify her tail, but it was a Sunday, and there was simply too much pedestrian traffic. He approached the bathrooms, which were two plastic booths side by side, waited around looking for threats, and then slipped into the right booth when a lady in a brimmed hat and a white dress walked out.

Cindy joined him there a few minutes later. He unlocked the door as soon as she raised her hand to knock and let her in.

They hugged and kissed and looked at one another as if they hadn't seen each other for years.

"Do we have time for a quickie?" she joked.

Frosty smiled. "I wish."

"So, what is going on? Please tell me," Cindy reproached.

"I am being accused of treason," he said, looking into her eyes.

She looked at him dumbfounded. "Why? What did you do?"

"Damn if I know," he said, raising his palms in the air. "But in the meantime, I'm being blamed for Kruger's death."

Cindy shook her head as if to clear it. "This is unbelievable. Why can't you talk to someone? Set them straight?"

"To be honest, Cin, I don't think they want me alive," he said solemnly.

"Who are they?" she exclaimed, exasperated. "These people have been your colleagues for over twenty years! Surely, they know you are no traitor."

"I cannot walk in there to exonerate myself if I don't know what I'm up against," Frosty reasoned. "If they went through the trouble of forging my visit to Kruger six months ago and making it seem like I killed the man, then they must be sending search units after me by now," he complained. "This thing is no random occurrence, and we have to be extremely careful."

"How do you know they'll send search units after you?" she asked, looking frightened.

"It's what I would have done," he admitted. "I know Bishop is personally involved and is most likely sending MI5 and everyone else after me…"

Cindy stared at him, suddenly looking helpless, tears welling up in her eyes.

"Who's everyone else?" she questioned.

"The police and whoever else they can recruit. Maybe even MI6."

The tears were now falling freely on her cheeks, and Cindy began wiping her eyes. Frosty took her in his arms and held her close for a few seconds so she would calm down.

"Did you find out who the bystander who was killed was?" he asked softly, trying to be more practical.

She nodded, wiping her eyes again. "His name was Simon Lewis; worked at SO1 for ten years until a year or so ago."

"Wow! Protection branch. How did you find out?"

"Hacked into the morgue at St. Thomas's Hospital," she said. "Got his name, then checked his employment record. He was listed as a government employee, but without designation, so I checked the security organizations and found he worked at SO1 until last year."

"So, it was no coincidence that he was there," Frosty marveled out loud. "He could have been the Tompkins meeting."

"He very well might have been," Cindy said thoughtfully. "And he might have gotten killed for it."

They looked at one another as the revelation sunk in.

"A definite path to pursue," Frosty said.

His wife nodded.

"Now listen to me, Cin," Frosty continued, hastily grabbing her shoulders. "You need to leave now; fetch the girls and go home. Assume you are being followed, so act naturally. I am going to see Jemma, then I'll come home. Leave the back door open and turn off the lights in the house. I'll try to sneak in. If I don't make it, I'll call you and we'll figure out what to do."

Cindy looked at him, then flung her arms around his neck and kissed him urgently on the lips.

"We'll get through this together," she whispered to him. "I love you."

Then she turned and reached for the door. Frosty stopped her.

"I almost forgot," he said. "I need you to look up an officer Reuben Santana. He's the officer who disappeared from the hospital. Get me an address."

Cindy nodded.

"I love you," he said, and let her go.

*****

Jemma entered Embankment Station at half-past seven that evening, having spent her Sunday at the office with everyone else, looking for Frosty. She joined the flocks of tourists going down the escalator to the Northern line, most likely back from a visit to Trafalgar Square or the London Eye or some other tourist attraction.

"Keep looking straight ahead," she heard a familiar voice talking to her. "Are you being followed?"

She did as she was told and did not turn her head.

"I most probably am," she replied, looking straight ahead, unable to contain a half-smile.

"Then shake that tail and meet me in an hour at Costa Coffee at Liverpool Street station."

She nodded, and he walked past her down the escalator. He was wearing a gray overcoat with its collar up to cover half his face and was carrying a black umbrella.

She did not get to see his face.

She entered the Northern line toward her usual destination, Camden Town, watching carefully for her tail. At the next station, Charring Cross, she stepped out and back in before the train moved, noticing a woman in a pink overcoat do the same. At Leicester Square, she got out again and stepped back into a different car. The woman in pink remained in the car Jemma had left, but a man in a blue parka stepped in after her.

At Tottenham Court Road, she got off the train and transferred to the Central line, taking the train to Oxford Circus, where she got off and took the escalator to the top level. She walked around the packed station until she was certain no one was following, then took the escalator back down and took the Central line to Liverpool Street, making it there in just under an hour.

Costa Coffee was situated next to the escalator in a square below street level, the only open shop among a row of retailers; it being a Sunday. She entered, ordered a cappuccino, and sat down at a corner table, her back to the wall.

Frosty joined her a few minutes later, an espresso in his hand, looking around. He smiled and sat down facing her.

"If you see anything suspicious, we split!" he said.

"Good to see you too," she said, smiling.

He reached out his hand to hold hers. "You, OK?" she asked.

"As well as can be expected," he said, with a tired smile.

"Bishop's got people out looking for you."

"How many?"

"Half the damn TFB," she informed him.

"What's your part?"

"Oh, they don't trust me," she said, smiling. "Left me in the office to dig up stuff…"

"What kind of stuff?"

"Reed assigned me to track your movements twenty years back."

Frosty smiled. "And what did you find?"

"That you got married in New York," she said, smiling.

"Well, you should know." He smiled back. "What about the rest of our guys?"

"Taylor and Edwards are investigating the policeman's murder at the hospital. Lucy Shepherd and Chapman are looking for you, along with GI, Harriet and the rest. Even Olga was asked to join the search."

Frosty's stare turned serious. "Did you know the bystander who was killed was SO1?"

Jemma registered surprise. "No, they wouldn't tell us who he was."

"Well, Cindy dug it up. His name was Simon Lewis, and he worked at SO1 for ten years until last year."

Jemma stared at him.

"Can you find out what he did there and what made him leave?"

"I can try," Jemma said.

"Also, can you get hold of prison records and tapes of Kruger's visitors in the last year?"

Jemma looked perplexed.

"Cindy found out that I had visited Kruger six months ago, which I never did. Someone went to the trouble of using my badge and forging my signature in the visitors' log to make it look as if it was me, so I need to find out who was there under my name."

Jemma was nodding her head.

"And it could really help if we could get a look at that tape of Kruger and me in the interrogation cell."

"Reed asked me to get that tape, but it was confiscated by some Homeland Security folks this morning. The commandant said they had a warrant for it."

"Well, there goes the evidence," Frosty sighed. "Can we find out who took it?"

Jemma studied him. Not three days ago, they were casually going about their business, gathering evidence and following leads. Now they were sitting across from each other trying to figure out how to survive.

"I need you to tell me what's going on, Frosty," she said quietly.

"I wish I knew, Jem," he said, and as if reading her mind added, "One minute I'm head of a major task force, and the next, I am wanted for treason."

"Did you kill Kruger?" she blurted, unable to stop herself.

Frosty looked at her with surprise. "All these years, and you need to ask?" She shook her head. "I'm sorry, Frosty, these people got to me…"

"Someone is trying to get rid of me," he whispered, moving his face closer to her over the coffee table. "There's a bigger picture here which we cannot see at the moment, and if we want to survive, we need to find out what's going on real fast."

"You think I'm in danger too?" she asked.

"Yes, I do. You, especially, are far too close to me for whoever is running this show to leave you alone. If they catch me, you and possibly the rest of our crew will be strung up as well."

They fell silent for a long moment before Frosty went on. "Take a look at what's happened. A deputy minister is assassinated with three others, one of whom is an SO1 guy who possibly met with him beforehand. Tompkins sends us to Kruger, who swallows a cyanide pill right in front of me. I get blamed for killing him, and the video of the interrogation is now confiscated. Meanwhile, there's another assassination attempt on the two police officers who were at the scene when the deputy minister was killed."

He stopped to take a breath of air.

"Now I am being accused of treason by the people I have worked with for twenty years without so much as a hearing, and what's more worrying is that it seems this charade was set in motion a long time ago."

Jemma took his hand between both of hers. There was deep concern in her eyes when she spoke. "I hear what you're saying, Frosty, and I agree. Sorry, I doubted you; but where do we go from here?"

"Obviously, we are key to this mess, otherwise why would they be after me? So, as long as you still have some credibility, you need to use whatever means and authority you still have to make this go away before it gets out of control."

"It's already out of control," she pointed out, "but I'll do whatever I can to help fix it."

"And you need to be extra careful, Jem! The minute you feel the slightest threat, you take off, promise me."

She nodded.

"And this includes Jake and the boys," Frosty added. "Don't leave them on their own or whoever is behind this will use them as leverage. If we don't make progress in the next day or two, and I have to get away to buy some more time, I'm taking Cindy and the girls with me."

They hugged before they split, Jemma kissing him on the cheek. Then each turned and disappeared into the crowd.

Chapter Thirteen

James Flanagan was six foot two and looked well kept under his black suit and blue tie; he sat erect, his gray curly hair cropped short, his hardened face creased with lines and his steel-gray eyes focused and concerned. He was sixty-three, Chairman and CEO of the London-based Europe Investment Bank, and the general partner of the Chelsea Capital Management Limited, Hedge Fund.

His black Jaguar approached his house at Hempstead; it was more a mansion than a house, with a small roundabout in front of the tall, sheltered entrance.

Flanagan was all ready for a glass of bourbon and a quiet family evening at home after a tiring day of burying George Tompkins, who shared a school bench with him at Oxford. His driver pulled up to the front door, and Flanagan stepped out with his black briefcase, signaling the driver that he could leave.

He rang the bell, and the housekeeper opened, her face deathly white. Flanagan was about to ask her what the matter was when he was forcefully pulled into the foyer by a man in dark clothes, a second man quickly shutting the double doors behind.

"What in the name of..." Flanagan began, then opened his mouth in utter surprise as he saw his entire family seated on the large L-shaped sofa in the living room, staring at three men with pistols.

A fourth man got up from the living room television seat, flashed a distorted smile, and gestured to Flanagan to join. He was a tall man with blond hair, clear blue eyes, a masculine jawline and a wide mouth with a perfect set of white teeth.

Flanagan hesitated just a bit before he was pushed forward again and stumbled toward the sofa, Gabriella, their Columbian housekeeper, hurrying behind him to take her place on the sofa as well.

His wife was there along with his two sons, their wives and three grandchildren, all squashed together on the large L-shaped leather sofa. The oldest of the grandchildren, Robbie, was eight, Sarah was six, and little John was four.

The men holding them at gunpoint all wore black, including black gloves and black wool headcovers. Their leader wore a black suit with a black shirt and no tie. He produced a large bracelet from his pocket, the size of a large watch, and signaled Robbie to step forward. Flanagan and his son Jenson, Robbie's dad, reacted instantly, attempting to rise from the sofa, but that caused the three guns to be cocked and aimed at their heads.

"Please don't interrupt again or someone will die," the man said in a calm yet menacing tone with what seemed like an Eastern European accent, signaling the kid over.

Robbie got up from the sofa and moved hesitantly toward the man.

"Pull up your pants and put your leg on the table," the man said when Robbie stood in front of him. Robbie did as he was told, and the man fit the bracelet around his leg below the knee. There was a metallic click, and a small red light began to blink.

"This is an ankle bracelet similar to those used for house arrests, which your grandson will now permanently wear," the man addressed Flanagan. "But unlike the bracelets used for house arrests, this particular bracelet is a sheet of very delicate and very powerful explosive that will trigger if tampered with. It is also equipped with a GPS tracking device that will transmit a signal to the child's whereabouts at all hours of the day. So, if, for example, we see a deviation in his daily routine, we can instantly blow him up from a distance."

The man looked around at the horrified faces and continued as if nothing had happened.

"All three of your grandchildren will be wearing this bracelet, Mr. Flanagan, and will remain in good health as long as you do as you're told."

The family on the sofa cringed in fright and held on to one another.

"Furthermore, our men will be escorting you around and should keep you pretty much in line," the blond man added.

The men in the black outfits nodded their heads at the fearful family staring up at them as if they were performers in a play.

"To save you the speculation, Mr. Flanagan, or is it Sir Flanagan?" the blond man continued, "there are a few things we need you to do that will not coincide with your bank's policies or with any policies for that matter, but as long as you promptly perform, no one will be harmed. Is that clear?"

The banker looked ill. He began opening his mouth to say something but thought the better of it.

"There will no longer be any loyalty to protocol, Sir Flanagan," the man continued. "Your only loyalty will be to what we tell you to do. If you go astray in any way, your kids die; if you mention anything to the police or the press, the same result. Is that understood?"

Robbie's dad, Jenson, could not contain himself any longer. He lunged at the man, jumping over the living room table, but the man was quick, moving to one side. He swapped the attack, using Jenson's momentum to throw him to the floor. Jenson tried to get up, but the man kicked him on the side of the head, sending him back sprawling on the floor, then lunged at him with extreme quickness, pinning him to the floor with his knee, then hitting him hard in the face with his elbow, causing Jenson to momentarily lose conciseness. Jenson's wife, Abby, let out a scream and jumped to her husband's aid, but one of the gun-bearers grabbed her and pushed her back on the couch, pointing his gun inches from her forehead.

The blond man stood up over Jenson, putting his shoe on his chest like a warrior who had just conquered his prey. "Do not attempt to fight this," he said, addressing Flanagan, as Jenson regained conciseness under his shoe.

"So when will it end?" Flanagan asked in a trembling voice, speaking for the first time since he walked into the house.

"When we achieve our goals," the man said, allowing Jenson to sit up on the floor.

"And what are they?" the banker asked.

"All in good time, Sir," the man said, flashing his distorted smile again. "Now allow the children to come to me so I can put on their bracelets, and we'll be out of your way."

Chapter Fourteen

Friday, January 25, 2019

Frosty inched his way into the dark. His house in Edgware loomed hostile in front of him. Never before had he needed to sneak into it like a thief in the night. He had walked from the Northern line Burnt Oak station several blocks to his house rather than get off at Edgware, where he would normally disembark, figuring anyone waiting for him would most likely wait for him there.

He took several back alleys once he got close, going through a few darkened neighborhood parks, jumping over and crawling under several fences before he reached his street and sat a while to watch for surveillance.

His street was S-shaped, and on an incline, and he had to get to both ends to detect the tail. Two darkened cars stood at the curb at both ends of the street, and there was no way to tell if there was anyone on foot watching as well.

He moved silently to a parallel street and surveyed the area a while for any movement before he leaped over a small gate and climbed a shoulder-high fence to his backyard.

Now he scooted low and ran to the back door.

Cindy and the girls ran to him as soon as he entered. He hugged all three and received a bundle of kisses on his face before he was able to spring free, his youngest daughter, Zoe, still hanging on his neck.

It was past midnight.

"Let Daddy breathe," Cindy whispered, and Zoe let go, sliding down to the floor.

"We missed you, Daddy," Gabi said accusingly. "Where have you been?"

"Well, it's not as if I have never gone away before, is it, dear?"

Gabi smiled in the dark and hugged his waist.

"Why are we whispering?" Zoe asked. "And why are the lights out?"

"Didn't mommy explain?" Frosty whispered.

"She said you got in trouble with some bad people and that you did not want them to know where we live," Gabi recited what her mom had said.

"But why do the lights have to be out?" Zoe insisted.

Frosty stared at his wife, who made a face in the dark. He sighed and sat on a kitchen chair, taking both girls on his lap.

"Now, girls, this may be a little difficult to explain, but you are both grown up enough to deal with it, so I am going to tell you what's happened, and then you need to go up to your rooms, pack a small bag with whatever you need for a short trip, and wait there until we call you. Is that OK?"

Both girls nodded, and Frosty did his best to explain in vague terms, so as not to frighten them, what had transpired and what they needed to do.

When the girls darted up to their rooms, he hugged Cindy, and they kissed intimately.

"You took a big risk coming here," she whispered, hugging him.

"I figured it's the last place they'll expect me to be."

"I've seen at least one car parked at the end of the street," she said.

"There's another at the other end," he informed her. "But I did not detect anyone on foot or anyone at the back. I was out there for an hour before I came in."

She smiled at him and hugged him some more.

"You need to pack a bag too," he whispered to her. "We must be ready to get away from here real quick."

"But where will we go?" she questioned. "Your parents?"

"Out of the question," he said. "They will be waiting there as well. What we'll do, if all else fails, is go to the country somewhere and hide until this thing is resolved."

She looked at him thoughtfully. "They may send out a countrywide alert."

"They probably did already, but out in the country, we'll have a better chance of dodging them for a while, and I'll feel a lot better if you and the girls are with me."

"But we can't run forever, darling," she said dubiously. "They'll catch us sooner or later..."

"We'll deal with it when the time comes, love," he smiled weakly. "But at least we'll be together, and they won't be able to use you girls to coerce me."

Cindy sighed and held out her hand to him. There was a long pause as they sat in the dark around the kitchen table.

"I've got an address for the motorcycle officer," she finally said quietly. "I also have his home phone number."

"That's great," he said. "Give it to me."

"It's in a file on the computer. Let me get it for you."

They walked in the dark to her study, and she sat in front of her laptop and turned on the darkened screen. Frosty looked quickly around, realizing she had closed the shades and curtains, and there was no possibility of seeing them from outside.

"Can you show me a photo of him?" he asked while copying Santana's address and phone number into his phone.

She quickly hacked the keyboard and came up with a photo of a large, well-built, handsome man with olive skin standing in a swimsuit next to a much smaller woman in a bikini. The woman was quite striking herself. She was tanned, had straight black hair, a well-shaped figure and an engaging face. They were both smiling happily on a white sandy beach with green-colored water in the background, holding a coconut with a straw between them.

"That was quick," he commended her.

"Quite easy, dear, when you have a full name and an address," she said modestly. "This is an Instagram photo taken in Rio only a month ago, as you can see." The photo was tagged with Rio de Janeiro and Brazil. It was impossible to miss.

"Do you have an address and a photo for this Tompkins' aide who visited Kruger?" he quickly asked while she was at it.

"You mean Andy White?" she said. "Let me check real quick."

She brought up another file she had designated "Andy White" and began to move around Windows with her mouse until she found what she was looking for. It took a little longer to dig up than Santana's photo, but she eventually found the address with a passport photo in the Home Office secure address book she managed to hack into. Andy White had long red hair covering his ears. His face was gaunt with bulging eyes and a long chin.

"It's a London address as well," she said as Frosty copied the details into his phone.

Cindy turned to him. "You need a rest," she declared. "You look awful. Why don't you take a nap, and I'll pack us a bag and watch over things while you sleep?"

As soon as she said it, he realized how tired he was. He nodded and looked at his watch. "It's midnight," he reckoned. "Give me three hours, and then wake me up. I'll need to get out of here well before sunrise."

"What shall we do tomorrow?" She asked.

"I'll try and find these two guys at their homes early," he acknowledged. "I'll let you know if I learn anything. You take the girls to school as usual. Take all our bags with you in the car in case we need to make a break for it. Go to the bank and take out as much cash as you can, then wait for my call. Don't use the house phone or your usual mobile, only the new one you got, and let's hope they haven't tapped into it yet. Make sure your regular phone is shut but take it with you. We can use it to divert them when the time comes. I'll call you from this new phone I got like we did at Covent Garden today."

They hugged and kissed again, and he lay on the sofa in the living room, instantly falling asleep.

Chapter Fifteen

Saturday, January 26, 2019

Frosty slipped out of his house at four in the morning, having had a nap, a shower, a shave, a change of clothes and a quick breakfast with a cup of sweet tea Cindy had prepared for him before he left through the back door.

He had to brace the wall at the side of his neighbor's house after he cleared the fence at the back when a car drove slowly by its lights breaching the darkness and illuminating the narrow street.

He waited a few minutes, checking for pursuers, then ran across the street and disappeared among the row of houses on the other side.

He reached Santana's Condo at six in the morning, having spent an hour at a 24-hour coffee shop a few blocks away in the Ruislip area.

He found the small street off Victoria Road and once again checked for tails, not sure what to expect. He settled in a small children's park that had a view of the address and waited there, watching his surroundings closely.

At seven, he saw the girl from the photo walk out of the Condo toward the nearest Underground station, Ruislip Gardens. She was dressed in jeans, a dark pullover, a short fleece overcoat, a large brown bag on her shoulder, and an umbrella in one hand.

As soon as he saw her, he called the home phone but received no reply. He hesitated a few seconds, then decided to follow her. She walked fast, and Frosty had to keep up, all the while checking his flanks for followers.

At the station, she stopped to get a ticket and pushed through the gate to the escalator that took her up to the trains. Frosty stood a few steps below her and kept his distance at the overpass station as they waited for the train. When it arrived, he shadowed her closely and sat next to her in the half-empty train, which filled up quickly at the next station.

"I want to meet your boyfriend, Rueben," he said to her when the Central line train left South Ruislip. Up close, she looked even more striking, her skin a smooth bronze and her eyes a dark brown with a small nose and enticing lips.

She looked at him in shocked surprise but did not utter a word lowering her gaze to the floor.

"I may be in the same trouble as he is, so it would help if we met," he said again calmly. "Do you know where I can find him?"

She still would not look at him, and he could see she was struggling to remain calm. At the next station, she got up and moved to another seat. Frosty remained in his seat but moved at the next station when the seat next to her vacated.

"You have nothing to fear," he said to her as she tried to look away. "He may need my help as much as I need his."

At the next station, Hanger Lane, she got up and stepped off the train. Frosty followed her. She walked quickly down the stairs and left the station, walking briskly down a busy street, opening her umbrella as rain started pouring down. Frosty kept up when she finally entered a coffee shop and sat down at a corner table.

"What is your name?" she asked in English with an obvious Latin accent, when he sat across the table from her.

"Adrian Frost," Frosty said. "What's yours?"

She hesitated, studying him intently. "Camilla," she finally said.

"Listen," Frosty said, "I don't even have to see him if you are suspicious of me. Just take my phone number and ask him to call me. I work for British Intelligence; he can check me out. I think we are both in danger as a result of the Tompkins assassination. Something we did or saw is threatening some dangerous people, and I believe we can help one another find out what it is."

Camilla did not immediately reply, but her gaze became a little bit more relaxed. The waitress came over and they each ordered an espresso, Camilla asked for water as well.

"OK," she said when the waitress left with their order. "I'll take your number, and Reuben will call you if you check out. You seem like a good guy."

Frosty smiled for the first time. "Is he OK?" he asked. "How bad are his wounds?"

"He'll survive," Camilla said. "He's strong, my Ruby," she smiled back, flashing a beautiful set of white teeth, her high cheekbones adorning her attractive face.

"Here's my phone number," he said, showing her the number on his mobile. She took her phone out from her bag, clicked the number into it, and put it back.

"May I make a suggestion?" he asked.

"Go ahead," she said. "It's a free country."

"Ditch the phone and tell Reuben to do the same."

"It was the first thing he told me to do," she said.

"Good man," Frosty commended.

"He is," she agreed, smiling again.

They drank the rest of their coffee in silence and asked for the bill.

"It's best we don't leave here together," he said before the waitress came with the bill. "I'll pay for this. You leave first."

Camilla nodded and got up. "Thank you," she said. "I hope you check out." He smiled at her as she turned and walked out of the restaurant.

*****

Andy White lived near Rathbone market in Canning Town, an up-and-coming neighborhood situated in the area of the former London docks on the north side of the River Thames. The neighborhood, for a long time, was one of the most deprived areas in the UK, but thanks to the many Docklands development projects, it became a sought-after commodity in recent years.

Frosty exited the Canning Town Tube station along the Jubilee Line in mid-morning rush hour, crossed over the Docklands Light Railway tracks, and walked toward Rathbone Street.

He had been in the neighborhood a few times in the past but not in the last five years and was surprised to see the progress. Replacing the rundown buildings and shops were new fashionable structures with famous brands, attractive restaurants and trendy coffee shops.

He walked a cobblestone alley toward the market, identifying White's address on a renovated two-story brownstone building that had a red-painted entrance with glass doors.

He tried the glass doors, but they were locked, so he waited a few minutes until a woman in a training outfit with a dog on a leash came running out, leaving the doors open just long enough for him to slip through.

He quickly looked at the names on the mailboxes in the small lobby and found White's name on apartment 2C.

There was no elevator, so he hopped the stairs two at a time to the second floor and peeked at both sides of the corridor before he approached White's door.

He knocked and heard ruffling inside. "A moment," a voice said. Frosty stood to the side, so he could not be seen from inside by the pip hole.

The door opened after a few seconds by the red-haired man with the bony face Cindy had found in the address book. He looked at Frosty, registering surprise, and hesitated for a moment before he pulled the door wide open and asked Frosty in.

He was wearing a gray undershirt, black slacks and shoes. His flat was painted white; it smelled new and looked rather empty, with a television set in front of a lone sofa in the living room and clothes thrown about on what looked like a kitchen table to the side by a small gas stove and a refrigerator. There were carton boxes stacked near a small hallway Frosty guessed led to a bedroom and a bath.

On one of two chairs that stood between the living room and the kitchen, he noticed a gun hanging in a shoulder holster.

He shut the door behind him and stood facing White, who was quite tall and wide but scrawny. He looked Frosty up and down with his bulging eyes, studying him closely.

"You know who I am, don't you?" Frosty stated.

White nodded. "What is it you want?" he asked hoarsely.

Frosty came straight to the point. "You saw Kruger a week before he killed himself in my presence," he said slowly, studying White's face for a reaction. "What were you doing there?"

White's gaze remained non-committal, but his eyes darted toward the place where he hung his gun.

"I am afraid it's none of your business," he said.

"It certainly is my business since I head the task force that is investigating the organization he used to be part of."

White flashed a crooked smile. "Used to be is right, now that he's dead."

"Why are you smiling?" Frosty inquired.

"Before he died, he was still a member," White said, sending a cold shiver down Frosty's neck.

"How would you know that?" he asked, surprised.

"Because he sacrificed himself for the good of the cause."

Frosty was dumbstruck but held his manner in check.

"So, you know I did not kill him," he blurted out.

"Of course, I do," White spat. "I gave him the pill."

"Now why would you do that?" Frosty asked, genuinely startled.

"You will soon find out," White said, flashing his crooked smile again.

"Meanwhile, I need to bring you in," he said and reached for his gun, moving backward, his long arms reaching for the holster without taking his eyes off his target.

Frosty was ready. He turned the doorknob and was out of the flat in a flash, racing toward the stairs, clearing them three at a time, bursting through the glass doors out of the lobby, and running full tilt toward the market to his right.

He risked a look back and saw White racing after him, gun in one hand and the other holding a mobile phone to his ear.

He reached the market and turned left, running along the various stands, bumping into people and moving them out of the way. He saw a small alleyway between two food shops and turned to run through it. Coming out the other end, he found himself in front of the DLR railway overpass and climbed the steps.

White was not far behind, reaching the steps only a few seconds behind Frosty and climbing them two at a time.

Frosty continued racing through the overpass to the stairs going down the other end and hopped down toward the Canning Town Tube station. Racing down its steps, he jumped over the entry gates toward the escalator. Moving people out of his way, he hurled down the moving stairs, hearing the brakes of a train at the bottom.

He jumped down the bottom part of the escalator, ran along the connecting tunnel, and burst through the waiting crowd as the train stopped and the doors opened. He got into the cart and stood at the entrance expecting White at any second.

White burst from the tunnel seconds behind, as the doors were about to shut. He saw Frosty and ran toward the cart, expecting to fit through the closing doors.

Frosty did not remain passive. He met White at the door with a massive kick to the groin, and when the man doubled over, he kicked him in the head, sending him flying on his back onto the station's concrete deck. A gunshot rang out as White hit the floor, but by then the doors had shut, and the train began gathering speed away from the station.

Frosty turned and began moving along the cart as people moved out of his way, staring at him in fear. He opened the compartment's door, the train's noise becoming evident, and moved to the next cart.

He knew he could not afford to disembark at the next station. White had surely alerted the troops, and they would be waiting for him at the next stop.

He reached the front compartment and stood at the front door, watching the tracks fly by, waiting to see the welcoming party. As the train skidded around a bend, he saw the lights from the station, which was announced over the loudspeaker as North Greenwich.

The train slowed and entered the station; nothing seemed amiss until the doors opened. He stepped out among the crowds going to visit the O2 Arena for music and sporting events and was about to head for the stairs when a group of three men in black clothes burst through the opening, pushing people left and right. He eased back, careful not to draw attention, and disappeared along a narrow pathway that extended from the station's embarkation deck into the dark tunnel, not sure if the driver noticed him, but without much of a choice.

The path ended after several yards with a steel latter that he climbed down to the tracks. He waited a moment, looking toward the station, then began moving along the tracks, finding a door in a niche further ahead that he could fit into when the train moved by. The train, however, remained at the station longer than usual, and at one point, he saw a figure on the narrow pathway staring in his direction but did not climb down.

Finally, the train moved, and Frosty clung to his niche as the carts gained momentum inches from his face, causing a vacuum that almost sucked him in. When the last of the carts disappeared in the dark tunnel ahead, he breathed a sigh of relief and took a peek toward the station, wondering whether it was safe to go back there or wait a while longer.

His head was spinning with what he had heard from White and the manner in which it was said. White had seemed so cocky and sure of himself...

He waited another hour in the tunnel. Several more trains passed by before he inched back to the latter and climbed it, straddling the narrow path and peeking into the station, which looked innocently at peace. From his vantage point, he tried to identify a threat but could not detect any. He decided to wait for the next train to arrive and blended in the crowd as soon as its doors opened, but rather than head for the exit, he decided to hop on the train for another stop just in case.

He got off at Canary Wharf and carefully climbed the stairs, expecting an assault any minute, which did not occur. He walked to the ticket inspector at the exit door to report that he had lost his ticket, paid the fee at the ticket booth, and walked out to a bright, sunny day, the first in almost a week. It was only noon time.

He called Cindy, who was waiting at home all packed and having drawn several thousand pounds in cash from their bank account. He instructed her to take the girls from school, leave their car at the Boardwalk Center parking lot, take the Northern line from Edgware station to King's Cross, and wait for him there at McDonald's. He explained that they should try and shake their tail by getting off the train at a particular station, and then get back on again on the next train. That should at least flush out their pursuers, he reasoned, who may just choose to let them go rather than get exposed—though after the events of the morning, he doubted they'd leave them alone for a second.

He next called Jemma, advising her of what had happened and what he had learned, suggesting she should consider leaving London with Jake and the boys.

"White would not have said what he said to me if he was not certain he could get away with it," he told her. "And that's the worrying part because it means he's got support from higher up."

"It also means Kruger must have remained involved from inside all these years and was part of the plan to set you up," Jemma remarked.

"Kruger did say something quite odd, now that I think of it," Frosty recalled. "I asked him if there was a call sign or a signal for the day they would be expected to perform, and he said he didn't know but that maybe I did. I thought he was trying to tell me something, but now I realize he was setting me up, knowing everything said in that room is recorded."

Jemma asked if she should inform Bishop or Reed, but Frosty argued against it, reasoning that it would expose the fact that she has contact with him and would only get her in trouble.

"We do not know how high this conspiracy reaches or who's involved, so it's better to keep a low profile for the time being until we know more," he maintained.

She began telling him what she had managed to dig up, but he stopped her short, asking her to save it for a later time, not wanting to spend any excess time on the phone.

He promised to call her when they had settled somewhere and clicked off, backtracking his way to Canary Wharf to take the Underground to King's Cross.

Chapter Sixteen

Sunday, January 27, 2019

The following morning, Jemma was at her desk when Andy Taylor came rushing in, his face flushed pink.

"There's been an explosion at the Oxford Circus station," he exclaimed, out of breath. "We need to get going. Take your gun."

Jemma shut down her computer instantly, stuffed a Walther from the safe into her purse, locked up, and ran after Taylor down the flight of stairs and out into the street. Three police cars were waiting. She jumped into the first car and found herself facing her boss, Alan Reed, with a concerned look on his face.

She looked at him questioningly as the car sped off, siren blaring.

"This just happened; we don't have any details yet," he said to her, looking out the window as the police car sped past Charring Cross to Piccadilly Circus, then onto Regent Street toward Oxford Circus.

Regent Street was completely jammed, and the police cars barely made it to Hanover Street. The lead driver managed to bypass the traffic by driving on the sidewalk, grazing two streetlights in the process, siren howling, and blowing his horn at the crowds, but the closer they got to Oxford Circus, the more difficult it became until they had to stop. Both sides of the wide boulevard were blocked by curious pedestrians and frustrated car passengers, who simply abandoned their cars on the street and gathered around, realizing they were not going anywhere for a while, trying to figure out what was happening. Double-decker buses, delivery trucks, taxis, and cars were literally parked between the posh facades of the street, and to Jemma, it seemed like a canyon whose water had just stopped all of a sudden, held in place by an invisible dam.

Reed jumped out of the car and led his team on foot to Oxford Circus, which was by now humming with ambulances, police cars, and fire trucks. There was a foul smell in the air of burning, and black smoke was coming out of steam vents, filling the street.

They flashed their TFB ID cards at the police personnel who were guarding the entrance to the Tube station and went down the stairs.

They found mayhem. The entire passageway was dark, lit by emergency lighting; emergency personnel were tending to people lying on the concrete floor, using flashlights, trying to locate those still moving.

As they inched their way forward searching the station, the incredible damage became apparent. The small shops and booths encircling the area were in shambles, clothes, and merchandise were blown to pieces, spread everywhere, windows blew, and fragments of glass covered the entire floor among puddles of water and other fluids that were seeping from all sides.

And people—wounded, some seated on the floor pleading for help, some lying unconscious, blood-covered bodies, clothes ripped, faces registering shock.

"Spread out," Reed commanded. "Let's give a hand to the wounded."

Jemma picked her way carefully along the passageway. The ticket booth's windows, which had fortified glass, were smashed to bits. All around the booth, people were lying on the ground, none of them moving. She began checking for pulses, going from person to person. There was a woman in a white dress lying on her back, her dress thrown over her face, exposing her long legs. Jemma pulled the dress down, shuddering when she saw the hole in the woman's chest, blood crusting around the wound. A man in a suit was lying face down, still holding a brown briefcase in his right hand. She looked closer and saw shrapnel sticking out the back of his neck, and a pool of blood formed on the floor around his head.

She counted seven dead around the ticket booth, then looked inside and saw the attendant sitting on the floor, not moving, among ticket stubs and open drawers, his face and neck riddled with glass. There was nothing she could do for him.

She looked around and gingerly continued past the ticket booth and the entry gates that were smashed open, reaching a dark crater that formed in place of the escalator going down to the Central line. The top half of the escalator had disappeared. Further down, the bottom half seemed in place, with bodies lying across it. Below that, she could hear cries for help. The roof above the escalator was cracked, pieces of concrete falling down into the gaping hole.

A fire chief appeared by her side. "We need to try to get down there," he said, and she nodded.

Two firefighters appeared with an extension ladder, which they began to lower toward the undamaged part of the escalator. It barely made it, but the two did not hesitate and began climbing down the ladder over the black pit, while pieces of concrete continued to fall intermittently from the ceiling above them.

"Let me help them," Jemma said to the fire chief, who was holding the ladder in place.

He looked at her quizzically for a long moment, then made a gesture with his free hand. "We can't afford to be picky, can we? But you need to be really careful, miss."

Jemma, glad she did not wear high heels for work—not knowing where she could end up in all the confusion after talking to Frosty—climbed down the ladder in her Blundstone boots and began descending above the black tunnel. At a certain point, she felt she was losing her nerve and stopped. Looking back up, she saw that she now had as much distance to climb back up as she had to climb down, so with a deep breath, she continued down until she felt the strong hands of a firefighter grab her waist.

The fire chief and two paramedics climbed down behind her. The paramedics began checking the bodies piled along the escalator and at the bottom while the rest ventured into the passageways leading to the tunnels. Further into the tunnels, they began to find life in the dim light. People were seated along the walls, in shock; many wounded were being tended by others who were relatively unscathed.

Jemma entered the westbound Central line tunnel, finding it relatively empty for such a morning hour, figuring a train must have just left. She moved among the wounded, talking to them, encouraging them, promising that help was on its way.

An old man in a torn suit was tending to a woman his own age, sitting with her back to the tunnel wall.

"She won't talk," he said to Jemma, his voice quivering. "She just keeps opening her mouth like a fish."

Jemma looked closely at the woman, whose face was deathly pale. The woman moved her cracked lips as if trying to say something but made no sound. There was a smell of burned skin, and Jemma could see burn marks on the woman's clothes; her raincoat was partly burned, as well as the dress underneath. She sat trembling, her stockings exposed, and she was barefoot.

"Is she your wife?" Jemma asked the old man, who was hugging the woman with one arm.

He nodded. "We were just coming into the tunnel when this giant explosion tossed us in here—threw us on the ground. My Iris almost fell onto the tracks, but I managed to grab her."

"Where are you from?" Jemma asked, trying to calm the old man, who she noticed, was trembling himself.

"We're from Kensington. Just went for some shopping," he said, stroking his wife's hair. "I need to get her to a hospital."

"She's in shock, but she'll be OK," Jemma comforted him. "Just keep her warm and keep talking to her. She will come around. I promise."

"Will you get us help?" he pleaded.

"We'll get you out of here very soon," she said, squeezing his thin hand.

She continued to the end of the tunnel, then crossed over to the eastbound tunnel, which was quite a bit fuller, with many more wounded and shocked. To her relief, she realized that, apart from the area beneath the escalators and the passageways leading to the tunnels, there were no fatalities in the tunnels.

More paramedics and firefighters began to appear, and a discussion began on how to evacuate. It soon became apparent that lifting the wounded on ladders above the damaged escalator was not an option, and further inspection of the elevators revealed they were damaged as well and, in any case, not functional with the power down.

It became clear that the best way to evacuate was to bring in a train, move everyone to the nearest station, and evacuate from there. The fire chief sent several firefighters to inspect the outbound tunnels in both directions and called the control center, asking them to send a train through the eastbound tunnel and prepare to evacuate Tottenham Court Road.

Andy Taylor and AVM Reed joined Jemma down in the tunnel when the train arrived and assisted in getting the wounded onto the train. They would evacuate the dead separately.

They boarded the train with the wounded. The train moved off slowly. At Tottenham Court Road, more emergency personnel waited by the tracks to begin evacuating the wounded to hospitals in the vicinity.

They emerged wearily from the station into the fresh air at the Dominion Theater, having spent over four hours below ground, helping restore order, tending to hundreds of wounded, and helping to carry victims on and off the train—without any breaks, food, or water.

Just then, AVM Reed received a call.

Explosions were reported at Covent Garden, Camden Market, and at Heathrow Terminal 5.

London became paralyzed.

Major arteries such as the M1, M4, the M40, and all the major streets were completely gridlocked by traffic that accumulated in all directions as law enforcement agencies, firefighters, health control authorities, and government personnel tried to get a handle on the situation—with little success.

The explosions at Covent Garden damaged half its central market, blowing up the entire sector that displayed its arts and crafts and antiques, completely destroying an adjacent coffee shop, and striking a group of onlookers enjoying a street performance under the glass roof, killing several and wounding many more. The adjacent Apple Market and a variety of stalls at Jubilee Market were hit hard by the blast, demolishing their contents and injuring most of their attendants.

Jemma reached Covent Garden by foot from Tottenham Court Road with Andy Taylor and one other member of their task force, Kevin Edwards, as the special task force teams split up. Reed caught a helicopter with Trevor Bishop from the roof of Selfridge's to Heathrow to evaluate the damage at Terminal 5; Lucy Shepherd, GI, Chapman, and several others were taken by police cars toward Camden Market, not sure they would ever get there.

Two ambulances were at Covent Garden, a few police cars, and a single fire truck—not nearly enough to deal with the disaster, but London was bleeding in four different places, its transportation lines cut off, and it was now more or less each borough on its own.

Jemma and her colleagues immediately began tending to the wounded with whatever means they had cleaning wounds with water and napkins, blocking bleeding arteries with tablecloths, and doing whatever they could do to save lives and ease pain. Mostly, they tried to comfort the suffering, encouraging them, and promising help was on its way.

After an hour, a group of doctors and nurses from the Great Ormond Street Hospital and the Royal London Hospital came on foot, carrying medical supplies in backpacks and nylon bags, and began administering first aid to the victims. Soon, more ambulances began arriving, breaking through the blockade of immovable traffic in streets all around. Along with a few volunteers whose cars were accessible, they began moving the wounded through a narrow corridor the police managed to secure via Kingsway to the cluster of hospitals by Russell Square.

At Camden Market, the explosion had ripped through the Stables Market, destroying a large part of the enclosed section that housed its famous booths of jewelry, clothing, tattoo parlors, musical instrument shops, and memorabilia collections. Power was lost, and in the dark, it was difficult to distinguish the wounded from the dead. Paramedics, police, firefighters, government personnel, and volunteers had to dig through heaps of debris to get to the people who were trapped underneath the fallen structures. Here too, the streets had become congested in minutes, the troubled area completely blocked, which made it extremely difficult for emergency vehicles to slip through. Many of the emergency personnel reached the area on foot, including doctors and nurses from the neighboring St. Pancras Hospital.

At Heathrow's Terminal 5, the explosion occurred near the check-in counters, the only area in the airport not entirely secured. The many passengers waiting at the check-in counters or at the self-check-in machines were thrown to the floor by the explosion. But due to its unique construction, the enormous hall contained the blast, its glass panels shattering but the overhead and side structures kept the building from collapsing. Only those passengers standing at or near where the bomb had exploded were killed or seriously wounded.

Reed and Bishop could see the commotion from the air, quickly realizing that, unlike the troubles in the city, there were no traffic jams around the terminal, and the airport was equipped to deal with such disasters. Before they landed, they could see the flashing lights of fire trucks, ambulances, and emergency vehicles surrounding the terminal as their helicopter lowered itself toward the landing pad.

Still, it was chaos. As they reached the check-in counter area where the bombs had exploded, they could see numerous bodies lying motionless on the floor, luggage thrown about, an entire line of check-in counters uprooted, with airline personnel lying among the ruins, wounded travelers being tended to in all parts of the terminal, escorted to evacuation areas by troops of paramedics and firefighters.

All flights in and out of Heathrow were immediately halted, hundreds of flights rerouted to nearby airports, and thousands of passengers funneled from all five terminals out onto the tarmac among the parked airplanes.

At eleven that night, the Prime Minister declared a state of emergency for the Greater London area. The military was called in to assist the police in clearing the congested streets of the endless traffic jams that accumulated around the city, opening corridors, and directing traffic through them to the suburbs away from the city. People were ordered to stay indoors. Helicopters assisted, bringing in troops to the damaged zones and transporting the wounded and dead to hospitals.

Chapter Seventeen

Monday, January 28, 2019

At eight the next morning, a TV anchor for the BBC received a Facebook message with an attached YouTube video which quickly went viral and was broadcast on the BBC an hour later.

A man in black clothes with a black hood covering his head sat behind a small empty desk, only his eyes visible through holes cut in the hood, speaking English with a slightly Eastern European accent; he took responsibility for the London bombings and delivered a message to Prime Minister Webster and the world:

"We, the 'Sons of Jihad,' intend to rule over Europe within a very short period of time. The United Kingdom is our first objective and this first act, the bombing of London, is our first step to achieving our goal."

The man became silent for a few seconds, his eyes intent on the camera, then he continued:

"To Prime Minister Webster and the people of London and the United Kingdom, there is more where this came from. There are several more locations around your capital that are wired with high explosives ready to go off."

He stopped again to let the message sink in.

"Do not look for them or try to disarm them for they are remotely controlled and will be set off if anyone as much as goes near them."

He took a deep breath and continued:

"To the people of London, yesterday you experienced our long reach into some of your most treasured sites. We do not feel remorse for the infidels who were killed and we would not hesitate to kill more if you disobey our orders. You are to stay home. Do not go anywhere. You may visit your local supermarkets to purchase your basic needs but otherwise do not leave the premises of your home until further notice."

The man flashed a crooked smile.

"Your famous Underground, airports, and all public transportation in the London area will soon cease operation and will remain inoperable until further notice. You may only use your cars to get to your local supermarket but soon the fuel supply at your petrol stations will run out and you will need to find other means to get your food. While you do that, we will deal with your government, which we hope will be reasonable by having your best interests in mind."

He stopped again as if considering his next words.

"We intend to demand that various laws will be passed allowing free passage for our people into the UK and Europe where they will be given respectable jobs and housing. We also expect to be given key positions in the corporate world and in Her Majesty's government and we intend to get rid of the monarchy once and for all, which is nothing but a wasteful burden on your taxes."

He stopped again and quickly looked sideways as if staring at someone. "I am advising you, the people, of our intentions so you know what your government will be negotiating for. That way you will know what you're up against and not allow your elected representatives to mislead you, as they normally would. Once we have reached an agreement with your government, life will resume as usual."

He stood up from his chair.

"Keep this in mind: by disobeying our orders, you will be putting your brothers at risk. Remember, we are watching you."

The picture went black.

"So, there it is," Frosty said, feeling mesmerized by the boldness of the events. "This is what they have been planning for over thirty years."

"Notice they did not threaten with any limitations on the use of the internet or the media," Cindy remarked.

"Of course not. How else would they get their message out? They need coverage and public opinion to divide us and scare us," Frosty observed.

The headlines on the screen read: "A Crisis of Immense Proportions" and "London Under Siege" as TV crews attempted to bring forth coverage of the incredible sequence of events taking place at the heart of the United Kingdom.

******

They had reached their hideout the previous night after dodging their tail at Kings Cross and taking a train north to Cambridge. Cindy and the girls identified their pursuers on the train but could not shake them. They reached their rendezvous destination at McDonalds at the King Cross train station and sat down to wait for Frosty who walked in a half hour later while they were munching on their fries.

He kissed both girls then Cindy who kissed him back and quickly gave him a description of their two pursuers, and where she thought they were positioned. Frosty kissed her again, instructing her to buy four train tickets to Cambridge for the train leaving in half an hour.

"They will come after me," he whispered to her, looking into her eyes, "so as soon as that happens, you go to the ticket office. I'll meet you on the train."

She nodded and he took off walking briskly out of the station to the taxi line, making sure the spectators were after him expecting an assault any minute. To his relief, he was third in line with a long line of black cabs waiting for passengers. He jumped into the taxi before it came to a halt, pulled out a fifty-pound note, and gave it to the driver who was a young man who looked a bit like Elvis with puffed hair and long sideburns, instructing him to run the red light at the end of the taxiway out of the station, take a quick left, go around the block, drop him off and keep going as if he was still in the cab. Elvis looked at him a little surprised, then smiled and nodded his head.

"It's about time we had some excitement in this old taxi," he said enthusiastically.

His two pursuers managed to grab the cab immediately behind him as Elvis took off. He slowed toward the red light, then pressed the gas pedal and screeched past it turning left nearly hitting an oncoming bus. The driver behind hesitated a moment too long and that proved enough. They now had a few seconds advantage and the bus between them allowed them a few precious seconds out of the pursuing cab's sight as they turned left again and were hidden by the station's outer wall. Frosty opened the door and jumped out of the cab onto the sidewalk, throwing the door shut behind him as Elvis kept going, ducking behind a newspaper stand, praying he would not be seen. The pursuing taxi came rushing by seconds behind, but his pursuers' attention was entirely focused on the taxi ahead getting away.

He rushed back into the station, finding Cindy and the girls waiting in line to purchase tickets.

From Cambridge they took a train west to Northampton, changed trains, and headed southwest to Bristol, and from there took a bus to Bath and from there a taxi south.

They ended up at a Bed & Breakfast a few miles south of Bath reaching it well past midnight, pleading with its owners, an old couple sprung out of bed, to allow them to stay the night.

In the morning, after a hearty breakfast made of eggs, bacon, sausages, fried bread, baked beans, and mushrooms, they treaded out to inspect the premises realizing they were on the edge of a wood on top of a hill overlooking green rolling hills surrounding a peaceful valley, a dirt road leading down the hill to the narrow asphalt road they had arrived on, which disappeared further along among the trees.

The sun had come out absorbing the low fog over the valley when Frosty and Cindy looked at one another and nodded.

It was a perfect place to stay for a while.

Only later that morning, when reports began to appear on their telephone screens, that they become aware of the immense terrorist attack in the center of London, and in the next few hours the rumors solidified, and video feeds began to appear in all the online news agencies and on the television, mostly from helicopters hanging above the city.

Toward midday, Noah Chisholm and his wife Mary, the couple who owned the guest house, came running into the house looking anxious, taking off their raincoats and sinking on a vacant sofa in front of the TV.

"We were shopping in Bath," Mary said out of breath. "We just heard the news. What in the name of god is going on over there?"

Mary was a small, fragile-looking woman, with long gray hair gathered into a bun; her skin was wrinkled white, and she had kind blue eyes and spoke softly. Noah was her opposite; a large man with broad shoulders, he had a high forehead with a receding hairline, a large nose, and deep-set brown eyes, whose booming voice could be heard from miles away.

"Yeah," he concurred out of breath himself. "What is going on over there?"

Both Frosty and Cindy nodded toward the TV. There was no need to explain.

From above, the center of London looked like a giant parking lot as the cameras from the helicopters captured the gridlocks that had formed the previous night, across all the major motorways and streets. People could be seen in clusters out of their cars in the middle of the motorways looking confused and helpless.

The Oxford Circus attack, the first to be reported, was being dissected, as helicopters tried to fly as close as possible, zooming in their cameras but it was impossible to tell what was going on below street level. The incredible gridlock around the condemned area and flashing lights from fire trucks and ambulances could be seen from miles away but it was impossible for the reporters to assess the damage.

Then the networks began covering the explosions in Camden, Covent Garden, and Heathrow Terminal 5, all at the same time, a cacophony of video tapes from the night before and live feeds showing parts of London in ruins.

The helicopters were scrambling in all directions. The BBC played a tape showing Camden market's blasted roof and a host of terrified people scrambling around between heaps of bodies lying on the ground from the night before, then switched to a live feed from above Covent Garden showing smoking ruins.

ITV was sending live feeds from the chaos at Camden Market and Sky showed a tape of its chopper hovering over Heathrow, videoing the emergency vehicles around terminal 5, frightened passengers being hauled out to the tarmac among the parking planes.

"This is our 9/11," Frosty remarked to Cindy who at the age of twelve lived through the nightmare in Manhattan when two high-jacked commercial planes crashed into the Twin Towers destroying them, another crashing into the Pentagon, and a fourth who was believed to be on its way to the White House crashed in an open field in Virginia, diverted by its passengers, in a heroic act of self-sacrifice.

They sat captivated by the events, in the small guest house by a burning fireplace, the wind whistling outside, watching the TV, feeling helpless and scared, the girls on the mat at their feet unable to draw their attention away from the screen.

At one point, Mary got up to heat up some supper made of roast beef in hot brown gravy and mashed potatoes, but their plates remained mostly untouched.

They fell asleep past midnight and watched the hooded man come on screen at nine the next morning, while the girls were busy exploring the meadow outside.

Chapter Eighteen

Tuesday, January 29, 2019

London resembled a ghost town.

The dynamic British capital was all but empty except for government vehicles, firefighter trucks, ambulances, and military and police patrolling the streets.

Firefighters and volunteers were still busy digging through the rubble looking for bodies and unlikely survivors at the sites where the explosions occurred, and ambulances were rushing about in and out of nearby hospitals delivering the remains of those found to be identified so the anxious families who milled around emergency rooms looking for their loved ones, could be notified.

Bishop called a meeting in the auditorium, and everyone was seated there at half-past seven. Nigel Scott came in with a man not familiar to many of them and introduced him as Tompkins's replacement.

It was the second time within a span of a few days Jemma had stumbled upon the name Ross Dixon whom she knew by name but had never actually met.

"We are facing our biggest challenge since the battle of Britain," Scott declared, adding drama to the already volatile state of affairs.

He looked around at the rows of secret agents all eying him tensely from their seats, somewhat embarrassed, he thought, at their own incompetence.

"This is first and foremost," he continued, "an intelligence failure which we are all to blame."

He swallowed hard and continued.

"However, we have an opportunity to show just how resilient we are in the face of adversity."

He swallowed again and coughed. Beads of sweat were coming down the side of his cheeks even though it was cold and damp.

"We will now recruit all available forces to overcome this fiasco with all of you here and anyone who is not present for whatever reason. I have just come from the PM who is busy assessing our options with world leaders but make no mistake; the resolve will come from this room. You people need to use all your skills, knowledge, and experience to return order to this country before people here lose faith in us."

The Home Secretary observed the room from his place on the stage behind the podium. One could hear a penny drop.

"Mr. Bishop with Mr. Dixon's assistance will handle matters and report directly to me on an hourly basis. At this point, no idea is too stupid to voice and no action too risky to try. I trust your competence and I am sure you will find a way to defeat this. Now let's get to work."

He ended his speech, turned and walked off the stage, two bodyguards following close behind.

Bishop took the podium and there began one of the most bizarre brainstorming sessions the security service had ever known.

******.

Jemma was at the computer in her office again when Frosty called on her reserve phone.

"Where the hell are you?" she exclaimed in a whisper. "This place is falling apart!"

"Yes, I've noticed," he replied. "How are you holding up?"

"Hang up," she said urgently. "I'll call you in half an hour from a pay phone," Jemma continued to whisper. "We don't know what we're up against and whether they have the means to tap our phones."

Frosty hung up.

Half an hour later, she called him from a payphone at Embankment. The commonly lively promenade by the Tube station was deserted. The coffee shops and restaurants were closed shut and only the newspaper stand at the entrance to the Tube was open with outlandish headlines flashing about but no one entered the Tube, and no one was buying newspapers.

He picked his phone up as soon as it rang.

She unloaded her grief at him describing what it was like to tend to the wounded and dying; the confusion and panic; the atrocious scenes at the bombing sites; the darkness, the smoke and the smell of burning limbs. She had held her nerve throughout but talking to Frosty, who had been with her for so long, caused her a release of emotions she did not even allow herself with Jake and the boys who she saw briefly late at night before falling into exhausted sleep.

"It was awful," she sighed, wiping away the tears. "There was nothing we could do for them…"

Frosty listened in silence waiting for her to calm down.

"We had a big meeting this morning with the minister and Bishop," she finally said. "They introduced Ross Dixon as Tompkins' replacement."

Frosty knew Dixon and thought it was a bit surprising he was nominated at such a crucial hour but realized they did not have time to look for someone more fitting.

"We've been assigned tasks," she continued briefly describing the overall plan.

Teams were assigned to monitor satellites and reconnaissance sensors aboard UAVs. Other units were sent to collect data from the forensics of the bomb sites. Emails and social media sites would be heavily scrutinized. City-wide surveillance camera data will be monitored closely. Alerts will be sent and information will be shared with similar task forces around Europe and the US.

Jemma was put in charge of gathering all relevant history and leads collected since Fleming's task force was established. The army was brought in. Troops were on their way to London to mind the streets while civilians were asked to stay home. Food and Gas supplies will be escorted. Major sites will be searched for explosives. The stock exchange will not be open for trading, and it too will be searched for explosive devices being one of the sites considered high risk.

MI6 was tasked with interviewing all collaborators with any links to Middle Eastern, Eastern European, or Russian-descent terrorist organizations since it was established the messenger's accent was Eastern European.

"Ross Dixon was insistent on bringing you in for questioning," she divulged. "Claims you may be the key to exposing the network and they are also looking for that police officer who escaped from the hospital, who Dixon suggests may have seen something during the attack on Tompkins or in the Hospital."

"So, who's in charge of bringing me in?" Frosty asked.

"Dixon said he will be personally responsible," Jemma informed him.

"The man does not waste any time, does he?" Frosty remarked.

"I encountered Dixon's name when I was researching Simon Lewis, the bystander who was killed in the Tompkins's assassination," Jemma said.

Frosty perked his ears.

"Lewis was let go because of a quarrel with Ross Dixon," she revealed. "I managed to log on to the protocol of the testimonies given in Lewis's dismissal board deliberations. They determined that Lewis had disobeyed an order due to differences of opinion with his superior, Dixon, regarding a certain individual who was used as an informant."

"I had no idea SO1 dealt with informants," Frosty remarked.

"Well, Dixon's responsibility under Tompkins' was Homeland Security and they are the people whose job it is to coordinate with customs and immigration," Jemma explained. "It had to do with a Russian network smuggling illegal immigrants into the UK by ships through certain ports of call. The dispute evolved around which ships and which ports were used after the UK customs and immigration officials set an ambush at Southampton and twice came up empty, finding no trace of any illegal activity on the ships that were specified by the snitch."

Jemma stopped for a moment looking around the phone booth, having gotten so engrossed in the conversation she forgot to check her surroundings for colleagues who might spot her, but the street remained empty.

"According to Lewis," she continued, "the snitch led them in wrong directions and several illegal immigrants did come through on the same nights but on different ships and through different ports, but he could not prove his claims.

"Dixon argued that the snitch was reliable but that someone else had alerted the network causing a last-minute change in plans. Lewis disagreed and confronted the informant using force. Two weeks later, he was fired."

"So, a year goes by and both Lewis and Tompkins get killed by a bomb assault within a few yards of one another," Frosty reflected. "Coincidence?"

"Not bloody likely," Jemma uttered

"What did Lewis do after he was dismissed?" Frosty asked.

"There's no record at the MOD." Jemma informed him.

"Can we check other records? Did he have a Facebook account? LinkedIn? Instagram maybe? Twitter?"

"Can you ask Cindy to do it?" Jemma asked. "I will not have a second to breathe in the coming days and besides, I would not want to leave any tracks at the office."

"Sure," Frosty said. "But I still need you to try and find out who visited Kruger on July 29th last year using my name, and prison records and tapes of Kruger's visitors in the last two years?"

"I'll do my best," Jemma promised. "But I got to go now. They'll come looking for me if I stay here any longer."

"Can we agree to talk once a day, at say, six in the morning, before you leave for work?" Frosty asked. "Can you get to a payphone near your house?"

"We can certainly try but you need to tell me what you plan to do?" she said. "They'll eventually catch on to us…"

"We know two things for certain, Jemma," Frosty recounted. "One that I was set up and two that the organization we had been following for twenty years has struck big time. So, I am assuming that for reasons yet unknown to us, I must be in the way of whoever is instigating all this and if we can find a link, we may find who's behind this and be able to stop this."

"Go on," she said.

"Therefore, I really don't think they want me in for questioning but rather to get me out of the way, so I need to stay alive long enough to find this link, so we know what we're up against."

"Makes sense," Jemma agreed.

"By giving you these supposedly trivial research duties, keeping you away from the primary effort, they are actually playing into our hands," Frosty added. "So, we need to take advantage and try and piece together these bits and pieces to get the bigger picture. At this point, our best bet is to focus on Kruger and Simon Lewis because both were involved and both have died in close proximity to this vicious attack."

Two policemen appeared at the end of the promenade, heading toward the phone booth. Jemma eyed them.

"OK, I need to go," she said hurriedly. "I'll look into this whenever I can and we'll talk in the morning. You keep safe, you hear."

She hung up and left the phone booth before the policemen were close enough to identify her.

Chapter Nineteen

James Flanagan received his guest at his private conference room adjacent to his office. It was a rectangular room with ten leather chairs around an ellipse glass table with large glass windows adorning two sides.

Four guards in black clothes stood at attention, two at the office door, and two at the conference room. They had escorted Flanagan to his office from his home in Hempstead.

Flanagan looked anxious; his eyes puffed and red from lack of sleep; his face unkempt; his suit crumpled, and his expression defeated.

"Explain to me if you will," the guest began without preamble, "what will happen if you buy billions of Rubles with your English pound?"

Flanagan looked confused. "Well, it depends…" he began, and then stopped.

"Yeah, go on," the man urged him. "What effect will this have?"

"Well, the pound will lose value if you sell enough of it," Flanagan said, his eyes darting from his guest to the guards. "Theoretically that would increase the cost of imports and decrease the cost of exports."

"Yeah and…" The man urged him on.

"Well, it also depends how fast you sell it…"

"How much will you need to sell for the pound to depreciate quickly?" the man inquired.

"I really don't know the exact amounts but regardless of how much you sell, the central bank can always step in to support the pound if they feel that the speed of the depreciation is destabilizing…"

"What will it do?" the man asked, flashing a crooked smile.

Flanagan offered an explanation despite suspecting his tormentor already knew the answers.

"The central bank can buy back vast amounts of British pounds, or it can raise interest rates to support the currency…"

"But that might not always work," the man argued, "markets can take them on, and raising interest rates may slow down growth, increase the cost of capital, and may also increase unemployment."

Flanagan gave him a tired look. "If you know all this, why do you bother asking?"

"Because I want to make sure we both know what we want to accomplish."

"And that is?" Flanagan queried in a sarcastic tone.

"I would like you to start buying Rubles by the billions, against your English pound, and allow your hedge fund manager friends to get a whiff of it so they will join in to make a profit."

Flanagan looked flabbergasted.

"But traders will jack up interest rates almost instantly and if rates go up high enough that can choke the economy..."

Even before he completed his sentence, Flanagan knew this was what he was being blackmailed for; they were using him to try and destabilize the British economy. The man kept smiling.

"You plan to turn us into a banana republic? Is that your plan?" he asked angrily.

"If you want to look at it that way," the man said looking smug. "In the meantime, I need to know how much we need to sell to get this process started."

Flanagan looked at him in dismay, but there was nothing he could do. Keeping his grandchildren alive took precedence.

******

The phone rang and Frosty who was watching TV witnessing British troops being mobilized toward the capital took it outside. It was an unidentified number.

"Adrian Frost?" a man's voice came through some static.

His heart missed a beat and for a second he thought he had been tracked down. "Who wants to know?" he asked carefully.

"This is Reuben Santana." the voice said and Frosty relaxed.

"Oh, good day," he said.

"You wanted to talk to me," the police officer stated.

"Yes I did," Frosty acknowledged.

"Well go ahead," Santana said in a neutral tone.

Frosty had been thinking about the wounded police officer for quite some time now wondering whether he would cooperate and if he could be trusted, realizing he had to tread carefully around him.

He first inquired about the officer's health and the condition of his wounds then asked about the events at the assassination site and later at the hospital.

Santana was not easily swayed though he must have done his homework, as Camilla, his girlfriend, promised he would. He described the events at the Ritz and in the hospital in short concise sentences, not including any of his own impressions or opinions, but rather describing the chain of events as they occurred, a few of them were familiar to Frosty from the TV reports.

"Did you notice anything suspicious before the bomb went off?" Frosty inquired.

The line became silent for a few seconds and Frosty held his breath, imagining Santana's inner struggle to trust him.

"I thought I saw someone in a black outfit on a bicycle chucking something in the direction of the car just before the explosion," he finally said. "But it was really obscure, and I may be imagining things."

Frosty stopped to digest this new piece of information before he continued. "And did you happen to see who Tompkins was meeting?"

"No, I did not. He went in and out of the hotel by himself as far as I could tell,"

Frosty decided to risk it.

"The bystander who was reported killed was ex-SO1," he disclosed. "I think he was the Tompkins meeting."

There was more silence on the other side. "And what if he was?" Santana finally asked.

"I think he may have had things to tell Tompkins others wanted to keep from leaking out..."

"Those must have been extremely serious issues if they both got killed for it," Santana pointed out.

"Just look what has happened since..." Frosty reminded him. "And they came after you and your partner, didn't they? Meant to silence you as well."

"Someone did, that's true," Santana said thoughtfully.

"These events are connected, Officer Santana," Frosty stated. "Make no mistake about it. You are a wanted person just like I am."

"Why you?" Santana asked.

118

"It's complicated, but in a nutshell, I am, or was, a task force leader at MI5 responsible for protecting against the organization that took responsibility for the very thing that had just crippled London."

He let his words sink in then continued. "Somebody intended for me to take the fall for all this but so far I have managed to stay clear…"

There was a long pause before Santana responded.

"So, who's behind all this?" he asked simply.

"It's obviously someone on the inside, high up," Frosty shared. "I have my suspicions but there are things I need to look into before I can be sure."

"So, what is it you want from me?" the officer questioned.

"I thought you might have noticed something important otherwise why would they come after you?"

"Well, I did not," Santana sounded flustered. "And for all I know you may be one of them too."

"I thought you had me checked out or else why would you call?" Frosty pointed out, keeping his cool. "And why would I be sharing such vital information with a person who could damage me?"

"I checked to see if you were who you said you were," Santana remarked. "Beyond that, I need to keep myself alive…"

"Listen, Officer Santana, I understand your dilemma; I have a hard time trusting anyone myself these days, but we are being hunted by the same people and I think we could help each other."

There was another long pause before Santana finally spoke.

"Assuming you are on the level, Agent Frost, and believe me I will disappear the second I suspect you are not, what did you have in mind? Keep in mind I am a wounded man on the run."

"You are the only other person I know, besides me, whose fate is not randomly dependent on the outcome of this," Frosty reminded him. "We both live if we can beat this otherwise we will most likely perish along with a multitude of random casualties."

Santana did not respond but Frosty suspected he was intently listening.

"I know your situation and I promise to refrain from asking for your help unless it is absolutely necessary. However, I would like your permission to contact you if I need anything."

"That would be okay," Santana agreed.

"How would I contact you?" Frosty inquired.

Santana became silent for a few seconds again then he gave Frosty a phone number.

"Camilla or I will be at this payphone twice a day at six in the morning and at three in the afternoon. We will wait five minutes and then leave. If you need to contact me, do it at these times."

"Fair enough and much appreciated," Frosty said. "You take care, and I truly hope we beat this for our sake and everyone else's."

"I'll be here if you need…" Santana was getting ready to hang up the phone when Frosty stopped him.

"One last question if I may?" he interrupted him.

"Go ahead."

"In the hospital, what language were those guys outside the toilet door speaking?"

"It sounded like Russian," Santana recalled. "But I cannot be sure."

Chapter Twenty

That afternoon, Andy White paced the floor of the control room like a caged lion berating himself for allowing Agent Frost to slip through his fingers.

He had been caught off guard when the man appeared at his doorstep but he felt he should have caught him and that would have saved everyone a ton of worry.

Now, he was conducting a major tracking operation in a room full of communication equipment; monitoring satellites, mobile phones, landline phones, email traffic, internet traffic, social network traffic, train stations, airports, car rental outlets, cab companies, and whatever else they could monitor to bring him in.

Agent Frost proved a formidable adversary and White should not have been surprised. He was ex-SAS, an MI6 operative, and an MI5 task force leader for over ten years. After the second time Frost had managed to escape his men at the Oxford train station, White had been reprimanded. A third time was unacceptable. White would be punished and left on his own. He had no more opportunities to screw up, he was told. He had also put feelers out for any traffic from Cynthia Cunningham-Frost, a well-respected web researcher who in her past had been involved in working for the American task force responsible for tracking "the outfit," as his superiors often referred to their own organization.

White had been recruited while serving in Afghanistan. He had received his training in the paratroopers where he fought as a private in the First Iraq War and was a platoon sergeant when NATO forces entered Afghanistan in 2003. He then transferred to the Special Reconnaissance Regiment, serving two years chasing Taliban leaders in Southern Afghanistan before he was transferred to Kandahar to the NATO Intelligence Corps after an incident that changed his outlook on accountability within the military ranks when he claimed he had been abandoned by the troops he was leading after his vehicle was ransacked by an IED and he was left by the side of the road unconscious. He even took it to court, but the field court ruled that the officer in question, Lieutenant Rick Mosby, who following the explosion had engaged the enemy in a firefight, had come back to extract the mutilated bodies, but since it was getting dark, he had not noticed White who was thrown into a ditch away from the vehicle. White had survived the incident with minor injuries and had made it back to forward command under the cover of darkness, but it remained that Mosby had acted appropriately under the circumstances, leaving White troubled and disillusioned.

He was approached in Kandahar by a Lebanese building contractor whose outfit was repairing the damaged airport. His anger and frustration at what he viewed as desertion drove him to accept the offer knowing he could never reverse his allegiance. He was offered a cool one-million-dollar flat fee to join the ranks which he did figuring he owed nothing to the people who in his view had abandoned him in battle. Aside from that he was from Canning Town, at the time one of the poorer neighborhoods of London and the entire UK, and figured it was his opportunity to get ahead.

They initially had him doing odd jobs while he was at the Foreign Office until he was sent to Tel Aviv, where he had a chance to meet actual collaborators in the West Bank which unlike Gaza was relatively access-free. He would make up excuses to visit the Old Town in Jerusalem, Bethlehem, and Jericho, and arrange to meet messengers who would cross over from Jordan with messages which he would send to his handlers in the UK in the diplomatic mail in typed memos using "work-related jargon" that was code. It was a risk-averse operation that left no electronic traffic trails for bodies such as the NSA or its British equivalent and White could not have been more impressed by their efficiency and meticulousness.

When he first met Ross Dixon, immediately following his return from Israel, he realized for the first time what the million-dollar payoff was for as they began to recruit operatives, inserting them into SO1.

Currently, to enhance his reach, he had Jemma Stone-Hammond under full surveillance as well, having acquired special permission from his superiors. All her computer searches, phone calls, and internet traffic were monitored, and she was regularly followed to and from home and anywhere else she went. But so far, he regretted admitting, she too has yet to be caught making contact with Frost.

The Home Secretary Nigel Scott, the head of MI5, Steven Bishop, and the head of the Task Force Bureau, AVM Alan Reed, were also among the people being tracked, their offices, phones, and cars, all bugged but for reasons other than finding Agent Frost. For the time being, they too were convinced Frost was key to the entire affair and that it was essential he was brought in, so White had all the backing he needed to use whatever means he deemed necessary to locate Agent Frost along with the massive undertaking led by the Ministry of Defense to stop the organization terrorizing the British people. AWACS planes with signal and communication detection equipment were hovering over London; Recce pods with powerful daytime and infrared cameras were put into use by fighter aircraft sweeping over the city and choppers were transferring troops to suspect locations in search of explosives.

"It is like fighting an invisible enemy," the Prime Minister had said in one of his many interviews and White wondered how long it would be before they realized the enemy were in their midst.

He currently had a secret SO1 detachment numbering four operatives on standby in a dedicated 212 helicopter at a landing zone north of the city in case Frost was spotted. Two men were staking his home in Edgware and two more were on standby to follow Jemma Stone when she left the office. In addition, he used MI5 operatives, unaware of his deceit, stationed at the main train stations, Heathrow and Gatwick airports, and the sites where the bombing occurred figuring Agent Frost might want to pay them a visit but White had to admit it was a drop in the ocean. Frost can be anywhere, including far away from London, and the only chance of finding him was intercepting a phone conversation or netting something on the web.

******

In the early evening, three days after the initial London bombing attacks, another attack took place at the London Stock Exchange at Paternoster Square near St. Paul's Cathedral.

The exchange had been shut down since the initial attacks and the explosion occurred below the FTSE 100 index big board by a bay of computer stations when a group of soldiers were searching the premises.

It rocked the empty hall destroying the famous board killing five troopers and wounding ten others. Emergency vehicles with bomb squads were rushed in and troops were immediately mobilized to search the area around the city of London but nothing of consequence was found.

Home Secretary Sir Nigel Scott called an urgent meeting and was at his office with Bishop and Dixon when a video of the attack was uploaded on YouTube and was immediately broadcast on all the stations. It was a shot from above showing the soldiers spreading out around the hall methodically going through each of the computer bays. Several soldiers can be seen searching through one of the bays when the explosion occurred sending them sprawling to the ground with great force, decimating the surroundings, causing the entire hall to shake, a gray cloud of debris mushrooming around obscuring the view from the camera recording the scene.

The hooded man in black clothes with an Eastern European accent appeared following the horrific video scenes.

"We have warned you," he declared. "But you have defied us, so this is the result. It is also obvious your government has no intention of negotiating the terms we imposed so further measures will be taken until you accept our demands."

"I urge the people of London to stay home and not test our resolve. Remember, we are watching you."

The screen became dark.

Scott looked from Bishop to Dixon and back to Bishop. They all had their suit jackets off, exposing crumpled shirts and loosened ties, their looks weary with bags under their eyes from lack of sleep.

"The PM wants the royal family out of harm's way," Scott said. "Where do we put them?"

"We've already made arrangements at Windsor Castle," Bishop informed him. "We're moving them out there tomorrow morning."

"Do it tonight," Scott urged them. "They're weighing heavy on our efforts."

"That won't happen," Dixon put in. "We've been trying to convince them to move since this disaster struck but they insist on staying at Buckingham and Kensington to show solidarity and not to give in. Now, they've agreed to move the women and kids in the morning, but William and Harry intend to stay here and fight."

"But that would only complicate matters," Scott bickered.

"William intends to join a search and rescue helicopter squadron. He's already contacted the Sea King squadron commander at Boscombe Down, so it looks like he'll be flying around," Dixon remarked.

"I wish he would listen to reason," Bishop complained. "I mean, we've got enough helicopter jocks flying around already and he would only be in the way with all of Dixon's guys around him."

"What about Harry?" Scott put in.

"Has contacted his old Apache squadron as well but that may prove a little trickier considering it's an attack helicopter and he has not been active for several years," Dixon explained. "Still, he intends to stick around if only to encourage the troops."

"You keep me updated on all this," Scott said to Dixon. "I want to know where they are and what they are up to at all times. Is this clear?"

Dixon nodded. "We put in place a multi-tier security plan. Where-ever they go we will scout and secure the areas beforehand and deploy a commando outfit in plain clothes to enhance their perimeter."

"This sounds OK," Scott said. "What will they be driven in?"

"We'll put them in the series 9 Jaguars which are bulletproof, can run on flat tires, and have fuel tanks that do not explode when hit by bullets or shrapnel. In extreme emergencies, the cabin turns into a gas-proof chamber as well but there's not much we can do once they deploy with their helicopters other than send on board one or two bodyguards from the close proximity team if they allow it."

"Well, I guess they'll have the troops protecting them at that point, won't they?" Scott remarked.

"Well, Sir, there are numerous threats they can encounter including chemical-bio threats, frontal attacks, IEDs, and even fires and medical emergencies. There's no telling what can happen once they leave our perimeter."

"Have you explained that to them?" Scott demanded.

"We certainly have and not for the first time. Their highnesses know what they risk once they leave their protective shields, but they have done it before, so we'll just have to do our best."

Scott looked at Bishop. "You happy with that?"

"Can't say that I am, Sir, but at this point, we are spread thin with everything we need to deal with, so that'll have to do."

The Home Secretary sighed. "Are we making any progress finding these hoodlums?"

Bishop and Dixon looked at one another before Bishop spoke: "The troops are out there combing the city. Most civilians are cooperating and staying at home. We've got practically all our experts covering the web; all internet and phone providers are monitored; satellites are being watched and Intelligence is using all SIGINT and COMMINT resources at their disposal. We've so far apprehended numerous suspects linked to terrorist networks and we're questioning them. It's just a matter of time before we get a break."

"This has to happen very soon," Scott said as he picked up his phone signaling his colleagues to leave him alone.

Chapter Twenty-One

Wednesday, January 30, 2019

Jemma rubbed her eyes with both her fists hoping to dissolve the fatigue.

She had been in her office in front of the computer screen from early morning till late at night for three consecutive days, traveling home for a few hours each night to drop in on Jake and the boys and nap.

Jake had set up an office in the den and was running things from home. Her boys, Colin and Ian, had set up camp in the living room, sprawled in their pajamas on bed sheets and blankets they had dragged in from their rooms, going through an array of home videos and Nintendo games they were transmitting to the TV screen from their iPhones, taking advantage of the upheaval.

Nylon bags with bread, canned food, cartons of cereal, half-empty boxes of cookies, and plastic bottles of water, their primary nourishment, were scattered all over the kitchen, the sink full of dirty glasses and dishes.

Too tired and bothered even to comment on the state of affairs, she would have Jake make her a cup of tea which she drank with some cookies and bread with jam and fell asleep under the blankets between her boys in the living room in front of the TV.

In the morning, Andy Taylor picked her up at seven and they drove through the mostly empty streets to Whitehall on Northumberland Avenue, encountering army troops and police scouting buildings entrances and storefronts.

For three days, she had been intermittently, amid her official tasks, trying to crack the British prison system database to find testaments of the apparent Frosty impersonator visit to Kruger that took place six months before. She figured she had to find a video of the visit that clearly identified a person, but the video library could not be easily accessed.

In fact, it proved impossible to break into the prison digital video system which was a closed-loop internal system not connected to the outside world. The videos, she found out, were all stored in a digital video recorder, or DVR, and even if she managed to break into the system, she would need to find an access code for the particular video according to the specific day and time of the visit.

She got her break when she found a reference to the contractor responsible for installing and servicing the system, having examined a list of the prison suppliers and sub-contractors when despairingly she realized, it may be the only way in.

It was a high-tech company, Digital Solutions Limited, based in Wrexham, Wales, that specialized in secured digital cameras and DVRs of the kind installed in the prison system and when she looked on the company's internet site she saw the items advertised as being installed at the Blackpool prison.

It became apparent to her that the only way to find a video of the visit and identify the person impersonating Frosty was via this prison contractor and she needed to pass on this information to Frosty as soon as possible.

She could not wait for their scheduled phone rendezvous at six in the morning which they had agreed to conduct but so far have exercised only once. She looked around the office. Taylor and Edwards were busy at their desks with whatever they were tasked with, everyone else was out of the building as far as she knew.

She shut down her computer, took her coat and purse, and marched out the door without explanation. She took the elevator two floors down and stepped into the entrance lobby which was empty except for two staff ladies behind the glass partition who issued passes to visitors and two guards near the x-ray machine who since the bombing have been practically out of work. Two soldiers with machine guns and ceramic vests stood outside the entrance behind large glass doors.

She walked out pushing the heavy glass doors open, stepped between the armed guards, smiled at them, and hopped down the stairs to Northumberland toward Embankment. As she crossed the wide avenue, she noticed two men sitting in a black Suburban watching her from behind the darkened windshield and as she turned the corner underneath the over-path into Embankment she noticed one of the men out of the car walking in her direction. She quickened her step and entered the empty Underground station looking for the lady's room which she found adjacent to the ticket booth and entered it.

She waited there a few minutes then stepped out looking carefully in all directions spotting the man half a block away talking urgently on his mobile phone searching both sides of the promenade. She ran from the Underground station's entrance to Costa Coffee across the small square and entered the public telephone booth next to the coffee shop without being seen by the man who had his back to her. She quickly dialed Frosty's mobile number and gave him the details of Digital Solutions Limited, explaining their role in the prison video scheme, and giving Frosty their Wrexham address and phone numbers.

When she was done, she inspected her flanks and slipped from the booth into the coffee shop which was the only one open, to order a cappuccino and a chicken wrap she paraded back to the office noticing the man in the car watching her from behind the dark screen.

When she entered her building, she saw his partner reach the car looking in her direction.

She thought she had seen a similar car on two previous occasions when she left the building for lunch at the Embankment Costa Coffee she regularly ate at and on her way home. It was no surprise to her that she was being followed but it dawned on her that she would have to find another venue to communicate with Frosty.

******

Cindy watched the girls playing outside in the small yard, racing one another from one side to the other, through the window of Noah and Mary Chisholm's little office next to the guest room on the ground floor. In the background, beyond the clearing and within the mist, she could see the great forest expanse, spreading toward the valley and beyond.

She had connected her laptop to their Wi-Fi internet access and sat exploring the virtual net among neatly stacked folders marked with a variety of accounting data, office gear, and cleaning appliances.

It was their fourth day at the Chisholm guest house which had four available rooms, two on each floor, and so far, they were the only guests that week, creating a type of bond with their hosts in lieu of the disturbing events taking place in London. The Chisholms never pried about their business and never asked how long they intended to stay, happy to have company at such trying times.

Cindy watched Zoe slip on the wet grass, Gabi helping her get up while inaudibly laughing. Zoe who had a competitive streak, hated to lose and was complaining as her sister pulled her up.

It was her second day using her laptop, trying to gather information on Simon Lewis and figure out what had gotten him killed. She tried to minimize the use of her computer, knowing any of her actions could get her traced and their whereabouts discovered, but she and Frosty agreed Simon Lewis was key to establishing who was involved in the brutal attack on their homeland, suspecting that some were working inside sensitive government departments, compelling her to recruit all her knowledge and experience to unearth them.

She had already collected the basic facts about Simon Lewis from the personnel files at SO1 that she hacked into while still at home. He was from London, born and raised in East Ham to a Jewish family. He joined the military right out of high school and did three tours in Afghanistan from 2003 to 2006 in the Special Reconnaissance Regiment after his basic training and two years in an airborne battalion in the Falklands.

He was discharged in 2006 as a sergeant and was recruited to the security service where he was assigned to SO1 after passing his training courses in 2007. There was no mention of a spouse, or children and his permanent address was the same one he had grown up in East Ham not far from the Synagogue in Brampton Park. Cindy knew the area well.

His discharge from SO1 in 2018 was well documented in the protocol of testimonies given in his dismissal board after his quarrel with Ross Dixon but documentation of his years as an SO1 operative was not as easy to come by and Cindy had to dig deeper into SO1 and MI5 files to find testaments of his service and possible motives for his eventual demise but after two days of plowing through endless documentation she could not find any indications as to what he might have had to reveal to Tompkins if indeed he had been the reason for that fateful meeting at the Ritz.

They needed to break into his home computer, if there was one, she surmised, so she called Frosty who was at the Bristol train station waiting for a train to Liverpool and they agreed to try and recruit Officer Santana for the job. In doing so they realized they were taking an extreme risk, having to disclose what they knew over the phone to outsiders but they had no better alternatives and time was running out.

She waited until the agreed time, three in the afternoon, and called the payphone number given to them by Santana.

A female voice answered, catching Cindy by surprise but she quickly recovered realizing it must be Camilla.

"Hi," Cindy said cautiously. "This is Cindy Frosty's wife."

"Frosty?" the woman questioned.

"I mean, Agent Frost," Cindy corrected herself. "Are you Camilla?"

There was a short silence before Camilla replied, her Latin accent becoming apparent. "Ah, yes, sorry I was expecting a man."

"So was I," Cindy said. "But my husband is away and something came up."

Cindy explained to Camilla what they were looking for and why; emphasizing that breaking into Lewis's computer was an instance of last resort. She gave her the address and if they agreed, encouraged her to make contact while they were at it if they needed guidance and to bypass obstacles such as passwords and the like.

Camilla listened quietly not saying much then confirmed she understood but added that the final decision would be Santana's.

Cindy thanked her, asking to be notified of their decision, and hung up the phone.

The girls had come in wet and hungry and she could hear them in the kitchen talking to Mary Chisholm who was encouraging them to go clean up, promising to prepare them something sweet when they came back down.

Chapter Twenty-Two

The train from Bristol to Liverpool was full when Frosty hopped on and found his assigned seat by the window. An elderly lady wearing a flowery hat and a fur coat sat facing him next to a young boy wearing a fleece jacket over a Liverpool football shirt, his attention entirely on his mobile phone moving his thumbs with fantastic speed entrenched in a game of sorts. The lady smiled at him apologetically, her clear blue eyes and wrinkled white skin in stark contrast to her red-painted lips.

The seat next to him remained empty until the train began to move when a middle-aged man with a wad of white hair and black-rimmed glasses, dressed in jeans and boots fell into the seat panting apologetically, thanking the Lord he had managed to catch the train.

Frosty looked around his cabin marveling at the run-of-the-mill behavior on the train, as if people were unaware of the ongoing drama which was paralyzing London and threatening all of England. It seemed to him, that people were going about their daily lives sticking their heads in the sand and hoping for the best, trusting a government that was all but dysfunctional, but on further reflection realized there was not much they could do but go about their business and it was a comforting feeling to observe that life does go on despite the horrors and threats.

The overhead TV monitor came to life with breaking news and everyone in the cabin, except for the kid who was busy attacking his video game, focused on it. Taped footage of London was shown as reporters recounted the situation and experts gave an array of opinions.

The screen changed to a live report from in front of the crippled stock exchange, a young female reporter wrapped in a gray overcoat fighting the wind and sleet was reporting that in the last two days, the British pound has lost more than fifteen percent of its value and there were reports that several banks were selling the British currency short by the billions. She transferred the broadcast back to the studio where a well-known financial personality from the Central Bank of England, was being interviewed.

"It would be reasonable for the pound to lose value," he was saying, "during such turmoil, but we have reported that various hedge funds were selling off the pound in the billions, mainly against the Russian Ruble, causing it to lose almost twenty percent of its value by now."

"Then shouldn't the Bank of England be buying the pound back to remedy the situation and restore confidence in our currency?" The Sky anchorwoman was asking.

"Well, obviously some greedy hedge fund managers got a whiff of some pretty big sellers out there and are scrambling to make a profit. We could definitely buy back very large sums and raise interest, but the danger is that traders in the financial markets have jacked up interest rates already and if they go up high enough it could choke the economy and totally kill domestic confidence and demand."

The two anchors, a woman and a man, looked at one another in genuine surprise and then looked at their guests expectantly.

"So, what does the central bank intend to do about it?" they asked in unison.

"The Governor will have to decide after his meeting with the PM this afternoon," he informed them. "Right now he is in an emergency conference with his counterparts from the EU and the US to draw up a strategy which he will present to the PM."

"Meanwhile, the wolves are getting richer," the lady anchor remarked but the man was not amused.

"This could be part of an overall scheme to ruin our country and take control as was promised in the first terrorist video," he reminded her. "This together with the current London bombings can cripple our country for years and take Europe down with it."

The two anchors were caught off guard and were left speechless for a few seconds before the screen changed back to live footage of London from above.

Frosty looked out the window, not seeing the gray pastures they were passing beyond the drops of rain being brushed aside by the wind, thinking that what he had just heard was not beyond reason; however, he put it aside for the time being needing to concentrate on a plan to approach the video company and obtain the information he needed from them.

******

He reached Wrexham Central early afternoon after changing trains in Liverpool then again at Bidston to the Arriva trains.

He emerged out of the brownstone train station building with the slanted tile roof through the ticket hall and began walking east toward Holt Street to make sure he was not being followed, finding a Pub by Yale College which he entered deciding to quench his hunger.

The place was rowdy, filled with students affixed to their laptops sitting in groups around long oak tables eating and drinking while doing their assignments.

The TV monitors scattered above were all tuned to different news stations reporting the latest from London. Frosty walked up to the bar, ordered a Tuna salad with fries and a glass of ale, and sat at a corner table to watch the proceedings while his food was being prepared, once again mesmerized by the lackadaisical attitude of the occupants. It was almost as if whatever was happening in London, did not register elsewhere.

He turned on his mobile phone and chose the Google Maps application which brought up the company's address he had stored in advance realizing it was walking distance from the pub.

Half an hour later, he exited the pub and proceeded west on Mooreland Avenue following his GPS until he reached a high-tech park with glass buildings and vast parking lots, in stark contrast to the old-fashioned town he had passed through adorned with cobblestone pavements and low brownstone buildings.

It was four in the afternoon when Frosty identified the Digital Solutions Logo in black letters with an orange frame, on the side of one of the buildings and he entered its posh heated lobby approaching a young receptionist dressed in a company shirt, white with its orange-black logo etched across her chest, sitting behind a low orange counter, the company logo looming large on a glass partition behind her, a mobile phone glued to her ear while she chopped away on a keyboard in front of a large computer screen. Her name tag revealed she was Becca.

To Frosty, she looked in her twenties, pale face with a touch of makeup, dark flowing hair and blue eyes. She smiled politely and signaled for him to take a seat while proceeding to talk quietly into her mobile.

Frosty sat on a low black synthetic leather sofa in front of the reception counter, looking around at an array of posters across the lobby's walls displaying company products, security cameras hanging from the rafters purposely on display. A little further to his right was a spiral flight of stairs, and beyond was a bank of two elevators.

When she completed her phone conversation, Becca turned to Frosty who walked up to her post and explained who he wanted to see, flashing his official TFB badge at her insisting the matter was urgent.

Five minutes later, a man in a brownish suit and a tie that matched his company's colors, walked down the spiral stairway, hurrying to greet Frosty, presenting his business card to him after warmly shaking his hand.

Marc Nash was the vice president responsible for Operations. He was a lanky man with gray hair and a gray mustache under a large nose who walked a little bent as if feeling guilty for being too tall.

"What can I do for you, Agent Frost?" he asked politely nodding to the receptionist and leading Frosty to the elevator, pressing the button to the third floor.

Frosty waited until they entered his office before he began speaking.

"Am I to assume that due to the nature of your business we are now being recorded?" he asked matter-of-factly.

"We most certainly are," Nash said ceremoniously, pointing to a small monitor on his office desk, turning it so Frosty could see.

"Well, this meeting is confidential, so I need to ask you to turn this off," Frosty said, looking around for the cameras that were recording him.

Nash looked a bit disappointed hoping to impress his guest, but he turned off the monitor all the same then approached the two cameras affixed to the ceiling, turning them off using a remote control.

"Thank you," Frosty said.

"Please take a seat," Nash offered placing himself on his luxurious office chair, leaning back in it with a mischievous grin.

"I thought I'd give you a taste of our products," he said. "Would you like some coffee? Tea?"

"No thanks," Frosty said, "I am very short on time and this is an urgent matter that has to do with the events taking place in London."

Nash became serious. "Yes, I suppose so," he said, his face taking on a grim expression. "We were just asked by some of your colleagues to come up with ideas of how to rummage through the endless mass of recorded data to extract critical information," He said looking at Frosty, then added, "Our president, Mr. Owen, is in London for just that purpose."

"It's good to hear Mr. Nash," Frosty commended him. "But I am here on a very specific mission which I will need your full cooperation."

"Shoot," Nash said, straightening up in his seat. "We'll do whatever we can to help."

"What I need, Mr. Nash," Frosty said with a serious expression, "is access to a video recording of a certain visit made in Blackpool prison."

He let the request sink in before he continued. "This visit took place about six months ago and it is crucial that I take a look at it."

Nash looked thoughtful for a moment. "Six months ago you say?" He repeated once again.

"Give or take," Frosty offered. "The exact date is July 29 last year."

Nash picked up his office phone, dialed a few numbers, and waited. "How far back do we have access to recorded data at the prisons?" he asked whoever was on the other line with him. He listened for a few seconds, then nodded. "OK then, I'll be right there. Don't go anywhere."

Nash led Frosty to the spiral stairway and they descended one floor down, walked through along a carpeted corridor passing several people rushing by, and rooms with monitors and electronic equipment, entering a lab of sorts at the very end which had a row of large monitors on a counter, with several people seated on swivel chairs working on keyboards attached to those monitors.

Nash walked to the end of the room and stood over a red-haired man with freckles, wearing a company orange shirt, examining the monitor in front of him.

"I'd like you to clear out the people," Frosty said to Nash, receiving a host of surprised looks from the others in the room.

"You heard him people, clear out," Nash commanded. "This is official business. Take a break; you can come back in in a few minutes."

The four other people in the room, two men and two women, all wearing orange company shirts, got up in unison taking their mobile phones with them, and left the room swearing under their noses, leaving Frosty with Nash and the red-headed man who Nash introduced as Rees.

"We've got a direct connection to the stored data in the prison for up to a year," Rees was explaining. "After that, they store it in our DVRs in their stock rooms somewhere. What date did you say you were looking for?"

Frosty repeated the date and Rees began to navigate through an array of files on the monitor accessing the video annex trying to pinpoint the date and time of the visit in question.

When he finally found the actual video of the particular visit, its data seemed to be missing.

Frosty watched carefully as Rees accessed all ten recorded visits of that day, all sequentially marked with the name of the visitor and the prisoner's name, witnessing that there indeed was a tape marked with the name of Adrian Frost visiting Kruger but when Rees tried to play the video, it revealed a dark screen. He played all ten tapes and all showed the visitation chamber with a certain prisoner and his visitor sitting across an empty table from one another, except for the video marked Adrian Frost which ran a blank tape. Rees tried to look for breaks in the tape where some footage may have been left, but it was all deleted. He went over all ten tapes a second time with the same result.

All three men looked at one another.

"Who was responsible for storing these tapes? Can you tell?" Nash asked Rees who began to scan a file until he settled on a screen that listed names and dates.

"Dylan Oliver was on duty that day," Rees said studying the monitor. "He is signed off on those items."

"Is he here today? Can we call him?" Nash asked.

Rees Dialed a number on his work phone and waited. "Oliver, can you come see me for a minute?" he spoke with authority and put the handset back in its cradle.

A short, stocky man peeked in a minute later, stepping into the lab and looking curiously at the visitors who were eyeing him. Oliver wore black pants tucked into high cowboy boots, a wide leather belt with a shiny silver buckle, an orange shirt with the black company logo over his left breast, and a thin blue scarf around his neck. He had large blue eyes darting about, a receding hairline above a high-creased forehead and an extremely wide jaw.

"Hello, Mr. Nash," he mumbled as he stood at the entrance not knowing what to do.

"Come take a look," Rees invited him, Nash making room next to the monitor. "We were looking for a certain video from about six months ago which seems to have been deleted," Rees continued while bringing the prison video annex back up on the screen, accessing the recorded digital videos of July 29th.

"Would you have any idea why one of these videos has been deleted?" Nash inquired.

Oliver looked at the screen as Rees brought up the deleted "Adrian Frost Visit" video after going through two other proper videos from the same batch.

"I am Adrian Frost," Frosty said introducing himself. "Do you have any idea why this video was deleted?"

Oliver looked at Frosty his eyes registering a flicker of surprise, and then he looked at the screen as if trying to recall something and turned away from the monitor.

"Why are you asking me this?" he inquired, his eyes darting between everyone. "How should I know?"

"Because you were on duty that day and you signed off on storing these videos," Nash told him harshly. "Why would you want to delete a video?"

"It wasn't me," Oliver stuttered, defending himself, "I don't recall any of this…"

"Do you deny being on duty that day?" Nash pressed him pointing to the screen. "You are listed on the duty roster."

Oliver turned to the screen again and looked at where Rees was pointing his finger. "Yeah, I guess that was me, but I did not erase any tapes. Anyone could have done it before or after."

Both Nash and Rees looked at Frosty. "He's got a point there," Rees commented. "It could be anyone who has access from here."

"Or at the prison before it goes into storage," Oliver added.

"And how long is it before a video goes into storage?" Frosty asked.

"A week at most," Rees said. "Sometimes just a few days."

"And how many people have access from here?" Frosty asked.

"Oh, there must be at least twenty people, maybe a few more," Rees offered.

Frosty looked at the three company men facing him realizing he had no way of sticking the blame on their man, not at this juncture, but having faced his share of liars and cheats, his intuition told him Dylan Oliver was lying, and he intended to wrench a confession out of him in any manner necessary.

Chapter Twenty-Three

Frosty thanked his hosts at Digital Solutions for their cooperation and walked into the darkness out of the lobby, waving goodbye to Becca the receptionist who was glued to her phone again. He walked past the visitors' parking lot rounded the building to the back parking lots, inspected the building for auxiliary exits, returned to the front of the building, and settled between a tree and a bush in a green meadow at the edge of the parking lot making sure he had a direct line of sight to the main entrance.

While he waited, he called Cindy asking her to look into Dylan Oliver.

She called him back after half an hour as he was starting to feel the frostbite on his skin. She had accessed the Digital Solutions personnel files and found him under technical support. Dylan Oliver was thirty-eight and had worked in the British prison system, namely Blackpool prison, for ten years before being employed by Digital Solutions. He was a Wrexham native where he still had his permanent address, and he was a widow with no children.

It was denoted that his wife, Gwendolyn, had been deceased for eight years without indicating the cause of her death. There were additional personal details, parents' names, employee status, pay grade, and two telephone numbers, a work phone, and a mobile one.

Frosty inquired about the girls and asked how the Chisholms were doing. Old Noah Chisholm had given him a lift to the Bath train station and volunteered to drive him back when he returned.

They exchanged a few more words about the girls who were missing him terribly, and he was sorry to let her go, but they had to disconnect keeping their contact to a minimum as a precaution, so they clicked off and he settled in to wait for his man.

Dylan Oliver came out an hour later, draped in an overcoat, walking quickly toward the back parking lot.

Frosty followed him at a distance, watching his flanks for passersby and onlookers but the lot seemed to be empty. Oliver rounded the building walking among the dwindling rows of parked cars, stopping in front of one, activating his remote keys as the car flashed its side lights with a muffled yelp. Frosty hurried along a parallel path and lunged forth between two parked cars, startling Oliver who was getting ready to step into his Hybrid Toyota. The two men measured one another, Oliver holding the car door open frozen in his stance.

"It wasn't me in the video, was it?" Frosty demanded.

"How would I know?" Oliver shot back.

"You do realize that you are cooperating with an organization that is terrorizing this country?" Frosty asserted.

"That is a reckless accusation Agent Frost, don't you think?"

Frosty moved a step forward, putting his right hand into his jacket as if reaching for a weapon of some kind.

"I need to know the identity of the man in the video you deleted," he hissed threateningly. "The fate of this entire country depends on it, so you better come forth or you'll be charged with treason."

"I thought I made myself clear in there," Oliver resisted, taking a step back but holding his ground, pointing toward the building. "Anyone could have done it…"

"You made yourself clear with your colleagues not with me!" Frosty tore at him. "Did you report the malfunction to anyone? Clearly, this was the first time anyone in your company has ever seen the glitch."

"We don't go through each tape to see its contents when we store it," Oliver argued. "And this could have been done after it was stored…."

"Yeah, yeah, you've said that before now tell me the truth!" Frosty demanded.

"That is the truth," Oliver insisted. "I had nothing to do with deleting that tape."

Frosty studied him in the dark contemplating what to do next. The use of force was always an option and it tickled his fingers to violently shake the truth out of him but Dylan Oliver did not seem like a man who would scare easily and threatening him with the Walther he carried in his inside coat pocket seemed superfluous since he had no intention of using it.

He tried a different tactic. "Whoever is using you will not let you run free for too long now that you've been talking to me."

"That's assuming someone is using me," Oliver retorted.

"You should be careful now," Frosty continued ignoring his comment. "These people don't like leaving evidence behind."

"I've got nothing to worry about," Oliver said and Frosty detected a mild shutter in his voice. "I've done nothing wrong. Now could you please let me go?"

Frosty took a step back and Oliver stepped into his car but Frosty caught the door before he had a chance to shut it. "If you change your mind, call me at this number," he said, flashing his mobile number in front of Oliver.

"If you insist," Oliver said and took his mobile phone out of his coat pocket, keying in the numbers.

"You take care now," Frosty said, allowing Oliver to shut the car door, turn on the ignition, maneuver out of his parking spot, and drive away.

******

Camilla reached Brampton Park in East Ham on her bicycle at half-past eight in the evening, hoping she would not be intruding too late but not wanting to loiter around the city during daylight.

London was ghostly, on its fourth day after the bombing, the streets were empty except for law enforcement vehicles, ambulances, military foot soldiers manning street corners, and the occasional cab on a special assignment.

She kept looking around for tails but could not identify any except for others like her on bicycles who were few and far between. No one was walking the streets; all shops were closed shut, Tube stations were shut down and buses were nowhere to be seen.

She and Reuben had agreed that it would be less threatening to Simon Lewis's family if she came rather than he and that he still needed time to recover from his wounds and though he was recovering nicely, was not yet fit to handle a bicycle.

She found the house and peeked through its windows seeing several people gathered in a lit living room. It was a two-story brownstone with several windows facing the street, all completely dark except for the living room.

She gathered her wits and walked up to the door, knocking gently, almost hoping they would not respond but the door opened instantly and Camilla, dressed in riding gear, gloves, and a fleece jacket, faced a small woman wearing a long white dress, a black blouse, her hair bundled up under a black knitted shawl. She had a kind face under wire-rimmed glasses.

"May I help you?" the woman asked gently.

"Is this the house of Simon Lewis?" Camilla asked, not sure how to phrase the question.

"Yes, it is," the woman said, looking sad. "I am his mother and we're sitting Shiva for him since he had just passed away."

Camilla looked into the room. Several men wearing white shirts and black slacks were sitting on sofas and chairs silently praying, their faces hidden behind prayer books, their heads covered in black knitted domes. In the middle of the room were several low tables with dishes of food and drinks but no one seemed to be touching any of it. A few young children were sprawled to the side on the carpet talking quietly among themselves.

"Yes, I know, my condolences," Camilla said unsure what to do next.

"Would you like to come in?" the woman asked. "I can make you a cup of tea. Did you know Simon?"

"Thank you," Camilla said. "No, I did not know Simon but some of my colleagues did."

A dark shadow ran over the woman's face but she remained gracious and led Camilla into the living room offering to hang her jacket in the foyer.

"This is Rabbi Gabriel, Simon's father," she introduced her to a man sitting on one of the sofas; he had a white beard with white bushy eyebrows and he looked up from his bible and nodded.

"My condolences," Camilla said again; the Rabbi nodded in gratitude.

"Please have a seat," he said making room next to him on the sofa. His wife left to make tea.

"So did you know my Simon?" he asked when Camilla sat down.

"No I did not," she said gently and took a deep breath. "And I am very sorry for your loss but if I may, I need to talk to you in private regarding an urgent matter that involved your son and may help us resolve the cause of his death."

Gabriel Lewis closed the book he was reading and eyed Camilla.

"We were very proud of him you know," he said to her after a few seconds.

"Served his country well before they threw him to the dogs…" the other men in the room looked up from their books for a moment and nodded in her direction.

"He certainly did, Mr. Lewis," Camilla said, though she was not familiar with Simon's background. She lowered her voice. "And we believe his death has to do with the mayhem that's been going on here lately…"

The mother arrived with the tea. "Would you like some sugar dear? Something to eat?" she offered.

"No, thank you, Mrs. Lewis, this is very generous," Camilla said, reaching for the China cup with the small China plate underneath.

"Let's go," Gabriel suddenly said getting up from the sofa. "You can leave the tea here. We'll be back in a minute."

He limped ahead draped in religious apparel climbing the stairs to the second floor.

"This is Simon's room," he said, pointing to a door when they were alone in a small hallway with two rooms at both ends. He led her to the end of the corridor and opened the door to his right, turning on the light.

The room was simple with a narrow bed, a work desk with several shelves above it, an office chair, and a wall closet taking up one side of the room. There were several pictures and photos hung on the walls and a cricket bat lying on the floor.

She could not see a computer.

"Has your son been living with you?" She queried. "Or did he have a place of his own?"

"There was no need for him to rent a place since he was always away. But when he was home, he lived here with us," the father said and sat on his son's bed stroking the covers.

Camilla shut the door and sat on the office chair facing Simon's father.

"Did he have a computer?" she asked staring into the old man's eyes.

"He certainly did but they took it away," he said, a gloomy look in his eyes.

"Who did?" Camilla asked alarmingly.

"His unit," Gabriel said. "Some of the people he worked with. Came here the day he died. Reasoned they needed to check it for classified information and simply ripped it away. Did not even stay to commiserate."

"But your son left his unit a year before, didn't he?" Camilla stated.

"Yes, he did. There was an inquiry and he had to resign but he kept in touch with them."

"Did he involve you in anything?"

"Nothing at all but I knew he was unhappy to leave…"

"So, what did he do with his time?"

"I don't really know but he spent quite a bit of time locked up in this room this last year."

"I was hoping to check his computer to help us figure out things, but I guess we're too late," Camilla said desponded.

The room became silent, the children's voices from the living room below becoming apparent. Rabbi Lewis kept stroking his dead son's bed looking down at the floor.

"What are you looking for?" he suddenly asked. Camilla saw no reason to hide the truth from him.

"We think your son was not randomly killed in the explosion at the Ritz, Rabbi Lewis," she said. "We think he was targeted because he had information that could have stopped these ghastly attacks. We believe there are some high-ranking people in his organization that are responsible for this chaos and we think your son had information that might have exposed them."

"Who are the 'we' you keep referring to?" Rabbi Lewis asked.

"If I tell you, I'll be putting your life in danger," Camilla said rising from Simon Lewis's office chair. "You've suffered enough and I would not want to add more suffering to your lovely family."

Rabbi Lewis looked up at her from his place on his son's bed then got up and motioned for her to follow him. He entered the room across the foyer while she waited by the door and came back out a minute later holding something in his fist.

"Simon left this with me," he said, taking her hand in his.

"Told me to make good use of this so here you are," he said, placing the little device in her hand. "I hope I am doing the right thing."

Camilla looked at the disc-on-key he had put in her hand and smiled at him gratefully. He smiled at her as she put it in a side pocket of her bicycle suit and they went back down to join the others.

She drank her tea, politely refusing various savory pies and stuffed vegetables from a flock of women who congregated in the kitchen, maintaining she had some distance to ride, then said her goodbyes and left the house.

She mounted her bicycle, checking she still had the device in her suit pocket and took off along the park. She rode quickly looking in all directions but had to slow down two blocks away in order to cross a wide intersection, when two black cars emerged from two sides, one blocking her path, the other screeching to a halt behind her, figures jumping out of both cars simultaneously catching her before she could gain any speed with her bicycle, throwing her to the ground, thumping on her, pinning her hands behind her back, cuffing them and carrying her kicking and screaming, throwing her on the seat in back of one of the cars, with two goons securing her from two sides.

Seconds later, the intersection was scrubbed of any wrongdoing as the bicycles were thrown in the second car and both took off with a burst of speed.

Chapter Twenty-Four

Thursday, January 31, 2019

Frosty went back to the center of town, bought a set of warm clothing including a heavy parka coat with a hood, and checked in at the Ramada Motor Inn, a few blocks away from Wrexham Central. He took a shower, put on his new clothes, stuffed the used clothes in a nylon bag he had from his shopping, and sat down to delete all messages and incoming and outgoing calls from his phone. He called Cindy quickly updating her on what had evolved and what his plans were, promising to watch his back carefully, deleted that call, then took out the SIM card, punctured the glass screen, and left his phone switched on under the bedsheets.

He left the hotel, found a convenience store on Regent Street, bought a thermos, filled it to the rim with coffee, added a box of Oreos to keep him awake, and went looking for a place where he could hide from the cold and watch the proceedings at the Inn which he anticipated will begin late at night.

After circling the area twice in the dark, he decided on a niche between two adjacent, two-story apartment buildings, which faced the hotel at an angle from across a roundabout. It was as close as he could get without compromising himself. He checked and made sure his niche had a getaway path and sat down under a low parapet which would provide some cover in case it started to rain. He had a clear line of sight to the Inn's entrance and could see his window illuminated by spotlights on the second floor, second from the end.

He pulled out his original phone, which he thankfully kept charged, switched it on, put it in flight mode, zoomed in, and took a few photos of the entrance area, checking to see if it was possible to photograph whoever came along. The photos came out quite dark, but he estimated that with a little filtering, he could make out a face if he got a good shot.

He settled down, drinking the coffee straight out of the thermos and nibbling on the cookies once in a while.

He was convinced Dylan Oliver was guilty as a sin and it was only a matter of time before they tracked the mobile phone and came storming in. At that juncture, he felt, Dylan Oliver would become a marked man like himself.

He looked at his watch. It was half-past ten. There was light traffic on the street and once in a while a taxi or a small shuttle bus would stop at the entrance to the Inn to offload or pick up passengers. At midnight, he felt himself fighting to keep his eyelids open, losing conciseness for periods of time, and having to check his watch from time to time to see how long he was out.

The troops came at two in the morning. Two black sedans which he instantly identified as security service vehicles, appeared from opposite directions, their lights off, followed by two mini-vans who let off several troopers who took positions around the Inn blocking both sides of the street and any footpath or trail access. Troops in place, the company vehicles approached the hotel entrance; several dark figures leaped out of the cars and entered the lobby. Frosty aimed his phone camera at the happening across the roundabout from his hiding place, and shot several photos in succession, videoing and photographing the stretch around the hotel with the troops lined up at their positions and zooming in on the lead cars and the figures that entered the hotel.

A few minutes later, he saw the light being turned on in the room he had used then they were back outside the hotel lobby huddling around their vehicles.

Frosty aimed his phone camera and once again zoomed in and took several additional photos before they gathered the troops back into their vehicles and took off in a small convoy, mini-vans in tow.

He lingered in his hiding place another hour making sure no one remained behind to ambush him, then slipped through the narrow gap between the buildings away from the open street and the hotel and made his way in the dark toward the center of town hoping to find an open coffee shop or a convenient store where he could wait out the rest of the night until public transportation commenced and he could slip away from the town. He took a wide berth around Wrexham Central expecting a welcoming party at the train station and ended up at a bakery that propagated savory smells. He waited outside the establishment for a few minutes then entered finding two young lads and a woman busy baking pies, fresh buns, and bread for the emerging day ahead.

"Care for some scones with jam?" The burly red-headed woman asked smiling at him under a tray of buns she was about to throw in a large oven. "Looks like you've had a rough night." She commented.

"That would be lovely, thanks," Frosty said. "Any coffee to go with that?"

"Help yourself," she said, expertly sliding the tray into the oven.

"There's a thermos and paper cups next to the scones over there," she tilted her head toward a side counter that had the condiments next to a cash register.

"Boys could you hurry up with that dough already, we've got customers in just over an hour."

The two boys, who were both red-headed and looked to be high-school age, were standing at a round wooden counter breaking a pile of dough into loaves, putting it on trays ready to bake.

Frosty went to the counter, sliced a warm scone in half with a plastic knife, pasted some butter and jam, poured himself coffee, and sat on an office chair by the cash register, eating hungrily.

"Is there a bus from anywhere here to Liverpool?" he asked when he was done with the scone, he thought tasted heavenly and was preparing another.

One of the boys raised his eyes from the dough and said: "Yes, there's a stop near the McDonald's on Regent Street. It leaves at seven and eleven."

"How long does it take?" Frosty asked, stuffing the second scone into his mouth hungrily.

"Oh, it takes quite a while. You're better off taking the train from Central." the boy said.

Frosty took another swig from the coffee. "I might just do that then," he said. "These scones are the best I've tasted," he commended.

The two boys smiled and the woman looked at him. "It's because they are fresh and you had a bad night, but thanks anyway."

Frosty looked at his watch and stood up. "I guess I'll go catch me a train," he said, reaching for his wallet and taking out a twenty-pound note to pay.

The woman took a paper bag that was hanging by the display stands and stuffed a few fresh buns in it, throwing in a small box of cream cheese from a rattling fridge and a clean plastic knife, handing it to Frosty.

"You take care now," she said, declining his money, sending him on his way. "And better get some sleep," she added as he stepped out of the shop and into the street.

It was still dark outside but with shades of gray and he debated with himself what to do next but the first thing he needed was to call Cindy. He stepped back into the bakery and asked the boys where he could find a payphone. They looked at him funny and pointed him toward Yale College where he found an alcove of beat-down pay phones that still worked.

Cindy was wide awake when he called and he had to calm her down with explanations before she began to make sense and they started assessing the pros and cons of staging a second meeting with Dylan Oliver if the snitch remained alive long enough.

"I have not heard from Camilla or Santana yet," Cindy informed him before he hung up.

"Call them at the agreed hours," Frosty suggested. "They must have had a late night like I did."

"I will do just that," Cindy said. "You watch yourself. Love you," she said and hung up.

It was still dark enough for Frosty to walk the streets and he hurried along back to the Industrial park, hoping to catch an hour of sleep under the bush before people began showing up at Digital Solutions.

It was still quite dark when he got there. He set the alarm on his watch for seven thirty and crawled under the bush by the meadow at the edge of the parking lot making sure he was hidden by the branches from all sides. When he woke up it was daylight and cars began arriving. He peeked through the bushes covering him and caught Becca the receptionist, dressed in a smart blue outfit and high heels, walking in the lobby door. Soon after people began showing up including Rees with the orange-black company fleece and Vice President Marc Nash in a gray suit with a red tie.

Half an hour later, Oliver appeared in his Hybrid Toyota, driving excessively fast screeching to a halt in front of the lobby, leaving the car on the curb, and running into the building.

A black sedan followed less than a minute later, braking behind Oliver's Toyota, two men in suits leaping out, chasing after him.

Frosty leaped into action. Without considering the consequences, moving on instinct, he left his hiding place under the bush in the meadow, ditching the nylon bag he had carried with him, and ran toward the two cars parked in front of Digital Solutions. Both cars' engines were still running.

He opened the sedan's back door and slipped in, taking out his Walther in the process, lying low on the back seat.

He did not have to wait long.

He caught a glimpse of Becca the receptionist and a few others in black-orange shirts, standing in the lobby with shocked expressions as the two men came out dragging Oliver screaming and howling; no one dared to interfere.

As the party descended, the wide stairs toward the cars, Frosty knew he would not get a better chance to catch them unawares, as they did not have their weapons out, straining to contain Oliver. He came out the back door of the car with his Walther out, aiming at the men who halted in surprise, still holding Oliver between them.

"Let him go," Frosty said, calmly raising the gun. The two heavily built men, one bald with sunglasses, the other with straight blond hair, combed to the side, with piercing light green color eyes, hesitated a second too long. Frosty pulled the trigger, hitting the concrete next to the bald man's foot.

"The next one won't miss," he said threateningly, raising the gun at them.

They released Oliver who fell forward, losing his balance, nearly falling to the ground. Frosty caught him with his free hand, still aiming his gun with a steady hand at the goons.

"Open the passenger door of your car and its window and get in the driver's seat," he commanded.

Oliver looked at him with a mixture of surprise and relief and did as he was told. Frosty backtracked toward the car, keeping his adversaries in his gun sight. He sat in the car, aimed and fired his gun hitting the black sedan's two front wheels shouting at Oliver to take off.

The car screeched away as Frosty shut his door. He kept aiming his gun at the two men through the open window until Oliver made a sharp turn behind some parked cars, seeing them jump into action, drawing their guns out and firing in their direction.

"Keep your head down," Frosty shouted at Oliver who stooped low but kept his eyes on the road, racing the car through the parking lot and out onto the street.

Frosty looked back, seeing the two goons jumping in their car, going after them with two blown front tires.

They were quickly lost behind.

Chapter Twenty-Five

Andy White thought he had finally gotten his break.

The woman sat in the corner of the room on the floor in a black and red sports outfit, head between her knees, hands hugging her legs. He was not sure if she was asleep since she did not stir when he entered so he walked to her and touched her shoulder.

She raised her face to him, giving him a weary look, and tried to move away along the wall.

He noticed her exquisite looks, dark skin, and shapely body.

"Since we found this in your pocket," he declared without preamble, crouching down and flashing the disc-on-key in her face. "It would be pointless to deny your involvement in the Tompkins assassination affair, or would it?"

Camilla looked at him uncomprehending. They had dumped her on the floor in the dark, heatless room, the previous night, and now this ghost of a man, with a deathly pale face and long red hair, was trying to get her to say things.

She figured she was better off shutting up.

White looked at her expectantly and when she did not respond, he tried a different angle: "Why were you at Simon Lewis's house last night?"

"He was an old friend," she retorted. "I went to pay my respects."

"And did that include coming away with this?" he insisted, showing her the disc again.

Camilla looked bravely into his gray eyes. "Who are you?" she spat. "And why am I being held here?"

"Agent White, Homeland Security," the man introduced himself, flashing an ID card in front of her eyes.

"Now I need some answers," he said.

"I am a Brazilian citizen and I demand to see someone from my embassy," she declared, straightening up. "You can't hold me here like this!"

"You are a Brazilian citizen with an expired length of stay," he countered her. "I know, I checked, and besides that minor infringement, you are also shacking up with a fugitive."

Camilla was suddenly at a loss for words. He was right. She did overstay her visitor's permit but that was because she and Reuben intended to get married, she thought, but did not dare say.

"Still, it does not give you the right to ambush me on the street and throw me in here like a dog!" she howled at him.

"Yes, it does," White said. "Especially now, when this country is in a state of emergency."

Camilla looked at him with burning eyes then retreated to her withered sitting position without any comment.

"Who gave you the disc and did you see what's on it?" White demanded, standing over her.

It was impossible to deny the existence of the disc in her suit pocket, though she had not gotten a chance to look at its contents. She looked up at him trying to decide how to tackle her predicament when he continued: "You do realize withholding information from me puts you in the same boat with those terrorists violating this country!" He warned. "Now, I have a situation that I need resolved so I need you to share with me what you know."

"I know nothing," she uttered deflated, lowering her stare to the floor.

White stooped next to her and pulled her face up by her chin. "Where's your boyfriend?" he demanded, hissing at her, so close that she could smell his body odor. "Did he send you to get the disc?"

It was obvious they had the Lewis house under surveillance and that they knew about her relationship with Reuben but what had just occurred to her was the fact that their hideout was not compromised, otherwise, he would not be asking about Santana's whereabouts, and neither was their contact with Agent Frost and his wife. So far, she realized, it seemed they were clueless about their dealings with Agent Frost.

"I will not answer any questions without proper representation from my embassy," She repeated her earlier demand.

It made little impression on White. "In a state of emergency such as this, I am authorized to interrogate anyone who I deem to have the potential to threaten our national security and since we found this disc in your possession, you are deemed as just that! Now, either you cooperate or I will declare you an accessory to these terrorist attacks in which case they will lock you up and throw away the key and no one, not even the distinguished representatives of your native country will be able to help you."

Camilla did not reply to White's threats. The disc obviously contained incriminating material, she thought, scolding herself for not taking extra precautions, realizing it must be the evidence Frosty was looking for, but there was nothing she could do about it now. They had her trapped and her only hope was to try and talk her way out of it.

She replayed in her mind what Cindy had said: that they suspected sensitive governmental positions in the Home Office such as Homeland Security, may have been infiltrated, and were now being used to launch the attacks. The same people, who may have been responsible for the Tompkins murder, in an effort to keep the deputy minister from exposing them, would not hesitate to hand her a similar fate she now realized, and if indeed it was Simon Lewis's information that got Tompkins killed, then whatever was on that disc was obviously extremely crucial in battling these people.

However, the disc was in the wrong hands.

"You would never let me out of here, will you?" she confronted him, raising her face to him bravely, tears forming in her eyes. "And Reuben will end up the same if I tell you where he is. Won't he?" she reproached and started crying.

White stood up and pulled her onto her feet.

"If you lead me to him, I will let you go," he hissed. "You obviously care for him but he is damaged goods."

The remark stung but Camilla remained silent until he spoke again, this time harsher. "You need to distance yourself from him, Camilla, because he will never be a free man. He may manage to avoid us for the time being, but he will eventually be caught, tried, and put away for life. He has nowhere to run because even if he flees the country, he will eventually be extradited back here. After all, no country can allow itself to be associated with people responsible for the attacks that have taken place here."

"All that assuming he has done something wrong," Camilla remarked backing away from White.

"Well, if he hasn't then he should come clean," White observed. "But so far he has been hiding."

"Maybe it's because he's worried the people, who killed his partner and meant to kill him, would try again?"

"Then why doesn't he seek our protection?" White reasoned. "That's our job, to protect people."

Camilla stared at the tall bony man wishing the charade they were staging would stop. It was obvious White and whoever he was working for were intent on steering the attention away so they could execute their plan and would stop at nothing to achieve their goals including shifting the blame onto innocent people such as Reuben and Agent Frost. It was clear to her now that they were using the upheaval to justify their actions; no one would receive a fair trial and she wasn't about to subject her future husband to these criminals.

But White was a dangerous man. She could feel it. He was going to use whatever means he had at his disposal to get the job done and she was a tool he could use.

"I'll give you time to think it over," he finally said, heading for the door, knocking on it, and waiting for whatever sentry was on the outside to open it. When the door opened, he turned to her saying: "When I return, you had better make up your mind."

He went out and she flipped a finger at his back and sat on the floor defeated, her back to the wall.

Chapter Twenty-Six

Frosty and Dylan Oliver ditched his car in Warrington and hopped on a train to Birmingham where they caught a train to Bristol and from there a bus to Bath.

Dylan Oliver, grateful to Frosty for saving his life, revealed all that he knew on their long journey back to the Chisholm's guest house.

Oliver was twenty when he applied for the British prison system after completing high school in Wrexham and traveling the Far East for a year where he met his future wife Gwyn who was a Scott from Edinburgh.

He started working at Blackpool prison in 2001 after completing his course as a guard but soon exhibited exceptional technical skills and was transferred to technical support where he dealt among other things with surveillance cameras and video storing devices that were products belonging to Digital Solutions, a company from his hometown.

He revealed to Frosty that he had met Max Kruger, the notorious terrorist inmate, in person on two occasions during his time at the prison; once when he was escorted into his cell to fix a surveillance camera and a second time when Kruger was brought into the visitor's chamber and he was there fixing some wiring.

In 2008, his beloved Gwyn was killed when she came to the prison one day with their car, to pick him up for a weekend trip to her parents in Edinburgh. A prison bus that had just offloaded some inmates stormed out of the prison gates just as Gwyn was entering hitting their car head-on. She was killed instantly in her second month of pregnancy.

Oliver who would be devastated and heartbroken for many years to come, was still suffering from depression, was denied the compensation he was seeking from the prison system including the termination of employment for the reckless bus driver who he later sued but lost his case.

After a year of dealing with lawsuits and endless court appearances which he ended up with nothing to show, Oliver quit the prison system and was hired by

Digital Solutions who knew his technical capabilities and were sympathetic to his loss. He was put in technical support and was part of the technical team responsible for installing new equipment on order, some of which were installed in Blackpool prison itself.

On Christmas Eve, 2017, a man showed up with a briefcase at his doorstep in Wrexham. Since the death of his wife and stillborn child, Oliver had stopped celebrating holidays or going to church and he normally spent his time alone at his apartment or off trekking somewhere which was one of the few activities that kept him sane.

He remembered the man as tall and bony with a pale face and red hair dressed in a suit. He offered Oliver a hefty sum of money for a single act that at the time seemed quite benign and harmless, but, its ramifications were now becoming clear as Frosty filled in the gaps. It became clear that he was approached for two main reasons: the first was that he had access to Digital Solutions storing media and had the skills needed to delete the required segment leaving minimum footprints.

The second was that he was the only one at Digital Solutions who had ever seen Max Kruger. The request was very specific. He was to be given a date in July of 2018, roughly six months from the time he had been approached, at which time he was to delete the video of a visit by a certain individual to Max Kruger at Blackpool prison. He would be given the exact date and time of the visit shortly before it was to occur and was to wait a week before deleting the digital recording from all storage devices. That was all.

For that, he received half a million English pounds, half of it on the spot, as the man had opened a briefcase full of fifty-pound bills, and the other half after he completed his task.

The only stipulation was that if anyone ever inquired about this affair, he was to report it without delay. The red-haired man gave him a mobile phone number he should call if he was ever confronted about that deleted tape, promising that the likelihood of such an occurrence was one in a million.

It was the first thing he did after their encounter; he admitted to Frosty, and he had been saved by Frosty, of course, and by a rare deviation from his routine when he went out early for a morning run, rather than his usual evening one which he missed being distracted by their meeting at work and wanted to make up for it. As he was approaching his apartment that morning on foot after his run, he noticed the alien black car parked across the street from his building with the two goons sitting in it.

It did not feel right so he made a detour and came in through a back entrance, got ready for work at his apartment, and rushed out of the garage with his car. They saw him and gave chase. He panicked, not knowing where to turn, thinking the police were the last people he needed to involved in this, so he did the only logical thing he could think of, he raced to his workplace hoping he would be protected there, but the goons flashed some formal ID's and dragged him out.

"They would have disposed of you, you know?" Frosty remarked as they disembarked from the train at Bristol, checking their flanks before hurrying to catch their bus to Bathe.

"I know that now," Oliver admitted. "But I had no idea what I got myself into a year ago."

"But you had to be asking yourself why such a large fee for such a simple job?" Frosty questioned as they were walking toward their bus station.

"An amount like this, kind of makes such a question uncalled for, don't you think?" Oliver argued, hurrying to keep up with the taller Frosty. They reached the bus station and remained silent for the duration of the wait until they boarded the bus.

"Can you describe the man in the video you deleted?" Frosty inquired once they were seated on the back of the half-empty bus.

Oliver looked at Frosty a moment considering the question. "I've thought about that ever since you showed up in our labs," he said thoughtfully. "And the one thing that stuck in my mind from that video, even though I saw it only once before I deleted it, was that the two men in that video looked extremely alike."

******

Noah Chisholm waited for them at the bus station in Bath and drove them to the guest house, no questions asked.

Cindy and the girls greeted Frosty with hugs and kisses and they were all invited to a mouth-watering supper.

Dylan Oliver was introduced as an old acquaintance of Frosty from the military days who came over from Wales to catch up on stuff with his old mate and meet his wife and kids. After supper, he took a room on the bottom floor, excused himself, and went to wash up.

157

Frosty and Cindy went up to their room. The girls remained in the guest room by the fireplace to watch television while the Chisholms cleaned up.

"I had to wait until three in the afternoon to reach Santana," Cindy said as Frosty lay on their bed with his clothes, exhausted. "The six O'clock morning call went unanswered."

"Why? What happened?" Frosty asked.

"Camilla did not return," Cindy said sitting on the edge of the bed. "Santana is worried that she has been caught."

"Oh god," Frosty sighed sitting up.

"Santana says they must have been watching the house," Cindy relayed her conversation with the police officer. "He went there this morning and spotted at least two company cars."

"We should have anticipated this…" Frosty said.

"Well we didn't and he is beside himself," Cindy divulged. "I asked him to wait to speak to you before he does anything rash but I don't know if he listened."

"We'll call him at six," Frosty sighed, putting his face between his hands. "I hope he doesn't do something foolish until then. I just have to get some sleep; I just can't think straight right now."

Frosty undressed and took a long-needed shower. Drinking hot tea, she had brought to their room, he told Cindy what had happened with Oliver and asked her to check some photos and names.

Then he put his head on the pillow and slept like a log.

Chapter Twenty-Seven

Friday, February 1, 2019

The following day, February 1st 2019, became one of the most traumatic days in the United Kingdom's recent history.

Rumors began circulating early morning that Prince William, the Duke of Cambridge, heir to the throne, had gone missing together with his Sea King, Search and Rescue helicopter crew, but it was later established that he had been on his way to join his crew when he disappeared.

They had been flying missions over London, assisting in various evacuation activities, and flying troops around. William insisted he join them and his squadron operations center at Boscombe Down accepted and had been in direct communication with him as he was making his way from London by car when they had lost contact.

Prime Minister Webster called an emergency meeting with his military advisors, intelligence aides, and cabinet members to try and control the potential turmoil once word got out. Prince Harry joined as well.

Sir Nigel Scott returned to his office at ten that morning accompanied by Trevor Bishop; both were awoken at five that morning after only a few hours of sleep, to urgently get to 10 Downing Street.

Back at the Home Office, they were met by Ross Dixon and AVM Alan Reed and convened in Scott's office.

The Home Secretary's face conveyed the foul mood he was in.

"Have you heard from your people?" he addressed Ross Dixon whose responsibility it was to safeguard the Prince.

"He took off on his own from Windsor just after midnight," Dixon reported. "I sent two cars after him covering both possible routes the M3 and M4, and both reached Boscomb without finding him."

The Home Secretary looked at him expectantly. "He may have already reached the base," he pointed out.

"We checked but he wasn't there," Dixon said. "So, I sent my teams back via the same routes, asking his chopper crew to look for him as well. The chopper received clearance to take off and searched the area until we finally found his Bentley on a dirt road off the A303 but he wasn't there."

"Christ all mighty," Nigel Scott muttered. "So what are we doing now to find him?"

"We've got whatever military units around Boscombe combing the area and Special Ops teams spread along the routes monitoring any signal that may be transmitted and ready to pounce once a signal is identified and the position traced," Dixon informed the minister.

"You don't strike without a direct order from the PM," Scott reminded him. "We may be in for a long hostage negotiation session if indeed we find him alive."

"Anything at your end, Alan," Scott addressed Reed.

"I've got my entire staff working this, Sir," Reed said. "We're monitoring cellular lines, email traffic, and the internet. I've sent people to air traffic control and to the military crisis headquarters here in Hyde Park. I've also personally asked Ken Harper at MI6 to contact our counterpart allies' task forces and see if they can provide us with anything."

"Bishop?" Scott addressed the head of MI5.

"We've taken over an entire Black Hawk squadron," Bishop informed them, looking haggard. "I've got crews on these choppers combing the area where his car was found. His own search and rescue squadron is out looking for him along with a host of UAVs. If he's in the area, we'll find him."

"We are at our wit's end," Scott said frustrated. "The treasury people are estimating the pound had lost half of its value and these hedge funds are still buying Rubles and anything else they can get their hands on by the billions. London is all but paralyzed and now this!"

"What's the central bank doing about the sterling?" Dixon asked.

"They are buying billions back and they have raised interest rates, but it seems too little too late. Our economy has come to a standstill with this London siege. No one's offloading any cargo at any of the ports, sea or air, since nothing can be shipped into London. Food is becoming scarce as well. Petrol is just about run out in London and worse of all the people are beginning to lose patience and will soon go to the streets, and now England's favorite son has gone missing. What else could go wrong!?"

There was a short pause as Scott stared at his aides and they avoided his gaze.

"We have not been able to locate any explosive devices anywhere, have we?" He addressed them and they nodded in unison. "Nor have we been able to find an end of a rope to anyone from the organization responsible," he reproached.

"Is the PM negotiating with anyone?" Dixon asked.

"He will be if it turns out they have the Prince!" Scott remarked. "They stipulated he bring their demands to debate in the house on national TV but so far he has refrained, preferring to negotiate directly."

"Who with?" Dixon questioned.

"It's classified to cabinet ministers only," Scott said. "But I can tell you he hasn't made much progress."

A secretary rushed in without knocking, her face pale white.

"The TV Sir, turn on the TV," she mumbled, standing in the middle of the room shaking.

Scott hit the button on his remote and the TV monitor on the wall came to life.

All heads turned and on the plasma screen they saw their Prince in a flight suit sitting on the ground, looking into a camera; a gloved hand holding a gun pointed at his head.

The camera shifted and a man with a black hood and holes for his eyes appeared standing above the Prince.

"It has been six days and we have made no progress," the man began with his Eastern European accent. "Your Prime Minister is responsible for this. We have presented our demands but so far no one is taking any action."

The camera shifted to the Prince again who stared bravely ahead, the gun still pointed at his head.

"So now you have an ultimatum," the man continued. "Three days to accept our demands and put a plan into action or your Prince dies."

The camera moved back to the compromised Prince who now looked intently into the camera and it seemed he was slightly shaking his head.

The screen went blank and for a moment remained dark until the BBC anchor appeared again looking dazed.

Scott's secretary suddenly sighed and dropped to the floor where she stood. The four men in the room jumped up from their seats and rushed to her, kneeling by her side, trying to revive her.

"Someone get us some water," Scott commanded and Dixon stormed out of the room, coming back in a flash with a pitcher of water and a secretary in toe with a first aid kit.

They poured some water on her face, and she came awake, looking at the faces above her in surprise.

"Did I just pass out?" she asked.

"Yes you did," Scott said. "But you'll be all right, just relax for a bit."

The men moved away allowing the other secretary to assist with the first aid kit then helped the woman up and escorted her to her desk.

"Take her to the ministry doctor," Scott said to the other secretary before he shut the door to his office and turned to look at his three colleagues.

"Was he shaking his head?" he boomed at them. "Or were my eyes toying with me?"

"He shook his head," Reed said in admiration. "He certainly did that, Sir. He certainly did."

It was a barely perceptible gesture of self-sacrifice that millions saw, or thought they saw, on the screen by the man who was destined to one day be the King of England, but it had a mammoth effect and people began voicing their objections to the terror, over the net. Hundreds of thousands, if not millions of posts were launched through Facebook, Twitter, and social networks, even on Instagram where thousands of photos of Prince William and his family were posted. That same night people gathered on streets everywhere, lighting candles, praying, and calling for the British Government not to give in.

The Prince's humiliation had a negative effect on what it had intended to achieve, or so it seemed. It gave strength rather than cause panic. A simple, almost unnoticeable resistance of a beloved figure under extreme duress rallied the people to voice their support and repel the oppressors.

It was no longer earmarked England's problem. It was now the world's problem.

Chapter Twenty-Eight

Jemma managed to dodge her tail once more and find a payphone to call Frosty not far from her house at seven that evening. Frosty had been signaling her on her spare phone to call all day but she could not get away. On direct orders from the PM, they were gearing up for a major push to flush out the hostile organization and put an end to the saga following the Prince's hijacking, and she had only a few hours at home before joining her colleagues at the makeshift crisis center where they would get their assignments.

"You at home?" Frosty inquired as soon as he heard her voice.

"Not far, why?" She questioned, looking left and right surveying the area.

"I am two blocks away," Frosty revealed, "We need to talk face-to-face."

"You know the back way?" she asked.

"Yes I do," he said. "Leave the glass door from the garden open and shut your lights. I'll be there in a flash."

"Give me ten minutes," she said and hung up, carefully walking away from the phone booth.

Frosty appeared from the shadows of their garden sneaking through the back door into the kitchen a half hour later. Jake was in the den working as usual and the boys were on the living room floor in front of the TV.

Jemma made sure the curtains were drawn and the blinds shut before turning on the lights.

They hugged and kissed on both cheeks and Jemma poured coffee. Jake came in and they shook hands.

"You, OK?" Jake asked.

"Not really but making progress," Frosty sighed with a tired smile.

Jake was Frosty's height with curly gray hair and sunken brown eyes behind round wire-rimmed glasses that slipped down his nose. He was wearing slippers, red trainers, and a black t-shirt. He grinned at Frosty and padded him on the back.

"I'll leave you to it," he said and turned to go back to his den.

"How are the boys holding up?" Frosty asked and Jake turned.

"Having the time of their lives," he said jovially. "Have not moved an inch from the TV in a week." He mocked and left the kitchen.

"It's Ross Dixon," Frosty said without preamble as soon as Jake was out of earshot.

"Dixon is who…?" Jemma mumbled confused, not sure what Frosty was referring to.

"The man who impersonated me at Blackpool prison visiting Kruger six months ago. The reason I am being hunted, as you may recall," he said scornfully.

"How do you know?" she asked focusing.

"I've met the man who deleted the tape. His name is Oliver and he identified him."

"Dixon? The SO1 chief? Are you sure?"

"Sure as I have ever been about anything," he said. "And it all makes sense now. Dixon is the guy! Don't you see? He's the sleeper agent. The one behind it all."

"You think he's one of those kidnapped babies sent back from Beirut? The ones we've been after?"

"Yes, I believe he is Jem. After Oliver identified him from a bank of photos we looked at as the man who visited Kruger, we ran a search to find out his background. Guess what? He has no background! The man appeared in a London high school at age sixteen, just like was written in Fleming's report. We then searched for missing children reports under that name dating back forty years and found his name. Ross Dixon was reported missing in 1980 and was never found."

Jemma caught her breath.

"It's a perfect setup," Frosty continued. "SO1, the Special Protection Branch, responsible for protecting dignitaries, government ministers, and the lot, including the royal family? No wonder they were able to trap the Prince with such ease. His escort detail must be part of the group responsible for all this. Andy White is definitely one of them."

"Simon Lewis must have suspected something," Jemma said thoughtfully.

"He probably did…" Frosty sighed despondently.

Jemma stared at him inquiringly from across the kitchen table.

"We asked Officer Santana to go check his house," Frosty divulged. "He is still recovering so he sent his girlfriend Camilla. She went there and apparently got caught…"

"Caught by whom?"

"We don't know. She never came back home, and we don't know if she found anything. Santana went looking for her there early the following morning and reported to have seen some company cars lurking around but now that I know who's involved I am assuming Dixon's people are holding her somewhere."

"Now that's an ugly turn of events," Jemma remarked. "Santana must be devastated."

"He's itching to go shoot someone, anyone, but I asked him to hold off until I talked to you."

"Does he know about Dixon?"

"Not specifically, but obviously we had to explain why we were interested in Simon Lewis…"

"What about Reed or Bishop? Shouldn't we fill them in?"

"Not yet," Frosty cautioned. "We have a weak case at best since the tapes were erased so it's basically the word of one extremely vindictive man…"

"Who is this, Oliver?" Jemma asked. "What happened with him?"

Frosty quickly recapped the events that occurred in Wrexham drawing admiring remarks from his colleague of twenty years but when he was done, she said accusingly: "You could have been killed you know?"

He flashed a tired smile and nodded: "It never crossed my mind."

"So, if we can't or don't want to use this knowledge right now, what should we do?" Jemma questioned.

"Oh, we definitely will use what we know but without involving the brass until we can bring conclusive evidence."

"Meanwhile, Prince William's life is on the line and this country is in the shits," Jemma observed. "I don't think we have the luxury of collecting enough evidence, Frost. We need to act and we need to do it now!"

"Wholeheartedly agreed with one exception," Frosty said. "We must find out what Simon Lewis had on them and for that, we need to get to Camilla."

"Why not go to his house again?"

"Because it's under surveillance and the minute any of us shows his face around there, we'll be caught too, and we can forget calling there because their phones must be tapped so we need to find out if Camilla came out of there with something."

"If she came out with something, they must have it by now," Jemma observed.

"Or she could have seen something or been told something by a member of the family."

"In which case they would make her talk..."

"She seemed like a tough cookie to me so she might hold up a while but that is why we must get to her fast plus the fact that I owe it to Santana. It was my mistake asking them to go there not thinking the house would be watched."

"Any ideas?" Jemma asked.

"I thought of something, but we first need to know where they are holding her. Could you find out?"

"We've got a major assembly in two hours at the crisis center in Hyde Park. They will be handing out assignments and dividing us into various task forces. I doubt I'll have time to breathe."

"Then you skip it," Frosty said simply.

Jemma looked at him as if he had lost his mind. "Have you lost your mind?" She asked.

"Not really," he said. "It's you and me who possess the critical information to put an end to this. Everyone else will be led, as they have been so far, down a fabricated path, so why bother?"

"They'll be after me in a flash," Jemma argued.

"Then you go under like me," Frosty suggested. "They suspect you anyway and would not leave you alone or let you do anything noteworthy so at this point, you'll be much more useful joining me."

"What about Jake and the kids?" Jemma asked, suddenly looking frightened.

"We'll give Jake directions to our retreat, and he can drive there tonight after you and I leave, or is he being followed as well?"

"I don't think he is," Jemma said uncertainly. "I mean, he hasn't left the house in a week except to go buy some groceries."

"Then they won't suspect anything," Frosty noted. "You go to your meeting then find a way to escape from there. Meanwhile, Jake and the kids will leave, and you meet me wherever we agree to meet."

Jemma took a deep breath. "You will need to help me convince Jake," she said. "He won't give up his den so easily."

Part Three

Chapter Twenty-Nine

Saturday, February 2, 2019

The Russian sat smoking among the snow-covered steel tables outside the Crown Hotel in Jyvaskyla, Finland.

It was minus 20 degrees Celsius outside with a light breeze and weak rays of morning sun reflecting off the frost-covered lobby windows. Across the snowy yard, on the street, a short procession of cars was gingerly following a snow-clearing tractor, shoving piles of snow to the side of the road from the night's heavy snowfall.

He looked at his watch. It was five minutes to nine. He had arrived the previous evening on a short flight from St. Petersburg and was expecting his contact to show up any minute.

The man showed up at the appointed time, heavily wrapped in a long cashmere coat, gloves, and a wool scarf. The Russian threw the cigarette butt in the snow, and they shook hands.

"Have a seat," the Russian said, pointing at the seat opposite him, putting a glove back on his bare hand, and shoving the snow from the top of the garden table.

The man looked hesitant for a moment before he heavily sat down on the steel chair.

"You've done well so far but you should not have taken the Prince," the Russian stated without preamble making the younger man perk up.

"Thank you, Comrade," the man said in fluent Russian. "But the British remained insolent."

"You woke up the demons," the Russian said.

"We thought it was necessary." The man replied.

"You should have consulted," the Russian insisted. "Their currency has lost more than half its value, London is paralyzed, and their government is in complete disarray. That should have been enough. We had them where we wanted but there is no telling how they will react now that their precious monarchy has been humiliated."

"You trusted our judgment," the man argued weakly.

"We allowed you too much leeway," the Russian admonished. "But what's done is done and we must continue."

The man stared at the Russian from behind his scarf, his blond hair blowing in a breeze that kept intensifying.

"The Ruble has gained over twenty percent compared to the US Dollar," he boasted, trying to save some of his pride.

"Now comes the big test," the Russian continued, ignoring the comment. "We will approach Webster discretely."

"What's with all our demands?"

"Those demands were just smokescreen," the Russian revealed. "We were never serious about those. Does eliminating the monarchy or giving those Muslims government jobs seem realistic to you?"

The blond man looked confused. "So, what will we ask for?"

The Russian snickered and then became serious: "When we took Crimea in 2014, the Americans led a series of sanctions against us with their European allies, primarily high-tech equipment for our gas and oil production. We were not worried then because we felt we could reach proper levels of production with our own newly developed equipment by the time conventional oil reserves were exhausted. But last year when we threatened to annex the whole of Ukraine, the Americans and their allies began building new Liquefied Natural Gas, or LNG, terminals in the UK in order to supply Europe with oil and natural gas from America as an alternative to our pipelines. These new ports will be operational by the end of this year and once this happens, our natural gas exports to Europe will drop from about 200 billion cubic meters of gas to about 50, almost three-quarters of the current supply, and we cannot allow that!"

The blond man looked at the Russian astonished. "So, all this Muslim religion exploitation is just a front to save the Russian economy?"

The Russian nodded. "In addition, Russian banks are in heavy debt to Western banks, almost half of it to banks in the UK. The Americans and the European Union have intensified their sanctions in retaliation to our threats on Ukraine and our recent military maneuvers on the Polish border. We were lucky they did not boycott the football games last year."

"So, these dormant spies calling themselves 'Sons of Jihad,' were really a Russian plot?"

"No, they were not, but when they were found out and compromised in Beirut by allied Special Forces in '96, their primary supporters in the Arab world abandoned them and ceased all funding. They needed help, so they turned to us."

"And how did you know what would happen so far back in time?"

"We did not. We just financed their actions and directed them where they should infiltrate with the understanding that we would use them when the time comes. There are still others waiting dormant for future opportunities."

The blond man wiped some ice that had accumulated on his face. "So, what will you do?" he finally asked.

The Russian took off one glove and lit another cigarette.

"We will commit to stop the bombing and return order to London, free the Prince, and get the international hedge fund managers to get out of their short positions on the Sterling and buy it back, squaring it up sort of say, to bring the Sterling levels up to where it was before it got dumped. Confidence will be restored, which will help the pound rally. For that, we will demand the Brits sign a document where they commit to drop their initiative of supplying American gas to Europe, write off our debt, drop all sanctions, and convince their allies to drop theirs as well."

"What will they do with their new LNG ports?" The blond man questioned.

"There will always be a need for such ports for Arab gas. Remember we supply only about 40 percent of Europe's gas and we hardly supply any gas to the Brits."

"What will the Americans do? They probably invested billions in increasing their gas supply capacity to include Europe. They could start a war over this."

The Russian sucked hard on his cigarette inhaled and continued.

"It's a risk we have to take but I doubt the Americans will be seeking another conflict after their campaigns in Iraq, Afghanistan and Syria. They are still licking their wounds and attacking Mother Russia is an entirely different affair. Our experts believe they would have to swallow their pride, take the loss, and look for other markets."

"They may continue the sanctions regardless and convince the others to do so as well. I mean, you don't really believe the Brits have such influence," the blond man argued.

"That is a very real scenario which we fully expect is possible, but our main goal remains blocking the gas supply; everything else will be a bonus."

"And what if the British renege?" the blond man asked.

"Then we'll boost the pressure until they give in. So far they haven't a clue where all this is coming from…"

"Does that include using the Prince?" the man interrupted.

The Russian looked at him intently, clearly struggling with an internal dilemma. He had criticized them for abducting the Prince but now it seems this radical move could allow them significant leverage.

"Only as a last resort," the Russian muttered, threw away his cigarette, and opened the leather pouch he had on his lap taking out a large brown paper envelope in a nylon casing. "This is the agreement," he said, handing it to the man. "There are two copies in here. You are to make sure it's delivered to the PM when we give you the word. Is that clear Vadim?"

Four years before, when the Russians took over Crimea, Vadim Petrovich crossed over the lines. He had been a member of the Ukrainian Security Service, the SBU, stationed in the Crimea as an intelligence officer, but switched alliances as soon as the Red Army marched into Simferopol and took over the Crimean parliament and police stations.

For two years, he and his colleagues were treated with mistrust by their new employers, often used on insignificant campaigns until Russia threatened to annex all of Ukraine, and they began training for a classified operation in which they would be given a primary role. For eighteen months they trained, practicing every relevant skill, anticipating various scenarios, brushing up on their English and even spending three months in London getting to know specific locations.

Six months before the scheduled launch, they were brought in confidence with the "Sons of Jihad" scheme and introduced to Ross Dixon and his team, learning their system within the British Home Office and becoming acquainted with the operatives Dixon had managed to plant in SO1, the Special Protection organization, learning their methods and techniques.

None of them were ever told, until today, the real reason for the undertaking, thinking they were supporting the Muslims in creating disorder with the Brits for a list of demands that were truly outrageous, but they were there to carry out orders not to make policy and never questioned their calling.

It all suddenly seemed contorted to Vadim, but he could see the genius behind the plan: Use the Muslim religious fanaticism which for almost twenty years had terrorized the globe attracting most of everyone's attention, to further Russian interests.

"They could stop me at the airport with this thing," Vadim said, studying the parcel in his hands.

"It's probably the safest method today, even better than those small discs," the Russian observed. "We would not want this document bouncing around the net and besides it's the president's original letterhead which we must have back signed otherwise we know it's forged."

The Russian stood up. He was rather short but looked sturdy dressed in a suit under a long overcoat.

"Why did you choose us for the job?" Vadim asked, standing up himself, as they both wiped away tiny icicles that had formed on their clothes.

"You will figure it out in the end," the Russian said, extending his bare hand toward Vadim who shook it with his gloved hand. "But if we pull this off you will be honored by the state and receive a luxury apartment in Moscow next to Edward Snowden."

Vadim chuckled. "And if not…?" he ventured to ask.

"We don't accept failure," the Russian stated and turned to go.

Vadim watched him as he trudged through the small yard, knee-high in snow, and disappeared into the hotel. He had no doubt he had meant what he said. If they failed, they would be discarded most likely somewhere in Siberia.

Snow had started falling again and it became strangely dark. He looked at his watch. He had an hour to kill before he needed to go back to the airport.

Chapter Thirty

Jemma and Frosty sat huddled in the car across the street from SO1 headquarters near Trafalgar Square. It was a mild winter day without rain, occasional gusts of wind propelling the flags in the square which was quite bare and void of human traffic.

They had spent the night at Jake's office on Marylebone then taken one of Jake's company cars from an underground parking garage nearby and settled in a strategic position allowing them a view of both pedestrian and garage exits of the Home Office Special Protection annex.

Jake and the boys had made it safely to the Chisholm guesthouse near Bath.

At Jake's office that night, they had tried to work out where Camilla could be held. There were several sites used by MI5 for the detention and interrogation of suspects before they were transferred to a conventional jail where they would undergo formal procedures and be allowed legal advice.

The difficulty was that in these preliminary detention centers, nothing was ever recorded and they could find no trace of a detainee named Camilla Paredes, so they decided the only way to tackle the problem was to tail the one person they knew for certain was part of the pretentious conspiracy they were up against, namely Andy White, and they figured the most likely place to pick up his tail was SO1 headquarters, though they knew he could be anywhere and they might never get a glimpse of him. A further hindrance was that if by chance he happened to be at the headquarters while they were there, he would most likely leave by car from the underground parking lot and would be difficult to spot.

But they had no alternative so they found a parking spot and settled in their car to wait for their target at five in the morning and as luck would have it, they spotted him getting into a car at the pedestrian exit three hours later.

Frosty ignited their car and they began following the black company car, keeping it in sight from a distance, the streets being almost empty of traffic. It was Frosty's first glimpse of London in daylight as he had never seen his hometown before: virtually empty. There was an eerie feeling to the place, like a deserted cowboy town in the American Old West, the wind blowing sage bushes across the street and debris accumulating along the sidewalks.

There was no pedestrian traffic to speak of and little or no vehicles except for military, police, and the occasional ambulance or fire truck going by. Shop windows were closed. There were no coffee shops or restaurants open; no double-decker red buses and just a few taxis driving by. Neon signs were extinguished; advertising billboards were dark and unattractive and traffic lights were all flashing yellow lights.

Troops could be seen meandering on major street corners, their military vehicles parked close by but no one seemed to pay any attention to them as they drove on tailing the black sedan.

White took the A4 following Strand to Aldwych then back to Strand until he reached Fleet Street, a ride that on a normal day at that hour would have taken almost fifty minutes, took them less than fifteen. He made his first stop next to a four-story office building.

As Jemma and Frosty watched White jump out of his car and enter the building, they debated whether to drive by and bypass the waiting car to inspect where White had gone to, but decided against it and sat waiting until White came out a half hour later. As they continued after White passed the building, they noted its marble façade and a glass entrance with a lone sign in red letters that read: Europe Investment Bank.

White's next stop was an address they had researched and knew to be one of MI5's interrogation sites. He drove as if he owned the town, not in the least bothered, not worrying about checking his flanks allowing Frosty an easy time tracking him. He crossed Holborn and took it via High Holborn to Oxford Street, driving the length of it to Hyde Park then across the park to Kensington where he was admitted through the guarded post to Palace Avenue at Kensington High Street. MI5 kept a place there among the mall of foreign embassies where among other things they monitored the activities inside those embassies.

Frosty and Jemma continued on Kensington High Street past the guarded entrance to the Embassy Mall and parked by St. Mary Abbots on Kensington Church Street.

"I've been in there," Frosty said, turning off the engine. "There's a basement with some secure rooms."

"Can we break in there?" Jemma asked, turning to him.

"You or me, not a chance, but someone who's got credentials and who's not a fugitive might."

"Do we know anyone like that?"

"No, but Santana does," Frosty observed.

"What did you have in mind?"

"If he's got guys in his outfit he can still trust, I think we can give it a shot," Frosty said with a mischievous grin and sketched out his plan.

******

At five that afternoon as the long afternoon shadows turned into darkness, Officer Murphy led a detail of four motorcycles through a deserted path of West Carriage Drive along a column of bare trees in Hyde Park. They reached Kensington Road and took it west toward Kensington High Street, turned into Palace Avenue, and stopped at the pillbox where a guard stepped out to meet them.

"Anything the matter, officer?" the guard inquired.

"No, everything's OK, just here to escort someone," Murphy said, roaring the bike impatiently.

Barrier raised, the column of motorcycles rolled along Embassy Row toward the MI5 building that nestled in between the Russian and Romanian embassies.

It was a modest building, dwarfed by the enormous Victorian structure that encompassed the Russian embassy and other embassies close by.

Murphy stopped at the fenced gate and waited patiently knowing their arrival was instantly recorded by an array of surveillance cameras as a powerful searchlight was directed at them. A few minutes later an MI5 operative appeared his pistol in plain sight in a shoulder holster over a dark sweater.

"Evening officer," he greeted Murphy from behind the gate. "What can I do for you?"

"Crisis Center sent us here to escort a detainee to Brixton," Murphy said.

"Escort a detainee? From here?" the guard said, looking surprised. "I don't know that we have any."

"Why don't you check with your superior?" Murphy suggested. "And let us in while you're at it. I need to use the john."

The MI5 man hesitated looking warily at the four officers, took out a mobile phone from his back pocket, and dialed. He listened for a minute then pulled on a hidden knob and the gate slid open. The procession of motorcycles roared into a small yard in front of the building and shut off their engines dismounting in unison and followed the guard with their helmets still on.

The MI5 man punched a code on a keypad and they were buzzed into the building through a heavy steel door that instantly shut behind them.

They stood in a large foyer with a shiny marble floor, a wide staircase going up along one end to their right, and several arched openings without doors, two facing them and two along the opposite end to their left.

Frosty had sketched the outlay from memory indicating there was a staircase that went down to the basement through one of the openings facing them. He thought it was the right one but was not sure.

A man dressed in jeans and boots, a dark gray sports jacket over a black t-shirt, and a gun in his shoulder holster bobbing visibly, came out of the closest opening to their left and greeted them. It was the opening Frosty had marked as the sentry room where they had the monitors and surveillance equipment with a 24-hour armed watch.

"What can I do for London's finest?" the man joshed, taking an expression out of the American lexicon. "And why don't you take off your helmets so we can see who we are talking to?"

Besides the operative who let them in and was standing to the side watching the proceedings, there were no other agents visible in the foyer. Apparently, a detail of motorcycled policemen was not considered a threat, which was exactly what they were hoping for.

"We've been sent by the crisis center to escort a suspect to Brixton," Murphy repeated what he had already said, leaving his helmet on.

The MI5 supervisor looked at him as did the operative from the gate; skeptically.

He said: "First of all there are no suspects to speak of in this facility and if there was, why would anyone send troopers to escort a suspect to Brixton of all places, when we are perfectly capable of doing it ourselves if need be?"

Murphy, who was standing a bit in front of the others, looked back at his colleagues and nodded. All four policemen drew their pistols simultaneously aiming at the two MI5 men, who gasped in surprise and went for their guns. Murphy, who at six feet three inches towered over most people and was a rugby player to boot, hit the supervisor with his gun on the right temple with lightning speed thrashing him to the floor, kicking him in the head unconscious, and leaped toward the guard room bursting in, gun at the ready.

The second MI5 man, who was going for the exposed gun under his armpit, froze in mid-motion raising his hands up and taking a step back as all three policemen surrounded him relieving him of his weapon.

"To the basement," one of them said, as a shot was heard from above and one of the troopers gasped in anguish grasping his shoulder. The policeman stuck his gun at the man's head and repeated his request pushing the guard toward the openings on the far end of the foyer. Two more shots were heard and the wounded policeman fell to the floor, his mate crouching next to him looking up to identify the shooter and firing blindly toward the staircase.

Murphy appeared in the opening of the guard room aiming his gun toward the stairs and firing in quick succession, signaling his colleague to pull the wounded trooper to safety.

The MI5 man with the policeman at his back reached the right opening and leaped through it as bullets grazed the floor behind them. The policeman, maintaining his aim at the guard's back pushed him toward a dimly lit staircase that spiraled down and shoved him down the stairs. They practically slid down the steep stairs and hit bottom in a heap, the trooper losing his balance and falling on the agent's back. Looking up, in the dim light he could see a small corridor with four doors, two on each side.

"Where is she?" he seethed, grabbing the man by his hair and pulling him up.

The agent gasped. "Where is who?" he asked and, for a second, it seemed he was genuine when he struck the trooper in the face with his fist and twisted underneath the weight going for the gun.

But the policeman who was almost as big and as heavy as Murphy, managed to keep the gun from his grasp and strike the man in the face with it. He moved back aiming the gun at the agent who remained on his back on the floor, blood oozing from his cheek.

"Camilla," the policeman shouted, his voice reverberating in the small enclosure. "Camilla," he shouted again and heard knocking from behind one of the doors.

He walked back, keeping the agent in his gun sight and looked at the door where the knocking was coming from. All four doors had the same keypad mechanism, similar to the one the guard had used to open the front door.

"Stand back!" The policeman shouted, aimed his gun and shot the keypad twice. The door squeaked open and a woman's head appeared through it, looking left and right, seeing the injured guard on the floor then looking up at her savior.

"It's me," the policeman said gently and held out his hand to her without taking his eye off his target. "Reuben?" She said surprised and hugged his large frame.

"Keep behind me at all times," Santana said and led her toward the stairs. He stopped towering over the agent sprawled on the floor, reached for a pair of handcuffs on the back of his belt, pulled the man toward the stairs and cuffed him to the railing, then headed carefully up the stairs, Camilla in tow, hearing the battle raging on the ground floor.

As they reached the ground floor, crawling up the stairs, Santana stuck his head carefully from below studying the area around the stairs seeing the exchange of fire raging in the foyer, however, the room they were in, was seemingly empty. He jumped up and ran toward the opening, gun at the ready, and peeked through seeing Murphy caught in a cross-fire from above but holding his own from within the sentry room. Caldwell was sprawled on the floor by the front door, not moving and Jimmy was nowhere to be seen.

"I've got her!" He shouted to Murphy, drawing his attention and seeing a smile spread across his face.

"You hear that, Jimmy?" Murphy called to Jimmy whom Santana could not see but heard shouting.

"Yes, I heard it!" Jimmy called out from his post by the front door. "They need to come out," he added as several shots rang from above.

"You chuck the smoke grenade and give us cover," Murphy called. "We're coming out."

"What about Caldwell?" Jimmy shouted.

"You leave him be," Murphy commanded. "He's done his job."

Suddenly, white smoke began spreading in the foyer, mushrooming toward the ceiling. Santana held Camilla's hand and ran straight through the smoke pulling her after him, bullets hitting the floor around him. He could see the door opening in front of him through the cloud of smoke when he suddenly felt a sharp pain at the back of his neck and felt himself losing control of his motions. With a last effort, he propelled Camilla toward the opening and crashed face-first on the floor, half his large listless body sliding through the door.

Murphy who had followed suit and was only a second or two behind Santana and Camilla, dashing for safety, shooting his gun blindly toward the stairs at his back, almost tripped over Santana's fallen body but somehow managed to stay on his feet coming out of the smoked filled building running straight ahead, snatching Camilla who had rolled on the ground in front of him, raising her with one hand and jumping on his motorcycle, Jimmy doing the same.

As the two remaining troopers roared away from the scene not ten minutes from the time they had first arrived there, with the girl held by Murphy for dear life, crying and calling her boyfriend's name, two agents came running out of the building firing after them, missing their targets.

Chapter Thirty-One

Sunday, February 3, 2019

The skirmish at Embassy Row did not receive any headlines.

It was mentioned on the morning news the following day as a minor altercation whose details were fuzzy. Not a word about any wounded or any casualties and no mention of the drama that took place among a host of foreign embassies who employed strict security measures around their perimeters with elite security forces to guard their premises.

Any other time, on any other day, the fierce shooting battle that took place at Kensington Palace's backyard would have been headline news for days, with TV coverage from helicopters and panels of experts.

There was sufficient argument to claim that with London being under forced curfew following several deadly attacks that claimed hundreds of lives; the British capital being paralyzed for over a week and the media being strung out, such an event could have gone unnoticed, but Frosty suspected word had not leaked out, deliberately.

Someone made sure the event went unnoticed.

A lone BBC crew that showed up was not allowed past the pillbox at Embassy Row and only managed to record a single ambulance leaving the premises and several official cars driving in and out. No helicopter coverage from above and no interviews with any police or Home Office officials.

Murphy had brought Camilla to Frosty and Jemma who waited for them in an underground garage in Chelsea, delivering the unspeakable news and taking off with his partner in his private car, changing to civilian clothes and leaving their motorcycles tucked underneath a tarpaulin cover they had brought with them, in a dark corner of the garage, fleeing to an undisclosed location where they hoped to lay low until matters cleared up.

Santana had warned them they would be passing a point of no return but they went ahead and did it anyway after hearing the shocking suspicions regarding SO1 involvement and looking for payback for their partner who was murdered in St. Thomas' hospital.

Before they took off, Murphy took Frosty aside and hastily described in brief the sequence of events estimating that both Santana and Caldwell did not make it but admitted his prognosis could be inaccurate and that they might only be seriously wounded.

Camilla was beside herself, stricken with grief; Frosty and Jemma had to force her into their car kicking and screaming. They drove back to Jake's office without incident, Frosty driving, Jemma in the back with Camilla who kept pleading with them to go back and look for her boyfriend.

They promised they would do so once she told them what had happened at Simon Lewis's house and what her abductors wanted from her, regrettably learning that the disc given to her by Simon's dad was taken away.

"We need to go after Dixon," Frosty concluded when they finally managed to sedate Camilla with some Volume pills Jake kept at the office and put her to sleep. "He's the key."

"So, they know what we are after," Jemma concluded.

"They don't necessarily know it's us," Frosty observed. "They could be thinking Santana was looking for payback and sent his girlfriend to find out why Simon was killed. Camilla did say White's line of questioning was aimed toward finding her boyfriend and never connected them with us."

"Yes, and she also said he accused her of being involved in the Tompkins assassination."

"Which means the disc shows a connection," Frosty surmised.

"Damn shame we don't have that disc," Jemma complained again.

"I think it's time we approached the old man," Frosty said. "He could point us in the right direction."

"Do you know where he's at?"

"Most likely fishing somewhere."

"At times like these!?" Jemma reproached.

"With his heart condition, he doesn't need the excitement. After his second heart attack, they moved south near Brighton to what they now call an 'assisted living' facility, which is basically a nursing home where he gets treatment. I doubt he could do much from there but he still knows a few people and he may tie a few strings for us."

"Do you have an exact address?"

"Cindy probably has somewhere in her files. We'll call her and then one of us can drive down there. I doubt we'll attract much attention in Jake's car."

"What about roadblocks?" Jemma pointed out. "We're most likely high on their wanted list and with the trifling traffic these days they'll easily identify us if we get stopped."

Frosty considered her argument. She was right of course. It was a big risk for them to drive out of town with the kind of measures taken around London, but he worried that a train ride would lose them too much precious time they did not have.

"OK then," he finally said. "I'll take the train down there and you stay here with Camilla; see what we can find out happened to Santana."

"They could be keeping an eye on Fleming as well, so you watch yourself," Jemma said before he left.

"I'll do that," he assured her. "You take care of the girl and make sure and let me know if you find out anything about Santana."

******

Retired Group Captain Harry Fleming was busy fishing when Frosty finally found him. He was sitting on a folding chair dressed in a heavy sweater, a coat, and a scarf on a wooded pier that protruded out into the Atlantic with a bucket of bait next to him, his fishing rod stuck in a slit between two planks of a wooden railing that swayed in the wind and made creaking noises.

The male nurse had escorted Frosty across a grassy field to the shoreline in the back of the nursing home to the secluded pier and left him alone.

"Grand old place you got here, Sir," Frosty said as he climbed down a few small steps to the little pier and walked gingerly toward Fleming who had turned his head to him and was smiling.

"Figured you'll show up eventually," Fleming nodded at him as they shook hands. "Quite a mess you got over there."

Fleming looked a fraction of his old self; his hair was thinner than Frosty remembered it and completely white, his face scrawny and pale, his blue eyes bulging and his body thin and fragile-looking.

"And how's the Missus?" Frosty asked. "Looks like you've got it made over here."

"Taking a nap," Fleming said. "She doesn't like my fishing habits so I get this place to myself."

Frosty looked out to the vast gray waters that converged with the cloudy sky at the horizon.

"How's your health?" he asked, leaning on the railing.

"Could be better I suppose," Fleming said, "but enough about me. Tell me what's been happening over there."

Frosty checked the railing to see if it would hold then sat on the landing and leaned back against the fragile fence. He recapped the events of the past week in detail trying to fill the gaps for his former boss and outlay his suspicions.

Fleming sat quietly listening to Frosty's briefing and thought a while before he spoke.

"Why do you think Tompkins sent you to Kruger of all people?" He wondered aloud. "You would think he would have kept you away from him if he had information that things are disquieting at SO1 and you might be in danger."

"Maybe he was given skewed information," Frosty suggested. "Maybe the information he was given was meant to cause him to send me there and have me framed."

"Then Simon Lewis, if indeed he was the guy meeting him at the Ritz, which makes sense, was given skewed information himself which could mean the information Simon Lewis might have had cannot be relied upon," Fleming concluded.

"You might be right," Frosty admitted. "But in any event, Lewis's disc is not in our possession. Either way, we need to go after Dixon."

A flock of seagulls hung in the air above the pier for a few seconds then flew down in formation attacking the waves, looking for food.

"We know what schools he went to and where he was employed, from when he arrived back here at age 16 and we have found his missing person's report but that might not be enough to convince people he is what we think he is."

"What do you think will be proof?" Fleming asked.

"If we could somehow connect the man with the missing child, for example," Frosty suggested. "Should we talk to his biological parents? Did he know they exist? Kruger didn't when we caught him. Did Kruger ever try to make contact after we told him about his real parents?"

"Kruger never did," Fleming said. "And by the looks of it, he kept in contact with the organization somehow and even sacrificed his life for them," Fleming observed. "It seems to me you need to find out who Kruger's contact was! That'll give you proof."

"We could try and find out what means he used to make contact," Frosty said thoughtfully. "But that would mean we'll need to find help at the prison."

"You could also try and follow his trail. Talk to people at his school or at his university; find out where he lived and who he stayed with." Fleming suggested. "This may lead to uncovering the network itself."

"It's a question of time and resources, both of which we don't have. But we might be able to find someone honest at SO1 who can check."

Fleming was shaking his head. "If SO1 is indeed compromised, you need to stay away from them because you obviously cannot tell the good guys from the bad and since none of the good ones are aware of the mess they are in, it would do no good to approach anyone."

"Should I talk to Reed?" Frosty asked, shifting his pose on the wooden planks of the pier.

Fleming considered the question, looking out into the choppy gray waters.

"They have obviously gone to great lengths to set you up to divert the attention from them," he finally reasoned. "So, you would need concrete proof, such that he can use to convince Scott and the others, otherwise it's your word against Dixon and you are the one accused and gone AWOL."

They remained silent for the next few minutes looking into the ocean, the wind picking up, howling around them, each straining to find a remedy for the situation.

"I will try and contact some of my colleagues from back when, see if they have any ideas, though my phone is probably tapped," Fleming said after the long pause. "But I still think the prison is your best bet. If you can figure out how Kruger communicated with the outside world, it will lead to his contacts and give you the proof you are looking for."

"And I need to do it quick now that the Prince is at risk and London is on the verge of anarchy," Frosty remarked.

"Goes without saying," Fleming agreed, gingerly getting up from his chair. Frosty jumped to his aid supporting the fragile form of his former boss as he grabbed the fishing rod and began rolling the empty line back onto its roller.

When he was finished, they went ashore and stood on the rocks, Fleming staring along the coastline away from the nursing home.

"About a mile from here," he said, pointing along the coast, "the road comes mighty close to shore and there's a bus station where you can catch a bus to the train. You are better off taking this route, in case somebody decides to come take a look since you arrived. They do it now and then; I've seen them." Fleming said above the howling wind.

Frosty nodded and they shook hands.

"How can I reach you in case I find out something?" Fleming asked. Frosty read him his alternate phone number and map coordinates to the Chisholm farm near Bath, which Fleming keyed into his mobile, and walked away along the coast.

******

That night, they all convened at the Chisholm guesthouse.

It was raining and howling out; Cindy and Jake sat by the fireside looking at the kids playing a trivia game ever since the internet connection had gone cold and their smartphones were confiscated and shut off by the adults with a vague explanation why live phones could be used to trace their whereabouts. Zoe was making faces at Gabi trying to make her comprehend the image displayed on her card. Ian and Colin were following her attempts watching the sand clock carefully as its topside emptied to its bottom.

Jemma had come in from London two hours before with a disconcerted Camilla who she put to bed in one of the guestrooms. Frosty came in from Brighton an hour later and now they sat around the heavy oak dining table together with Dylan Oliver, hungrily devouring Mary's savory dishes.

Noah had brought both parties from the Bath train station and was now sitting quietly with his wife listening as Frosty brought them up to date on who they all were and what's been happening, filling in any gaps their hosts were not aware of. And though the Chisholm's never asked for explanations, Frosty insisted they know what was going on and what the risks were since they had inadvertently involved them and put them in danger.

"Well, you've filled up our guest house. That's a good thing." Mary Chisholm commented when Frosty concluded his brief, looking at her husband for support.

"It certainly seems our nation's in a real predicament at the moment so it's the least we can do to help," Noah Chisholm added. "You look like good people and we trust you," he added, looking back at his wife. "Had we thought you were on the wrong side of things we would have reported you a long time ago."

Frosty, chewing on a large piece of meat, nodded thankfully and waited to swallow before he spoke.

"Much appreciated, Noah," he said, gravy dripping out the side of his mouth. "But the minute you feel this is too much for you, you let us know and we'll be out of your way."

"Just don't forget to pay the bill," Noah concluded with a half-smile, the first time they had seen him do that, looking at his wife for approval; Mary nodding her head, smiling herself, got up to refill the empty mashed potatoes bowl.

Frosty turned to Oliver. "Do you still have any connections at the Blackpool prison?"

Dylan, wiping the gravy from around his mouth with a paper towel, stared at him in surprise.

"I might know a few people. Why do you ask?"

"We need to try and find out how Kruger communicated with the outside world," Frosty said. "If we knew that we may get to the people he communicated with…"

Dylan studied Frosty intently. "I would have to go back there and get someone to talk. You think it's wise?"

"I don't think we have much choice." Frosty reasoned. "We have our suspicions but we need proof if we are to convince anyone…"

There was a large cheer from across the room as Gabi and Zoe hugged one another having managed to outsmart the boys. Colin and Ian looked embarrassed.

Jake said, "Get them next time boys."

The kids began collecting the cards from the table into a pile, tempting the girls to go another round.

Frosty turned back to Dylan who was looking over at the proceedings by the fireside, eyeing him expectantly.

"I can call someone and try and set up a meeting somewhere," Dylan suggested but Frosty shook his head. "No phones!" He declared. "We'll need to go back there and find someone willing to talk. Do you have anyone in mind?"

"If there is such a person then he's a liability and is likely being watched or they have already disposed of him," Jemma interjected.

"That's true," Frosty agreed. "But we're out of alternatives and we'll have to take that chance."

"There are a few people I know inside that may be able to help," Oliver said. "These guys have it rough dealing with inmates on a daily basis but on the outside they are still patriotic to their homeland. They all know about the Kruger incident and I am sure they are aware of the developments in London and would be just as concerned as us to the future of this country."

Frosty nodded looking at Jemma for approval. "How would you contact them?" Jemma asked.

"We'll find a way." Dylan said and scooped some more of Mary's food onto his plate.

Chapter Thirty-Two

Monday, February 4, 2019

Home Secretary Nigel Scott was awoken by the phone at four in the morning.

It was from the Prime Minister's office asking him to urgently show up. His wife Gina, sat up in bed bleary-eyed as the minister hurried to get up.

"What's happened?" she asked.

"Not really sure," Scott said, standing in front of the mirror, tucking his shirt in. "But whatever it is, it must be progress."

"Positive or negative progress?" Gina questioned, rubbing her eyes with both hands.

"It can't get much worse than what's been happening so I am optimistic," Scott said. He took his mobile phone from the bedside table and dialed the driver on duty asking him to prepare.

He then walked into his bathroom, brushed his teeth, and sprinkled his face with water. He had only managed three hours of sleep, having come home from the previous challenging day at half-past midnight.

He fixed his tie in front of the mirror, put on his jacket, then leaned over the bed to kiss his wife and stepped out of the bedroom into the darkened hallway, gingerly walking down the wide stairway holding on to the railing.

Willie Hancock, his driver, was waiting by the Jaguar.

10 Downing Street was in full swing at five in the morning when Scott walked in the door past the guards, the foreign secretary and defense minister showing up as well.

Prime Minister Webster was waiting for them in his private office leaning on his wide mahogany desk.

"The cat's out of the bag," he said as the door shut behind his three top ministers. "It's the Russians." He handed Scott an official-looking document with a Kremlin Logo and they crowded around to read it.

The Prime Minister waited patiently as his three top ministers read the document and then looked at them expectantly.

"So this is what it's all about?" Scott remarked.

"Those got damn LNG terminals?" He swore out loud. "We should have known."

"What did you expect?" Webster asked. "It'll cost them almost their entire gas supply to Europe."

"How do we know this document is not a hoax?" Defense Minister Sir Alistair Banks questioned. "How did it get here?"

"It was left in Ross Dixon's private mailbox outside his home." The PM informed them. "He rushed it here an hour ago."

"Can we check its authenticity?" Scott asked.

"Dixon did," Webster said. "Took it to the lab across the street first thing to check for prints. Informed me there were no prints and confirmed it was an official Kremlin letterhead. The president's signature is authentic as well."

"Well, this is an act of war if I ever saw one," Minister Banks snapped. "Several acts of war," Foreign Minister Charles "Charlie" Draper put in.

"I count seven, Charlie," Webster said. "Five London bombings, the abduction of our Prince, and the financial attack on our currency. Hell, each one of these is reason enough to turn to violence, but we won't do it; do you know why?"

The three ministers remained silent.

"We won't do it because we do not have the means or the longevity to engage the Russians in an all-out war…"

"Well obviously, but we won't do it alone, would we?" Scott remarked. "The US Dollar has lost twenty percent of its value and the Americans have much to lose if those terminals don't fulfill their purpose."

"President Trump won't engage either," Webster stated. "They are still hurting from ISIS not to mention Afghanistan and Iraq. The American public will not support a third world war, which is what this could easily turn into, and the Russians know it. They are threatening to annex the whole of the Ukraine and are now threatening Poland, and we are still sitting on the fence."

"Well it's time we put our foot down, don't you think?" Defense Minister Banks retorted. "If we allow them to get away with abducting our Prince and bombing London, we may as well give in to their demands on the gas terminals."

"There are other ways," Prime Minister Webster cajoled the tense atmosphere in the room. "Now that we know who's attacking our currency, we can fight back especially since Russian debt is accumulated mostly in British and American financial institutions. Then, there is Cyber. The west still owns the majority of web applications which can cause enormous havoc in the east. And we can negotiate the supply of gas in such a way that will appease the Russians. It's not in our interest to see them go belly up, is it? We don't want millions of Russian immigrants knocking on our borders like those poor Arab refugees from Syria and Iraq, do we?"

The room became silent for a few seconds as the three ministers mulled over the PM's words.

"So what do you intend to do?" Foreign Minister Charlie Draper finally asked. "You going to sign the document and give in?"

"We'll need a conference with President Trump, but it is my opinion we should discretely approach the Kremlin and offer to negotiate before signing anything."

"If you do that," Home Secretary Scott remarked. "You are playing into their hands, accepting the current state of affairs as the status quo. We cannot begin negotiations over the terminals before they free the Prince and remove the threat on London, otherwise, they've already got what they've set out to get."

"That's very true, Nigel," Webster agreed. "But what is it you think we can do to remove the threats?" the PM asked in a derogatory tone.

Nigel Scott looked at his two colleagues and then back at his boss, realizing where the blame lay. The PM would consider him the fall guy if the mess was not cleaned up.

"Give me two more days," he pleaded with the PM. "If London is still under threat and I don't have Prince William back by then, I'll resign and I guess we'll need to approach the Kremlin."

PM Webster looked hard at Scott then turned to his two top ministers. "You give him everything he needs! Charlie, call back all your MI6 guys and, Alistair, you consign all Military Intelligence outfits to the Home Office! Is that clear!?"

The two ministers nodded.

"Nigel, you've got 48 hours…" the PM said and turned to his desk, indicating to them he wanted to be left alone. He picked up his desk phone and asked his secretary to get him Washington.

Chapter Thirty-Three

Tuesday, February 5, 2019

Blackpool lay on the banks of the Irish Sea, solemn and gray, its darkened streets whipped by the eternal wind and salt, its famous Blackpool tower erected over the coastal promenade, seen from almost anywhere.

Frosty and Dylan Oliver took a single room at Hotel California, a two-story Victorian establishment, several blocks inland from the coastal promenade, keeping away from the various attractions that lay along the walkway, where small flocks of tourists wrapped in winter attire under tattered umbrellas, were meandering among the various restaurants, coffee shops, fish and chips joints, tattoo parlors, discount stores, and the central pier with its dripping amusement park.

They had reached the town by train the previous evening making a long detour from Bristol via Leeds to Blackpool, to avoid possible tails, had dinner at Seaside Fish & Chips, and turned in early. Dylan Oliver would wait for the prison morning shift at the Blackpool bus terminal at five in the morning.

At a quarter to five, when it was misty and dark, the streetlights still shining from within the fog, rainwater dripping from roof gutters, twenty people covered in heavy coats, wearily waited for the bus to the prison, most of them with their heads down to cover a burning cigarette. Dylan did not have to do much to conceal his identity. No one paid any attention as he stood several feet from the bus station partially hidden in the mist, his coat collar raised.

There were two he recognized easily. Both were prison guards who were there during his ten-year stint. Gus "The Bear" Nicolas, of Greek heritage, was a burly man with a thick layer of hair over most of his body, neck, arms and back. The common joke about him was that by the time he completed shaving one side of his face the other side would already grow whiskers and vice versa. The second man was Jimmy Morgan, a giant Welshman from Swansea, with a heart of gold who treated the prisoners almost as if they were his equals. Morgan was easy to spot as he towered over everyone, so Dylan approached him first.

He walked up to the big man and stood in front of him lowering his collar. "Hey Jimmy, remember me?" he asked in a low voice, looking up at the man's face.

Morgan seemed to wake from his reverie focusing his stare at the smaller man. It took him a few seconds to recognize his former colleague and when he did, a big smile formed on his face and he made a gesture as if he was about to call out, intending to announce Dylan's appearance to the boys, when Dylan caught his arm and put his finger to his own lips signaling he did not want the attention. He motioned for Morgan to move with him away from the crowd and Morgan did as asked.

When they were several paces away and into the fog, Dylan shook Morgan's hand and addressed him carefully.

"How you been mate?" he asked, tapping the big man on his shoulder.

"How've you been?" Morgan replied, hitting him back on the shoulder. "Heard you left Digital Solutions in a hurry…?"

"Why, what have you heard?" Dylan asked worriedly.

"Heard there was some kind of an altercation. The Feds came after you or something…?"

"Well, not exactly but I did leave in a hurry."

"Are you on the run mate? Because I'll help out if you are! Those assholes treat us like dirt…"

"It all has to do with that mess going on in London," Dylan said. "And, yes, I do need some help but just information."

"Whatever you need mate. Do you have a place to stay?"

"Yes, thanks, I am OK. You are familiar with this Lifer who was in for trying to bomb a Thai plane? Who swallowed a cyanide pill during an interrogation?"

"Who isn't?" Morgan snickered.

"No, I mean, were you ever assigned to his section? Were you ever in contact with him?"

"Not me," Morgan shook his head, "I never dealt with those guys."

"Do you know who did? What about Gus? Did he deal with them?"

"Gus did actually," Morgan acknowledged. "He's right here. Do you want me to call him?"

"Please but do it discretely. I don't want this to get around."

"Hold on," Morgan said and disappeared into the fog coming back after a minute with "The Bear" at his side, complaining that the bus was due in five minutes.

"Remember Dylan?" Morgan asked as Gus stepped in front of Dylan looking confused. He studied him for a moment then smiled.

"I sure do. Hey, mate, long time…"

"Yeah, Gus, how've you been? Look I'd love to shoot the breeze over a beer with you guys, but I've got an urgent matter I need to resolve before your bus shows up."

Gus looked up at Morgan who was nodding his approval. "Shoot, mate, whatever I can do."

"It has to do with that Kruger guy who swallowed a cyanide pill a week ago."

"Yeah, what about him? Heard he did it right in front of an MI5 guy."

"It's a long story that has to do with the mess down in London. What I need to know is did that guy have a channel to the outside?"

"You mean, was he sending stuff out or getting stuff in?"

"We're not talking drugs here or anything of that sort. I need to know if he was corresponding with anyone. Sending out messages or getting any messages in?"

"Well if he was, it wasn't through me," Gus said defensively.

"Would you know of anyone who might have helped him?"

Gus looked up at Morgan again. "Can I get in trouble for this?"

He eyed Dylan suspiciously.

"Not in the least!" Dylan assured him. "But we need to know if he had access to the outside…"

"Who's we?" Gus cut him off. "I don't like where this is going."

Dylan could see the bus lights in the distance pulling into the station.

"Listen guys, I am here by myself so no one would know who I talked to and I will never give you up, but if you don't give me something helpful, there's a good chance Kruger's friends will take over this country."

The two prison guards looked at one another, then looked back hearing the bus pull in.

Gus said, "You better be on the level Dylan or I'll hunt you down."

Dylan looked at him pleadingly. "I am Gus. No one except Jimmy here will ever know we talked."

"There was a guy, a guard, who disappeared, the day Kruger killed himself. His name was Sonny Bertram, though I doubt it was his real name because he had a Russian accent. He always said he was a Brit who grew up in Russia and we never thought any of it until he disappeared. That's all I know and we need to get on the bus, Jimmy."

"Do you know where he lived?"

"Oh, sure, he invited some of us to watch football at his house a few times. Even gave us nuts and beers. Corner of Dryburgh and Worcester, right here in Blackpool."

With that, the two prison guards turned and hustled to the bus which was shutting its doors. Dylan remained in the shadows watching them go.

******

The house was a modest two-story brownstone where Gus had said. The entrance door was painted bright white as were the window sills. Frosty and Dylan watched it from the corner of Dryburgh and St. Leonard's Road at a small diner, a block away. They had a direct view of the entrance and were scrutinizing it for inhabitants from seven in the morning when the diner opened.

At seven thirty, a girl stepped out of the brownstone, blond hair fluttering under a wool hat, covered in a puffed pink overcoat and a red backpack strapped to her back. She seemed no more than twelve or thirteen, and she stood in front of the house talking on a mobile phone until a yellow school bus stopped near her and she hopped in.

They gave it another half hour before they moved in to inspect.

Dylan rang the doorbell, as Frosty kept to one side of the entrance so he would not immediately be seen. A woman in a gray uniform, pants and a short-sleeved shirt with the Blackpool Amusement Park logo impressed over a breast pocket, opened the door after a few seconds. Dylan guessed she was in her late forties, with blond hair tied in a bun, wide blue eyes, and a friendly face.

She looked at Dylan in surprise. "Can I help you?" she said politely.

"Yes mam," Dylan said a little unsure of himself. "I am looking for Sonny Bertram. Is this his residence?"

"It is," she said, becoming a bit guarded. "What do you want from him?"

"Just to ask him a few questions regarding an inmate at the prison."

"And who are you, if I may ask?"

"My name is Dylan and this is Frosty." He introduced them as Frosty moved into view, causing the woman to take a step back. "And we need to urgently talk to him. Is he your husband?"

The woman studied them holding on to the door handle as if contemplating shutting the door.

"Yes, he is my husband," she said after a long pause. "But he is not here."

"Where is he?" Frosty pitched in. "We really need to talk to him, Miss..."

The woman looked embarrassed all of a sudden. She lowered her stare to the ground.

"I don't know where he is," she mumbled. "He's been gone a whole week and hasn't even called."

Frosty and Dylan looked at one another. "Would you have any idea where he could be?"

She raised her stare to them, her large blue eyes looking hurt and shook her head.

"I have no idea where he's gone to. Just disappeared without as much as a word. Not to me and not to his daughter."

"Did you report him missing?" Frosty asked.

She shook her head again. "Didn't want to make a fuss you know. This is a small town and we have a reputation to keep."

"May we come, Mrs. Bertram?" Frosty asked gently. "Your husband may be involved in something quite troubling."

"Who did you say you were?" she asked again suspiciously.

Frosty took out his TFB credentials and MI5 badge and showed them to her. "I am agent Adrian Frost from London, and this is my associate Dylan Oliver, if you let us in, we'll explain to you what this is all about."

She studied Frosty's credentials for a few seconds looking up at him and then down to compare with the photo on his TFB ID, before she stood aside and indicated they could come in.

Chapter Thirty-Four

She led them through a narrow foyer simply decorated with the usual family photos and a couple of obscure paintings of Blackpool Pier. Frosty stopped to look at a family photo. It featured a man, Frosty assumed was Sonny Bertram, seated on a hammock, a tropical beach in the background with the woman standing next to him in a full-body black bathing suit on one side, and the younger daughter in a pink bathing suit in his lap. They were all smiling. Sonny was quite thin, clean-shaven, in bathing pants, his white skin gleaming in the sun. He had crew-cut blond hair and blue eyes, and seemed quite tall, his legs dangling, touching the sand.

"That's Florida, the Keyes, five years ago," Mrs. Bertram mentioned, seeing Frosty and Dylan studying the photo. She showed them to the living room inviting them to sit on an L-shaped beige couch that had several blue pillows thrown over it. A low glass coffee table stood in front of the couch and a large TV screen was hung on the wall across it, turned off.

"Should we call you Mrs. Bertram…?" Dylan began asking.

"Ruby will do fine," she cut him short. "Would you like some tea? I have an hour before I need to go to work."

"Milk for me with one sugar," Dylan said as Ruby headed to an adjacent room, they assumed was the kitchen.

"What about you, Mr. Frost?" she asked, stopping before stepping out of the living room.

"Milk, no sugar, thanks," Frosty said, as Ruby disappeared.

Besides the TV, the guest room walls were quite bare, painted bright white, with two Rothko reproductions above the couch, and a ray of sunlight poking through the glass window that faced a small backyard. Frosty got up to look, seeing a grassy lawn with a wooden table and some chairs to one side and a swing hanging from a thick branch that extended from a large tree stump on the other side.

Ruby was back with a tray carrying three China cups filled with tea, a small milk jug, and some biscuits. She set it on the low glass table and sat next to her two guests.

"I took the liberty of adding your sugar," she said to Dylan who nodded agreeably. Then she looked to Frosty.

"Does your husband have any family, Mrs. Ber... I mean, Ruby?" Frosty asked, adding the milk to his tea.

Ruby looked at him thoughtfully. She reached for the milk jug and added some milk to her own teacup.

"No, he does not," she admitted. "At least not here in the UK."

"Where does he have family?" Frosty persisted.

"In Russia," she said without hesitation. "He grew up there and his family is still there."

"Have you ever met them?" Frosty continued. "How long have you been together?"

"Ella is Twelve," Ruby said thoughtfully. "So we are together fifteen years."

"And where did you meet?" Frosty went on.

Ruby suddenly became impatient. "What's this interrogation? Do you have something to tell me or not?"

"You mind switching on the TV?" Frosty relented. "It'll explain much...."

Ruby looked at him irritably but took the remote from the table and switched the TV on. It was the BBC summarizing the London destruction of the last week with clips from helicopters above Covent Garden, Heathrow Terminal 5, Camden, Oxford Circus, and the stock exchange. A panel of experts was assessing the chances of finding the Prince alive.

Ruby was transfixed by the visions on the screen for a minute, then looked expectantly at Frosty.

"Are you aware of what's going on there...?" Frosty inquired carefully so as not to offend their host.

"Of course I am," Ruby said irritably making Frosty feel foolish. "Who isn't? You think we're so out of touch here?"

"It's just that I expected your TV to be on..." Frosty defended himself. "Most people are glued to their TVs these days."

"Well, I've got a job, a house, and a twelve-year-old to take care of and now my husband is gone, so I don't have time to sit around watching TV."

"We believe your husband may be connected to all this," Frosty said.

"Connected? How?" she asked incredulously. "He's a prison guard for Christ's sake! Here in Blackpool!"

"Ruby, what I am about to tell you now, you cannot repeat to anyone, especially not to your daughter so as not to put her in danger."

Ruby looked dumbfounded.

"Is this clear?" Frosty asked again. Ruby nodded her head submissively and sat back on the couch.

"And when I am done, I need you to consider very carefully if there is anything that may be of assistance to us."

Ruby looked at him. There were tears in her eyes but Frosty ignored them and went on. "We believe your husband may have assisted an inmate who was instrumental in launching these attacks." He began looking hard at Ruby for her reaction.

"Assisted? How?" she asked, bewildered, looking from Frosty to Dylan and back.

"We suspect the inmate used your husband to send out messages he needed to be delivered to the conspirators."

"Sonny? My Sonny?" She queried, unable to grasp what was being said to her. "Why would he be involved in something like that?"

"I don't think he was honest with you, Ruby. I think he used you to do what he came here to do. I don't think he is who you think he is," Frosty surmised.

"Then who is he?" Ruby hissed at them; fear reflected in her eyes.

"We believe he's a Russian spy," Frosty said without mincing words.

"Oh my god!" Ruby said, crossing herself. "You mean I have been living with a spy for fifteen years?"

"Afraid so…" Frosty confirmed. "And he's most likely back in Russia by now."

"But that can't be!" Ruby retorted. "What about Ella? He will not just abandon her. Would he?"

"That may be a weak point we can exploit to lure him back, or at least make contact," Frosty said. "Were they on good terms?"

"Oh yes! He loves her so much!"

"Look here, Ruby, the only way to make contact with this ultra-secret group that's terrorizing London and has taken the Prince hostage, was through this inmate. Sonny, your husband, whoever he is, was planted as a guard in the prison so he can deliver messages from his Russian controllers to him and from him to the outside. We believe that even this inmate did not know who these conspirators on the outside were, but he had a method to contact them and we need to uncover this method and we need to do it quick." Frosty insisted, pointing at the TV for effect.

Ruby had her head down and was shaking it.

"Can you think of something that could help us?" Frosty continued. "A routine of some sort? A place where he went? Things he has in the house?"

"I need to think," Ruby said. "I can't think straight at the moment, but something may come up…"

She looked up at them in despair. "What do I tell Ella? That her dad will never come back? That he's the reason this country is in a rut? She's sure to ask questions. She's already asking."

"You tell her nothing!" Frosty commanded. "You'll just make it worse for her and for you. You need to focus on helping us find out how this inmate communicated with the outside world. Your husband is key, so we need you to be strong right now."

Ruby nodded wiping away her tears, the mascara staining her cheeks.

"I'll leave Dylan here with you. Is this OK?" Frosty asked. "He knows the prison and he can help you recall things."

Ruby looked at Dylan hesitating a moment, then nodded. "I'll need to go to work in a few minutes. Ella comes back at three…"

"You need to take a day off," Frosty said. "Things are getting out of hand in London and we have no time to waste."

Ruby looked confused. "But my boss, he doesn't approve…"

"I'll take care of your boss," Frosty said as gently as he could but looked impatient for the first time. "You need to put your head together and give us some clues. Dylan, you contact me as soon as you have something."

With that, he got up and went to the door. "What if Ella asks about this man?" Ruby called after him.

"Tell her he's an old schoolmate or something," Frosty suggested and slipped out the front door.

Chapter Thirty-Five

Harry Fleming watched the sunset over the Atlantic as he sat on his veranda in the Old Veterans home sipping his tea seemingly enjoying the moment, but very much alert as he waited for his new burner to ring.

He had bought a spare mobile phone, a burner, of the ancient Talkman variety where he could buy limited time from the phone company. He figured he had a day before whoever was tailing him would catch on. The devastating developments in London and Frosty's account were weighing heavy on his mind though his demeanor remained calm both in front of Frosty and his wife.

As soon as Frosty was out of sight, he took a taxi to the outskirts of Brighton, slipped into a crowded mall, and bought himself the mobile phone he now held in his hand.

His first call was to Mike Devlin. The ex-SAS man who replaced Colonel Joe Harley after he was killed in the Sinai, as leader of the ultra-secret British outfit who freed Sam Baker's son, little Sammy, and led the attack on the "Sons of Jihad" stronghold in Beirut. Devlin was now retired and living with Ali, the once irrepressible physical training guru for Harley's men, on a farm that belonged to Ali's parents, a two-hour car ride from their old training grounds in Scotland.

Fleming briefed Devlin on the developments and Frosty's predicament and asked if he could help.

Joe Harley's unit, for lack of a better name, had since merged into MI6 as operational enforcers of the organization's covert policies and were no longer a distinct unit, so to get access to them one had to approach MI6 and that obviously could not be done, without exposing Frosty.

Devlin offered to get in touch with several retired veterans who were his subordinates at the tail end of his reign, a year after most of the original members retired, largely due to their falling out with the security services, and Fleming who had insisted they join MI6. These men, Devlin reasoned, had retired before the unit joined MI6 and were as loyal as ever, discrete, fit, and young enough to see action. He also suggested Fleming get in touch with Lizzy O'Leary, the veteran unit's sergeant who now resided near Edinburgh, Scotland, and with Malcolm Rolston who had moved to New York after marrying Mai-Li.

Lizzy and Devlin met twice a year; on Christmas and on the anniversary of Harley's death, a gathering to which a few of the ex-operatives came including Rolston and Mai-Li, Ali, of course, was there, retired Colonel David Kessler, the Israeli spy, Sam Baker and his wife Elena who played a major role in the Beirut operation, Christine Patrese, the French journalist, Natasha, and Jack Preston from the original "Center for Missing Children". The operation to release Jack Preston, Black Jack, from Egyptian hands near Dahab was the one that got Harley killed.

The group would get together, "crossing the pond" on alternating years, to have a ceremony at a New York bar one year and a London pub the next, establishments they knew would be more than acceptable to their admired, and long departed, leader and mentor.

Fleming was unable to contact Rolston and did not want to leave any messages but did manage to find the old sergeant at his home near Edinburgh.

Now he was waiting to hear back from both Devlin and O'Leary after sketching out the grave situation to them over the phone.

There were others Fleming could have called. Old air force buddies, MI6 and MI5 subordinates, and piers, but he hesitated not knowing who could be fully trusted. He estimated they would need a high government official if Frosty was to convince anyone of Dixon's involvement, one that has the PM's ear, but he was worried others in government could be in on the scheme. He also knew this was an Atom bomb in waiting which would wipe out the entire security service's leadership, a scenario none of the current kingpins would accept.

Devlin called first and Fleming hurried down to the beach to take the call.

"I have three guys ready to go at a moment's notice," Devlin said without preamble. "They have gear and are ready to finance their own expenses."

"Damn gallant of them," Fleming said. "I had not even considered the financial aspect, but I guess this is no time to demand pay."

"I doubt anyone would consider it," Devlin agreed. "I also spoke to Lizzy who told me you called him. We combined forces so whatever you get from me, it's from him as well."

"Saved me an extra call," Fleming joked feebly. "Could buy me another few hours with this phone."

"Can you give us their hideout?" Devlin asked. He had no patience for chit-chat.

Fleming gave him the map coordinates Frosty had given him. "It's a house in the country just south of Bath," he divulged. "They will not answer phone calls so your guys need to get there on their Recce skills alone."

"Oh, I am sure they can do that Harry," Devlin said. "Have you heard from Malcolm?"

"No reply on his mobile. Did not want to leave any message."

"I'll try him as well," Devlin offered. "He and Mai-Li are still active with the Missing Children organizations together with Sam in New York, so they may have some clout with our cousins across the ocean."

"When will your guys be getting there?" Fleming asked. "So I can alert Frosty."

"They can be there by midnight," Devlin said, not disclosing any additional information about his volunteers.

"Right," Fleming concluded. "I'll let Frosty know right away."

"What else can we old folks do?" Devlin asked.

Fleming was silent for a moment. "I guess we'll need at least one heavy hitter in government to help convince the PM about Dixon once the shit hits the fan." He observed. "If and when Frosty's arguments may be hampered well before it reaches the right ears. SO1 is everywhere and will probably not let anyone near."

"We'll look into it," Devlin promised. "Let us know when you change phones. We'll do the same so we can be in touch."

"Will do," Fleming agreed, hung up and immediately rang Frosty who he hoped would pick up his unlisted call.

****

Cindy was busy scanning the internet. They allotted ten-minute increments for six hours for a total of one hour a day, to try and extract information that would serve their purpose. Convinced that Simon Lewis had hidden a file with the disc's information somewhere on the net since he had to download it from somewhere, she kept plowing through piles of SO1 information trying to locate the file at great risk of exposing their location but was unwilling to remain idle.

She scanned the organization's Bulletin boards, unclassified and classified sites, any public notice sites, and even virtual garbage bins, knowing she could restore any deleted files if need be.

Jemma and Camilla were sitting at the table picking at Mary's food, Jemma trying to uplift Camilla's spirits for she looked like a ghost. They had waited at Jake's office for the remainder of the day after Frosty left to find Fleming, hoping to learn of Santana's fate. There was no word on any of the major news channels and they could not find anything on the net regarding a skirmish with casualties at Embassy Row. It was bizarre but not unexpected with all the mayhem going on around them.

Photos of Prince William kept appearing everywhere on all TV stations, in all news bulletins, on most internet sites, as well as on Facebook and Instagram. There were panels of experts, prayer sessions in churches around the world, and five-minute formal updates by British officials on all British media. Foreign correspondents swarmed the airports unable to enter the city setting up shop at airport terminals, ship ports, and train stations outside London.

Jake was out with the kids, playing rugby in the meadow behind the house.

Mary was busy cooking and Noah was looking over some bills in the corner office.

"I may have something!" Cindy called out, making Jemma jump out of her seat and join Cindy in front of the computer.

"This is a deleted Zip file I found in Lord Tompkins' personal Gmail files. It does not have a title, and it was sent from an anonymous site but the date fits. It was never opened by Tompkins who I guess could not open it or missed it somehow and trashed it."

Jemma looked at the screen as Cindy was working to open the file.

"Are we past the ten minutes?" Jemma asked, following closely as Cindy worked the keyboard in a frenzy.

"We may be but I've got to open this file!" Cindy said, talking through her actions as she tried to crack it open. "It's a bitch, this one, but I don't think it has a password since I doubt Lewis would have risked informing Tompkins of one."

It took her another five minutes, with Jemma holding her breath over her shoulder, but she managed to crack it. The file opened and it was a gold mine! It had no title and no addresses but had a list of fifteen operatives recruited to SO1 over a period of three years, their background, and who recruited them.

All were recruited by Dixon.

"Bingo!" Jemma said and hugged Cindy's shoulders.

Cindy did a "print screen" and turned to Noah who was sitting in the small office.

"Is the printer working?" she asked.

"Last time I checked," Noah said, raising his eyes to her from the pile of bills he was working on.

"Quick," Cindy said to Jemma. "Let's connect it!"

She raised her laptop moving closer to Noah's printer and switched cables pressing the 'enter' key twice.

When two copies of the list were printed out, she shut off the laptop and breathed a sigh of relief.

Chapter Thirty-Six

Andy White was perspiring, though the room temperature showed 20 degrees Celsius. He kept pestering his tracking experts to give him a lead that he could pursue but it seemed an exercise in futility. For the last week, he has been desperately trying to track the rouge agent Adrian Frost without success, having failed twice when he had him in his grasp.

With his SO1 conspirators and Dixon at the helm, they had pretty much everyone fooled. Four of the guys were holding the Prince well away from any of the major search areas which both he and Dixon were fostering, and their Muslim collaborators were well hidden in London waiting for a signal to detonate another bomb.

The chaos was complete with all the top policymakers and party leaders in total disarray beginning to blame one another for their shortcomings, everyone pointing a finger at the Home Secretary and the PM for failing to resolve the crisis.

With MI5 leading the way, the military, SAS units, the air force, the navy and MI6 were all taking part now, putting a siege on all ports of call, airports, train stations, and roads; checking all moving vehicles, trains, ships and planes, combing the city for stray bombs and the likes, analyzing endless databases of all known and unknown terrorist groups, and collaborating with foreign emissaries for any leads they might supply, without any success. Dixon sat on all the major committees, received all the delicate, urgent reports, and knew exactly what to watch out for and how to steer the momentum away from his operation.

The one thorn in their side was Agent Frost, who knew for certain of White's involvement and no doubt connected the dots but was unable to cause any harm, yet, due to his renegade status. That would be short-lived, White knew, and he had to find him and his people before they appeared with the truth.

Dixon himself was not giving White any slack, demanding results immediately before it all blew in their faces.

"Sir." Someone called from the array of computer screens and communication devices situated along the four walls in the damp operations room at the basement of Thames House, a section designated exclusively to SO1 personnel.

"Yes!" White called out from his post at the entrance to the room by the fortified glass doors. No one entered the room without his approval.

"I may have something," the thin, bald-headed operative raised his voice over the hum.

White had been called over by different operatives several times a day to examine their suspicions, and was losing hope, but made an effort every time, in case something real popped up.

He stood over the man and looked at his screen.

"Tracked a site from a place near Bath that connected to Deputy Minister Tompkins's Gmail account," the man said. Tompkins was one of the accounts they had been tracing.

"That's the late Lord Tompkins for you," White corrected him. "Can you show me the link?"

The man punched a few keys and brought up the Tompkins Gmail account bringing up the Inbox with hundreds of unread emails. The operative went to the Deleted files which had several hundred deleted mails in bold. He scrolled down until he reached an untitled file among the bold, yet-to-be-trashed files, which was not in bold.

"You see, Sir, this file has been restored and sent back to the deleted section."

"Can you open it?" White demanded.

"It's a Zip file which will take a while, but yes, I can open it."

"So why do you suspect it?"

"Well, Sir, I've been tasked to track the Tompkins account for a while now, and it has not been tampered with until today."

"And how would you know where the inquiry came from?" White insisted, though he began to suspect the agent had something.

"Someone was able to remotely enter the account, no small task in itself without a password and all and was able to open the Zip file and restore it. However, whoever hacked into it was unable to conceal the name of the site and where it came from. Our algorithms are programmed to track not only the designation of the site on the web but its physical location as well, which is exactly what it did."

"OK, son," White said, his voice turning excited. "You do whatever you need to open this file ASAP and call me right away when you do."

******

Frosty received a signal from Dylan Thomas' phone and quickly rushed back to the Bertram home.

He had remained at the B&B for most of the day and into the evening, dozing off in front of the TV and waking up to the mobile phone's buzz.

Dylan was sitting on the same couch he had left him in the morning looking dejected somewhat, looking in the direction of Ruby fussing around her daughter Ella, who was at the kitchen table having her dinner.

"Would you like some tea or coffee?" Ruby called to him when he entered the living room.

"Coffee would be great," Frosty said, looking at Dylan questioningly. Dylan, who looked tired and beat, flicked his head focusing his eyes toward the kitchen but said nothing.

Frosty sat next to Dylan and the two waited patiently for the girl to finish her dinner before Ruby came with the hot beverages.

"Well," Frosty said impatiently as he added some sugar to his coffee. "What do we have?"

Ella came over and sat on her mom's lap.

"Ella remembered something just now which I thought may be of interest," Ruby said, extending her hands around her daughter's waist from behind.

"Tell him dear," She encouraged.

"Dad gave me an address in case he disappeared one day, and I wanted to go to him."

Frosty looked at the girl who seemed older than her 12 years as she turned her head to her mom. "He made me swear not to tell you unless I never wanted to see him again."

"When was that?" Frosty asked.

"About a year ago. I entered it into my address list in code but I can still find it."

"And will you?" Frosty asked carefully.

"If I do I'll never see him again, right?" she stated.

"You will never see him again either way…" Dylan said in anger. "I told you that already, didn't I?"

"And I told you that I will not speak to you!" Ella retorted.

"The damn country is in shambles…" Dylan started to complain but Frosty stopped him, putting a hand on his lap.

"You will have to give it to us you know," he said matter-of-factly, in a gentle but firm tone.

Ella looked back at her mom who studied the two guests carefully before making a choice.

"I am afraid we'll have to help these gentlemen dear," she said hugging her daughter tightly.

"And I'll never get to see Dad?" The girl whined, her eyes becoming wet.

"Your dad made his choice before you were born," Ruby said to her daughter. "So, there's nothing we can do for him."

"But I miss him," Ella cried, tears running down her face. "I want to see him again."

"It's out of our hands, love," Ruby said, trying to comfort her daughter, stroking her hair. "You saw the destruction in London. We cannot let that happen. It's our home too and if we can do something to help, we must do it."

Ella looked torn but she took her mobile phone out of her pant pocket and activated it. It turned on with a chime and she bore into it looking for the address given to her by her father.

It took a few minutes but she managed to decrypt it and showed it to Frosty.

It was a London address Frosty recognized easily, on the north side of Hyde Park, on Bayswater Road near the Lancaster Gate Tube station.

Part Four

Chapter Thirty-Seven

Midnight, Wednesday, February 6, 2019

Three men burst into the house.

Jemma and Cindy were sitting on the carpet in front of the fireplace, the kids, asleep, sprawled around them. Jake and Noah were resting in their rooms, and Mary was, as usual, in the kitchen, washing the dishes.

"We need you to pack up and come with us!" One of them said in a cool but firm tone hurrying to look out the back window, while another flew out the back door. The third was left standing by the front door entrance, looking out the adjacent window behind the curtains.

"What's going on!?" Jemma asked incredulously, jumping to her feet. "Who are you guys?"

"Friends of Air Vice Marshal Fleming," the man at the back answered her, keeping his stare out the back window.

"Harry Fleming?" Jemma asked in surprise.

"Yes! And you need to pack up your things and move out of here in the next fifteen minutes! That's all of you including the landlords!"

"I am not going anywhere!" Mary squealed from the kitchen where she stopped wiping the dishes.

Jake and Noah appeared from their rooms looking concerned. Jake came rushing down the stairs from the second-floor guest rooms and Noah from his bedroom on the first floor.

"Jemma, you OK?" Jake asked, eyeing the strange men in their midst with concern.

"You can't barge in here like this!" Noah said indignantly, moving next to his wife in the kitchen.

The man at the front door spoke up.

"We've been sent here by friends to protect you," he said, nervously turning to look out the window all the while.

The third man returned through the back door. "All clear!" he announced and took a position by the door.

"How do you know Harry Fleming?" Jemma spoke aloud, she and Cindy had the kids in their grasp.

"We are ex-regiment and served under Devlin in Harley's unit after that." The man at the door replied. "We've been briefed on your situation and we're here to help."

Jake looked toward Jemma who nodded. She and Cindy relaxed a bit. They were both well-versed in the history of the covert unit that had years ago been formed by the late Joe Harley and later when he was killed, was run by Mike Devlin.

There was an awkward silence for a few seconds before the man went on.

"I am Barry, and these are Blake and Bond," he pointed first at the man by the back window, and then at the man who had searched outside the back door, who like the famous Ian Fleming character, was quite striking with neatly combed hair and a handsome face.

They were all dressed in hiking gear and carried large backpacks.

"We were told you would not answer phones, so we had to come in without warning," Barry went on. "Just as we got here, we intercepted a communique received by a regiment alpha team giving them the exact coordinates of this house."

"How did you get the position of this house?" Cindy asked.

"Your husband gave it to Fleming and asked for our help," Barry said.

"It won't be long before they get here so you do as we say if you want to survive," Bond said from over by the back door.

"What's an alpha team?" Jake asked.

Andy looked at Jake away from the window. "It's a hit team," he said, "extremely efficient."

A frenzy of activity ensued as Jake, Jemma, and Cindy ran upstairs with the kids to pack and arouse Camilla.

"Pack only essentials you can carry on your back," Barry called after them. "And destroy any computer equipment you have with you."

Noah and Mary remained standing in their kitchen not moving an inch.

"This is our home," Noah addressed Barry, who kept watching nervously through the window. "We have nowhere else to go."

"It's your call," Barry said from his position at the door.

"They won't dare shoot us, will they?" Noah inquired.

"Do you have any kids? Relatives?" Barry asked.

"No kids and no family who would take us in," Noah said.

"Look, these guys may use unorthodox methods to get information out of you," Blake said from his position at the back window. "I would not stick around for that."

Noah looked at Mary who was shaking her head but grabbed her anyway and ran to their bedroom.

Ten minutes later, they all burst out the back door into the dark meadow. Cindy had borrowed a hammer from Noah's toolbox and smashed her computer keyboard and screen to bits, taking out the hard drive and smashing it as well, throwing away the pieces in the meadow as they ran. The only pieces of evidence she kept were the two copies of the printed list of fifteen SO1 operatives recruited by Dixon, which they had recovered from Simon's deleted email to Tompkins.

Bond was in the lead and Barry was in the back carrying a lethargic Camilla on his shoulders. Blake would remain near the house hoping to learn something when the troops arrived and would catch up with them later.

They ran down the meadow in total darkness tripping occasionally over rocks and the uneven ground but kept on going until they reached the line of trees and disappeared in the forest.

Blake took a position among the closest line of trees, at the crest of the hill, where it abruptly descended toward the main road. He was within earshot, roughly thirty meters away, and could see the house from above.

They came within minutes. He heard a distant engine being shut off on the roadside of the house. Minutes later they came, in total darkness. Blake had his infrared goggles at the ready, instantly switched them on, and studied the scene.

He saw them rushing to the house. Split into three teams, five men each, they approached swiftly, one team circling from the far side of the house, another heading across the meadow toward the back door, and the third circling to his side of the house.

He had to admire their pace and their stealth. Almost without a sound, they were at the house, bursting in from both sides on cue only to find it categorically empty.

He watched them rummage the house, first in darkness, then the lights came on and some talk began among them. Someone was giving orders to ransack the place for any clues and another came out the back door talking on his mobile.

The man was dressed in civilian clothes and stood looking across the dark meadow speaking angrily on the phone. Blake could not make out his face or his hair color but could tell he was thin and quite tall.

"Looks like they were warned..." The man said, listening to the reply. "Yeah, left in a hurry..."

"Looks like a short time ago..."

"There's a pickup out front belonging to the owners..."

"We'll have to wait for some daylight to search the area..."

He listened intently for quite a while before ending the call then entered the house coming out accompanied by a soldier a minute later. Blake was able to identify the gun strapped around the neck, the military vest with its bulging magazines, and the helmet, items the civilian did not wear.

They spoke softly and Blake strained to hear picking up only partial sentences.

He heard the name "Agent Frost" mentioned several times as well as "Agent Stone" which he knew to be Jemma. He also heard a mention of the Home Secretary and AVM Alan Reed and bits and pieces of "...a need for a search of the immediate area..."

Then, he heard something that alarmed him: The civilian who did most of the talking mentioned the need to interrogate one Harry Fleming.

******

Blake caught up with the fleeing entourage at six in the morning when it became a trifle light.

He had waited to see what the raiders would do, watching them rummage through the house and then send scouts to look for tracks scanning the entire line of trees surrounding the meadow, then across toward his position on the hill above.

At that point, he decided to split taking a wide birth through the forest aiming for the updated GPS coordinates sent to him by Barry. He found them asleep, all bunched up and covered with two sleeping bags provided by his mates who were guarding their flanks.

They were well hidden along the banks of the Avon River near a small creek surrounded by heavy vegetation and lofty trees. They had taken a track northeast, into a forested expanse for about a kilometer, then crossed several open fields and two roads before stopping by on the riverbank just south of Freshford, a spot both Bond and Barry thought was safe enough to rest for a few hours.

Bond, Barry, and Jake took turns carrying Camilla until she came to and could carry herself.

They conferred for a few minutes before anyone awoke.

"They came minutes after you left," Blake whispered. "The standard alpha team with a civilian who seemed to be calling the shots. They'll start searching the area at daybreak. We should have hidden the owner's car…"

"There wasn't enough time," Barry rationalized, "anything else of importance?"

"Yeah, I think they may be going after Fleming. The civilian wants to interrogate him."

The two veterans looked at their colleague in alarm. "Fleming!?" Barry asked in surprise. "How would they know about him?"

"Well, it seems they do mate," Blake maintained. "I called Mike and alerted him to the fact. He'll warn the old man."

"Well not much we can do about it now," Bond pointed out. "So I suggest we focus on avoiding these assassins who would be out looking for us just about now."

"Right," Barry agreed. "Noah here knows the area quite well so we could follow his lead. Said he knew several proper hideouts."

"My guess is they'll comb the area with a chopper or two and send in several teams at once. Maybe they'll bring in the dogs as well. Come daylight, they'll spot our tracks in the meadow in a jiffy and follow on from there."

"How long did it take you to get here?" Barry asked Blake.

"About an hour," Blake said. "Had to be careful at those road crossings."

"Yeah, it took us double that time," Barry concurred. "So, we have an hour head start on whoever will follow our tracks but they may come from other directions as well."

"You do realize their main target is not here," Blake pointed out. "And I don't think they are aware of that. They mentioned his name and Agent Stone's name at the house as well. Did you let him know?"

"His wife did," Bond informed him. "Did he say what he was going to do?"

"Said he was going to London," Bond said. "Kept it very short."

"You guys realize his entire family can be used as leverage to bring him in if caught," Blake remarked.

"Well, then gents," Barry proclaimed, "we simply can't afford to get caught!"

A sudden reverberating sound rumbled toward them from the south along the river and after an initial anxious moment, they relaxed realizing it was an oncoming train.

The three ex-commandos looked at one another and nodded in unison. A train escape was something they had not considered but looking at their GPS map realized the Freshford train station was only a kilometer away.

Chapter Thirty-Eight

10 AM, Wednesday, February 6, 2019

A second appearance of the abducted Prince William was broadcast at ten that morning, this time via Sky News.

As in the first broadcast, he sat on the ground in his flight suit, his hands cuffed behind his back, a pistol aimed at his head, looking up at the camera. He looked quite exhausted, unshaven, and dirty, but his eyes radiated confidence.

The man with the black hood appeared again, standing above him.

"It has now been eight days with no progress," the man began with his Eastern European accent. "Your Prime Minister has all our demands but so far has yet to take any action."

The camera shifted to the Prince again who stared bravely at the camera, the gun still pointed at his head.

"So now you have one day," the man continued. "Or your Prince dies!"

The screen went black for a few seconds then a video of London from above appeared with no sound as the camera zoomed in on various locations as it passed above the center of London.

Then, the man in the black hood was back standing over the Prince.

"There are more explosives in the city that can cause great damage. You are not safe at train stations, restaurants, office buildings, public areas, and even hospitals. Your fuel supply is depleted and soon the city will lose all electricity. There will be chaos. I promise you!"

The camera focused on the Prince again, and again he looked up and seemed to be shaking his head. Then the camera returned to the man in the hood.

"You have one day!" he warned again and the screen went black.

Air Vice Marshal Alan Reed stood among his operatives in the Task Force Bureau operations center in the Whitehall basement among a cluster of monitoring equipment looking at the TV screens overhead as the broadcast ended.

"Get me that tape!" he said to no one in particular. "How on earth are they able to fly over the city?" He wondered out loud as everyone returned to their computer screens after watching the broadcast.

He walked to his corner behind a glass partition and slumped heavily on his chair.

Through the glass, he could see his people working frantically. All his operatives with the addition of dedicated MI5 and MI6 people, were focused on locating the Prince and the ticking bombs. Other security services people under Bishop were attached to Special Ops and SAS units combing the country, searching designated suspect areas across the UK using RAF choppers.

It perplexed him greatly how with such a force out and about they could not, for a full week now, locate anything of substance including his rogue agents Adrian Frost and Jemma Stone. There was a city-wide curfew and everything was monitored; the web, all social networks, any and all internet correspondences with assistance from Google, mobile phone communications with assistance from the NSA, landline phone communications, satellite aerial data, and fast jet Recce data. The police placed roadblocks on all major traffic routes and on all routes leading in and out of London. Immigration and customs were closely monitoring all ports and airports, and the military was combing every street in London and beyond.

PM Webster, Home Secretary Scott, and Bishop had open communications to its allies in Europe and the US who had most of their intelligence assets available and were assisting, and still nothing materialized.

Something was greatly amiss and he had less than a day to uncover it. Meanwhile, the Sterling was slipping further having now lost more than half its value from a week ago. Treasury officers were going after international hedge fund managers to buy it back and bring its levels to where it was before it got dumped but that too would take some time and there were no guarantees with such matters.

Chaos would not even begin to describe the state of affairs, he thought to himself. Andy Taylor was signaling to him from behind the glass partition. Reed motioned him in.

"The tape you asked for. It's on the grid," Taylor said.

Read punched in a few keys on his computer and brought up the video. Taylor looked over his shoulder. They watched it for a few minutes then Reed said in disbelief: "This was taken after the bombings! How is that possible?"

Taylor looked baffled.

"Can we tell what airframe this is taken from?"

"Well at that speed it must be a helicopter…" Taylor suggested.

"It could also be a small plane," Reed commented. "Could you check?"

Taylor nodded and started to leave.

"Oh and Andy," Reed stopped him, "after you've figured it out, have all the team leaders assemble in the conference room will you?"

"Sure, Sir," Andy said and hurried out the door just as the phone rang at Reed's desk.

It was Bishop. "Did you see the clip?" he asked without preamble.

"Sure did. It was taken after the bombings and we're checking to see if we can determine which airframe it was taken from?"

"Scott is livid!" Bishop said. "How can this happen?"

"We're looking into it as we speak…"

"What are you hoping to find?" Bishop interrupted him in mid-sentence.

"Look, Trevor, it is next to impossible for an unauthorized airframe to enter the no-fly zone over London at this time. Air traffic control would have identified it and sent the fighters after it. So I am guessing it was taken from an authorized airframe…"

There was silence on the line for a long moment before Bishop spoke.

"So the clip could have been taken from one of our choppers?" Bishop wanted to make sure he understood.

"That's my suspicion," Reed acknowledged. "And if it is, then we've got some adversaries on the inside, which would explain our running up dead ends all this time."

Again there was silence on Bishop's end. "So what's your plan?" He finally asked.

"If it's indeed a friendly airframe that was used and we can determine the time frame, we'll get air traffic to tell us who was up there at that time and take it from there."

"OK, keep me posted," Bishop said. "I'll most likely be with Nigel for the rest of the day so he'll be informed as well. And I don't have to tell you time is running out, do I?"

Andy Taylor rushed in as Reed was hanging up the phone. "I think we got something, Sir, you better come see!"

The team leaders were assembled in the conference room all watching the video on a large screen at one end above the TFB logo etched on the wall.

Reed took his place at the head of the table while Taylor stood next to the screen.

"We've identified the airframe's shadow as it passes over this roof here," he said, pointing a laser pointer at an area on a white roof, freezing the frame.

"It's a Black Hawk, Sir…" Andy said with finality, pointing the beam at a small shadow in the middle of the roof.

Reed got up and walked to the screen to take a closer look. "Are you sure?" He mused. "I can't really tell."

"We ran it by the intelligence crowd and some pilots. They all agree it's a Black Hawk." Harriet Gold put in from her place at the desk. She was older than most of the crowd around the conference room, with straight white hair down to her shoulders, intense blue eyes, and a motherly demeanor which was quite misleading as she was known as "The Bulldog" in the clandestine circles. Once she got her teeth on something, she never let go.

"I talked to air traffic control," Kevin Edwards, Jemma's office colleague, the redhead, pitched in. "There were a host of Black Hawk squadrons over the city the entire week obviously, so it's hard to pinpoint the day, but they seem to think it was taken exactly a week ago, a day before Prince William was taken, by someone from squadron 511 based in Boscomb Down."

Reed looked over the crowd. "Anybody thinks otherwise?" he asked. There was silence as everyone seemed to be in agreement.

"You must realize," Reed continued. "If this is true, we are dealing with a breach on the inside," he said, looking hard at the people around the conference table. "Which means we've got an entirely different ballgame on our hands."

Nobody spoke.

"OK then, Edwards, arrange a meeting with the squadron commander and get down to Boscomb Down. Harriet and the rest of you, do a thorough check on all squadron 511 personnel, pilots, flight engineers, and the lot."

Reed looked around the room as people began to collect their things.

"Now to Frosty and Jemma," he said and everyone froze in place. "Special ops raided a farmhouse they were hiding in near Bath last night, but it seems they managed to escape. I don't have all the details but there are strong indications that they are hiding in a dense forest area near that house so a large-scale search is being conducted. Taylor, I want you down there on the double! I'll be in the ministry to brief Bishop and the Home Secretary on our latest."

As he sat at the back of his Range Rover, his mobile rang. It was Frosty from an unlisted mobile who, without introduction, gave him the London address given to him by Ella, Sonny Bertram's daughter, and hung up instantly.

Chapter Thirty-Nine

Noon, Wednesday, February 6, 2019

Kevin Edwards and Harriet Gold hugged the wall behind the Special Ops squad, preparing to storm the upper floor apartment of a four-story blemished white building on Bayswater Road, an address provided to them by Reed who did not bother to explain but ordered them to thoroughly search the place and bring whoever was there for questioning. Guns at the ready and wearing ceramic vests, they scooted behind the last of the commandos and ran silently up the stairs. The entire building was surrounded by a Special Ops contingent including snipers across the street between the trees of Hyde Park.

The lock to the apartment was shot open with a silencer and the troop stormed into the suspect flat seizing all rooms in a matter of seconds without resistance.

As Edwards and Harriet walked in, they found two men on the floor being handcuffed.

Edwards escorted the apprehended duo back to the grid in a bulletproof Range Rover with two armed troopers riding shotgun while Harriet remained at the apartment and began a thorough search with Special Ops troopers guarding each floor not allowing any of the neighbors access to and from of the building.

She went through all the drawers, closets, shelves, and bags that were left stranded by the occupants. She searched the toilet, the kitchen, behind the few posters that were hanging on the walls, cut through the mattresses of the two beds and the living room sofas but found nothing incriminating that could be used to connect the occupants to anything that had to do with the current crisis. Finally, as she was ready to give up, she decided to upend the entire wall-to-wall carpet and found a small niche against the living room wall with a vintage Nokia mobile telephone in it.

There was a single number contacted numerous times in the outgoing memory so she dialed it.

A deep male voice which sounded somewhat familiar answered after two rings: "Not a good time Boris…" the voice said in Russian, which Harriet understood, "this better be good…" he continued, then realized something and became hostile: "Hello, who is this…?" he said anxiously and immediately clicked off.

Back at the TFB, Harriet went directly to the interrogation cells to watch through the glass the two men being questioned but both sat alone in their cells with Edwards outside standing watch.

"Anything interesting?" She asked matter-of-factly.

"Not so far," Edwards said, watching the cell intently. "We're to wait for Reed before we question them and so far, in the car, they have not uttered a word!"

"They are Russian!" Harriet said quietly.

Edwards shifted his gaze to her. "What did you find?"

"A mobile phone," she said, "with a number which I called and got a reply in Russian."

Edwards kept staring at her.

"A man answered addressing a person named Boris. He was about to reprimand him for calling when he realized something amiss and instantly ended the call."

"So one of these guys is a Russian named Boris?" Edwards queried.

"I believe so," Harriet said. "But why are they not being questioned?"

"Don't know exactly. Reed should be in any minute now. Anything else you found there?"

"No, the place was squeaky clean apart from this phone hidden in a niche under the living room rug."

"Good job Ms. Gold," Edwards said, smiling at her as Reed walked in with Bishop and Ross Dixon.

They all stood a moment looking at the two detainees then Reed spoke. "Anything in the apartment?"

"It was clean except for this mobile phone," Harriet offered, holding up the phone.

"Anything on that phone?" Reed questioned.

"A single number which I called and got a brief reply before they understood it was not one of them calling…" She informed them, pointing at the men in the cells.

"What was the reply?" Reed asked.

"It was a man who answered in Russian addressing a Boris, who I assume is one of these two…"

"Anything else?" Reed continued.

"No, he quickly realized something amiss and disconnected."

"You know Russian?" Dixon asked.

"I am head of the Russian desk." Harriet divulged. "I should know the language…"

"OK then," Bishop addressed Reed, "I suggest Ms. Gold interrogate one of them. Any other Russian-speaking personnel who can do the job with the other?"

"Can you get Olga in here?" Reed asked his agent.

Harriet walked out and came back after a few minutes with a striking blonde woman who towered over both Bishop and Dixon.

"This is Olga Mitanova," Harriet introduced her. "She is my FSB expert."

Edwards pitched in. "What exactly are we looking for, Alan?" He addressed Reed by his first name.

"The apartment you searched is an address given to me by Agent Frost." Reed divulged causing the three junior operatives to raise their eyebrows.

"He called me with the address from an unlisted number and said no more. I didn't even manage to put in a word before he hung up."

"So what are we after here?" Edwards insisted. "I mean, Frosty is considered damaged goods right now, wanted for treason, why would we follow his leads?"

"Good question," Dixon said. "I can't see how this would boost our quest. On the contrary, we should be aware he may want to lead us astray."

"It's worth a shot, Ross!" Bishop declared, having been briefed by the Home Secretary about the demands from the Kremlin, a little vexed by Dixon whom he knew, knew as well.

Dixon gave him a menacing stare before he conceded. "Of course, at this point, anything is worth a shot."

"Right then," Reed said. "Harriet, Olga, try and find out which one of these is Boris and see if they would give us the person who answered the phone, apart from anything else of value you can extract. You have an hour; after that, we bring in the druggies. There's no time to waste."

******

226

As soon as Dixon left, Bishop asked Reed to accompany him for a smoke outside the building.

Reed waited patiently as Bishop lit a cigar he retrieved from his inner coat pocket cut off its end and fought the wind to light it up.

"I thought cigars were smoked only at the gentlemen's club," Reed commented.

"It is," Bishop said, "and I don't ever smoke them outside."

Reed looked at him questionably. "So what's the occasion?"

"You need to know this," Bishop confided, "the PM received a demand from the Russian president to sign a document in which we commit to dropping our initiative of supplying American gas to Europe, write off Russian debt, drop all sanctions against Russia for threatening Poland and Ukraine and convince our allies to drop theirs as well."

Reed looked at him in surprised shock.

"The Russians…" he began to murmur.

"Yes, Alan, it's all a Russian plot to keep us from using these new Liquefied Natural Gas terminals for US oil."

"So 'Sons of Jihad' and all this Muslim mumbo-jumbo, is just a cover?"

"The threats are real but the culprits are Russians using that Muslim organization as a front. It's yet to be determined how they hitched up but these outrageous demands eliminating the monarchy or giving those Muslims government jobs are just a smoke screen."

Reed looked flabbergasted. "When did you know of this?" he asked angrily.

"Yesterday. The document was put in Dixon's home mailbox and he brought it in."

"Did he check its authenticity?" Reed pried.

"He sure did. It's an original Kremlin letterhead signed by their president."

"Why wasn't I informed immediately?"

"It was the PM's call," Bishop said. "Wanted to keep it under wraps. He gave Scott 48 hours to remove all threats or he will negotiate with the Russians."

"And how does Scott intend to remove the threats without informing the TFB?"

"Well, I am informing you now! Got damn it! I realized it was a mistake as soon as Ms. Gold said they were Russian. We have less than a day for god's sake!"

"Why would Dixon question this then…?" Reed asked after a short pause.

"I presume he does not trust Agent Frost's tips," Bishop said. "I wouldn't either for that matter…"

"But the intel was spot on," Reed observed. "If Frost can't be trusted then he would have led us astray."

"That remains to be seen," Bishop remarked. "You took quite a chance following his lead."

"Beggars can't be choosers…" Reed observed.

"Quite true," Bishop agreed, "now you go back in there and get these guys to talk! We are due for a break… and Alan…"

Reed who began to climb the stairs to the building, turned and looked down at the MI5 head.

"Do not disclose the Russian involvement to your people yet. Wait until we see if this lead is legit."

Reed nodded looking thoughtful. "Sure, but if this is legit, we may want to rethink our assessment of Frost's involvement."

Chapter Forty

1 PM, Wednesday, February 6, 2019

James Flanagan sat on the sofa sipping coffee watching his grandkids fool around on the living room carpet, seemingly oblivious to the ominous bracelets adorning their ankles.

Since that dark evening, a week or so ago, when his entire family was taken hostage by a menacing group of foreigners, Flanagan had lost track of time.

He was still aware of the days of the week and so forth, but time was now measured by his and his family's personal nightmare and the spell it would take to remove the bracelets safely off his grandchildren's ankles.

He had since met all of his captors' demands, ensuring the British pound devaluated against the Russian Ruble and all other currencies as a result, as hedge funds hounds and other investors he had unleashed, pounded the currency market and brought the pound to an all-time low in a week.

He was also quite aware of the correlation of his actions with the sweeping London chaos that had, so far, cost many lives and had paralyzed the British capital, but he could not place his captor's direct involvement in the affair, except for one thing which he thought he knew for certain:

The man with the hood, who held Prince William captive, was the same man who had put the bracelets on his grandchildren's ankles, and he guessed he and his family were among the few who could make the connection. They had known it as soon as the first BBC clip aired and discussed it among themselves but could not come to terms with it. It was an impossible dilemma that further tormented their spirits for how can one trade the life of his children for that of the Prince.

Besides, they now had a 24-hour watch at the house of at least one person, so it was impossible to do anything without scrutiny. In fact, Flanagan was the only one allowed out of the house once London was attacked and since there was nowhere they could go in the mayhem and imposed curfew, they all remained at the house watching over the kids who were delighted at not having to go to school and having their elders pay so much attention to them.

Flanagan would be allowed to take his son Jenson to do the shopping at the nearest shopping center once in a while and he would visit the bank on occasion with an escort in tow. Few of his workers made it to work and the ones who did, did not stay for long. All transactions were made via the web and he was required to give a report to his captors on the deals that went through. All his phone conversations were monitored, so no one could sneak out a call.

There was a commotion near the front door; a few seconds later, the blond man burst into the living room with two of his goons in tail.

"Did you talk to anyone?" he fumed, looking hard at the banker.

"Certainly not!" Flanagan replied instantly. "What's this about?"

"Some woman called my private phone," he seethed, raising his mobile toward Flanagan. "Spoke Russian. Now two of my men are missing!"

Flanagan studied the man. "How would I do that?" He asked quietly, careful not to further upset the man.

"I have no idea but my phone is compromised and because of that, so are these children!" He wailed then picked up little four-year-old John, who was rolling around on the floor, by his leg and held him hanging upside down.

Jenson and Abbey appeared on the staircase leading from the bedrooms on the second floor, looking horrified. They both ran down toward little John but the two goons stopped them from reaching their son.

"Did you talk to anyone? Call anyone?" The blond man addressed them, holding on to John's ankle, who was kicking and squirming trying to free himself.

"Talk to who? Call who?" Jenson called out. "We have not spoken to anyone in a week!"

"What about you?" the blond man addressed Flanagan's wife Sheila, who followed her eldest son and daughter-in-law alongside her younger son Michael and his wife Jenny, Sarah's parents. All three shook their heads.

"Did you meet anyone, talk to anyone, inside the supermarket?" the blond man insisted, looking back at Flanagan who shook his head.

Sarah and Robbie were sitting on the floor, looking up at Robbie's little brother dangling above their heads.

Flanagan stood up. "We have abided by your rules and would never put our children in danger."

He called. "Now, please put the kid down."

There was a silent moment as the blond man studied the frightened family all huddled together looking at their helpless child swaying above the floor.

"Well," he finally said, "we may have been compromised so new measures are now in effect."

He put little John down. Abbey ran to him and picked him up, hugging him closely.

"You are to disconnect all internet access, hand over your mobile phones and you are not to answer the landline phone. Is that understood?"

They all nodded but for Flanagan who pointed out that he would not be able to communicate with his people at the bank or provide any status reports.

"So be it!" the blond man asserted. "All of you are to stay in the living room at all times. No one goes upstairs. Use the restrooms and rooms down here and shower here if you need to."

With that, he addressed his two associates in short concise sentences in their language, turned, and left the house.

******

Harriet and Olga walked into Reed's office and sat down heavily on the small office sofa in front of his desk.

"Anything?" Reed questioned, raising his eyes to them, having been occupied looking at a file sent to him by Andy Taylor who had reached Boscombe Down to check on the Black Hawk squadron and was now on his way to the Bath area where an extensive search in the bush for Jemma, Frosty and the lot was already being carried out by Special Forces.

"Would not say much, I am afraid," Harriet said. "Both gave their names but not much else."

"And… is there a Boris?" Reed demanded.

"Yes, there is," Harriet said. "Boris Kushnir, a Ukrainian. The other one's Vladimir Melnyk, also Ukrainian."

Reed started to say something when the phone rang and he picked it up instantly pressing the speaker.

"Andy, I am here with Harriet and Olga. Got your report. What's the latest?"

"Well, it looks like the choppers over the city from where the video was taken were Sea Kings; not Blackhawks. The two squadron commanders verified it and

231

it's most definitely the Sea Kings and…" Taylor paused for effect, "It was Prince William's squadron! The one he usually flies with on reserve duty."

There was a stunned silence in the room.

"Alan, you there?" Taylor persisted after a few seconds.

"Yes, we are," Reed said, "trying to comprehend the news."

"We checked flight patterns from the day Prince William was taken but found nothing out of the ordinary. The squadron commander will question his men as soon as they return to base."

"Where are they now?"

"Out on assignments. Some are assisting in tracking Jemma and Frosty."

"When are they do back?"

"Afternoon. Sometime before dark."

"That may be too late!" Reed exclaimed. "Can the Group Captain call them back?"

"Doubt it, but I'll ask him. Got his mobile number."

"Where are you now?" Reed continued.

"Following a military jeep to a temporary ops center near Bath. Be there in about thirty minutes."

"OK. We must find the pilot ASAP so work it from there. If you need assistance, call back, we'll assist from here."

"Yes, Sir!" Andy replied.

"And… let me know as soon as our agents are found! I don't want a field trial over there!"

"Will do," Andy said and clicked off.

A man stepped into Reed's office escorted by Edwards who introduced him: "This is Rob… what did you say your name was again?"

"Rob Walton, MI6," the chubby man in a black suit, with wire-rimmed glasses and gray hair, said, introducing himself. "Here to assist with the detainees…"

"Oh, you're the druggie," Reed said. "Nice of you to show up. Mike, please take him to the cells but wait for my signal before you interrogate."

When Edwards and the interrogator left the room, Reed proceeded to question Harriet and Olga about the two suspects.

"Anything else of interest before we hand them over to these MI6 guys," he said with distaste.

"Boris totally denied any knowledge of Tompkins's murder, Prince William's abduction, or the bombings," Harriet said. "He contends they were tourists who rented an apartment for two weeks and got caught in the city when the attacks began. Said they had lost their passports in the chaos near Oxford Circus and were waiting for a reissue from their embassy only no one is providing any service at this time there."

"Did you question him about the phone?"

"Not yet, I was waiting to consult with you guys before I went ahead with it but I don't foresee making too much headway. I doubt these guys will confess to anything of use… unless we force it out of them."

"It could be a dead end…" Reed suggested.

"I don't think so." Harriet contended, "Not with this phone I found. They have something to hide, I am just not sure what it is but…"

She stopped looking at her colleagues before she went on. "The guy who answered the phone…"

"Yeah, what about him?" Reed urged.

"I hope you don't think less of me but I had a premonition that I have heard that voice before. And not too long ago. I just can't place it."

"What about your guy Olga?" Reed asked, moving on. "Any discrepancies?"

"No. Vitaly related a similar account," Olga confirmed to Reed's dismay.

"So, either they were well prepared or we're going down the wrong trail." Reed surmised.

"But the phone…" Harriet started to say.

"You let the druggie deal with that," Reed directed. "Meanwhile, did you have the two numbers checked out?"

"Yes, we did," Olga volunteered. "Both are pay-as-you-go numbers impossible to trace the owners."

"I wouldn't expect anything else," Reed said in frustration. "OK, go back to the cells, brief the druggie and let him do his stuff. Hopefully, he'll get something out of them. And Harriet, if you do recall the man's voice, do let us know."

The two agents rose from Reed's sofa and left the room.

Chapter Forty-One

2 PM, Wednesday, February 6, 2019

Jemma stood with her legs spread above the running water and steadied each person as she or he passed over the little waterfall, preventing them from skidding on the slippery surface. Noah and Bond were ahead, already climbing the narrow chasm above the water, making their way up expertly along the nooks and crannies of the gorge's walls.

In front of them, to the northwest, the expanse was heavily forested, with dense vegetation adorning the hills around them. It provided a much-needed sanctuary but made the going sluggish and extremely demanding.

They had boarded the train at Freshford, splitting into smaller groups; Barry with Noah and Mary, Jake and Jemma with their two girls, Bond with Camilla, and Blake with Cindy and her two boys, making sure they had eye contact with one another on the train. The early morning trains were quite empty so they had no problem finding seats from which they could observe the entrances to watch for any sign of trouble. They all got off at Gloucester and boarded a second train to Berry Hill where they disembarked and made for the sanctuary of the Wye Valley. They began trekking toward the border with Wales, an area the three B's, Barry, Bond, and Blake, were quite familiar with from their military days and knew would provide them a host of hiding places and would buy them time.

So far, the kids had no trouble, but both Barry and Blake were glued to Mary and Camilla who experienced difficulties and had to be constantly helped, Cindy, Jemma, and Jake, assisted wherever they could.

"Watch that rock, it looks slippery," Jemma called after Gabi, her eldest daughter, as she began climbing, leading her sister Zoe, and the two boys, Colin and Ian, in the footsteps of the two-point men who stopped for a moment to give climbing instructions to their flock below. It was quite dangerous and rough going, but the only route they could make reasonable headway and leave minimum tracks.

They had been trekking for almost two hours, keeping to the forested areas, avoiding obvious trails, and sticking to the many creeks flowing with water. On two occasions they heard a chopper flying over but did not see it remaining still and hidden until it passed.

They had no particular destination in mind but strived to lose themselves in the thick bush and remain hidden for as long as possible, hoping their pursuers would eventually lose interest or enough time would elapse for Frosty to bail them out. The longer they remain at large, the more time they allow Frosty to exonerate himself and expose the real culprits, or so it seemed. Knowing what's at stake, they might also expect the whole lot of them to be wasted and left to rot in the woods.

Atop a rolling hill gorge, Bond could see the forest stretching endlessly in all directions. They had reached a ridge that stretched east to west, with a wide valley below, and a parallel ridge to the north roughly three clicks away. He took out his binoculars and surveyed the ridge and the valley below spotting a clearing just below the top and what seemed like a narrow trail leading to it from below.

Noah was helping the others clear the last hurdle to the top, a slippery step roughly a meter high. The bereaved Camilla looked utterly spent. She wore a parka coat over a hooded sweatshirt Cindy had given her, her pretty face wet and smeared with mud, her hands scratched red from the climbing effort. Mary was being tended to by her husband as she slumped on the ground trying to catch her breath. Gabi and Colin were sharing a secret away from the group, seated on a boulder facing the valley while Zoe and Ian were desperately trying to join them but unable to find room on the boulder.

Jake walked over to where Bond stood and was joined there by Blake, Barry, Jemma, and Cindy.

"I am thinking we should aim for that clearing over there," Bond said, pointing in the direction of the ridge across the valley. Barry and Blake took out their binoculars and Bond gave Jake his.

"Think we could make it there before dark?" Jemma asked after she and Cindy had a look through the glasses.

"It's rough terrain down and through the valley but there's a trail that leads up there from down below," Bond said. "If we could make it to the trail, before dark, we should be OK."

"I suggest we grab a bite to eat and continue on," Blake said. "It's two O'clock now so we'll need to be moving quite soon if we want to make it there before dark."

"What's wrong with staying here?" Mary asked, then coughed loudly.

"If someone's after us then we have to assume they'll pick up our trail sooner or later," Blake explained. "We need to keep moving otherwise we'll be sitting ducks. The people after us are good, very good, and they'll eventually get to where we are. The question is how long and at what cost because whatever resources are used to track us, are resources missing somewhere else. Someone may eventually decide that we are not worth the effort."

Camilla got up from her spot and walked over to the group to listen in. Everyone turned to look at her. Her eyes were tearful and her face damp but she looked determined.

"These guys will kill us if they catch us," she said. "I am a liability to them for sure and they would have killed me had it not been for..." She paused, fighting another emotional outburst, her eyes filling up with tears again. "...If it had not been for Reuben, god rest his soul, springing me out of that awful dungeon."

Jemma moved to her, hugging her shoulders. She had informed Camilla of their suspicions on the few occasions the young woman had calmed down sufficiently to comprehend what was happening around her and was encouraged to see her speak up, though she did not share Camilla's ominous insight.

"They are after Frosty and me," Jemma said, "especially Frosty who had been set up. I doubt they would have put in much effort going after us if they knew Frosty was absent."

"Well, things have evolved, love," Cindy addressed Jemma. "They could use us as bait..."

"I wouldn't put anything past these people, considering the fuss they have kicked up so far," Jake interjected.

"I wish there was a way to contact Frosty," Cindy remarked, looking over at the kids amusing themselves around their gigantic boulder.

"We have a SAT phone," Blake related, "but I wouldn't advise using it."

"They'll be on to us in a flash," Jemma said, and everyone nodded.

"So, we better get moving," Bond said, picking up his backpack and turning to leave.

"You OK there, Mary?" He asked. "Need a hand?"

Mary stretched her hand out and Bond helped her up steadying her until she regained her balance.

"You stick to Barry, and you should be fine," he said and vanished in the vegetation, Noah and the kids following behind.

Chapter Forty-Two

3 PM, Wednesday, February 6, 2019

Andy White found Harry Fleming at his favorite fishing post, sitting on a folding chair dressed in a heavy coat and a wool hat on a wooded pier that protruded out into the Atlantic, his fishing rod stuck in a slit between two planks of the wooden railing that swayed in the wind.

Fleming was not surprised to see him, walking briskly toward where he sat, across the grassy domain towards the shoreline in the back of the nursing home. He had been warned by Mike Devlin who recommended he split, but Fleming was past fleeing or hiding from anyone.

White climbed down the few small steps to the little pier and stood above the frail Group Captain who turned his head and looked out to sea.

"You've been assisting a rouge agent," White accused without preamble, sticking his hands in his coat pockets as the wind picked up.

"And who may you be?" Fleming asked into the wind, avoiding the man's gaze.

"Andy White, SO1," White introduced himself, taking out his badge which Fleming ignored.

"Why was Tompkins killed?" Fleming asked, looking into the wind. "To make room for Dixon? Or did he figure out by himself you guys were traitors?"

"We needed him out of the way," White said dryly. "Dixon's nomination was an added bonus."

"Do you even know who Dixon is?" Fleming asked in a harsh tone.

"No need to," White said. "All I need to know is that the people who abandoned me pay up," White said.

"Well let me tell you anyway," Fleming said, staring at White in disgust.

White remained standing, looking at Fleming, making no comment but seemingly curious.

"Dixon is part of a group that was trained in Lebanon to spy on us." Fleming began. "He is actually English, but brainwashed since he was a baby."

White suddenly looked perplexed. "That's a load of bull," he exclaimed. "How can that be?"

"He was kidnapped from here, London I mean, when he was a year old, smuggled to Beirut, trained there, and was sent back when he was sixteen. And he wasn't the only one. Kruger was one as well and there are more in Europe and the US we don't even know about."

"That's even more grandiose," White mocked, dismissing the notion.

"We freed three kids from there in 1996," Fleming said. "It's true!"

"So where are the rest?"

"Frosty leads a special task force, which I established, that has been looking for these sleepers for over twenty years," Fleming emphasized. "The only one ever found was Kruger, and he didn't know a whole lot. He may even have been sacrificed to check our awareness."

"So, Dixon is one of these sleeper agents you say?" White reiterated skeptically.

"Did he ever tell you his background? Did you ever ask or check before you fell in with him?"

"The 'Sons of Jihad' you mean?" White said dismissively. "Of course, I know of them."

"And were you ever told some were babies kidnapped from the west?"

"No," White admitted.

"So regardless, you cooperated with a group called 'Sons of Jihad' without any qualms? You, a British citizen!"

"I was left for dead by my own unit in Afghanistan and then thrown to the dogs!" White said menacingly. "I owe this country nothing!"

"And don't you realize you were set up for this many years ago without even knowing you were? You were the perfect target for these people, and you fell right into their trap."

White did not reply. Instead, he took out his revolver and proceeded to screw a silencer onto it.

"I need you to tell me where Agent Frost is!" he finally said, pointing the gun at Fleming who did not flinch.

"Do you honestly think I would betray the only person who could stop this madness?" he exclaimed, looking at White with derision.

"Give me your phone!" White ordered, cocking the gun and aiming at Fleming's head.

"I don't have one…" Fleming started to say when White pulled the trigger.

Fleming's head flew backward hurling his entire body off the pier through the meager railing and onto the rocks below. White jumped down, checked for a pulse, then frisked the Group Captain finding nothing but a small bag with some hooks in Fleming's coat's pocket. He rolled the body under the pier and walked away failing to notice the mobile phone, set on record, stuck in a makeshift pocket underneath Fleming's folding chair.

******

Olga barged into Reed's office without knocking.

"They are dead!" she exclaimed. "The both of them!"

Reed, hovering over his computer screen, looking at Google Maps of the Wye Valley area, looked up with concern.

"What? Who's dead?" he questioned, uncomprehendingly, still pondering over the information provided to him by Taylor from the search center near Bath.

"The Ukrainians," Olga said out of breath.

"The druggie…" Reed stood up in alarm. "The detainees? Dead…?"

"He poisoned them and left the building," Olga said, as Reed stormed past her on his way to the cell blocks.

He found the doors ajar, the two suspects slumped in their seats, foaming at the mouth, unconscious, two medics futilely trying to revive them. As Reed entered they both stood shaking their heads.

Reed looked over at Olga, who looked shocked and embarrassed, her pretty face whiter than normal.

"Where's Harriet and Edwards?" he barked.

"Ran out after him," Olga replied. "He had a five-minute head start before we realized what was happening."

"How could this happen?" Reed looked at his agent in frustration. "What exactly happened?"

"He explained that he was giving them the 'truth serum' and that it would take a few minutes to go into effect. After he injected them, he excused himself to the restroom and that was the last we saw of him. They started foaming at the mouth after about three minutes. We ran in and called the medics, then searched for him and saw him leaving the building on the building's video playback about a minute after he left here."

Reed stood a minute, perplexed, looking at the two bodies being dragged to the floor by the medics.

"Harriet and Edwards alerted everyone and ran after him…" Olga continued when her phone rang. She answered and put on the speaker.

"Olga," Harriet was saying out of breath. "He ran toward the Tube, at Embankment… we're not sure where he is."

They could hear her breathing as she nearly choked trying to relay the information. "We were too late… Get the guys to monitor all Northern line's northbound exists…"

"But the Northern line isn't operating," Olga reminded her. "They activated only the circle and metropolitan lines this morning."

"You're right, I forgot!" Harriet admitted out of breath. "Is Reed informed?"

"I am right here, Harriet," Reed said out loud, "Edwards with you?"

"Yes, he is, Sir," Harriet said, catching her breath. "We screwed up…"

"Come back here and we'll reorganize," Reed said in a controlled tone. "No point chasing him around. What's done is done. We'll look for him around Embankment on the street cameras."

He looked at Olga who hurried out of the cell blocks to the main grid to relay the instructions, then scooted over the bodies for a better look. Both were pale white, obviously of Russian descent.

"Strip them!" Reed commanded the two medics who by now had both bodies in one cell looking over them. They both looked up in surprise but did as instructed.

When both bodies were fully naked, lying on their backs, Reed scrutinized them carefully then ordered them to turn over and instantly noticed identical tattoos on their lower backs. Taking out his phone, he photographed the tattoos and turned to leave.

"Get them to the morgue," he ordered and hurried out.

Harriet, Edwards, and Olga were in his office waiting. He showed Olga the photo of the tattoos wondering about their meaning. Olga took one look and knew what they were.

"Ukrainian Security Service, the SBU," she said with authority.

"But these are prison tattoos, aren't they?" Harriet commented looking over her shoulder.

"Similar, yes, but not exactly," Olga said.

"They all have them?" Reed asked.

"Not sure, but I've seen a few of these, not all identical but similar. Some agents in the KGB had them as well." Olga said.

"So, the Ukrainian Secret Service is in on this?" Edwards asked, perplexed. "Why would they show up here?"

They all looked at Reed who considered letting them in on what he had heard from Bishop but decided against it.

"Olga, take the photos and find out who these blokes are and if they are indeed members of the SBU!" Reed instructed and turned to Harriet and Edwards.

Olga ran out of the room.

"Any luck tracking the chap?" He inquired.

"Not so far," Harriet said, an embarrassed look on her face. "Should we organize a search team?"

"Never mind that for now," Reed dismissed the notion. "I need you two to fly up to Wye country…"

"Wye country?" Edwards questioned, raising his eyebrows.

"Yes, apparently Frosty, Jemma, and their group took flight up there. Taylor just called before this Boris debacle happened. He is at the search center near Bath. Special ops teams were sent up to Wye country to track them down."

"How do we get there?" Harriet asked.

"I've ordered a copper. It should be landing on the roof any minute now. Take your weapons and get up there quickly. I'll have Lucy and Chapman go after the assassin. You two need to get to Frosty before anyone else does."

Chapter Forty-Three

9 PM, Wednesday, February 6, 2019

The descent had been even more difficult than the climb.

Mary held on to Barry for dear life but Camilla seemed to have gotten a second wind and kept up with Noah and the kids up front. Most of the descent was performed on their rear ends from bush to bush, tree trunk to tree trunk, and down wet surfaces of water drops that at times became like waterslides in a natural amusement park, sliding several meters down a slippery gully, Bond and Noah stopping their forward progress so as not to allow them to gather speed and be hurled further down the slope.

They reached the bottom two hours later and began to trek along a narrow water channel that drew in the smaller streams flowing from above. The forest became even thicker at the bottom, the sun unseen as the dense foliage obstructed its rays from filtering through.

And it was becoming dark, slowing forward progress almost to a crawl. Bond, Blake, and Barry put on their infrared gear, a thermal imaging camera, strapped to their eyes. But everyone else was practically blind. Noah, at the front, asked whether he could use a flashlight intermittently to allow the rest to pass problematic obstacles, but Bond relented, explaining that such flashes of light could easily be detected from above or from any vantage point by anyone looking for them.

Bond pushed forward trying to locate the path he had seen from above that led up the next ridge to the clearing they had spotted. He relied mostly on his sense of direction since the forest swallowed the few salient landmarks, he thought he had detected from above.

After a while, he decided to cross the stream and begin climbing hoping to intersect with the path leading to the clearing. They stopped for a much-needed rest, ate whatever rations were left, filled their water bottles from the stream, and continued to climb diagonally up the next ridge.

Both Barry and Jake had to assist Mary, who was weakening considerably and practically carried her up the slope with Blake who was bringing up the rear, assisting whenever needed. Cindy and Jemma walked behind Camilla who proved quite nimble and kept up the pace with the lead group of four kids, Noah and Bond. At several spots, they had to lift themselves up using tree roots and branches and at other spots, they had to bypass large boulders stuck in their path.

It was very slow going and they rested every few minutes making sure all were present until Bond reached the path that shot almost vertically up the ridge and though it provided a clear trail forward, its steepness proved no less difficult and once again they had to stop and rest every few minutes.

After six grueling hours, they made it to the clearing in total darkness and found a passel of boulders at one end, at the edge of the tree line, where it felt safe to stop and prepare for the night. Bond, Blake, and Jemma continued to the top of the clearing to survey the surroundings beyond the top of the ridge.

"That would be the river Wye," Bond said pointing at a dark snake-like channel in the distance to their right. "We have been heading north-north-west all this time so the border with Wales should be roughly three kilometers from here as the crow flies."

They rejoined the group who were slumped between the boulders fast asleep except for Barry and Cindy who were standing watch and updated them on what they could expect in the morning which was essentially more of the same. Then they divided the watch duties between them, two to a shift, every two hours, and retired to a much-needed sleep.

The dark figures appeared an hour later.

******

Barry went down without as much as a hiss as the bullet struck his forehead and exited the back of his head.

Cindy, who had left her post for a minute to go check on Zoe who was making noises in her sleep, found him sprawled on the ground bleeding to death and was about to shout out when a gloved hand covered her mouth and nose and she lost consciousness in a matter of seconds.

Blake managed to see the barrel of the silencer pointed at him before he was shot dead at point-blank range, and Bond was apprehended by two figures in black who cuffed his hands behind his back and tied his feet together.

The rest, kids and adults, were sat on the wet grass around the unconscious Cindy, all shivering and huddled together, as several men in black outfits took positions around them, weapons at the ready.

Not a word was spoken.

Cindy began to come around, whispering her daughter's names. Jemma holding her head in her lap stroked her hair; Gabi and Zoe who were worriedly watching her, curled up next to their mom.

The ghosts in black stood without moving looking up to the sky as a faint hum became noticeable and soon a large helicopter was swooping into the clearing, the wind from his blades tilting the trees around them. As soon as it made contact with the grass, opening its sliding doors, the group was herded harshly toward the flying beast, Bond being dragged along by two of the men.

It took no more than three minutes before the helicopter lifted up into the air and took off low over the trees, carrying its load of captives and hijackers. Down below, a large contingent of the black ghosts remained to clean up the mess.

An hour later, they landed in a clearing somewhere to the east of Wye, refueled from a large drum that had been carried inside the chopper, left it on the ground, and continued for another hour before landing in a dark field. The group was ordered out of the helicopter and was rushed several hundred meters across uneven terrain to a large wooden cottage in a forested area on the banks of a small lake and herded in. Bond's handcuffs and feet were released; he and Jemma were separated from the rest and steered into a side room where a man in civilian clothes stood waiting for them.

The man was tall and scrawny, with a wad of red hair, his face gaunt with bulging eyes and a long chin. He gestured for them to sit on two wooden stools in front of a small desk and took his place behind the desk on a swiveling office chair.

Two of the operatives stood guard near the door with their weapons ready and cocked.

"Did you disconnect all their phones and any likely tracking devices?" the man asked the guards.

"Took all the SIM cards and batteries out as soon as we had them, before boarding the chopper, Sir," one of the guards acknowledged. "Searched for tracking devices but found none."

The man nodded his approval and turned his attention to his captives.

"We need to find your colleague," he said, addressing Jemma wearily as if he wasn't about to accept denial for long. "He's key to our cause."

"And what cause might that be?" Jemma shot back angrily.

"You've seen the tapes on the television, haven't you?" the man reminded her.

Jemma didn't reply. She lowered her gaze to the floor and remained rigid, unwilling to acknowledge the foe.

"Now see here," the man continued, "we've now got his wife and his kids..." He went silent, looking at his two captives.

"We have no idea where he is," Bond informed him, taking up the slack.

"Is there a phone he can be reached at?" the man continued coldly.

"There's not," Bond replied.

"So how does he contact you? Surely you're in contact."

"He uses pay phones," Bond said. "Never revealing his whereabouts."

The man indicated to one of the guards in the back who exited the room and then came back with two of the mobile phones that had been confiscated at the ambush site.

The man held up Jemma's and Cindy's mobiles. "Does he contact you or his wife?" he asked.

Jemma looked up, fighting to hold her temper.

"One of us, Mr. White," she said as calmly as she could.

"And you, Mr. Zachary Bond, how did you get mixed up in all this?" White asked, ignoring Jemma's mention of his name.

"I keep an eye out for troublemakers like you," Bond retorted.

"Well, apparently you didn't do a very good job!" White derided.

"You don't expect to pull this off, do you?" Jemma remarked.

"Why we already have, or haven't you noticed?" White said calmly with a chuckle. "Now all that we need is to find that rouge colleague of yours and we've got it made, don't you agree?"

"It would not make any difference if you caught him," Jemma said. "Other people know the truth already."

"We've taken care of them," White maintained. "It's your colleague and the lot of you we need to worry about and since you all are here, it leaves him."

White's mobile phone rang. He fished for it in his jacket's inner pocket and hurried to leave the room leaving the two guards to watch over the captives.

Outside the small office, the group was huddled together. The kids lay in a row, eyes shut, clutching one another, their frightened faces awash with tears; Noah and Mary were hugging each other trying to gain strength from the horrors they had witnessed; Cindy and Camilla were talking in hushed voices.

"You recognize anyone?" Cindy whispered, looking up at their captors who had taken off their black masks and were milling around the room.

"The one that's with Jemma and Bond," Camilla said. "He was the one who interrogated me."

"Yeah, I recognize him too," Cindy whispered. "That's Andy White and he's with SO1."

"What's SO1?" Camilla asked.

"It's the specialist protection branch responsible for protecting dignitaries and the like and it looks as if they've all been recruited."

"But how's that possible?" Camilla marveled.

"We've been trying to prevent this for twenty years," Cindy admitted sadly. "It's obviously Dixon's doing first and foremost but how was this kept under wraps for so long I have no idea."

A tall man in a muddy flying suit and helmet was escorted into the cottage by two guards with White leading the way. His head and face were completely concealed by the helmet, yet everyone stopped and stared as he was led into the small office.

"Is that…?" Camilla whispered, looking hard at Cindy who looked up then lowered her gaze as the entourage disappeared into the adjacent room where Bond and Jemma had been taken.

"It must be…" Cindy whispered back, caressing Zoe's hair unconsciously.

Both Jemma and Bond stood up instinctively when they saw who it was underneath the pilot's helmet.

"Your Haines…" Jemma blurted in surprise as Prince William flashed a weary smile at them.

"Sir…" Bond uttered, bowing his head.

Prince William looked fatigued; his flying suit muddy, his face gaunt with dark circles under his eyes, but his look was still as determined as it seemed in the videos that had been broadcast worldwide.

"Well, your Haines," White said with contempt as he took his seat behind the small desk, "you now have company."

Prince William turned to him. "You better not harm these children," he said firmly, speaking quietly but with a great deal of authority.

"I will do no such thing provided they give me what I want," White retorted.

Prince William sighed. "You're not done ruining this country?" he remarked.

White ignored the remark. "I want their colleague who's running around the country threatening our cause."

Prince William looked at Jemma and Bond as if expecting clarification.

"He's a colleague, who they set up to take the fall for all this, only he got away and found them out," Jemma quickly said.

"We're hoping he'll expose this scheme…" Bond said then suddenly went quiet.

White sat back looking amused as the two agents nervously glanced from him to the Prince wondering how much they should expose.

"The more you know, your Haines, the less likely you'll get out of here alive," White remarked. "We could not afford to let you lose if you know too much."

"You can't afford to let me loose. Period!" Prince William pointed out bravely.

"That's not for me to decide," White replied. "Now, I need you to convince these two to give up their man or else suffer the consequences."

Prince William turned toward the two agents. "Don't be afraid for my safety now," he said reassuringly. "I am as compromised as I'll ever be so go on, tell me," he encouraged, but both Bond and Jemma realized instantly that they were putting the Prince in mortal danger if they kept talking so they clammed up.

"They know what's good for them," White said. "If it ever gets out they compromised you, they'll be locked up for life and then some."

"Sir," Jemma said, "I am afraid on this point he's right. I am sworn to keep you out of harm's way at any cost…"

"And what does this look like to you?" Prince William said irritably. "Could I be in more danger than this? If you fill me in maybe I can negotiate with these hotheads."

"If I fill you in, Sir, you may not survive this," Jemma insisted, "you not knowing, they may negotiate your release after all."

"And if you hand over your colleague," White called out from behind his desk. "You'll be getting the Prince a step closer to freedom."

Prince William sighed for a second time. Frustrated, he turned to White. "I will not allow them to hand over the agent, you hear!"

"Loud and clear Your Excellency, so unfortunately that leaves me his kin to deal with." White pointed out.

It seemed Prince William was going to lose his cool but he held back, sighing for a third time, and turned to Jemma. "Do you know where he is?"

"No idea, Sir," Jemma said. "Mr. White here knows it but seems to think I can do the impossible. I have no idea where he is."

"Yeah, I do know that," White admitted, "but I also know he calls you up from time to time, so I want to make sure that when he calls next, you tell him to give himself up for the sake of our beloved Prince here and for the sake of his kids."

"She will do no such thing!" Prince William retorted. "I won't agree to that!"

"Well, you have no say," White pointed out to him, "the best you can hope for is that he realizes what his colleagues here just realized and comes in."

"I'll do it if you free William," Jemma suddenly said. "He will come in, in exchange for the Prince."

"And all of the children I saw outside," Prince William added before White had time to digest.

White became quiet. He looked at his men who remained passive, then got up and moved to the door.

"Come with me," he ordered Prince William, who was manhandled by his two bodyguards. He stopped at the entrance and addressed the agents. "Stay strong," he said and was escorted out.

Chapter Forty-Four

11 PM, Wednesday, February 6, 2019

Frosty sat frozen, watching the television screen above the bar, as a newsflash reported the alleged murder of an ex-high-ranking Airforce officer at his nursing home near Brighton.

A nurse had found the body under a pier after Group Captain Fleming failed to show up for the four O'clock tea which he rarely missed, according to his wife, who became worried and sent the nurse to the pier where Group Captain Fleming frequently spent time fishing. He was found lying in a pool of blood under the wooden pier.

The Brighton police were investigating but so far there were no indications to point to any suspects or a motive in Fleming's death.

Frosty gulped the rest of his espresso and ordered a double shot of whiskey.

Sitting on a stool across from Frosty, Dylan Oliver watched him cautiously, realizing Frosty was stunned by the news, but he waited patiently not wanting to push further and upset him more than he already seemed.

They had arrived at Paddington train station late afternoon from Blackpool via Manchester having traveled most of the day, hopping off trains and changing carts, and were now seated at the Mitre Pub on Craven Terrace, a ten-minute stroll from Paddington Station; the only pub they found open in the area where they took a booth hidden from the front entrance, ordered dinner and were drinking their coffees when the newsflash aired.

Frosty gulped down the whiskey and ordered another.

"That's the guy I met down there," he finally said, "a long-time colleague and a dear friend. I guess they saw me there…"

"If they saw you there, they would have picked you up, wouldn't they? Why let you go and go after your colleague?"

Frosty considered it for a minute. It made sense. Whoever did it, had not seen him there, but knew enough to try and obtain information from Fleming who surely wouldn't give him away and paid the ultimate price for it.

Suddenly he was up on his feet hurrying to the pay phone for the third time since they had reached London. He kept getting a disconnected signal on both Cindy's and Jemma's phones and he was getting worried.

This time Jemma answered on the first ring.

"Everything OK?" Frost asked.

"Don't hang up!" Jemma said and, in a second, a man's voice came on the line.

"Agent Frost, this is Andy White. You got one chance to save your family, so you need to listen to this."

"Son of a…" Frosty said to himself but tried to keep his cool. "What do you want?"

"An exchange," White said, "your family and Prince William, for you."

"I want to talk to my wife!" Frosty demanded.

"You will if you agree," White said.

"I agree to nothing unless you put her on the line."

There was some shuffling and finally Cindy came on line. "Hey, Frosty, it's me." He heard her say and managed to relax his clenched jaws.

"You OK, love?" he asked, concerned. "Where are you?"

"I can't say, honey, but we're OK. The kids are OK. Jake and Jemma are OK as well. The Prince is here…"

She did not finish the sentence when White came back on the line.

"You heard her, now you listen to me," he said, outlining his demands, leaving Frosty little choice but to go along with the scheme.

******

Frosty walked the dark deserted streets of Bayswater, his steps echoing across the brick face sidewalks. He reached Bayswater Road and crossed into Hyde Park by a darkened Kensington castle where he stood under a large tree watching the dark grassy clearing.

The chopper didn't take long. It came down in a flurry shining a powerful searchlight on the landing zone before its skids hit the ground.

Frosty approached carefully, trying to ascertain whether whoever was coming out of the sliding doors was who they agreed upon. As he neared the helicopter, he could just make out the kids being smaller than the adults around them. He stopped several steps away and then walked into the light. Cindy saw him first, then Gabi and Zoe who were about to run to him, when he froze in place, then collapsed on the grass.

A wild shriek resonated above the rotor blades holler and across the empty park as Cindy ran to him, but she was caught from behind by the men in black who hustled everyone back on the chopper and took off.

******

Dylan Oliver reached the grid at about the time the chopper was taking off from its encounter with Frosty.

White had given Frosty an hour to make the exchange location and warned him not to try and make contact with anyone since they had all mobile phones and offices tapped and if a phone call was intercepted, they would abort. What he did not know was the existence of Oliver who was asked by Frosty to go and report, at considerable risk to himself. Frosty had decided against calling Reed on his mobile and they had rehearsed what Dylan would say so that he would be believed. Frosty had added a written note to AVM Reed outlining his proof, but it was a big risk Dylan was taking if he would be deemed a fraud.

A further worry was who would receive Dylan at the entrance and if he would be allowed to see Reed, who Frosty insisted was the only one he should report to.

Dylan stood at the Northumberland entrance below the wide steps and signaled to the cameras he wanted to enter. A loud metallic click was heard after the better part of three minutes as the heavy metal door opened and two armed guards came out.

"Your name?" One of the guards asked, approaching him down the stairs while the other remained by the door with a machine gun pointed at Oliver.

"Dylan Oliver," Dylan said and produced his expired Blackpool prison credentials which were looked over carefully by the guard.

"There's no entrance here," the guard said. "State your business."

"I am here to see Air Vice Marshal Alan Reed. It's urgent!" Dylan said with as much authority as he could muster.

The guard, trained to deny the existence of any MI5 or the Task Force Bureau personnel, waved him off and turned to go.

"Tell him Frosty sent me!" Dylan called out as the guard began to climb the steps back toward the entrance. The guard turned and hurried back down.

"Who did you say sent you?" he said in a threatening tone.

"Agent Adrian Frost," Dylan said without hesitation. "The one you are all looking for."

The guard, who was under strict orders to report any mention of the infamous missing agent, reached for his phone.

"Please don't do that," Dylan said quietly. "You need to go get him. I'll wait here."

The guard, phone in hand, looked at Dylan with a mixture of anger and surprise, then proceeded to dial, ignoring the request.

"Phones are all tapped, and you don't want this call to be intercepted," Dylan advised patiently.

The guard looked at him hard again and seemed to be debating within himself whether to trust the man or dismiss him as a lunatic. Dylan's quiet demeanor and unwavering stare never swayed from the guard who slowly shut his phone and ran up the stairs to alert the troops.

******

They found Frosty's body lying on its side, blood dripping from a hole in his back, and quickly called in a medical team.

Reed, who was driven in the lead car with Dylan and Olga, had felt a weak pulse when he reached him and immediately signaled for the ambulance in the back of the procession of unmarked agency cars and police vehicles who stormed in and took positions around the clearing hoping to retrieve the Prince and the other captives.

But all they found was rogue agent Adrian Frost, left for dead.

Once the initial excitement faded to colossal disenchantment, Reed retreated to his car, locked its doors, and began to drill Dylan, something he had not had time to do when Dylan informed him of the pending exchange and they all rushed to the spot.

Dylan, who was himself on the verge of tears, sat dejected in the back of the car and recounted his time with Frosty who had come to Digital Solutions looking to find out Kruger's mystery guest who had used Frosty's identity.

"I was the guy Frosty was looking for to identify the man who impersonated him at Blackpool prison visiting Kruger six months ago."

"It wasn't Frosty?" Reed inquired, surprised. "His TFB ID was used."

"His ID was certainly used but it wasn't him," Dylan said matter-of-factly.

"And how would you know that?" Reed insisted.

"Because I was the guy who deleted the tape. I saw the man who was there, and it wasn't your agent."

"Who was it then?" Reed asked, a sickening feeling developing in the pit of his stomach.

Dylan looked at the TFB head and shook his head. "It was Ross Dixon. Frosty was framed."

Reed froze looking hard at the man whose gaze never wavered. "You mean…"

"Yes, that's who I mean," Dylan acknowledged without hesitation. "Your SO1 head. The man you've been searching for, for twenty years."

Reed sat back with a sigh and looked out the window at the commotion outside. The ambulance with his dying agent had taken off in a flurry with police cars clearing the way, allowing police teams to search the area. He could see Olga directing traffic but knew they would not find anything of value. It was all becoming very clear to him now, only he didn't know how to go about it. The bombshell that had just been thrown in his lap, had repercussions far beyond clearing Frosty.

It was the principal reason they were blindsided and had not managed to deal with the crisis. The SO1 regime was in a prime position to cause such damage and make sure it stuck. It was his primary responsibility to flush out the sleeper agents that had been lurking since the early 90s, and he had failed. They all failed, Frosty and Bishop included. His entire TF bureau had failed. MI5 and MI6 failed.

Their primary specialist protection branch had been breached at the highest level and had thrown the kingdom into hell.

He looked over at Dylan who was studying him intently.

"Why didn't he come to me?" Reed asked in frustration.

"Do you really expect me to answer that?" Dylan said.

"No, I don't," Reed sighed. "And I guess there is no way to fix that now."

Chapter Forty-Five

1 AM, Thursday, February 7, 2019

Reed snatched his phone and rang Bishop.

"Trevor, you need to come here right now!" He said without preamble when he heard Bishop reply.

"We're trying to locate the chopper," Bishop said indignantly, having been monitoring events from MI5's grid.

"Drop everything and come here!" Reed insisted.

He heard Bishop sighing, trying to get a grip on the astonishing events of the last hour.

"What's this about that you cannot handle yourself or brief me over the phone?" he finally asked.

"No! No phones!" Reed seethed. "Just get in your car and drive. It should take you ten minutes."

Bishop sighed again, then Reed heard him distributing orders. "OK. I'll get Dixon and we'll be right there."

"No!" Reed hissed. "No Dixon. Just come alone."

"But…" Bishop started to protest but Reed cut him off.

"Please… just do as I ask!" he said and disconnected his phone.

He looked at Dylan then stepped out of the car walking briskly toward Olga who was talking on short-wave radio to the search teams with several police officers surrounding her. He tapped her on the shoulder and signaled for her to step aside with him.

"Seen any of Dixon's guys around?" he asked when they were away from the group.

"No, come to think of it, not yet, but they should be on their way…"

"Well, you let me know as soon as you spot them," Reed commanded. "I'll be in my car just there," he said, pointing to his black Rover parked to the side by some lofty trees.

"Anything I should be aware of?" Olga asked.

"Not yet, but soon. Just make sure you warn me as soon as they are here."

Olga nodded and walked back to the makeshift HQ they had set up on the spot where the helicopter with the captives had landed and taken off.

Reed walked back to his car. He leaned against its back side a moment watching the commotion on the small grassy hill in front of him, suspecting it was a waste of time, but wanting to question the SO1 guys before he drew a firm conclusion as to the inconceivable revelation Dylan had just shared with him.

He tried to piece together bits of information that had seemed odd, first and foremost, the assassination of the two Ukrainians by the imposter who had infiltrated the grid, and Dixon's insistence on Frosty's guilt, dismissing the notion that it was Frosty who had led them to two people of Russian descent who may have been involved, knowing full well the PM had received an ultimatum from the Kremlin.

The more he thought about it, the more it made sense, how Prince William could so effortlessly be abducted and how the investigation had come up against so many dead ends. Of course, it all started with the Tompkins assassination, for which reasons have yet to surface, however, that particular event ultimately led to Dixon's nomination and the five bombings that have paralyzed London and raged havoc in government.

Dylan came to stand by him. He pulled out a pack of cigarettes and offered one to Reed, who only smoked cigars at the gentlemen's club, but felt he could use one to ease the tension he felt.

Dylan produced a lighter and raised it up for Reed to light his cigarette when he noticed a trickle of blood on his hands and before realizing where it came from, felt a sharp crack to the back of his head and everything went dark.

******

Bishop reached the gathering of agents and police personnel, riding almost into their midst. His driver opened his window and asked for Reed's whereabouts. Olga was first to oblige pointing to Reed's Land Rover parked to the side by the trees, in the dark. Bishop's driver turned toward the spot Olga had pointed to, his headlights washing the SUV with light when they first noticed the two bodies in the back of it on the ground. Olga inhaled in surprise and sprinted down the grassy slope along with Bishop's car.

They found Reed seated with his back to the Land Rover, eyes open but blind to the world, a red hole in his forehead, and blood trickling down his face. The other man was lying in front of him, face down in a pool of blood, a larger hole in the back of his head. Olga quickly searched for a pulse on each man but found none. They alerted a second ambulance, parked at the entrance to the park, but the medics only confirmed what they all suspected. The head of the TFB and an unknown man were shot and killed. No one heard a thing.

Bishop stepped out of his car and looked down at his colleague in utter disbelief. More people showed up, police officers, MI5 agents, and a firefighter truck which flooded the scene with a blazing white light from a mounted searchlight.

The medics were making preparations to move the bodies but had to wait for the forensic team to show up before they could load them into the ambulance and take them to the morgue.

Dixon appeared out of nowhere surrounded by a detail of his men and looked at the carnage.

Bishop took him aside.

"I was coming to see him," he said when they were out of earshot of the cluster that had formed around the bodies. "He sounded mighty distraught. Asked me to hurry over, which I did, but not soon enough."

"Did he say what troubled him other than his agent being shot?" Dixon queried.

"No, would not talk over the phone. Insisted I come alone."

"I'll have my men comb the area," Dixon suggested. "We may find something of use, but I doubt it. This looks like a professional hit."

"He insisted I leave you behind," Bishop continued. "Any idea why he would not want you to be present when he obviously had stumbled upon something of value?"

It was dark and Bishop could not make out Dixon's facial expressions but the head of SO1 paused slightly before he answered.

"I guess he didn't feel I should be in the know," he observed. "He reports to you, not to me."

"Yes, but I offered to bring you and he was adamant I do not bring you along."

Once again Dixon hesitated but when he spoke he was utterly calm. "I guess we'll never know," he said and Bishop caught a hostile look in his eyes as they glinted against the light from the firetruck.

"Did you locate the chopper?" Bishop asked after a brief pause, as both men turned to look as the forensic team arrived.

"The only airframe flying away from London at the time flew east along the Thames for a while. We picked it up around Darford then lost it as it must have plunged low. My guess is it flew toward the channel. I asked the chief to send a squadron of Apaches after it."

"Why wasn't I informed?" Bishop demanded.

"You had just left the grid. I had informed the squadron and asked to send the posse when I was informed of the assault, so I came here."

"And are there any results? Who's running the Apaches?"

"The base commander is personally monitoring the search from Boscombe Down and two of my guys are on it as well from the grid."

"Reed's people know what's evolved?"

"Saw Reed's FSB woman over there talking on the phone so I assume they know by now," Dixon said, pointing his thumb back to the dreary scene.

"I want them all in my office when this mess is squared away!" Bishop said. "You make sure every piece of grass here is combed! I'll inform Scott and the PM."

"Shall I join you there?" Dixon asked.

Bishop hesitated slightly. "I am going to No.10 on my own but I do expect you to wait for me at the office with everyone else," he said then stormed toward his car.

Chapter Forty-Six

3 AM, Thursday, February 7, 2019

Edwards and Harriet arrived at the clearing in Wye country together with Andy Taylor at three in the morning. Taylor had requested they divert to the headquarters at Bath before continuing on north. He had finally managed to track the Sea Hawk squadron commander and wanted Edwards and Harriet in on the interview.

They met at a makeshift landing zone, near the Bath makeshift HQ, where choppers landed to refuel. A row of Jet Fuel trucks were parked to one side of the clearing, three of them were refueling the three King Sea helicopters parked on the other side, where the Eurocopter Dauphin chopper delivered Harriet and Edwards.

Wing Commander Connor Gilliam, in his flight suit, holding his helmet under his arm met them at a makeshift Cantina that had been erected by army personnel, a safe distance from the LZ. It served sandwiches and coffee to the pilots, flight engineers, maintenance personnel, and fuel truck drivers, and was the only decently lit site in the area.

They ordered coffee and moved away from the busy stall.

Taylor introduced them and quickly described to Gilliam what they derived from the clip of the London bombed sites shown by the terrorists on national TV.

"We have surmised the clip was taken from a Sea King helicopter flying over London, a day before the Prince was abducted."

Gilliam, a tall, gaunt man, with bushy dark hair and penetrating dark eyes, looked up toward his helicopters, digesting what he had heard. He sipped his coffee and looked thoughtful.

"My squadron has five choppers, three of which are here, one of which had just taken a team up to Wye country, and another back in the base for maintenance."

He said, "I will need to check my logbook but I am relatively sure we were flying sorties over London that day, though I cannot recall any specific routes."

"Who did you carry? What personnel?" Harriet asked.

"Oh, we carried mostly medical personnel, doctors and paramedics, and some wounded, if I recall. Those first few days were total chaos…"

"Was the Prince one of your pilots?" Harriet asked.

Gilliam looked suddenly hostile.

"I am not at liberty to divulge such information." He pointed out. "William's assignments are on a need-to-know basis only."

"Well, somebody must have known," Taylor remarked. "And we are looking for that person or persons."

Gilliam became annoyed. "Look I have orders not to discuss this with anyone," he hissed. "If you want disclosure talk to my chief."

"OK," Harriet said in a conciliatory tone, "just tell me this: On that day, other than paramedics and doctors, did you carry any other units?"

Gilliam looked thoughtful. "I believe we had one sortie with an SO1 team on board." He finally said. "Yes, I believe they wanted a tour of the sites…"

He suddenly stopped talking and looked at the three agents in horror. "You don't think…"

"I don't know what to think other than the fact that the video broadcast to millions was probably shot from one of your choppers," Harriet said.

"They were with me!" he blurted.

"Could they have shot a video from your bird without you or your men noticing it?" Edwards queried.

"Well, there's my co-pilot next to me, and the flight engineer in back. I am sure I would have been made aware had they noticed anything, but a video can be shot from an iPhone or an Android phone without us noticing it, for sure."

"And one last question," Andy Taylor said, seeing Gilliam dumping the rest of his coffee on the ground in disgust. "Assuming Prince William does fly for you. Does he have a detail of these Special Ops guys guarding him on board?"

"You don't expect me to tell you this, do you?" Gilliam said angrily and began to walk back to his chopper.

The three agents stood baffled when he turned to them and said: "But for your information, William didn't fly any sorties with us because he never made it to the squadron."

******

A contingent of Special Forces was searching the area when the three TFB agents made their way up to Wye country.

"We found two bodies," Group Captain Carter reported when the three agents disembarked from the helicopter. "Both are ex-SAS guys."

"Can we see their IDs?" Harriet asked as they were whisked to the crime scene.

"They had no IDs," the Group Captain informed them. "But we used face recognition, though one of them had lost a large part of his face."

"Who are they?" Harriet asked as they reached the bodies.

"Barry George age 48 and Tim Blake age 51. Both ex-SAS, both from Glasgow."

Harriet quickly wrote the information down in her WhatsApp and sent it to Reed's and Olga's numbers, before they all crouched to inspect the deceased under the Group Captain's flashlight.

"How long have you been up here?" Edwards asked when they straightened and moved away from the bodies.

"About two hours." the officer said.

"And who sent you here?" Harriet queried.

"We were looking for the fugitives down near Bath when I got a call from an SO1 team to rush up here. Apparently, they got here first."

"Do you recall who you talked to?" Edwards asked.

"Yeah, a bloke named Andy White; SO1 guy. I've been coordinating with him since day one," the Group Captain said, a little annoyed. "Don't you know the guy?"

"Oh, we know the guy," Harriet said. "But we didn't know he was the one handling you."

"Well, I figured since it was their bust losing the Prince, it would be their burden to get him back."

"It's everyone's burden, Group Captain," Harriet admonished. "The problem is we are no closer to finding him today than we were a week ago. Where is this SO1 team now? Are they here with your guys?"

"No, they left before we arrived."

"Now why would they do that?" Harriet asked.

"White informed me when we were airborne, they had gotten a lead and were relocating to pursue it. He gave me coordinates for this place and informed me of the two bodies. When we landed, they had already taken off."

"And where are they now? Do you know?" Taylor asked.

"Have not heard from them yet but I expect to hear any minute."

"Is there anything else of value here besides the bodies?" Harriet asked after an awkward moment.

"Not so far but my guys are still looking…" He did not complete the sentence when his mobile rang. He answered and listened intently, then handed it to Harriet. "It's for you," he said, looking glum.

It was Bishop sounding upset. "Reed's been killed," she heard him say causing her to catch her breath.

"Frosty's in intensive care barely alive," Bishop continued. "What we know is that Frosty was shot in Hyde Park, apparently by some hit team using a chopper. Reed and an unknown person with him, were shot and killed while investigating Frosty's shooting at the same spot."

She heard Bishop inhale. "I need you and whoever is with you to come to my office at once! We need to salvage this situation before there are any more killings."

"Right sir," Harriet heard herself say. "We'll leave right away," she said as if in a daze, and started running toward their chopper.

Chapter Forty-Seven

6 AM, Thursday, February 7, 2019

Frosty did make one phone call from the public phone booth before leaving the Mitre pub on his way to his rendezvous with death.

He called Mike Devlin.

Devlin, who, like most of England, became aware of Fleming's demise, decided he had sat idle long enough watching his country go to waste.

He was no longer an agile, 45-year-old, ex-SAS who kept in shape owing to his clandestine activity, but a rather heaver 67-year-old father to his beautiful 20-year-old Michelle, named after Sam's first wife, whom he and Ali had when she was 40.

His long SAS service and his intense activity in the later years with the late Joe Harley's outfit had given him all sorts of back problems, and after two herniated disc operations to his lower back, he was all but limited to very short walks with Ali's or Michelle's assistance, and he could not stand still for more than a minute. In fact, on several overseas trips, he had to be wheeled along large airport facades to get on and off airplanes.

His close mate and former sergeant, Lizzy O'Leary, who lived in Edinburgh, suffered a near-fatal heart attack several years back, and Malcolm Rolston, who lived with Mai-Li in New York, had lost a lung in a car accident in the Catskill mountains while on a leisurely weekend outing with Mai-Li who suffered only minor injuries. He had mostly lost contact with Jimmy the Driver who had moved to Alice Springs in Australia, a place so remote, it allowed him endless terrain for racing, mostly sport utility vehicles of all kinds. His other comrades, Long-John Evans and Lieutenant Brian Copeland, the communications experts from the Harley days, had both moved to the South Island of New Zealand, both marrying Kiwi girls.

In the waning years of the Harley outfit, it was Harry Fleming who had come up with the idea of merging the troops into MI6, a move strongly opposed by most founding members of the Harley team who wanted to keep the freedom to operate on their own terms, and not have to deal with the bureaucracy and long chains of command.

That had been the beginning of the end for the Harley outfit.

Fleming insisted and caused an irrevocable abyss between the British clandestine authorities and Devlin's men who resisted any government involvement in their business and who opted to retire rather than to merge with the British security services, a point of view they knew would have been applauded by Harley, had he been alive. To prove their point, they had performed, what turned out to be their last stint, a completely unauthorized operation against the IRA, abducting a top dissident in Belfast, and handing him over to MI6, a move that caused such a stir among the Irish rebels, that it ceased all peace talks for an entire year.

As a result, most of its founding members retired and became unwelcome personalities at No. 10 Downing Street, White Hall, and all of the security services that had supported their actions for so long. Devlin was asked to stay on for another year to transition the unit's merge into MI6, but he himself wanted nothing to do with it once the transition was complete.

Devlin and the majority of Harley's unit had disappeared off the grid and were no longer part of the efforts to uncover the "Sons of Jihad" sleeper agents who were always assumed to have remained in hiding, waiting to strike, but over the years, Devlin, Lizzy, and Malcolm Rolston had softened their position toward Fleming's Task Force Bureau efforts and had assisted when asked.

When Fleming had first approached him with Frosty's predicament, they had both agreed that Frosty would need concrete proof, such that he could use to convince Scott and the others, otherwise it would be his word against Dixon, which would not favor him being the one accused and gone AWOL.

Now that Fleming was dead, Devlin felt a strong sense of responsibility to pick up the slack and help eliminate the mammoth threat to his country, first and foremost by exposing Dixon.

Phone calls or internet communications, were out of the question, due to obvious tapping as Frosty had warned as well as immense loads on the security services phone and data lines, so Devlin decided to travel to London.

It was no simple decision for he knew Ali would need to come along and Michelle would never allow them to go without her. She had a stubborn streak like her mother, and he knew there was no way of keeping her from tagging along. It deeply worried him for it put them all in danger, but he did not see any other way he could make his suspicions known to the right people.

He and Fleming agreed that they would need to approach an influential figure in government or the Service to help convince the PM about Dixon. Devlin was concerned Frosty's arguments may be hampered well before it reached the right ears since SO1 had the means to keep people away and would probably not let anyone near the PM or the Home Secretary if they suspected someone could expose their leader.

Trevor Bishop, the MI5 head, was one man he could approach, and AVM Reed was another, but Devlin thought he should approach one of the ministers namely Nigel Scott the Home Secretary, or Defense Minister Sir Alistair Banks, neither of whom he had known on a personal basis but assumed his reputation would at least have them pay attention.

At six he was in his study preparing his arguments when Ali walked in, in jeans and a wool sweater, her hair still wet from the morning shower, ready to go over and have her morning coffee with her parents Beth and Martin, who lived in the big house across a wide clearing.

Devlin could not get enough of how fresh and vigorous she looked. At 60, Ali looked like she barely aged in twenty years, her face as pretty as ever, smooth as silk with only a few wrinkles around the eyes and down her neck, her posture straight, her body lean and sturdy, and her movements agile and effortless.

She smiled at him and gave him a kiss on the cheek, hugging him from behind.

"What's that look?" She whispered in his ear, kissing it, then kissing the back of his neck. "You seem worried," she said, leaning on his desk and studying his face.

"Frosty called me last night," he said, causing her to become instantly alert. "Said he was on his way to an exchange, himself for his family and the Prince."

"What!? Where? When?" She asked worriedly.

"At around midnight, while you were sleeping," he said quietly, "It should have taken place in Hyde Park, but I haven't heard anything. I did not want to wake you, but I've been up all night waiting for word. It's something that should have been reported by now, but it hasn't been."

Ali looked at him questioningly. "So you think…"

Devlin nodded his head. "It might have flopped," he said sadly, "otherwise we would have heard something."

"Can you call anyone? Find out?" Ali asked, knowing her husband would not be worried for nothing.

"I think we need to go there," he said shaking his head, looking into her blue eyes.

"Go where? London?" She asked surprised.

Devlin nodded. "Afraid so love. There's no one I could call, and we can't expect this thing to be resolved on its own now that Fleming is dead."

"And how would we do that?" Ali remarked. "Flights are all but extinct."

"Car or train," Devlin said.

Ali studied him. She knew he would have considered all options before taking such drastic measures, but she also knew what it meant for them to travel all that way.

"That would take almost a day," she pointed out. "Can't we call someone or send a text?"

"Lines are all busy and most likely bugged," he said with a tired smile. "We need to go, Ali. We've sat idle long enough."

"What about Michelle?" Ali asked.

"She can stay with the folks, but I suspect she will insist on coming along."

"That's putting us in the line of fire," Ali observed.

"Yeah, it is," Devlin agreed, "but we could suffer a worse fate if we don't do this."

"I'd hate to expose our daughter to such danger," Ali said.

"Well, we can stay here and pretend it's not our business," he said, looking at her, knowing she herself would never shy away from danger. "Or we can risk it and go to London."

He looked at her gray eyes as a ray of light swept across them, sympathetic to her great dilemma.

"This regime is threatening the entire country, Ali, and we can't remain passive with the knowledge we have."

"Well, let's at least try and convince her to stay." Ali ventured.

"Good luck with that," Devlin chuckled and turned to his laptop to inspect train schedules.

As he turned, he thought he noticed a flicker of light through the window, like a ray of sun glinting off metal. Years of combat experience had taught him never to hesitate when a feeling of extreme danger came to him, and though it was 20 years since he had been active, he reacted the same way he would have then.

"Get down," he shouted to Ali who was exiting his room, he simply tilted his chair sideways and crashed to the floor.

A harsh sound engulfed them when the bullet broke the glass and struck the wall in the back of the room with immense force, inches from the door where Ali had jumped through, face down on the floor.

"Stay down!" he called to Ali and went for the pistol he kept in his lower drawer.

"Get the gun from the kitchen and go for the tunnel," he called out to Ali, watching as she began to crawl across the living room floor.

For years, Devlin had been ridiculed by his fellow military buddies, family, and friends, of the tunnel he had insisted on digging under the clearing that connected their house with Ali's folk's home. Well before their house was erected, while the foundations were being dug, he had tasked the contractor to extend a trench, two yards deep and a yard wide, for almost 50 meters, leading from the back of their kitchen to the parents' back yard where he kept a getaway car for exactly such an event. He had fortified the tunnel's sides with concrete and covered it with wooden beams screwed to the concrete walls, creating a hidden crawl space from one house to another.

As a young girl, Michelle loved the "tunnel" and would often play hide and go-seek with friends and relatives who came over, and once in a blue moon, with her parents who felt quite awkward crawling such a distance in such close quarters.

But as she grew older, she abandoned the tunnel for grown-up activities such as tennis and hiking, and it had been a few years since anyone had been inside it.

Now, all of a sudden, it became their refuge, exactly how Devlin had anticipated it.

"Get Michelle!" Ali called to him as she scrambled into the kitchen and began looking for the gun hidden in one of the lower cupboards.

Another bullet went through the living room window and was lodged in the wall above the television set with a fearsome thrust.

Devlin began crawling toward the stairs to the upper floor when his daughter appeared in nickers and a t-shirt having woken up to the racket.

"What's going on, Dad?" She marveled at seeing him crawling toward the stairs.

"Get down on the floor and slide down here!" he commanded, trying to keep hysteria from his voice. Michelle hesitated for a second when a third bullet went through the same living room window hitting the wall again.

"I said get down!" Devlin hissed, and Michelle hit the floor, sliding head-first toward her dad.

"The tunnel," he said and began crawling, making sure Michelle was beside him. They both crawled swiftly and reached the kitchen. Ali was lying on her side holding the back door open.

"Your phone with you?" Devlin asked out of breath from the sudden burst of energy. Ali fished for the phone in her pocket.

"Call your parents and tell them to wait in the car out back for us," Devlin said and crawled out the door and down two steps to the wooden door that covered the tunnel entrance.

He opened it and signaled for the girls to crawl in, which they quickly did. He slithered into the hole after them but kept the door open so Ali could use the phone.

Her dad answered at once. "What's going on, Ali? Did I hear shots?"

"Get Mom, your gun and a phone, and wait for us in the car out back!" she said breathlessly.

"What's going on…?" He began to protest but her tone of voice made him stop. "Do as I say, Dad, or we'll be minced meat very shortly!" She hissed. "We are in the tunnel! Wait in the car, but don't start it until we're there."

She disconnected the call, and they began to move on their hands and knees through the darkened tunnel.

Chapter Forty-Eight

7 AM, Thursday, February 7, 2019

Frosty was fighting for his life.

Two bullets had hit him in the chest. One exited through the back of his shoulder, hitting no vital organs but smashing his collarbone. The second lodged in his upper back just below the neck. It was causing internal bleeding and threatening the spine.

He was unconscious, his pulse weak and his blood pressure was very low. He was given emergency treatment in the ambulance, oxygen, and an IV, and once in St. Mary's Hospital's emergency ward near Paddington Station, was immediately given several pints of blood, having lost much blood.

Later when he stabilized, they operated, removing the bullet, stopping the internal bleeding, and fixing his collarbone. Still, he was in bad shape.

He was put in the intensive care ward under severe monitoring, watching, among other things, his air intake, blood pressure, and pulse.

Frosty remained unconscious and the doctors were not sure if there was any damage to the brain from the lack of oxygen and blood. They took him for a CT scan and an MRI and hurried him back to intensive care.

Then, his pulse ceased, and they had to restart him with electric shocks, which he luckily responded to and remained alive, but only barely.

Reed, before his tragic end, had given strict orders to the TFB Special Ops unit residing at the grid to post themselves outside Frosty's room and to allow no one but doctors and nurses to come in. He also instructed them to take positions at the entrance to whatever floor Frosty would be on and at the entrance to the hospital, front and back.

The results of the CT and MRI came back, showing no ill effects on the brain, but Frosty was still in a coma.

Then two SO1 operatives arrived fully armed and demanded to see Frosty. Both the doctors and the TFB men refused adamantly, but the two were not to be denied.

"This man is a fugitive," one of them said to the lead surgeon who would not let him enter the intensive care ward. "I need to identify him and then make sure he cannot escape."

"With all due respect, Sir, this man had just been through a four-hour operation and he's in a coma, so I believe escape is out of the question for now. He is in a clean environment along with other patients. No one can enter this ward! When we establish his condition and he stabilizes a bit, we may allow a family member, or a colleague, to dress properly. But you cannot expect to see him until he stabilizes and wakes up, which may take an hour, or it may take a year."

The large bald squaddie with his vest full of magazines and an M-16 slung over his back, a knife in a sheath, and a pistol stuck in his belt, towered over the insolent doctor, staring at him menacingly, thinking that if it wasn't for the armed guards, he would have set him aside, charged in, and put an end to the audacious bastard lying there half dead anyway, but feared an altercation would attract needless attention which his bosses could not afford.

He was to make sure Frosty never left the hospital alive but realized he would have to postpone it for now.

"Right, we'll stay here until he stabilizes, then I expect to be let in!" He said irritably. "And doctor, I expect to be appraised of his condition from time to time."

The two men, dressed in black, pistols hanging from their belts in plain sight, sat down on two chairs in the waiting room, facing the ward entrance; the two TFB guards remained standing by the doors, submachine guns held pointing at the floor.

******

Bishop entered 10 Downing Street like a charging bull, demanding to see the PM at once.

PM Webster and Home Secretary Scott were in the PM's conference room with the entire cabinet of ministers, being briefed by Charlie Draper, the foreign secretary, on the flurry of support and assistance being offered to Britain by its allies.

The stern office manager opened the conference room door a crack and signaled to the PM who looked her way and was about to ask what she wanted when Bishop burst in breathless and stood a moment to catch his breath.

Scott was about to object to his subordinate's ill-mannered behavior when Bishop managed to speak.

"Reed's been killed…" He said, and everyone rose from their seats.

"Assassinated in the park right after the exchange debacle."

"Reed killed?" Home Secretary Scott repeated the revelation with indignation. "But how…?"

"Hitman, professional, one bullet to the forehead from a fair distance I suppose." Everyone looked to Webster for a comment, but the PM remained silent.

"Why that's an outrage!" Sir Alistair Banks, the defense minister, exclaimed and the room turned into a beehive of small talk.

"Brief us on the failed exchange," Webster finally said in a loud voice, making everyone silent.

Bishop looked around at the astonished forum of ministers and hesitated, not sure if everyone was in the know.

"Just do it," Webster urged him on, realizing what the hesitation was about. "This is everyone's problem."

"Reed called me from his car, saying there's going to be an exchange for the Prince in Hyde Park," Bishop blurted, hearing everyone catch their breath. "Said that Agent Frost had sent a man to him with the information and that he was on his way…"

Bishop took a deep breath and went on. "Dixon and I were heading to my car, a few minutes later, when Reed called again saying Agent Frost was down, shot in the chest, and that apparently, a helicopter had been to the spot where Frost was found. A police report confirmed a helicopter descending near the spot, some cop patrolling Embassy Row had seen it flying low over his head, but no one saw a thing."

"We rushed back to the grid to try and locate the helicopter when I got another urgent call from Reed demanding I come to see him at the landing site without delay, but when I got there, we found him shot…"

"What's Agent Frost's condition?" Scott asked.

"He came out of surgery, still alive, but just barely," Bishop informed them, "The doctors are giving him a good chance to survive though he's still in a coma."

"And the man Frosty sent to Reed?" Webster asked.

"Shot and killed as well. He was with Reed," Bishop said.

"Where is Dixon now?" Scott inquired.

"I left him at the scene. His guys are looking for the assassin or assassins, but I doubt they'll find anything."

"And why is that?" Sir Alistair Banks demanded to know. "I'll give you whatever you need to find these guys."

Again, Bishop hesitated, looking at Webster, who nodded his approval.

"We've been behind the ball ever since this crisis began. We have the air force, half the army, and Special Forces, all trying to locate this group for over a week now, not to mention Reed's guys, my guys, and MI6 personnel, and so far we have yet to find any significant leads and we allowed our heir to the throne to be taken."

Bishop stopped for a moment looking at the pitiful group of government executives staring at him.

"This… this outrageous affair, for lack of a better description, which had just taken place right under our noses in the middle of London, shows undeniable incompetence on our part, for which I take full responsibility."

He was silent again, looking at the disturbed expressions then went on addressing the Prime Minister. "I see no alternative for me, Sir, but to step down, but before I do that I'd like to say that it is my impression that we have been infiltrated at the highest levels and that whoever is responsible for this senseless attack on our nation, can frustrate everything we put forth with inside information, otherwise I cannot explain our incompetence."

Bishop stopped, then went on. "The ultimatum given to us ends in three hours and we have just lost the head of our TFB right here in our midst. So, it is imperative that if any of you has any suspicions regarding someone with access to highly classified information, such information that could in any way affect the current state of affairs, you should step forward and allow us to deal with it."

Once again, a flurry of small talk erupted as the ministers began to talk among themselves.

"Quiet, quiet everyone," Webster called out in his booming voice. "Let's try and be civilized about this…"

"Civilized?" Minister of Finance Professor Julian Grey admonished. "How can anyone remain civilized with such accusations? And I'll tell you another thing, Mr. Prime Minister, it's a sad day for the kingdom when your top spy has nothing better to suggest."

"No one is accusing anyone," Webster addressed his ministers, trying to appease the explosive atmosphere. "And in fact, it's the first time for me hearing this," he said, giving Bishop a scolding stare. "However, ladies and gents, we are not in a position to second guess MI5 now. They have been at it for a while and we could not afford to miss-trust them now. Therefore, Mr. Bishop, you will conclude this campaign as MI5 chief, and if you want to resign, see me after."

The buzz in the conference room subsided and everyone slowly sat down. Webster remained standing. He called Bishop over and hugged his shoulder.

"Now everyone in this room will give Bishop here, his or her, full cooperation if indeed you have something you think could be helpful."

He took a moment and looked around the table. There were no verbal objections but several of his ministers looked extremely unhappy.

"We are out of time so we will do everything in our power to assist MI5. Is this clear?"

There were nods around the table, but Finance Minister Grey was not convinced. "Sir, with all due respect, I believe Bishop should step down," he maintained.

"I second that," the Education Minister, Dr. Abigail Dalton called out; everyone else remained quiet.

"The attack on our currency is no less a debacle Professor Grey and no less a threat to our country, yet I didn't fire you," he reasoned looking sternly at Grey. "So, you have some explaining to do to this forum as well, and besides, it's not your call, Not in a state of emergency. Bishop remains and you all will cooperate."

With that, he gestured for Bishop to leave the room.

"I want hourly updates to Scott and call my private number if you need anything," he said, as Bishop turned and left the room.

Chapter Forty-Nine

Bishop arrived at his office to find everyone he had requested, present.

Harriet, Taylor, and Edwards had just made it, having been flown in by the helicopter all the way from Wye County.

Olga was there as well, having seen to it that both Reed's body and the man killed with him, one Dylan Oliver, be driven to the morgue.

Several of his MI5 agents were there, an MI6 contingent, the treasury department, and Dixon who sat with two of his men sitting behind him, armed with pistols.

"Who are these men?" Bishop snapped at Dixon, who looked alert and fresh compared to everyone else in the room.

"My guys," Dixon said, flashing an insolent smile.

"Well, get, your guys, out of here!" Bishop demanded and took his seat at the head of the table. "And all of you shut off your mobile phones!" He added in frustration. "Anyone with his phone left on should leave the room."

Dixon looked to be weighing his retort for a long moment before he turned to his men and signaled to them to leave the room. He then took out his mobile phone from his inner jacket pocket and shut it off. Everyone else did the same.

"I have just updated the PM and the entire cabinet," Bishop began when the door behind him closed. "We have less than two hours for the ultimatum to run out." He began solemnly. "And you've all heard by now that Reed's dead and Agent Frost is fighting for his life at St. Mary's." He continued looking at the four TFB agents in the room.

"I am really sorry guys, he was a good man, but we now need to focus on the task ahead. We'll have plenty of time to mourn later, that is if someone else doesn't mourn us first."

"Details are sketchy as to what exactly happened at this failed exchange in the park. There was a second man killed there with Reed; anyone find anything about him?"

"Yes," Olga volunteered, "his name is, or was, Dylan Oliver and he was an employee at a company in Blackpool called Digital Solutions. Before that, he worked at the Blackpool prison. He is a widower and I found no next of kin…"

"Thank you, Olga," Bishop acknowledged and went on. "Apparently, it was this Mr. Oliver who alerted Reed to this so-called exchange, but when they arrived at the scene, they found Agent Frost shot, and the chopper gone."

"Reed called me with the news then called me again demanding I personally come urgently to the site. When I got here, we found him and Oliver shot dead by Reed's Landrover."

A silence engulfed the room, and a few people lowered their heads as a sign of sorrow.

But Bishop pushed on, though he looked haggard and was short-tempered. "Dixon," he addressed the SO1 chief, "did you find anything at the site?"

"My guys found two bullet shells by some bushes fifty meters from the Landrover. They were 7.62 bullets most likely from a sniper rifle which we believe had an IR sight." Dixon offered, taking out the shells from his jacket pocket and rolling them on the conference table toward Bishop.

"Do we know the kind and make of the rifle?" Bishop asked.

"My guys are looking into it. They are also waiting at the morgue for the slugs to be taken out of the… deceased…They should be calling me with the results any minute," he said, pointing at his, now shut phone, on the desk in front of him.

Bishop addressed the issue. "If you need to take a call, take it outside, otherwise give the phone to one of your men out there and have them call you when they hear something."

Dixon made no attempt to go anywhere.

"Can you brief the forum on where that chopper had disappeared to?" Bishop continued.

"It flew southeast for a while," Dixon informed them. "We lost it around Darford. The air force chief sent an Apache squadron after it but I have yet to get a report."

Bishop continued to question the people around the table, each one in his turn. The MI6 deputy chief reported contact with foreign agencies such as

Interpol, the CIA, and Israeli Mossad. Old David Kessler who had been very instrumental in the initial push against the "Sons of Jihad" in Beirut and later in the US and Europe, and his protégée, Dovik Nissman, Frosty's counterpart in the Mossad, were being consulted via the British embassy in Tel Aviv using whatever means the Mossad had to assist the British.

Interpol and MI5 were monitoring border activity, studying security footage at airports, bus and train terminals. They had gone over passport data of suspected terrorists traveling to the UK and other European countries, going back months before the London attacks as well as checking dealings of explosives and weapons suspected to have been used by the terrorists.

Retired Colonel Doug Collins who had been part of the initial task force with Fleming and Kessler in the 1996 Beirut raid, had been contacted by the CIA along with anyone involved with the investigation over the years. NSA was monitoring a host of mobile phones, internet communications, and radio transmissions, transferring any suspected communique to MI5 for further investigation.

The treasury department was investigating all suspect stock and trade dealings, particularly through the use of the Russian Rubles, the initial cause for the drop in Sterling's value.

"Having investigated most of the hedge funds and investment banks doing business in the UK, who have recently invested heavily in the Russian currency, we have narrowed down the list of suspect institutions to two." A bald, lively looking man called Eckersley reported. "The Europe Investment Bank and the Chelsea Capital Management Limited, Hedge Fund. Both headed by the same man: James Flanagan who resides in Hempstead. We now believe the trade in Rubles and the host of rumors that started it all, initially came out of those two institutions."

"And have you talked to the man?" Bishop inquired.

"Unfortunately, he is not answering his phones and both workplaces are shut down due to the curfew. We were coming to you to get a judge to sign a warrant to search the premises of both banks and his residence."

"I'll get a judge to sign your warrant right after this meeting," Bishop said. "Anything else?"

Bishop was disappointed knowing the suspect "Sons of Jihad" sleeper agents were doing the Kremlin's work, possibly without even knowing it, and he had hoped the treasury department report would lead to the involvement of a Russian institution, but no such report surfaced, and the PM's ultimatum to begin discussions with the Kremlin was nearing fast.

"Ms. Gold, Mr. Taylor," he addressed the TFB team. "Anything to report?"

Harriet described their outing to Wye country, the two bodies found, and their conversation with Group Captain Carter.

"The two bodies were Barry George age 48 and Tim Blake age 51. Both ex-SAS, both from Glasgow," Olga intervened, having checked the information sent to her by Harriet via WhatsApp. "They were discharged with honors from the regiment and joined Mike Devlin at the ultra-secret Harley outfit, before the merge into MI6. The files I checked noted MI6 and MI5 had insisted they merge and caused a split between the secret service authorities and Devlin's men who most preferred to retire. George and Blake were of the few who had remained, though they too had retired after two years."

"Any idea how they got mixed up in all this?" Bishop inquired. "Any family members we can talk to?"

"Both were single men," Olga informed the forum. "George has a sister in Glasgow, married with two kids. The parents live in Glasgow as well. Blake has parents in Glasgow and a brother living in Edinburgh, single as well. I called both parents. They had no idea what had happened and after I informed them, they were obviously so distraught, it did not feel right to question them."

"Well, we'll need to talk to them!" Bishop observed. "Anyone else we can talk to? What about this Devlin guy? He may have been in touch with them."

"He lives near Inverness, I tried him but there was no answer," Olga said. "One other person who may have known something was Group Captain Fleming, whose murder was reported this afternoon. He was quite influential in forming the TFB and was involved with Devlin's crew long ago. In the files, he is mentioned as the person responsible for their merge into MI6."

Bishop perked up. "So, we have two ex-SAS guys, ex-Devlin guys, dead along with Group Captain Fleming, all in the same day. That may not be coincidental I dare say."

"Exactly our thinking," Harriet pitched in. "We are checking for other people involved with Devlin's and Fleming's past activities to see if they know anything."

"Well, get on it quick!" Bishop exclaimed.

"One other odd thing we learned," Harriet continued, "is that the Special Ops guys who found the bodies, said they were handled by Andy White, one of

Dixon's deputies." Harriet divulged looking at Dixon as if expecting clarifications.

"Why would SO1 be running the Special Ops guys?" She turned to Bishop.

"Well, since the Prince is our responsibility," Dixon said calmly. "The PM gave us a free hand to run these guys and so far we have been closer to finding him than anyone."

"It seems to me we are no closer now than we were a week ago," Harriet retorted. "And it seems anybody who can shed any light on all this is now dead."

"What are you suggesting?" Dixon growled at her, his dark eyebrows converging over his dark eyes. "It's your guy who is the prime suspect still, unfortunately in a coma, or we'd have the answers by now."

"Well, for your information," Harriet seethed, "the video shown to the world on Sky News of the terrorized sites, was taken from a chopper that had your men on it!" Harriet informed him. "And just so you know, Wing Commander Connor Gilliam, the Sea King squadron commander whom Prince William flew for, informed us that the Prince, who was on his way to join them, never actually made it. Now tell me you weren't aware of all that? And if you were, why weren't we informed?"

"Well, the Wing Commander had exceeded his authority!" Dixon fumed. "I cannot confirm or deny such information."

"What difference does it make now that he is held a prisoner?" Harriet raged before a flurry of discussion engulfed the room.

"Quiet! Quiet please…" Bishop called out but the people around the table were too astonished to quiet down.

"We need some explanations, Bishop!" The deputy head of MI6 called out, enraged. "Who knew about this? How can we solve anything if information of such magnitude does not reach us?"

Bishop looked at Dixon who was evading his gaze, fending off some of his colleagues. He realized he himself was on the spot, not being aware of such vital pieces of information. He had trusted Dixon with the task and even gave him full authority to act as he saw fit. Now Dixon's incompetence had marred him too.

Or was it incompetence? He thought as he played in his mind again the exchange with Reed before he died, thinking it was odd he had demanded he come without Dixon. Did Reed feel Dixon was a nuisance or was there another reason?

He decided to end the meeting and have a private discussion with both Dixon and the TFB team.

"Ladies, Gents…" He called out banging his palm on the mahogany table. "Can I have your attention please?"

The discussion quieted down slowly until finally, everyone looked to Bishop. He stood up.

"We'll get to the bottom of this just as soon as we adjourn," he said, raising his hand as another round of heated murmurs began to envelop the room.

"Each of us has a job to do and we have less than two hours for the ultimatum to expire!"

The room became quiet again.

"Treasury, you guys call Judge Roy Graham, wake him up if needed, and get that warrant!"

"MI5 people, you hook up with the Brighton police and see what we can find on Fleming's murder. Also, make contact with anyone on that former Devlin team, pre-MI6 days, and find out if there's any connection between them."

"Ms. Gold, any word on Jemma and Frost's family members?"

"We know they were at the house near Bath but the Special Ops guys up in Wye country could not find any trace of them. We believe they were with George and Blake but it's unclear where they have gone to."

Bishop turned to Dixon. "Your guys find any trace of them up there?"

"No, sir," Dixon said, looking directly at Bishop not offering anything else.

"Right, I'll instruct the Special Ops guys to look further up there. Dixon, how many operatives do you have working on this?"

"Oh, about fifteen," Dixon said offhand.

"What about the rest?"

"All assigned regular duties; now more than ever."

"Can you spare anymore?"

"Afraid not. We've increased protection for all high-profile people. I am afraid it's all I can spare."

"Well, then, get them to find that chopper! Get your guys down to Boscomb and have them join the search. Is that clear?"

"Yes," Dixon said. "I'll get on it right now."

"And when you're done, please come to my office."

Dixon nodded and got up to leave. Bishop waited until he was out of the conference room and turned to the ones who remained.

"I want all offices swept for bugs!" He said suddenly. "And that includes all communication lines; mobile phones, landline phones, and internet access. Olga, you're in charge. Make sure it's done here, at MI6, at the treasury, at the communication centers both here and in the park, and all our vehicles. Get the tech guys to start right away. You can start in this room as soon as we leave."

Olga got up and quickly left the room.

Chapter Fifty

9 AM, Thursday, February 7, 2019

Cindy had seen her husband collapse to the ground.

One moment he was there approaching them, the next he was on the ground, and she was caught from behind and forced back onto the helicopter.

The rotors spinning above them were making such noise she did not hear a thing and at first, could not comprehend what was happening. Zoe and Gabi were vivaciously walking to him, but when he fell, were also caught by the men leading them and thrown back onto the chopper.

Prince William was not even let off the helicopter. The trap was perfect. Frosty had spotted his daughters and thought they were in the clear.

The helicopter took off with the sliding door still open, its searchlight lighting the ground below and for a split second, Cindy could see her husband lying there, in the clearing below, unmoving. Both her girls were talking to her but she could not hear what they were saying.

It was too much to bear. She collected them to her chest, then came the tears.

She was in a state of shock, tears running down her cheeks, realizing her husband had just been hurt badly, possibly even killed, right in front of her and his daughters. Gabi and Zoe were in the nook of her arms, looking up at her, crying themselves.

Prince William was freed from his hold and lowered himself next to them, padding her back, but she couldn't feel anything but a great fear and a sense of loss she could not comprehend.

She had held her daughters' faces to hers and wept uncontrollably. The girls turned to the Prince, tears running down their faces, asking him to tell them what happened, but Prince William was not saying anything; he just hugged them to him and looked up at their captors with hatred and blame.

Then they were back in the cottage by the lake.

She could not recall the flight or when they had landed. She was hustled off the helicopter, Zoe and Gabi holding on to her, Prince William remaining back for some reason.

Suddenly, Jemma was there, in front of her, and she fell into her arms, weeping uncontrollably. All she could do was envision her husband collapsing on the grass before she could get to him.

In her grief, Cindy realized they never intended to carry out the exchange. She had been notified of it only after the chopper took off, and had no say in the matter, though she did try to think up ways to alter the decree while they were in the air but could come up with nothing short of grabbing her husband and girls once they land and getting away somehow, an act she knew would put them all at risk of being shot.

When the helicopter landed in Hyde Pary, Prince William was kept on board, held firm by two of their captors, while she and the girls were escorted off the chopper, each led by one of the black outfit men. She could not see Frosty at first but then he appeared in the chopper's beam smiling when he saw his girls, only to collapse a second later as he was about to go to them.

She remembered her scream being swallowed up by the noise of the chopper; beyond that, it was all grief. She could not put into words, for her girls, what had happened, though they were asking over and over again.

The Prince sat down next to them, on the chopper's floor, and tried to comfort the girls who turned to him for answers, but he didn't speak. Shortly before landing back near the lake by the cottage, he had whispered to her not to draw any conclusions.

"He may only be wounded," he said, but Cindy could envision only the worst.

Then they were separated.

The Prince was escorted by three guards to wherever they were keeping him; Cindy and the girls were taken back to the cottage as Jemma, Jake, and the rest tried to provide some comfort.

They had not been apprised of why Cindy, the girls, and the Prince were being taken away and were shaken to see their condition when they got back. They had tried to extract information from the men who had remained guard, but White was not around, and no one else would offer a word of explanation.

Later, after they sat back in their corner in the large hall, trying to lull the bereaved family into sharing what had happened, Gabi spilled out the words.

"We saw Dad," Gabi uttered. "Then he fell on the grass, and we were taken back…"

Jemma, who was comforting Cindy as best she could, held her hand out to Gabi who slid over and settled in the crook of her arm, new tears flowing down her cheeks.

No one said a word. It was not the time or the place, with the grieving girls in their midst, to figure out what exactly had happened and where, but it was obvious something had gone awfully wrong and Frosty was seriously hurt.

Finally, after what seemed like an eternity, Cindy managed to speak describing what had happened.

"He fell right in front of us," she told, sobbing. "The helicopter was making such a racket, I could not hear anything, and when we tried to run to him they caught us from behind and lifted us back onto the helicopter."

She wiped her nose with a handkerchief someone offered her. "Everything happened so fast… for a second, I saw him lying there on the grass unmoving, in the middle of the light beam as we took off, then it all became dark…"

She tried to keep her sobbing in check but was too overwhelmed, the girls whimpering in her arms.

"Where did this happen?" Jake asked as Jemma hugged Cindy's shoulders.

"Oh, it was in Hyde Park, in London," Cindy said, looking at the concerned faces watching her, seeming almost surprised they did not know. "It was supposed to be an exchange for the Prince and us…"

They all exchanged glances. "So, it was Frosty for the Prince and you?" Noah asked indignantly.

"Only in theory…" Jemma sighed. "They never intended to give up the Prince or anyone… Their target was Frosty who they knew would be drawn in seeing his family there…"

The men in black handed them a pile of ready-made breakfast with beans and some eggs, which they heated in a micro-oven standing on a shelf in the corner of the hall next to an electric kettle used to make coffee and tea. Cindy did not touch her food and her girls only nibbled, but everyone else devoured their shares having gone without food for more than a day.

"Have some," Mary urged her on. "You need to keep your strength." But it fell on deaf ears.

"She is too numb," Camilla ascertained, still desperately grieving for her boyfriend but able to digest some food.

Cindy did accept some sweetened tea, then fell asleep in Jemma's arms, Gabi and Zoe following suit on her lap.

White came in at nine in the morning, storming into his small office with two of his aides in tow. A half hour later, he sent for Jemma and Bond who groggily stepped into his office and shut the door behind them.

"Is Frosty alive?" Jemma asked before White could utter a word.

White looked at her testily, his expression a mixture of distaste and contempt, but she also noticed a hint of fear in his eyes.

"For now, he is but he will end up the same as your boss, same as you if you provoke me some more."

"My boss?" Jemma questioned uncomprehendingly.

"Yes! Your boss. Marshal Reed..." White said cruelly, making a cutting gesture across his neck.

Jemma's face contorted and she was about to retort, but Bond put a hand on her shoulder.

"And just so you know, I will not hesitate to execute anyone of you, including the kids, if you diverge in the slightest from what I tell you to do."

Chapter Fifty-One

Devlin loved to watch his daughter drive.

Despite her young age, she looked so confident and cool on the wheel, weaving the car from one lane to another, her pretty face glued to the road in total concentration.

Ali had her hands on his shoulders. Her parents, Beth and Martin, now in their mid-eighties, sat next to her in the back, both asleep.

They had barely made it out of the farmhouse.

Reaching the end of the tunnel, they burst out of it running full speed toward the getaway car, to where Ali's parents were waiting.

"Get in! Get in!" Devlin mimicked to them, signaling with his hands. He flung the car door open, taking the wheel as Michelle got in the back with her Grandparents and Ali in front with him.

The keys were in the ignition. Devlin turned them, praying the old Honda would start, having neglected to check the car for a while now. But the ignition caught easily and Devlin gunned the gas pedal, shooting onto the dirt track toward the gate.

The distance to the wooden gate was about 300 meters along an exposed dirt track in their little valley, which gave anyone shooting at them an easy target, but there was no back way through which they could escape, other than trying to drive through the meadow in back of the farm where a small creek flowed into their small lake and would have deterred their escape.

Devlin was gaining speed driving toward the gate and still no shots were fired at them.

"Hold on," he warned as he burst through the wooden gate smashing it to pieces then making a right turn onto the asphalt road, leaving a cloud of dust behind them.

A bullet hit the side mirror on Ali's side and a gray sedan came shooting at them from behind, gaining distance as Devlin put the gas pedal to the floor.

"Get down," he shouted as two bullets struck the back of the Honda in succession. Devlin looked in his back mirror, seeing two figures in the car behind them, the passenger pointing a gun through his window, firing at them.

A sharp bend in the road has his wheels screechin as they barely made it upright through it. Devlin looked through his mirror again and saw the gray car overshoot the bend and veer off the road stopping just short of a cultivated field.

He realized then that although he had the weaker car, he had the advantage of knowing the road and its terrain. He managed to see the silver car reversing back onto the road before another bend in the road hid them from view.

Minutes later, the gray car appeared behind a bend, gaining on them as Devlin sped along the B9014 country road across the river Fiddich to the B975 near Balvenie castle. They sped west just south of the famous Glen Fiddich distillery on the A941 past Dufftown then turned south on Old Military Road toward Cairngorms National Park hoping to lose their pursuers in the narrow winding back roads and trails at the park, a favorite venue for Ali and himself, to ride their bikes and hike.

Hoping to spot a police car, he refrained from using the mobile, not sure who else was monitoring them. The road was empty and their pursuers were gaining.

Then, at a familiar turnoff beyond a sharp bend, he veered off the asphalt road onto a dirt road that wound dangerously among the vegetation along uneven ground throwing himself and his passengers from side to side in the small car.

But the dust trail they left in their wake gave them away and the gray car managed to spot the turnoff and turn into it without mischief.

The road wound its way up an incline, the trees on both sides threatening to shut its path, converging on the speeding car, and soon the road became a trail with barely enough room for the car to go through. Suddenly the path opened, the trees remained behind, and they were speeding on a narrow dirt road along a steep bluff swerving around its side. Devlin hoped the road may be too narrow for his pursuers but realized they had no such luck as the gray car powered behind them.

He knew the road from their bicycle trips to the area and figured he could anticipate its trouble spots but soon realized riding a bike at a leisurely pace did not resemble driving a car at top speeds. They reached a fork in the road on a bare saddle and veered hard left down a steep decline back toward the forest below. Looking back in the mirror he saw the gray car overshooting the turn and surging up the saddle's far side before coming to a stop and reversing unharmed.

He stepped on the gas pedal as hard as he thought was possible without losing control, the Honda whooshing along the dirt road tilting from side to side toward the awaiting forest. Once back in the trees, he looked for a turnoff, finding one after several minutes, and slowing down considerably. He turned and stopped.

"Okay get out," he ordered his passengers, "quickly!"

"What are you going to do?" Ali questioned as she was getting out the passenger door, Michelle and her parents scrambling out the back doors.

"Shut the doors!" He ordered. "Wait in these bushes! Be back in a jiffy."

Without explanation, as the doors were slammed shut, he turned the car around, back to the road, making a left turn toward the chasing car. He stepped on the gas pedal and thrust the vehicle forward gaining momentum, eyes focused on the road ahead.

The gray car appeared racing among the trees unaware of the looming danger. Devlin turned on his headlights as soon as he saw they were on a collision course and kept going full throttle. It took his foes a few seconds to realize what was happening before the gray car broke to one side plunging into a ditch and crashing through the thicket by the road toward the trees behind. It managed to remain right side up only to be instantaneously halted by a sturdy tree trunk reducing its front end to rubble.

Devlin didn't wait around.

He stopped a short distance away, managed to turn the Honda around on the narrow road, and roared back to collect his people.

******

Exhausted from the chase, he was finally convinced by Michelle to take over the wheel, once they had crossed the Forth Road bridge at Queensferry, west of Edinburgh, and were safely on the M74 freeway south, toward Manchester.

He had even managed an hour's nap after they had stopped on the M6 to relieve themselves and fill the car with petrol.

As they were approaching London on the M40 driving east, he realized they needed to plan, but he took a minute to look at his daughter, an alert cool demeanor on her pretty face, looking back in the mirror from time to time.

"I believe we lost them," Devlin had said to her, noticing a worried stare when she looked in the back mirror.

"Better safe, than sorry," Michelle said, giving him a wry smile.

"You'll become a spook like me one day," he joked, feeling Ali's fingers tightening around his throat.

"Don't even suggest it," she said threateningly, hiding a smile. "Not even as a joke."

"Who should we approach?" Devlin asked his wife when a sign to London marked forty miles. "We've got an hour to decide."

"How well do you know the MI5 chief?" Ali queried.

"Not at all, though I did see him giving a lecture once, a few years ago in Edinburgh. I don't think he was even a field guy, though he may have had some operational experience I was not aware of."

"What difference does it make?" Michelle intervened. "If he's the head guy now. We should go to him."

"Well, for one thing, my dear, he may be suspicious if he doesn't know me. Don't forget these people are under enormous pressure right now."

"But I am sure he has heard of you," Ali put in. "From Fleming, the poor bugger, or from anyone else."

"He probably has," Devlin agreed, "and I doubt he would doubt me, but getting to him may be a whale of a problem right now especially if we can't use a phone."

"So, who else were you considering?" Ali asked.

"Well, there's Sir Alistair Banks, the defense minister, whom I know, but who may be as busy as Bishop if not more, and there's Julian Grey, the finance minister…"

"He may be busier than the first two," Michelle intervened. "The pound hasn't been at its best lately."

"Rightly so," Devlin agreed, "so that does not leave too many choices."

"I know Abigail Dalton, the Education Minister," Ali said after a short pause. "We took classes together in Glasgow at the university."

"Yes, you did," a voice called from the back. It was Beth. "You even brought her to the farm once," she added.

"Was she a physical education major as well?" Devlin asked, surprised.

"No, she was an English major, but we had some General Ed classes together and we actually shared a room for a semester."

"Will she remember you?" Michelle asked, keeping her eyes glued to the road.

"I am sure she will though we have not been in contact since college."

"Will she have access to the PM?" Devlin wondered out loud, addressing no one in particular.

"Of course she will," Martin said from the back in his hoarse voice. "They all do."

Devlin looked back at his wife and her parents, worried looks on their faces, awaiting his decision.

"Well, if she has access to the PM, she could be the better choice," Devlin reflected. "Being somewhat away from the spotlight…"

"I am sure she has her hands full as well, with the school system in London being shut down," Michelle remarked.

"Definitely so," Devlin agreed, "but she may not be scrutinized as closely as the others."

"Do we know where she lives? Or where her office is?" Beth asked.

"Well, the Ministry of Education is at Whitehall Lane, as I recall," Ali pitched in. "As for her private residence, I have no clue."

"We could assume she will be at her office today, couldn't we?" Michelle argued. "Mom could wait for her there."

"Or at Downing Street," Martin pitched in. "They're probably all there…"

"Not a bad thought," Devlin agreed. "We start asking for her at the PM's office, don't you think?" He looked at Ali.

"The place may be quartered off," Ali said. "Who knows what security measures have been taken? It may be off limits by now."

"We won't know until we try, but I think we should try and catch the snake by the head," Devlin said. "And if Abigail Dalton is not there, I may try and talk my way to the PM myself."

Chapter Fifty-Two

9:30 AM, Thursday, February 7, 2019

Dr. Abigail Campbell-Dalton had taught English Literature and Social Policy for 30 years before she went into politics. Having gotten her English and Social Policy Bachelor's and Literature master's degrees from the University of Strathclyde, she moved to London and began teaching high school in the city of Westminster, renting a flat near Liverpool station.

She soon made a name for herself with some dignitaries' children who attended her classes and was acknowledged by local politicians and even by some far-off relatives of the royal family. She completed her doctorate thesis at London University College, or UCL, where she began to lecture and received a host of accolades for her work, working her way up the academic scale until she became the Literature department head.

She had married a colleague, James Dalton, a professor of Physics at UCL University, and had two children with him, Mathew now twenty-five, and Lauren, now twenty-two, both on their way to PhD degrees.

Abigail Dalton was a thin woman, with short dark hair, and gaunt cheekbones, her large blue eyes were always behind a pair of black rimmed eyeglasses, that overextended her thin face, and her chin and neck now riddled with wrinkles were hidden behind an ever-present handkerchief glued to her neck.

She did not pose much of a presence behind the ever-present glasses and her simple dress code, but when she talked, people listened. Highly recognized and respected in both academic and political circles, as Minister of Education, she had made serious inroads into the British education system with an advanced outlook on adapting high-school studies to present-day needs such as internet communication and social networks studies, a direction criticized by old school university advocates, received quite a following in government and by many of the parents whose children attended high school, and was a favorite initiative of Prime Minister Webster, who liked futuristic thinking.

She had just left 10 Downing Street and was entering the Ministry of Education building, her SO1 escort remaining outside. She put her purse and computer carry case through the x-ray machine and went through the metal detector, collected them, and walked toward the elevators, when a tall blonde woman in a long overcoat joined her, then stood next to her as she pressed the elevator button to go up.

"Hi, Abby," the woman said casually, smiling at her, and for a moment minister Dalton was at a loss, thinking she might be a target of some kind, and looked back toward the security personnel milling at the entrance, but when she looked at the woman again, she thought she looked a bit familiar.

"Can I help you?" she asked politely, looking up at the woman who kept smiling at her, looking not unfamiliar.

"Ali Saunders, Strathclyde University. Do you remember me? We shared a room one semester…"

The thin woman looked quizzically up at Ali then her thin lips broadened into a forced smile. "Why of course Ali, of course, I remember. It's been quite a while…"

"Class of 1980," Ali reminded her. "You were Abigail Campbell then."

"Yes, Yes, how have you been?" She looked around. "And how did you manage to slip through security…?"

Ali showed her the "Special Ops" badge she had used to gain access into the building, an item she kept in the emergency kit she had managed to grab from one of the kitchen shelves along with her phone before she entered the tunnel.

Minister Dalton Shook Ali's hand hesitantly at first as if wanting to make sure she remembered correctly but Ali pressed on. "Minister Dalton, Abby, I wish we had time to reminisce but we don't, I am afraid. I am here with my husband, daughter, and parents. We drove all the way from Inverness to see you."

The elevator door opened, and the two women walked in and stood side by side waiting for the door to close. A man in a suit was hurrying to catch the elevator, but Dalton signaled him to let them be, and he stopped short, allowing the doors to shut.

"My husband is Mike Devlin," Ali said hurriedly, as the old elevator began to make its way up to the fourth floor. "I am not sure you ever heard the name, but he was a central figure in MI6 clandestine operations in the 90s."

Ali looked to the shorter woman to make sure she had her attention.

"The group he was out to get at that time were called 'Sons of Jihad'," Ali said, catching a flare of recognition in the minister's blank stare.

"We have proof that this group had managed to infiltrate the secret services here at the highest levels."

The elevator was reaching its destination.

Ali did not wait for the minister to acknowledge the seriousness of what she was saying. She just came out with it: "We believe the SO1 chief Ross Dixon is a "Sons of Jihad" sleeper agent who's behind this ongoing disaster, including the bombings, the kidnapping of Prince William and, I dare say, the recent devaluation of our currency."

The elevator door opened but Minister Dalton did not move. She stared at Ali as if not comprehending what she was saying then reached for the closing door.

"Come to my office," she said hurrying to exit the elevator, but Ali made no move to follow. Minister Dalton turned and stared at her.

"No, not your office," Ali whispered to her. "And don't use the phones, they are most likely bugged."

Minister Dalton stood a moment unsure what to do, a secretary was staring at her not sure how to proceed, when Dalton turned and walked back into the elevator without saying a word.

"We need to inform Bishop," Ali said as the doors shut and they made their way back to the ground floor.

Minister Dalton stared at Ali for a long moment. She remembered a striking tall blonde girl, who she knew in college, but she needed to make sure.

"What was your major in Strathclyde?" she asked.

"Physical Education," Ali said, realizing the woman was still testing her.

"What was the pub we used to frequent?" Minister Dalton asked.

"Blackfriars…" Ali blurted with no hesitation.

Minister Dalton smiled. "You must excuse me, Ali, but it's been a long time and at our age, memory can play tricks on us. Now, shall we go see the PM?"

******

Parked at a side street near Embankment, Devlin received a "thumbs up" message on his WhatsApp and knew Ali was successfully convincing her old college roommate, now Minister of Education, that the British security services had been infiltrated and seriously compromised. He had rehearsed with Ali the exact words she needed to use, and who they needed to inform, namely Bishop, but preferably, the PM himself.

Three pairs of eyes looked at him questioningly and he nodded and smiled.

"Looks like your mom was successful," he said to Michelle who grinned in relief. "They should be on their way to inform someone."

They waited impatiently in the car and it seemed time had come to a standstill. A half hour passed. Devlin kept looking at his watch nervously when Ali finally returned, almost an hour after leaving the car.

"Saw the PM," she said as she slid in next to her husband, kissing him on the lips.

"And…" they all said in unison.

"The short or the long version?" Ali asked

"Any version," her father said excitedly. "Come on, out with it girl."

"The minister, Abby, took a while to recognize me and even tested me to see if I was legit. But once she was convinced it was me, her old college roommate, she did not hesitate one bit."

"After I told her of our suspicions, she went straight to number 10, taking me with her. On the way she confided in me that Bishop had just briefed them about a possible leak and that all cabinet members were asked to keep an open mind and their eyes open wide."

"The PM was busy, so we were asked to brief his head of staff, but Dalton wouldn't hear of it. She demanded to see Webster at once and began making a scene before they let us in."

"Who was in the room with him?" Devlin asked almost out of breath. "There were Nigel Scott…"

"The Home Secretary," Her father intervened excitedly, making everyone smile.

"And Sir Alistair Banks…" She halted, looking at her father to provide his title, but Martin just smiled.

"The right people," Devlin said.

"Abby came right out with it, introducing me as your wife and reciting what I had told her. The three of them almost passed out! Their faces became white and none could produce a sound, looking at us for a few seconds not comprehending as if all words were stuck in their throats. Then they asked Abby to repeat what she had said."

"When they got over the initial shock, the PM sat down and started drilling me for proof and to the source of my information. All three have heard of you of course, and knew Fleming, so the authenticity of the revelations was deemed legit. Also, it seemed that what Abby, Minister Dalton, had told me regarding Bishop's suspicions, were weighing heavily on their minds."

"One anecdote that I must share with you," Ali said smiling. "Is that once the PM was convinced, he picked up the phone to call Bishop but Abby let out a muted shriek, suggesting he put down the phone for fear all phones may be tapped. The PM was so surprised; he immediately did as he was told looking at Abby like a kid in a classroom caught by his teacher."

"That a girl!" Martin said, grinning from ear to ear. "So, what will they do?" Michelle asked.

"The PM sent a messenger to Bishop…"

"Not to one of the SO1 guys I hope…" Devlin remarked humorously.

"I doubt it, honey," Ali said caressing his cheek. "They did ask us to stick around and offered to pay for accommodations at the Ritz of all places."

"The Ritz!" Beth mused. "Why that would cost a fortune."

"Abby told me it was mostly empty now…" Ali explained.

"So did you agree?" Michelle asked.

"Of course, I did," Ali said. "We have been at it for a full day with hardly any rest. And besides, I once told a dear friend that I've never been to the Ritz. So, it's about time."

"Lead the way, girl," Martin said jovially, and Devlin put the car into gear.

Chapter Fifty-Three

Olga stuck her head in the door.

"Sir, I need a minute," she said. "It's urgent!"

Bishop was sitting across from an unfamiliar woman who turned in alarm as she heard Olga's voice.

"Would you…" The woman began to speak but Bishop calmed her. "It's OK she works for me."

"Can I speak freely?" Olga inquired, looking hesitantly at the woman.

"Go ahead, what did you find?"

"The conference room is bugged, and so are most landline phones," Olga informed him.

Bishop did not look surprised.

"Any mobile phones?" he inquired.

"We're checking the few who are here," Olga said.

"Any other buildings bugged?"

"The TFB grid and several company cars."

"Good enough for me," Bishop said. "Olga, fine job. Now get Harriet and the rest of your people into my office. Any word from treasury?"

"Not yet sir. Judge Graham was not happy but he signed the warrant anyway. I guess they are on the way right now. I'll get Harriet and the guys."

Five minutes later they were all in Bishop's office, door shut, phones off.

"I assume my office is not bugged?" Bishop addressed Olga.

"First room we checked sir. All clear."

Bishop introduced them to the woman, Maggie Fox, who was sent by PM Webster with the information supplied by Minister Dalton and Ali Devlin.

Maggie recited what she had told Bishop and not a sound could be heard in the room.

"So here's what we know," Bishop recapitulated. "Dixon is the head guy. Apparently, he recruited people into SO1 for some time now and has control of the outfit. He also may have others working for him. To cover his tracks, he may have eliminated Tompkins, SO1 agent Simon, Fleming, Reed and Oliver; seriously wounded Agent Frost and came after Devlin who managed to escape and bring the information to our attention."

The room was deathly quiet.

"So Ross Dixon has masterminded this entire onslaught right under our noses, but to what end?" Harriet wondered out loud.

"These people don't need much of an excuse to kill innocent people," Edwards noted.

"Well, it seems this is a well thought out plan Maggie informs me," Bishop acknowledged. "And these 'Sons of Jihad' fanatics are just pawns in a scheme which was set forth by the Russians."

"The Russians?" Taylor mused. "Are they considering World War Three?"

"Not exactly but close to..." Maggie said. "It seems they intend to force us to give up those Liquefied Natural Gas terminals which will supply Europe with oil and natural gas from America as an alternative to Russian pipelines. This initiative apparently will decrease Russian gas supply to Europe by almost three-quarters from the current supply, and they cannot afford that..."

"So all this... mayhem, bombs, kidnapping, and loss of life are to secure Russian gas supply to Europe?" Harriet asked in amazement.

"Could you find a more worthwhile reason?" Bishop asked her. "Gas and oil supply are what runs this world."

"So how did the Russians manage to recruit those 'Sons of Jihad'?" Olga asked.

"Apparently, they had recruited them years ago after we ransacked their headquarters in Beirut in 1996. Apparently, the Arab league severed its ties with them and left them with sleeper agents in the field and no sponsors..."

"A perfect setup for the Russians," Edwards remarked.

"It gets even better," Maggie said. "The PM received a secret letter from the Kremlin demanding he sign up to invalidate the US Gas pact in return for ceasing the attack on London."

"If we agree, are they going to pay for the damages here?" Taylor scorned. "This city needs fixing up. It will cost billions!"

"Now Andy, that seems above our paygrade for the moment," Harriet admonished. "Let's focus on putting an end to this nightmare and restoring order."

"She's right," Bishop agreed. "Our deadline is up so we need to apprehend Dixon first and foremost! We can call in a SWAT team or apprehend him ourselves when he shows up here, which I will make sure he does."

"If he comes in with those goons of his, it may get a little tricky…" Edwards remarked.

"A SWAT team will give it away," Harriet said, "who knows where he's got people and the extent of their monitoring? But if we get ready, we can disarm his bodyguards and take him."

"We need to move quick," Bishop pointed out. "If he's the guy giving orders, once we have him, it may capsize the threat on William's life."

"The PM and Scott have asked to be notified the instant we have him in custody," Maggie Fox informed them.

"Well, then you need to stick around until we have him, then go and inform the boss because we do not want to broadcast the fact in any form of cellular or wireless communication," Bishop advised.

"I'll do whatever is necessary," Maggie said, flashing a worried grin. She had sandy blond hair done up in fashion; and had on white Nike sneakers in profound contrast to the trendy black pants and white blouse she wore, with black buttons and a thin silver chain around her neck. Her brown eyes seemed to fill with guarded excitement, but her look remained sharp and Bishop could fathom why she became the PM's top aide.

"Anybody see Dixon? Or know where he went?" Bishop asked, looking at Olga.

"Last I saw him, he was down in the communication center talking with the Apache squadron commander at Boscomb," Olga said.

"When was that?" Bishop asked.

"When we adjourned from the conference room about two hours ago."

"Well, he can be anywhere by now and we need to stop him," Bishop complained. "Let me call him. He's probably the only guy we can call without worrying about being bugged."

There was a nervous cackle from the people in the room.

"Now, once I talk to him, we'll know where he'll be coming from and we can prepare. The best thing is to let him in my office. I'll make sure the goons stay out where you can disarm them. Then we grab him, in here. Maggie, does he know you?"

"He has seen me around the PM, yes…"

"In that case, you stay out of sight until we disarm him and lock him up. Are we all clear?"

Bishop did not wait for consent from the troop. They were out of time and all were resourceful agents with plenty of experience and nerve. They would know what to do.

He dialed Dixon's number.

******

Dixon was at the SO1 Communication Center across the street from MI5 headquarters, coordinating with White their next move. Time was up and he had to decide what to do with the ultimatum he had given.

Things appeared to be on track though there was room for concern if Agent Frost ever woke up from his coma. They had two men at the hospital ready to pounce but they would have to overcome the TFB guards and hospital staff before they could finish him off.

They were also yet to hear from the two men sent after Devlin, but Dixon did not figure he was a threat up in Northern Scotland, and if he did try to phone, they would handle the call.

Dixon was no stranger to operating in uncertainty. He had been living it his entire life. From the war-stricken city of Beirut where he and his friends learned to dodge shrapnel during air raids, bullets at neighborhood skirmishes, roadblocks, car bombings, IEDs, and suicide bombers; to the training base in Syria where among ruthless physical training he was put through psychological warfare which included physical and mental abuse by his instructors; to many years of clandestine existence in London moving through the ranks while waiting to strike.

Now, he was a heartbeat away from completing the mission he had been groomed to carry out for so many years; a mission that could not only put a major dent in the balance of global power but may convince his employers to bring him back and allow him to finally settle down.

He was under no illusion that, for all intents and purposes, he would be burned as a clandestine operator in the west once he was done with the mission, but was certain his knowledge and experience could prepare others for such missions. It took great patience and diligence to get to where he was and even more crafty maneuvering once he was in a position where he could recruit his operatives. Once out of college, it took him twelve years to reach the position of deputy to the SO1 chief; a position he held for three years before replacing the late George Tompkins.

As deputy chief, new recruits were his responsibility to approve, and in three years he managed to bring in no less than 15 of his cohorts, all dedicated to the cause. Three were sleeper agents like himself, and the rest were British, some disillusioned military personnel like Andy White who himself had recommended a few, and others were college graduates of Muslim faith who secretly supported organizations like El-Qaida and ISIS. Kruger too was part of the team, though he never knew who he was dealing with until they met six months prior.

Kruger's job was to transfer messages from the Russians via poems that he wrote and were published in various local rags in the Greater London area. He became the focal point of all their correspondence with the Russians who would send him word via several FSB collaborators both prisoners and guards, inside the Blackpool prison. It was the perfect set up and no one suspected a thing until word was given to proceed at which point Kruger agreed to give up a life that gave him nothing but grief, in order to frame Agent Frost and get the ball rolling.

In truth, his superiors had not approved executing the Prince but Dixon expected the threat would advance things. Andy White was in the cottage by the lake awaiting word from the Kremlin that Webster had caved and was ready to negotiate.

Furthermore, Dixon was not aware Special Ops, nor Bishop's people, knew the whereabouts of Jemma Stone, Agent Frost's wife Cindy, their kids and whoever else was with them, cards he could use to apply further pressure. White's people had managed to fly them out of Wye country before the Special Ops team arrived, leaving only the two dead ex-SAS guys.

The Prince was the ultimate reward but Dixon figured he could use the family members to better his position if things got sticky.

It took quite a bit of luck and sheer coincidence that allowed him to abduct the Prince, Dixon mused. The idea came to him when the Prince demanded to get to the Boscombe Down air base where his Sea King squadron was operating from.

The SO1 contingent assigned to him reported it to Dixon asking for guidance. Dixon ordered them to bring in a chopper but, in the chaos, an available chopper was difficult to find.

The Prince, losing his patience, had called his squadron commander informing him that he was coming down with a car, and asked if they could wait for him. The squadron commander, under enormous pressure, agreed to leave the Prince a chopper with a full crew for the two hours it would take him to get from Windsor Castle, where the royal family was rushed to when the trouble erupted.

Informing no one, the Prince walked to the garage, jumped in his Bentley, and took off. No one expected it, since, unlike his younger brother, William had never pulled a stunt like that before and it was his wife, Lady Kate, Duchess of Cambridge, who pointed out to them that her husband had gone.

At that point, his plan for the kidnapping was put in motion.

The entire contingent took off after the Prince in two cars. Dixon's people in one, and others in a second car. In all the chaos it was difficult to predict which way the Prince would take since the beacon in his car failed to transmit. It was the M3 to the A303 or the M4 and A336. The M4 exits were closer, but it was a longer route so Dixon sent the car with his men to the M3, and a second car with the Prince's MI5 personal bodyguard contingent, to the M4, realizing he was taking a chance he would get it wrong, but needing to decide on the spot.

He then sent a third car with Vadim and his men who were at the Flanagan residence in Hempstead, to carry out the abduction once the Prince was located, hopefully before he reached the air base. The car with Dixon's men caught up with the Prince an hour and a half later on the A303 south of Andover, a mere ten miles from the air base, and held the Prince for another hour taking refuge in the fields, before Vadim arrived and took him away to the cottage by the lake.

The second car reached Boscomb and having been told by the gate sentries that the Prince had yet to arrive but that they were expecting him, took off on the A303 toward their colleagues who kept feeding them false information sending them on a wild goose chase all the way back to the M3 while hiding in the fields.

The Prince had always been a target they had considered, Dixon recalled. In Dixon's eyes, he was a legitimate and rather easy target, who would bring maximum effect at minimum cost, and once he had established himself at SO1, there were various ways he knew they could pull it off. But the Russians kept putting it off.

Now, after undermining the currency and blowing up half the town, with a host of casualties to boot, including some of the ones threatening his existence, he had a golden chance to carry out his plan and grab the heir to the throne, politics be damned.

The second car was finally alerted to a dirt road off the A303 where they found their colleagues dumbfounded, standing around the Prince's empty Bentley.

The meager military forces that had remained in the Boscombe area and did not converge on London, were alerted to perform the search, but could not find a trace and in the evening, Vadim appeared with his black head cover once again to announce to the world that they had the Prince.

Dixon's phone rang, waking him out of his reverie. It was Bishop asking him to come to his office.

Chapter Fifty-Four

10:30 AM, Thursday, February 7, 2019

The MI5 main floor, known as the Grid, with its array of computer monitors, electronic, surveillance, and communication equipment, seemed to be in full swing with agents standing around monitors watching several large screens situated above with data running across, consulting one another and moving around frantically.

No one paid any attention to him as he strode in flanked by his two bodyguards.

Dixon reached Bishop's glass office at the edge of the grid and knocked on his door. Bishop sat alone at his desk talking on the phone seemingly unaware as Dixon allowed himself in with his guards.

Bishop, tense on the phone, looked up and motioned for him to take a seat and kept listening to whoever was on the line, not saying much.

A minute later, he put down the phone and, looking haggard, shook his head in disgust.

"Anything I need to know?" Dixon asked.

"Oh there's plenty," Bishop said, "but your guys need to get out of this room."

Dixon hesitated again.

"I thought I made it clear they can't be in on our discussions." Bishop admonished.

He took out his own phone, shut it off, and put it on his desk.

"Turn off your phone and have them wait outside," he commanded, waiting impatiently.

Dixon signaled his men to exit the room, which they did, then took out his mobile phone, turned it off, and put it on Bishop's desk.

Before Bishop could begin speaking, a commotion was heard outside and the door to the office burst open. Taylor and Harriet walked in, guns pointing at Dixon, who began to get up, but quickly sat back in his chair when he realized Bishop's gun was pointing his way as well.

"Show us your hands," Harriet commanded, taking aim at Dixon as Taylor approached him.

"Give up whatever you have under there, Ross," Bishop said, getting up from his seat, Glock in hand.

The look on Dixon's face turned from shock, to surprise, to anger, and finally to acceptance; all in a matter of a few seconds. He made a move to get up, but Taylor, already behind him, put a hand on his shoulder and began frisking him, taking out a gun from a shoulder holster and a second mobile phone, then he produced a pair of handcuffs and cuffed Dixon's hands behind his back.

"Get up!" Bishop ordered, rounding the table and standing over the SO1 chief. "It's time you start earning your pay."

Dixon stood up towering over the shorter Bishop. His black eyes were loathing as he stared at the MI5 chief. With his aquiline nose and wad of black hair, his entire demeanor became that of a caged crow ready to poke someone's eyes out.

They walked out of Bishop's office, Harriet leading the way with Bishop and Taylor in the back. Out on the main floor, the two bodyguards were lying face down on the floor, hands cuffed behind their backs; Edwards and three other agents surrounded them with drawn firearms.

"Put them in separate cages," Bishop directed as he followed his entourage toward the interrogation cells.

When the door to all three cells was shut, they all relaxed for the first time.

"Easier than I thought," Edwards pointed out as everyone gathered by the one-way-looking glass, watching Dixon seated by the lone metal table in his cell, cuffed to his seat.

"We'll need quick answers," Maggie Fox said. She had kept a low profile in one of the back offices and turned up as soon as the three men were apprehended.

"I am afraid that will not be so simple," Harriet remarked. "If Dixon is who we think he is; no doubt he had been preparing for just this consequence a long time. He will be a tough nut to crack if we crack him at all…"

"Let's run a check on the two bodyguards," Bishop suggested. "Also, Harriet, get Olga to organize a team, go down to the SO1 command center, and cease it. Get everyone out of there, lock them up somewhere, then check whatever data exists there that could lead us to any of the bomb locations, the Prince, of course, and to Jemma and Frosty's people. Do not allow any SO1 people to flee or erase data. Report to me as quickly as you can of any findings. I'll have a crack at him first. Then we'll see."

With that, he entered the interrogation cell and took a seat in front of Dixon, everyone watching from behind the looking glass.

"So far," Bishop began, addressing Dixon in a serious but somewhat cynical tone. "There are over four hundred people killed and more than two thousand injured. The Sterling has dropped in value by half, the nation's capital has been paralyzed for a week, and our heir to the throne has been abducted. I do believe you have fulfilled your purpose. Don't you?"

"It's unprecedented to accuse your SO1 chief of such treachery," Dixon stated, staring at Bishop coldly.

"Are you denying involvement?" Bishop asked.

"Of course, I am denying it. This is insane!"

"You left a trail of blood, Ross; and quite a substantial one I dare say: starting with Tompkins, your guy Simon, Officer Evan Wilson, Officer Santana, Fleming, two ex-SAS guys, one Dylan Oliver and our colleague AVM Reed, not to mention the casualties from the bombings, a top agent you tried to frame who is now in a coma, and whatever else you managed to cook up."

"All this does not pertain to me, Trevor," Dixon said lethargically. "How in the world did you connect me to all this? I am the one trying to put a stop to all this."

"We'll get to that later, but I am afraid we've got urgent business to conduct before we discuss reprimands," Bishop said and got up circling the table to stand behind his prisoner.

"Now you know there are chemicals that will make you talk and we normally refrain from using them unless the entire country is seriously threatened and our dear old Prince William is being held hostage. Now if you talk and help us put an end to this, the best I can give is your choice of prison to spend the rest of your days in because I doubt anyone will be forgiving when you are sentenced."

"You got nothing, Trevor! This is an outrage! I want to see Martin. He'll straighten you out."

Bishop moved from behind Dixon signaling his audience to open the door. He poked out his head and signaled Maggie Fox to step in.

"You know Ms. Fox, don't you, Ross?" Bishop said.

Dixon nodded. "Yeah, I know Maggie."

"Well then, Maggie here is Martin's emissary, and it was she, on his behalf, who tied the strings for us as to your involvement. Now, anything you have to say to the PM you can say to Maggie. She has his full authority."

"I was appointed by Martin," Dixon declared. "You people have no right to accuse me of anything and least of all interrogate me!"

"Give it up, Dixon," Maggie Fox said. "The PM knows enough and we are out of time. I'd love to shoot the breeze with you some other time and learn some of your methods. I must admit, you had us fooled. But I am afraid time is of the essence. So let's cut the small talk and you help us restore some order to this ongoing chaos? Ha, what do you say Ross? Does that suit you?"

Dixon chuckled, "Do you really believe I had anything to do with this? You are quite mad, you know."

"Look here, Dixon, or whatever your name is," Bishop began losing his patience. "The longer you hold out, the more money your Russian benefactors will have to pay us to restore this mess. Now you need to start cooperating or we'll need to exploit some extraordinary methods which I am sure are not alien to you."

There was a knock on the cell door. Bishop opened the door and called Maggie to step out. It was Harriet.

"We've run into trouble at SO1 headquarters. Olga went down there with Taylor and some agents and apparently, there was a shootout. Not sure about what evolved or if there are casualties…"

Bishop looked at a loss for a brief moment then he regained his senses. "Harriet, you stay here with Maggie. See if you can milk anything out of him," he said, pointing to Dixon's cell. "I am going down there. Who else is around?"

"Edwards is at the grid collecting people. There should be a few still around." Harriet informed him. Bishop checked his Glock making sure the magazine was secured.

"You do not leave him alone whatever happens!" He ordered, then he turned and ran along the corridor.

Edwards had six men and two women agents huddling around him when Bishop burst onto the main floor. He stopped for a brief second; looked his people over, then took off toward the stairs.

Chapter Fifty-Five

11:30 AM, Thursday, February 7, 2019

They ran in a column down three flights of stairs and emerged at the main lobby, exiting the glass doors past the security station, which was remarkably empty, crossed Whitehall lane, and entered the building where SO1 retained the two bottom floors and the basement.

Past the building's security station, empty as well, Bishop stopped in the lobby and stood quiet for a moment trying to detect any sounds. Everyone followed suit. Suddenly the elevator door opened and a bloody figure emerged from it toppling to the floor.

They all converged on the figure. "It's Sergeant Jeffries," Edwards said, recognizing one of the police officers responsible for security at the MI5 building.

Bishop knelt next to him but then had a thought. "You two," he pointed to whoever was closest to him. "Secure the stairway exits, and you," he pointed to a third agent, "disable the elevator. Keep it right here."

He then knelt close to the police sergeant seeing his shirt dubbed in blood from his chest down. The sergeant was looking at him.

"Medic, I need a medic..." he whispered. Bishop turned to Edwards. "Call in whatever ambulances are available. Are there any medics in the building?"

"I'll check," Edwards said, whipping out his mobile and dialing the emergency numbers.

"Can you tell me what is happening down there?" Bishop asked.

"I am not sure," Jeffries said, his voice barely audible. "We heard shots and ran over here. They came from below so we ran down..." He stopped wincing in pain. "As soon as we got there, two men rushed passed us up the stairs, then one turned and shot me..."

The lobby lights flickered. Most of the building was empty and the lights were darkened except for the main lobby and stairways.

"Who was with you?"

"Sergeant O'Neal, and the two security people from here," Jeffries whispered. "They ran after them I believe. I fell next to the elevator and managed to call it and come up here."

"We didn't see anyone running out," Bishop said, looking at his people who all nodded in agreement.

"Is there another exit out of this building?" Bishop asked as ambulance sirens were heard from a distance.

"There's a back exit one floor down," Jeffries said, gulping for air.

"GI," Bishop snapped at one of his agents, nicknamed GI Joe, "you stay with the sergeant until the medics arrive, then you hop on back to the grid, to the holding cells, and inform Harriet what is happening. You guard them with your life with this machine gun of yours. Nobody comes in or goes out of this building until we figure out what had happened."

The ambulances could be heard closing in and several more figures were crossing the street from the MI5 building.

"Sarah," Bishop addressed another agent, "you and Pearce round up whoever is still at the grid and run a street sweep around these buildings. Check out the embankment as well and along the river."

He got up. "Edwards you and Chapman come with me."

They took the spiraling stairway down three floors. Edwards in front pointing his gun down the stairs, Chapman and Bishop following close behind.

They reached the basement corridor and turned toward the communication center which loomed dark behind a shattered glass door.

Edwards took out his flashlight, stopped at the entrance, and surveyed the darkened interior shining the light slowly across its main floor.

Five bodies were sprawled in different postures; three were lying face down in the middle of the floor; one was flung across a control panel at the front of the room, and a fifth was on his back in front of a half-opened side door. There didn't seem to be any movement in the room.

The three agents, flashlights beaming, hurried to check the bodies. Taylor lay in a pool of blood, large holes in the back of his head and his back. Two other agents right next to him, suffered the same fate. A fourth agent lay on his back in front of the side door riddled with bullets. The fifth, an SO1 agent, lay across a large communications console, unmoving.

"Anyone see Olga?" Edwards asked, looking around him frantically.

They all shined their flashlights to the four corners of the equipment-filled room and all three saw the movement. Edwards lurched forward gun at the ready finding Olga behind an office desk, only her legs showing, lethargically seated, her back to the wall, her eyes shut, but her mouth moving, her mobile phone still in her right hand.

"Olga, it's us! You are safe now! Can you hear me?"

Olga opened her eyes and smiled weakly.

"I knew you would come," she said weakly.

"Where are you hurt?" Edwards asked.

Olga moved her lips. "My back…" She managed to whisper. "Can't feel my legs…"

Bishop whipped out his phone and called GI. "You still up there?" He asked urgently.

"Just left," GI said. "On my way to the grid."

"Who's up there?" Bishop demanded.

"Briggs and Shepherd, guarding the stairs."

"OK, you go on," Bishop said, disconnected and dialed Shepherd.

Lucy Shepherd answered after one ring.

"You see any medics?" Bishop barked.

"Sure do," Lucy said. "There are several patching up the sergeant."

"Sent them down here! On the double!" Bishop commanded. "We got five killed and Olga is barely alive."

"Right away," Lucy said and ran to the medics.

"Olga, can you tell us what happened here?" Edwards was asking her when Bishop turned his attention back to his wounded agent.

Olga weakly raised her hand, signaling to Edwards to lean closer which he did.

"We were surprised by someone…" She said weakly. "They cut off the power and came at us from the side door…"

"How many were here when you came?"

"Three I think…" She took another weak breath. "And another who they shot as well…"

"Did you recognize any of them?" Edwards pressed, as two medics burst into the room.

"I am not sure…" Olga said. "I had my back turned…"

The medic pushed his way toward her and Edwards made way. He got up and stood with Bishop and Chapman as the two medics carefully lay Olga on a stretcher.

Edwards relayed what he had just heard.

More medics poured in and started checking the carnage.

Bishop looked to Olga, needing descriptions but she was no longer conscious; The medics were securing her neck, fixing an air mask to her face, and an IV to a vein in her right arm.

"Chapman," Bishop snapped. "You escort Olga to wherever they take her. Sit with her in the ambulance as far as I am concerned but don't let her out of your sight! Is this clear?"

"I will if they let me…" Chapman started to say. He was a deceivingly fragile-looking agent, extremely bright with round wire-rimmed glasses and a thin body who was a triathlon champ of sorts. "They will get her into an operating room pretty quick."

"Then you sit outside the operating room until she's out!"

Chapman nodded and Bishop signaled to Edwards to follow him and he ran out of the communication room and up the stairs. Lucy Shepherd met them at the top of the stairs. She was athletically built with large brown eyes and long blond hair arranged into a ponytail, dressed in skinny jeans and a large overcoat.

"No one goes down there unless it's a medic or one of our guys!" Bishop ordered, out of breath from the climb. Lucy nodded

"Where's Briggs?" Bishop snapped.

Lucy pointed toward a second stairway across the lobby. Briggs was watching them from afar and Bishop made a sign for him to approach.

Lawrence Briggs, a burly agent with a crew-cut and enormous arms, came running.

"We need to watch the entrance to this building," Bishop said. "Get yourself over there and keep an eye on whoever comes in. If you suspect anyone or identify any of the SO1 guys, you apprehend him or her. Clear?"

Briggs nodded.

"I'll send more people to assist and search the basement and offices as soon as the casualties are evacuated. It seems Olga is the only one left alive down there."

Lucy and Briggs took their positions looking crestfallen at the news of the horrific fate suffered by their comrades, while Bishop and Edwards hurried out of the building.

"Call Sarah or Pearce and ask them to give us an update on the escapees. Also, I want to talk to that Sergeant O'Neal who chased after them."

Edwards nodded and took out his phone.

"I am going back up to inform the Home Secretary and the PM of the developments and we need to somehow neutralize all SO1 teams without further delay," Bishop said as he stopped with Edwards in the middle of the street between the two buildings.

"Then I'll get that traitor to talk!" He said angrily and hurried away.

Chapter Fifty-Six

Noon, Thursday, February 7, 2019

Holding on to Judge Roy Graham's signed warrant, department of treasury agent Bill Eckersley sat in the passenger seat of a black government Range Rover, watching the side mirror for the two cars following him, speeding along Finchley Road toward Hampstead. Eckersley was a short man who kept his head shaved religiously since his college days when a female student suggested it would be more appealing when his hair began to seriously thin out. He was a plump, five foot eight inches, numbers cruncher, or CPA, who joined the treasury department right after college and quickly climbed up the ranks to his current status of department head.

He had under him, in the foreign currency department, close to one hundred agents working the latest currency disaster and he finally felt they were getting somewhere, though Flanagan's silence was disturbing.

As they were veering onto Fitzjohn's Road, his phone rang. It was Harriet.

"Bill, Harriet Gold, TFB. Where are you?" she asked urgently.

"Just entering Hampstead…" Eckersley informed her. "We should be at Flanagan's house in three to five minutes."

"Don't go near the house!" Harriet warned. "Stop your car and call in a SWAT team."

"Why? What's going on?" Eckersley asked surprised, signaling his driver to stop, looking in the side mirror to make sure his entourage followed suit.

"Just do it!" Harriet said. "I don't have all the details, but you need to be extremely cautious approaching that house. Wait for the SWAT team, then follow their lead. I'll try and send people from my crew to assist. Flanagan may be in on it or he may be held against his will."

Eckersley looked at his driver then at the two agents in back. His three-car convoy had all stopped.

"OK, we're at Fitzjohn's corner of Lyndhurst Road. I am calling in a SWAT team." He informed Harriet. "I'll wait for them here."

"Good man," she said. "Now who is handling Flanagan's offices?"

"My deputy, Rita," Eckersley said.

"Stop her too if it's not too late. Call a SWAT team for her as well."

"Will do," Eckersley said, confused, but realizing he could not object.

"And keep me appraised. I'll be back if I have more to report. I hope this won't turn into a hostage situation."

Harriet clicked off before Eckersley had a chance to inquire more. He sighed and punched the phone keyboard quickly, calling in a SWAT team.

Then he called Rita.

Rita Garret was an attractive, tall brunette, thinly built, 40-year-old treasury agent, going through an ugly divorce. She had moved out of her house with her two children to an apartment in Shepherd's Bush from a posh home in that same neighborhood and was harassed endlessly by her husband, haggling over visitation rights and dragging her to court whenever possible.

Eckersley had worked closely with her in the department on various cases and had picked her as his deputy as soon as he received his posting as currency department head. She was a bright, relentless operator, who in the last six months, had had a difficult time focusing on her work. But as soon as the currency disaster emerged, she left the kids with her husband and focused all her attention on locating the source or sources, who threatened to destabilize the British economy. She immediately identified Russian Rubles as the source, acquired by the billions against the English pound, and began investigating a host of hedge funds and investment banks that traded in that currency.

It took them almost a week to pinpoint who initiated the trade and the host of rumors that caused traders and banks to sell the British currency short by the billions, reducing the sterling's value to half. She was now leading a team of treasury agents to investigate the source—Flanagan's Europe Investment Bank offices on Fleet Street.

She answered on the first ring.

"Rita," Eckersley said, out of breath. "Where are you?"

"Just managed to break into the building," she reported excitedly. "The place is completely empty as far as I can tell."

"Good god," Eckersley sighed. "The TFB just ordered me to call in a SWAT team for you to get you in the building."

"Why? What happened?" Rita asked, alarmed.

"I am not sure, but they think Flanagan may be held against his will. They asked me to wait for a SWAT team to enter his house and asked me to warn you as well."

"Well, there's no one here," Rita said. "My agents are searching the premises but have found no one around. Not a soul."

Eckersley thought a moment if maybe MI5 were overly paranoid but instantly dismissed that thought. They were in the midst of the worst week in Britain's history since World War Two, and no threat could be offhandedly dismissed.

"Shall I continue searching the place?" Rita was asking.

"By all means," Eckersley said, "just make sure no one ambushes you in the process. Put some people at the exists and make sure the place is secure."

"Got it. I'll keep you appraised." Rita said. "And be careful at his house."

"Sure will," Eckersley said and disconnected.

The SWAT team arrived forty minutes later, two armored vehicles led by a black Range Rover. A familiar red-headed man jumped out of the passenger seat and hurried to him. It was Agent Edwards whom Eckersley first met at the briefing in Bishop's conference room just a few hours ago.

They shook hands and Edwards quickly filled him in on the events that took place immediately after the briefing with Bishop.

Eckersley shook his head in wonder.

"Dixon?" he said, unable to stop himself. "It's all him?"

"He hasn't confessed yet, but yes, he's rogue."

Eckersley and Edwards walked over to the armored vehicles where Officer Walter "Wally" Wade, the SWAT team commander, stood outside the lead vehicle with two of his men studying a drawing of Flanagan's home and surrounding area on an iPad.

"…assuming we can get close enough without being seen, we go in through the balcony on the second floor…" Wade was saying. "There's a wall right underneath without windows which we can use to climb up…."

"Do we know who's at the house?" Wade addressed Edwards.

"The entire Flanagan family is unreachable," Edwards said, "which could mean they are all in there."

"Or it could mean no one is there…" Wade said. "Did we check their residences?"

"Flanagan has two sons; both are married with children." Eckersley pitched in. "One son lives in Chelsea, the other here in Hampstead. We tried calling them but all phones were shut off. Of course, with the state London is in, people may have shut off their phones or have no signal."

"I doubt that's the reason," Wade said. "The only form of communication these days is smartphones."

"I agree," Edwards said, "these guys made sure their threats reached everyone."

"Did anyone question the neighbors around here?" Wade asked. "They may have seen something."

Edwards looked at Eckersley who shook his head.

"First time we needed to come here," Edwards said apologetically. "Had no reason until this morning."

Wade looked at his two comrades and all three nodded, relaying an unspoken understanding between them.

"OK. There's no time so we go in." Wade concluded, "We'll have to assume the entire family is in there held captive by these maniacs."

"There could be small children there…" Eckersley pointed out.

"These are desperate times we're in," Wade reminded them. "Under typical circumstances, we would find out as much as possible and may even opt to negotiate. But to wipe out the city from this scum, we need to make sacrifices, children included, unfortunately. Our entire future hangs by a thread here and I've got orders straight from the top to put an end to this."

With that, Wade jumped into the passenger seat of the lead armored vehicle, his two subordinates got in the second vehicle and were preparing to move.

"Kevin," Wade called Edwards who stepped to his window. "You take the treasury man with you in the Landrover and follow us. I'll let you know when to stay clear. Leave everyone else here ready to move at a moment's notice."

Edwards nodded, signaled to Eckersley to join him and jumped in the Landrover, his driver looking questioningly at him as Eckersley ran to inform his people then jumped in the back.

Chapter Fifty-Seven

1 PM, Thursday, February 7, 2019

Home Secretary Nigel Scott stood at the unidirectional looking glass staring into the interrogation cell where Harriet Gold and MI5 head Trevor Bishop were waiting for Dixon to start making some sense. He sat cuffed to the table with his head thrown back, his eyes blinking in and out of focus, wincing in pain. A man was holding him firm while another was plucking a fingernail from his right index finger with a pair of pliers.

A second fingernail was pulled out making the subject faint before a syringe was produced, with some derivative of the notorious Sodium Pentothal, also known as the "truth serum," which was a range of psychoactive drugs occasionally used to obtain information from subjects who were a threat to national security. These drugs' effectiveness was never proven, never accepted by the courts, and were essentially banned, except for extremely rare cases where the threat to large groups of people was imminent. Its use also required the approval of the Home Secretary.

So far, Bishop had briefed Scott, but Dixon had not given an inch. He made a mockery of their questions, knowing exactly where to point them each time, easily deflecting blame, though it was obvious he was not who they thought he was. The ramifications of such treason were mind-boggling, Scott mused, wondering above all, how he had managed to recruit people who had succeeded in passing the extensive British security services personal background checks and polygraph examinations.

There was an obvious large displacement in his childhood whereabouts history, though he claimed to have grown up in London's west side, where he had been born, and that the government had the documents to prove it. In sixteen years at the Home Office, he had done border patrols, become a team leader, a section leader, the SO1 deputy chief, and now the SO1 chief. He had a Bachelor of Arts degree from Westminster University in London, worked in the Ministry of Defense procurement office for five years, got his master's degree in International Relations and Security at Westminster graduating with honors in 2003; joined the Border Force, within the Home Office, dealing with smugglers and immigration enforcement, then joined SO1.

But his name was also searched for, in missing children reports dating back forty years, and was found to be reported missing in 1980. A missing child who was never found according to the records. Was he the same man?

His parents were no longer alive. Perished in a fire at their London flat at the turn of the Millennium, right at midnight when the world was celebrating, from an apparent gas leak in the apartment that had caught a lighted cigar, an event that was not exclusive during those hours of celebration. And he had no siblings.

Board of Education records showed that at age sixteen he had reappeared in a London high school as if he never left. There were no records of previous years. Kindergarten records were not found. Elementary and junior high school either.

How did he survive all these years? Who paid his tuition? Where did he live?

Scott looked at Maggie Fox standing next to him, staring at the proceedings in horror. She looked at him.

"Is this going to work?" She asked.

"It should," Scott said. "Partially, at least. Hopefully enough to get a location on the Prince and those damn bombs still lying around London."

Bishop went ahead and stood over Dixon after he was brought back to consciousness by the interrogators.

"What's your name?" He queried.

"Ross Dixon," Dixon said weakly.

"And where are you from Ross?" Bishop continued.

"From London," Dixon replied.

"You ever live abroad?"

"Not really..."

"Where at?"

"Don't recall..." Dixon whispered. "Somewhere..."

"Where are your parents?"

"Dead, I think..."

"Do you belong to 'Sons of Jihad'?"

There was a pause. Dixon was trying to get a grip on his thoughts but seemed unable. He looked dumbfounded at Bishop then at the doctor.

"Sons of who…?"

"Sons of Jihad," Bishop repeated. "It's a group you trained with…"

Dixon was weakly shaking his head. "Don't think so…"

"Can you tell us where Prince William is?" Bishop continued.

Dixon suddenly produced a painful smile. "William? Must be with Kate…"

Bishop looked over at Harriet. "You want to give it a try? We don't have all day…"

"Can you tell us where Agent Frost is?" She asked.

"White…" Dixon began to say, then stopped, looking sheepish almost.

"Yes, Andy White," Harriet urged him on. "What about him?"

"He will kill Frost..."

"Where is he holding the Prince?" Harriet pressed on.

Dixon's eyes seemed to go out of focus and his head tilted back again. The two orderlies took hold of him once again forcing Dixon to look at his interrogators.

Suddenly, Dixon began speaking Arabic. It was a bit mumbled and incoherent but clearly Arabic.

Bishop looked at Harriet helplessly and she shook her head and backed out of the room quickly moving past Scott and Maggie to find someone who knew the language.

Dixon kept mumbling in Arabic until Harriet showed up with agent Rasheed Duranni from the Middle East department who stepped into the room and picked up on the conversation translating as best he could.

It almost seemed like Dixon was preaching a sermon, or praying. He had his eyes shut and was bobbing his head up and down.

"Ask him about the whereabouts of the Prince," Bishop pressed agent Duranni.

"With White… he says he's with White!" Duranni said.

"Do we have White's Mobile?" Bishop asked. "Can we track him somehow?"

"Afraid not," Harriet said. "White has gone off the grid. They must have had a safeguard in place for just such an occasion. The escapees from the Comms room must have alerted them all."

"Other ministers and royal family members could be hurt," Maggie said to Scott outside the cell. Scott was looking on intently, entranced in the drama taking place in the interrogation room.

"We've taken care of that…" He said offhand. "First thing we did…" He did not elaborate but kept watching Dixon and Rasheed.

"He's talking about a helicopter ride. Wait! North to a lake…" Rasheed was saying excitedly. Dixon's eyes rolled up, showing only white as he lost consciousness again, his head tipping back.

"Wake him up!" Harriet ordered. "Quick!"

The two orderlies gave Dixon something to sniff which startled him awake but he was still out of focus looking around the room, then he began to wet his pants.

Rasheed kept talking to him in Arabic but Dixon was back to English, his eyes focusing just a bit as he looked at Bishop.

"Your Prince is dead," he said suddenly and went for the syringe in one of the orderly's hands.

In one swift motion, he grabbed it and stuck the needle in his own neck, emptying its contents into his body before the orderly could pull it out.

He began to convulse almost immediately, foaming at the mouth as the two orderlies lay him down and began emergency resuscitation efforts, cutting a small hole in his neck and inserting a tube to allow him to breathe. It seemed to work as Dixon stopped convulsing, but he was past being able to provide any useful information let alone talk.

Scott hurried into the room.

"Where do you keep the videotapes?" he asked. Harriet pointed to the two cameras attached near the ceiling.

"Get them and go over them with Rasheed here. See if he can learn more from the Arabic parts that he missed."

Harriet nodded and leaped out of the room to alert the technicians.

"Bishop, you and Maggie come with me," he said and turned to leave. "The PM needs to know about this."

Chapter Fifty-Eight

1:30 PM, Thursday, February 7, 2019

Officer Wally Wade crawled to a vantage point where he figured he had a clear path to the wall below the balcony to Flanagan's Hampstead mansion. Several windows were facing both the front roundabout and the sides of the house, but Wade was counting on a blind spot that he hoped would allow him to reach the side of the house under the balcony without being detected.

They had taken the side streets and left their vehicles on a parallel street, moving carefully through several backyards, among bushes and trees toward their target.

The side of the house was now in front of them across a wide lawn approximately fifteen meters from where they were. They hid along a wall of a neighboring house, and Wade was preparing to send a team around the back of the house when a side door opened and a neighbor stuck his head out, looking awestruck.

Wade signaled him to keep quiet and step back in, then thought better of it, and stepped in after the man who was dressed in a robe and had a cup of coffee in his hand.

"You know the neighbor there?" he asked, pointing toward Flanagan's house, not bothering to explain his actions.

"No, not really…" The man, short and balding with a pair of thick glasses, said defensively. "I've seen him out on the lawn a few times in the past…"

"Seen him lately?" Wade asked.

"Not since the curfew…" the man said defensively.

"Seen anyone else lurking there? A group of men maybe?"

"No, I can't say I have…"

"Can we use your house to get to the other side?" Wade asked.

"Well…I suppose…" The man stammered. "You guys Special Forces… or something?"

"Yes we are," Wade said. "And we need to get to that house undetected. Can you give us a hand?"

"Does this have to do with… you know… the crisis?"

"It certainly does!" Wade said. "Now can you show us the way through? Anyone else in here?"

"Just my wife upstairs…" the man said, frightened.

"Well, run along and make sure she does not make a fuss. Then show us the way to the other side."

The man took off down a narrow corridor. Wade signaled for several men to step in and told them what he had in mind, then he stepped out and crawled to the edge of the lawn, his people behind him, getting ready to strike.

A few minutes later, he got a signal on his mobile that the team that had gone through the house was in position. He looked once to make sure no one was watching from Flanagan's windows then took off across the lawn, four of his men in pursuit.

They hit the wall below the balcony and halted for a brief moment to catch their breath and make sure they were not detected.

All was quiet so far.

Two of the operatives, with ropes with hooks at the end, chucked them up to the balcony's outer railing and pulled to make sure they caught.

Without hesitation, Wade pulled on the rope and with three mighty heaves reached the railing and climbed over finding himself on a wide empty veranda with just a couple of flowerpots adorning its vast space.

A sliding glass door beyond, which Wade could see a twin-size bed was the only entrance to the house and Wade quickly tried the lock.

It was unlocked. The glass door slid quietly to the side and Wade found himself in a wide bedroom with a white thick carpet that muted his movements.

He looked back to make sure his guys were following. They were all there, eyes focused, guns at the ready.

He inched toward the door, silenced Glock in hand, his assault rifle strapped on his back. He pressed the door handle and pulled carefully.

Voices could be heard from somewhere below. He took a peak, seeing a wide hallway covered in the same thick white rug. To his left were three rooms, their doors shut, and to his right a wide stairway leading down.

Wade had no idea what he would be facing. He hoped he would identify his foes in an instant and be able to drop them, the element of surprise on his side. But years of experience taught him to expect the worst, the unexpected. Worse of all he was afraid of hitting innocent hostages, and children worst of all. And he had no idea how many were there, friend or foe.

If the entire family was there, then there would be three children and six adults who he would have to watch out for, amongst who knew how many adversaries. Furthermore, they could be anywhere on the lower level; He had no way of knowing. Someone could pop out of a bathroom or the kitchen... He had the layout of the house and could anticipate where the different entrances were situated, but that was the extent of his knowledge. He had no intel on the type of firepower he could be facing or the type of weapons they possessed.

He signaled his men; each was assigned an entrance once they were down on the bottom level and began inching his way down the steps. The stairway spiraled around a stone wall decorated with family photos and the living room appeared below.

Wade could see Flanagan's white hair mane sitting on the floor with two of the children. One of them looked up. It was the girl. A look of surprise on her face, she started pointing catching the attention of a man in black clothes sitting in back of her on a sofa. He raised his head and looked at Wade, his stare barely comprehending what he was seeing when he tried to shout and reached for his gun.

Wade shot him in the head before he had time to utter a sound. Flanagan turned around, saw Wade, and reached for the kids. A second man in black clothes appeared from the bathroom and was shot by Wade as well but managed a shout before falling to the floor.

Wade jumped the rest of the way to the bottom and hurried toward the lower hallway, his men spread out bursting through the various entrances.

Wade heard shots from the kitchen area as he hurried toward the back door along the bottom hallway, unlocked it, and opened it, his second team waiting just outside ready to jump in. When he turned back, he saw a tall blond man with an assault rifle aiming his way and he did the only thing left for him to do; he fell to the floor. A burst of bullets sailed over his head hitting some of the men just coming in. Wade, unharmed, aimed his Glock from the floor and shot, but the blond man had taken refuge behind a wall and was spraying to corridor with bullets. The second team could not enter and had to retreat with two of its men lying on the floor next to Wade.

Low wailing could be heard now around the house. Wade jumped up and managed to enter a room along the corridor before another burst of bullets raked by. In the room were Jenson Flanagan, his wife Abbey, and a small child, cowering behind a king-size bed.

Wade made a sign for them to keep quiet but the woman screamed for her other son. Wade did not have time to deal with her. He looked through the opening and saw the blond man scoot for the living room.

Wade's man, Michael Brock, nicknamed "the Rock," who took a position behind the bathroom wall, shot at the blond guy as he went for Flanagan and the kids. The man spun around and delivered a burst of fire toward Brock, who had to retreat behind the bathroom wall.

Two more men in black, burst from the kitchen toward the living room spraying the room with bullets. Wade's man, coming out of a room adjacent to the kitchen caught a burst into the chest and was thrown backward.

It was now Wade and Brock, against three armed men; one of them, the blond man, was wounded in the shoulder. All three moved toward Flanagan who was on the living room rug sprawled over his two grandkids.

Then the front door burst open, and three operatives from the backup team burst through shooting their pistols at the three black figures. All three went down.

Two remained flat on the bellies, but the tall blond man was crawling toward something unseen by Wade and his men.

Then Jenny crawled from the kitchen pointing at the crawling man.

"Don't let him…" she whispered. "Don't…" Then she fainted.

Wade jumped forward with Brock covering and grabbed hold of the blond man who was inches away from a mobile phone that had flown out of his shirt pocket with the force of the bullet that had hit his back. Wade snatched the phone and kept hold of the man who was breathing heavily.

Flanagan raised his head, his face deathly white, and pointed to a bracelet on the children's legs.

The men quickly spread, searching the house for additional threats. Jenson, his wife Abby, and little John came out of their bedroom from the bottom hallway, gingerly approaching the living room afraid of what they would find.

322

Abby saw Robbie alive and well and ran to him. Sarah crawled over to her mother who was passed out on the floor near the kitchen, and hugged her tightly.

"Where's Dad?" she asked.

It was Gabriella, the housekeeper, who had opened the front door for the backup team and now went to kneel by Sarah hugging her closely.

Brock came out of the kitchen shaking his head. It caused Flanagan to rise and stumble there. His wife Sheila, Michael, the Flanagan younger brother, Sarah's father, and officer Brian Cook, known to all as "Cookie," were dead.

Cookie had gone there first and was met by two black suits who shot him from close range then finished off Michael and Sheila, his mother. Jenny, who was there as well was shot in the back but had remained conscious long enough to call out a warning to Wade.

"Anybody else here?" Wade asked, looking at Jenson who was holding little John, looking around at the carnage.

"No, I don't think so," he said in a daze, then hurried into the kitchen. His mother and brother were lying there, dead.

"Edwards, you there?" Wade said into his mobile.

"Right where you left us," Edwards said. "We heard shots. You guys OK?"

"We need ambulances, quick! There are casualties! Call 'em in and get over here quick!" Wade commanded.

"On the double!" He heard Edwards say and shut off his phone, then looked around to assess the damage.

Three of his men and three hostages were dead. One hostage was seriously wounded and he himself was shot in the shoulder. It would have counted as a disastrous mission had they had enough time to prepare, but under the circumstances, he felt they had done well.

Brock and the rest of the men were checking the fallen for vital signs but managed only a weak pulse on Jenny. First aid kits were pulled out and they began administering emergency CPR to her.

Flanagan came out of the kitchen with Jenson, both looked devastated but tried to keep their wits about them.

They sat all three children on the living room rug, away from Jenny who was being treated, and pointed at the bracelets.

"These are explosives," Flanagan said in a voice filled with rage. "They warned us not to touch and had some way of detonating them from afar."

Wade stared at the mobile phone he had snatched from the blond man.

"Yes," Flanagan said, seeing Wade's surprise, "they had us pegged from the start. Not much we can do you see. And we still can't be sure who else can detonate these, so we better get it off them quick."

Wade got back on his phone. "Kevin, get an explosive unit in here as well, on the double! They have the children booby-trapped…"

Chapter Fifty-Nine

2 PM, Thursday, February 7, 2019

Bishop, standing outside the interrogation cell where for the last hour, the medics and doctor were hectically working to save Dixon, answered his phone on the first beep.

"Boss, it's Lucy," he heard her distorted voice weakly with an echo. "Yes, Lucy, speak up. I can barely hear you."

"I am in the SO1 communications center like you asked, Sir," she said, raising her voice. "Most of the control boards are damaged from the shooting and whatnot, but I found a laptop that has not been damaged locked up in a cupboard. It works but it has a password we need to override somehow. Anyone you can send over?"

"Hold on," Bishop said, walking to the main floor and holding the phone to his ear. He looked around the room where several agents, sitting in front of TV and computer screens, were monitoring metropolitan London, simultaneously talking into microphones and mobile phones.

"Anyone here know how to hack a computer?" he asked, raising his voice over the commotion.

A few hands were raised all pointing to an athletic-looking man who was dressed like a boxer, in training attire and a hoodie, sitting in the middle of the grid working an array of computer screens in front of him.

The man was so involved that he seemed oblivious to the commotion around him, focusing on his job. Bishop walked over to him tapping him on the shoulder.

"What's your name, laddy?" he asked as the man turned and looked at him, surprised.

"I… I am Marcus," he said and stood up. "Pardon me, didn't see you there, sir."

"I need you to hack into a computer," Bishop said without preamble, noticing Marcus looking around uneasily.

"Where is it?" he asked, his blue eyes focusing on the MI5 chief. "It's in another building, can you go there?"

Again, Marcus looked around uneasily. "They need me here, sir," he said looking around. "Can it be brought here?"

"Lucy, is Briggs still with you?" Bishop barked into the phone.

"He's still up there watching the front door," Lucy said.

"Bring the laptop up here to the grid and tell Briggs not to let anyone into the SO1 area. I'll send another person to help him keep an eye."

"Be right up, sir," Lucy said and hung up.

"Marcus, Agent Lucy Shepherd is coming up here with a laptop. I need you to help her crack it. Top priority! Are we clear?"

Marcus nodded and sat back at his station. Bishop walked back to the holding cells.

Lucy showed up five minutes later, panting, holding a laptop under her arm.

She stopped at the entrance past the glass partition and stood a minute catching her breath, looking around. No one was paying attention, so she raised her voice asking where Bishop was.

"Lucy, over here!" The man with a hoodie called to her from the center of the grid, two other agents by his side looking up as well.

Lucy nodded then smiled, not recognizing him in his gym attire for a second. Marcus signaled her to approach.

"I am Marcus," he said, smiling as if introducing himself to her for the first time. "This the device needs hacking into?" he asked, pointing at the computer under her arm.

"Yes, please," she said gratefully and handed him the laptop.

Marcus connected the mobile device to his own 50-inch computer screen and began hacking away.

Bishop and Harriet came in to watch the proceedings. Dixon was still in and out of consciousness in the interrogation cell. The doctor was monitoring his condition but so far, they were unable to make him talk. His two bodyguards were being questioned in adjacent cells without much success.

Marcus was working on the laptop on his desk among his various gadgets.

After several minutes, he turned it off, pressing the power button for a few seconds shutting the system down. He then powered it up again and chose the

"Start Windows Normally" option, then shut it down again. Powering up again, he chose the "Launch Startup Repair" option.

The agents around him stared, mesmerized, as Marcus went about bypassing the password without hesitation.

The computer began trying to repair the Windows software. It took a short minute after which Marcus received the option to "View Problem Details," choosing the small arrow next to it, and opening a window with a link marked:/windows/system32.

He pressed the mouse pad opening a Notepad screen and pressed "Control O".

He chose several files and went to the local disc changing within the system 32 file "Sethc" to "Sethc1", then detected a cmd file, and pasted it, changing its name back to "Sethc".

He looked around the room at the astonished faces around him.

"Is this going to work?" Lucy asked worriedly.

"Let's wait and see," Marcus said shutting down all windows but for one he pressed on a small "x" on the bottom, then pressed "finish." The computer shut off again and then restarted. Pressing the shift key several times Marcus brought up a message window, closed the "Sticky Keys" window, and entered the Administrator window typing "Net User" and pressing the Enter key, shutting the computer down once again.

When he restarted it again, it booted up and uploaded the Windows Chrome screen without a password.

A large cheer went up from the agents watching and Lucy gave Marcus a kiss on the cheek.

"All yours," Marcus said, blushing, shaking some outstretched hands and accepting pats on the back.

Lucy grabbed the computer and began scanning its files as everyone went back to their tasks. Harriet came over to help.

The incredible feat took all of five minutes.

******

Jemma and Bond were marched out of the cottage to a wooden outhouse near the lake. One of the two guards unbolted the door and they followed White in, both the armed guards following, shutting the door behind them.

It took them a minute to adjust to the darkness and when they did they saw Prince William there, sitting on a small cot, leaning on the wooden wall covered by a blanket. A small electric heater on the floor next to the cot spread a faint light in the small cabin which otherwise was empty but for a small shredded rug in the corner parallel to the bed. There was a foul smell of wood rotting and Jemma shivered from the cold.

"We're planning to provide you some company," White said to William in a derogatory tone.

Jemma could not hold her tongue. "You have some nerve treating him this way!" She hissed and was immediately struck across the mouth staggering back but holding her own.

White was rubbing the back of his hand, cut by Jemma's front teeth. He was about to strike her again when William called out. "Hitting defenseless women Mr. White. Is that your thing?"

"She's TFB," White uttered, "she can take it."

But he refrained from hitting her again. Instead, he whipped out a pistol from his coat pocket and put it to Jemma's right temple.

"It'll go off the next time you open your mouth!" He hissed, then pushed her back. She almost stumbled to the floor if it wasn't for Bond who caught her and kept her standing.

In the dim heater's light, White's angry features were augmented. He wheeled from the agents and addressed William.

"Care to babysit?" He spat.

William shut his eyes and sighed. "I'll do whatever it takes providing you don't hurt any more people."

"Oh, there will be bloodshed…" White said mockingly. "You can count on that, which is why I need you to watch over their kids."

William opened his eyes looking hard at the rogue agent. "Haven't you ruined enough lives already?"

"Small change compared to lives ruined by the monarchy; I dare say…"

"Will you at least allow their mothers to stay with them?" Bond interjected.

White wheeled around to stare at Bond. "Now why didn't I think of that?" He mocked, then addressed Jemma. "The four children will be brought here to stay with his excellency. You make sure they behave. Are we clear?"

Bond squeezed Jemma's shoulder. She looked up at White in defiance but said nothing.

"I'll take that for a yes," he said and signaled his men to open the door and lead the way back to the cottage.

Gabi and Zoe were still curled up next to their mother when Jemma and Bond arrived back from the outhouse. Ian had his head on Camilla's lap and Colin on Jake's, spread next to one another on the floor, both fast asleep.

Jemma kissed both her boys on their heads, and sat between her husband and Cindy, explaining to the group in a whisper what they were expected to do. Noah Chisholm and Mary, sitting to the side, received the explanation from Bond who lowered himself next to them.

There was a moment of silence before the adults all began whispering angrily at one another. Cindy held on to her girls and was shaking her head, tears flowing down her cheeks again. Jake was beside himself with rage and was about to get up and stomp to White's office when Bond intervened.

"This is not up for a vote," he whispered to the group. "White is on edge, even frightened, and I believe something is going down. Maybe a rescue attempt. It's possible the children will be best protected staying with the Prince."

They all stared at him.

"What do you think is going down?" Jake asked, first to comprehend the possibilities.

Bond looked around making sure the guards were out of earshot. "Not sure but White said there will be bloodshed. That and his behavior may indicate they are expecting something."

"Sure they are expecting something." Camilla reflected. "They've been expecting something all along…"

"No, I believe they are expecting something very soon," Bond clarified.

"But Prince William is the primary target. They may want the kids as a human shield around him," Jemma argued.

"Not likely," Bond said. "Whoever's coming for us will make damn sure the Prince remains alive."

"They may threaten to harm the kids if anyone approaches William," Jake interjected.

"True, but they can do that regardless," Bond replied. "No, I think they want their most valuable assets together and those are the kids and Prince William. We on the other hand are expendable."

At that moment, White stormed out of his office. Signaling to two of the guards, as he approached the group who all stared up at him.

"Well, what'll be?" He asked impatiently. "I don't have all day."

Cindy shook the girls who awoke scratching their eyes.

"I want Daddy," Zoe said yawning and stretching. Cindy hugged them both and got up holding their hands. Jemma woke the boys who rolled over trying to avoid the nuisance.

"Come on, guys," Jake said pulling them up. "You can go on sleeping next to a Prince. Would you like that?"

Colin and Ian shook out of their reverie.

"We are going to see him?" Ian asked.

Jemma threw an insolent look at White.

"Yes, you are, my darlings," she said. "He's expecting you."

Both Cindy and Jemma took the kids by the hands but White signaled for them to remain. They looked at him astonished.

"This is not your everyday school drop-off," White snickered. "We'll make sure they get there safe."

"I'd like to tag along," Bond said.

White looked at him contemptuously. "You bloody will not!" He said and strode off, the guards steering the four kids after him.

Cindy held on to Jemma. Both had tears in their eyes. Camilla and Mary came over to give comfort as they watched the entourage disappear out the door.

"What if they take them somewhere else?" Noah said suddenly and everyone turned to look at him.

"Noah!" Mary said incredulously. "Don't we have enough to worry about?"

Everyone looked to Bond.

"Could that happen?" Jake asked carefully.

"Anything can happen when you're a hostage," Bond said exasperated. "But then why would they bother to notify the Prince if that was the case?"

The argument appeased them for a short while, though both Cindy, Jake, and Jemma, became more agitated than they already were. Jake kept pacing back and forth in front of their spot, Cindy and Jemma were whispering to one another out of everyone's earshot.

White and his two guards came back after a half hour. Bond watched them carefully. He guessed they would booby-trap the cabin and looked for signs on their hands and clothes but could not detect anything out of the ordinary. In any event, he intended to make it a priority to keep people away when a rescue attempt was made. He had no doubt an SAS outfit would lead the way and he thought he knew what to expect.

Chapter Sixty

3 AM, Friday, February 8, 2019

Three Blackhawks deposited the 45 trooper contingent at a location well away and hidden from sight of the cottage. The plan was to split into three squads and approach the cottage by the lake from different directions. All were SAS and SBS teams, with a police SWAT unit attached for negotiation purposes, if needed.

Their objectives were clear. Free Prince William alive; keep White alive; free everyone else and try and take as many of the perpetrators alive as possible. They had to keep White alive so he could divulge the bomb placement around the town, an undertaking they had yet to accomplish.

For the rest of it, they hoped they would be able to draw conclusions as to how so many subversives had managed to infiltrate the security services or were turned by Dixon on the job.

Dixon had died in the interrogation room. Bishop would not allow sending him to a hospital when it was clear he was critical. The doctor had tried to save him, but the additional serum he had injected himself was a death blow. He lost consciousness one final time and never awoke until his heart ceased to function.

The coordinates to the cottage were found in White's computer and a loud debate took place in Scott's office. The Generals wanted to send half the army, the air force, and Special Forces.

Bishop would not hear of it. He argued that a large force would be detected early and they would lose the element of surprise. The Generals argued that sending a large force in one thunderous swoop would paralyze the terrorists and make them surrender without resistance. Alternatively, they argued, they could simply surround the place and commence negotiations.

Finally, PM Webster walked in and settled the matter. It was a covert Special Ops operation, if he ever saw one, he had said, unwilling to consider negotiations as a primary directive, unless the rescue attempt was somehow botched. And so, the SAS was chosen for the task. Webster did agree to add a SWAT team to the force for negotiation purposes, but only as a last resort.

"The last thing this nation needs now," he had said, "is bargaining with terrorists over our Prince."

Colonel Carter, the commander who had led the SAS team up in Wye country and had found Blake's and Barry's bodies, was the chosen commander, but both Harriet and Edwards objected to his appointment, arguing that he had admitted to them taking orders from White for the length of the crisis and that he should at least be thoroughly queried before leading another assignment.

Major-General Sir Michael Bennet, Director of Special Forces, acquiesced, though he was not happy, some of the blame was bound to stick on himself as well. He appointed Colonel Gary Maddox, a regiment commander, to lead one of the most sensitive missions in the history of modern warfare; Freeing Prince William, Duke of Cambridge, the United Kingdom's heir to the throne, and one of the most familiar and loved figures, worldwide.

The coordinates on White's computer indicated a spot in Hertfordshire, just off Hollycross Road by a small lake where the River Lea and the River Ash converged, and a General Atomics Predator UAV equipped with electro-optical cameras and a synthetic aperture radar, or SAR, was deployed there, sending back Recce photos and a live feed to Ross's office indicating positive human activity at the location and a Bell 212 helicopter in a nearby field to the south.

The UAV was restricted to fly no lower than 20,000 feet so as not to awaken suspicions, but though hidden in the woods, the feed was good enough to detect human activity near a structure by the lake.

The premises were quickly checked for ownership and were found to be owned by one, Ross Dixon, who acquired the place ten years earlier. Under normal circumstances, no one would have suspected a prominent civil servant of owning such a summer house, quite common among the British elite. But now, it provided further proof of Dixon's long-term commitment to his cause.

An urgent request for drawings of the property and house was sent from Scott's office to the county and was received in no time and loaded onto Colonel Maddox's iPad.

The plan was to land the teams two miles east of the house beyond a large wooded area and circle from the north. The choppers would come in low from the east hidden below the line of trees and land behind a sizable knoll in the terrain upon which stood the All-Nations Christian College. The SBS team would circle northward and approach from the northwest hugging the river. The SAS teams would circle southward and approach from the east side of Hollycross Road, among the trees, then split; One team would circle and approach from the south-east along the River Lea; The team led by Colonel Maddox, with the SWAT team in tow, would cross the road into a wooded area just east of the house and attack from there once all were in place.

It was estimated that Maddox's launch position may be too close to the house and agreed that if that was the case, they would remain on the east side of the road and strike from there. Barring any sentries posted, Maddox's team would neutralize the two vehicles detected from the Predator parked on a narrow path leading to the house just off the road and take positions along Hollycross Road blocking any potential routes for hostiles fleeing the scene.

The second SAS team, led by Lt. Colonel Warren Kidd, would send two SAS operatives and a 212 chopper pilot, who was added to the force, to seize the hostile chopper. The rest would strike the main house from the south while the SBS team, led by Lt. Colonel Norm Guthrie, would strike from the north targeting the small cabin closer to the lake.

It was a dark moonless night with cloud cover making it a relatively simple approach. Everyone wore night vision goggles. Lieutenant Holly Pearson, one of only a hand full of women to be admitted as a full-fledged member of the regiment, passing the grueling SAS course third in her class, becoming the first female platoon leader, was walking point with an IR camera attached to her helmet, sending a feedback to Lieutenant-General Larry Fowler's office, the SAS chief at SAS headquarters, and to the Prime Minister's office at 10 downing street.

Another two feeds came from identical cameras on the helmets of Lieutenant John Ryan, who walked point for the SBS squad, and Kidd's point man, Lieutenant Jim Huxley. Additional IR cameras were fitted on several other strikers but would only be used in case of a malfunction in the active cameras.

The forces split at the designated spot and swiftly made their way among the woods toward their launch positions. Lt. Colonel Guthrie, known to all as Norm after the famous character from the Cheers Bar sitcom, using the tiny headset that allowed him to communicate with the troops who were all equipped with identical devices, was also carrying a water-proof cellular mobile phone with a dedicated frequency assigned only to him, Kidd, and Maddox, in the event that the headsets faltered and they needed to communicate.

Lt. Colonel Norm walked behind his point man Lieutenant John Ryan, known to his peers as Jack, as in Jack Ryan the Tom Clancy superhero, who was picking his way between the vegetation down to the Lea River's edge. The Special Boat Service, or SBS, SEAL team, all had special black rubber diving gear underneath their uniforms which enabled them to proceed in the water. The River Lea was quite shallow and freezing at their entry point and grew deeper as it neared the little lake.

Lieutenant Jack held up his fist crawling up the river bank for a look at the cottage. The temperature outside was a mere six degrees Celsius and it began to rain. He spotted the cottage and the cabin on the far side of the lake, dim lights emanating from the cottage. Then he spotted a man walking the perimeter who looked to be carrying a weapon of sorts. He watched him a while longer looking to spot more people but could not.

Sliding back to the water, he reported it to Norm who relayed it to the other teams via his headset, receiving confirmation from both Maddox and Kidd. They continued along the river circling the lake from the west reaching the launch spot agreed upon in advance, crawling across the river's edge through an expanse of bushes to where they had a clear path to the cabin.

By then, Maddox's team was in position stooping among the trees across Hollycross Road. Kidd had sent the pilot and two of his commandos to seize the chopper, had crossed the small open field, and was approaching his own launch spot sneaking along the bushes of the Lea River from the south.

Minutes later, he reported reaching his spot and all teams were in position to strike having reached their positions without incident. The chopper crew was to wait and strike at the same time as the main force, not before.

Holly Pearson was closest to the cottage and could see lights seeping through the one window facing her position. It was one designated entry point along with the main door facing south, a back door facing north, and another window facing the lake.

Maddox was on the net making sure all were ready, then he gave the agreed code word for the strike prompting his commandos into action.

******

Bond was restless. White and his men were on edge. At night they would normally sleep in shifts, two always awake to watch them, but this night none were asleep, walking nervously back and forth in the large hall, White's office lit with his men walking in and out of there.

The group around him, except for Jemma, were all in different stages of fitful sleep. She sat against the wall, waking up every few minutes to look around her. Jake was next to her, curled up on the floor in his parka, his back to the wall.

Cindy finally managed to fall asleep, her head on Camilla's lap. Camilla was asleep her back against the wall, her hand on Cindy's shoulder. It took a while for Cindy to calm down, terrified about her girls being out of reach now, and her husband's uncertain fate. Mr. and Mrs. Chisholm were asleep against the wall further away, Noah snoring lightly.

He counted eight men, including White. Two were always outside, most likely patrolling and watching the cabin; the rest were in the hall, munching on rations and drinking tea or coffee, now and then someone would go out for a cigarette.

Bond wondered about the cottage they were in, having seen White, at least once, going into his office, then coming through the front door without having left through there. There had to be another exit through White's office, Bond thought, though he hadn't noticed it when they were in there.

Coming in on the chopper the first time, their heads had been covered with a cloth of some kind and he had no idea in which direction they had flown or where they had landed. Cindy had been so distraught coming back from their outing to London that he did not even try to inquire about their route, though she did mention that the flight took about an hour.

He wondered why they had allowed them to remain un-cuffed, or at least himself and Jemma, knowing their background, but he figured that with the firepower they were carrying, each wore a handgun at all times, knives strapped to their thighs, and M-16 assault rifles carried at all times, except when they slept or had a bite to eat, they were quite content none of their prisoners, even himself, would endanger the rest, having kids around and the two seniors, Noah and Mary, whom they figured correctly, would be reckless enough to respond to a breakout attempt.

Bond had met Prince William in the past, even shook his hand, at a medal ceremony, awarded to his SAS team for exceptional courage, having invaded an El-Qaeda arms depot deep in the Afghani mountains, blowing it sky-high and taking several prisoners, one of whom was high on the most wanted list. They had traveled on foot with him, being chased by an El-Qaeda posse, but managing to evade them and reach safety.

William had come out to Afghanistan on an undisclosed outing to visit the troops; Dressed in his flight suit and jacket, he had commended them for their bravery and shook everyone's hands warmly, saying kind words.

Bond remembered being impressed by him. He was a chopper pilot himself, though he was not allowed to take part in the fighting, as his brother Harry later did, a chopper pilot himself, but his presence certainly gave them a sense of purpose, which was sometimes lost as the harsh conditions and loss of life took their toll.

Seeing him locked up in the outhouse, with that single heater for both warmth and light, made the entire affair hit home. It was his homeland, his heritage being humiliated, and it made him fume with rage, though he kept his cool, unlike Jemma who was slapped for it.

He tried to close his eyes and get some rest when he heard it.

It was a muffled cry from outside the cottage, causing White's men to go for their guns and jump up.

******

Bishop sat next to Harriet in the PM's crisis room, around a large round desk watching the feed from the troops on three separate screens, nervously bouncing his right leg. Just before going into the room where no mobile phones were allowed, he had gotten a report from Edwards on the confrontation at the Flanagan mansion and its dim results. The five hostiles were eliminated, among them a Ukrainian named Vadim Petrovich, who was the hooded man who delivered the terror threats on the TV, according to Flanagan, but Flanagan's wife Sheila and his son Michael were dead along with four SWAT team members.

Flanagan's daughter-in-law, Jenney, had been evacuated from the house in critical condition. Flanagan's three grandkids had been booby-trapped with explosive leg bracelets but successfully unshackled from them by the police bomb squad.

Bishop had not even had time to update Ross and the PM before they entered the crisis room and refrained from reporting to them until Prince William's fate was established.

Home Secretary Ross was there along with Defense Minister Alistair Banks, Major-General Michael Bennet, Director Special Forces, and the Chief of Police Bradley Nelson. Prince Harry was there as well, the PM instructing Maggie Fox to call him in. Maggie now sat next to PM Webster, whispering something in his ear, when over the loudspeaker in the room, they heard the SAS chief, Lieutenant-General Larry Fowler, from SAS headquarters, informing them that his troops were in place and were ready to strike.

"We need the green light, Sir," Fowler said, addressing the PM who was intently watching the screens.

"What are we seeing?" He asked; the infrared feed was quite hard to decipher.

"Straight in front of you, on the main screen, is the Dixon cottage, Sir," Fowler explained.

"I can see that," the PM said.

"There is a guard patrolling between the cottage and the cabin, which you can see on the screen to the right. He's now circling the cabin and we want to hit him as he appears making his way back to the cottage."

Webster looked hard but was not sure what he was seeing. He could see the cabin from the camera fixed on Lieutenant John "Jack" Ryan's helmet, the SBS point man, but was unable to see the guard.

"When the guard comes into view, you have the green light to strike," Webster finally said, and everyone in the room tensed, focusing on Ryan's feed, waiting for the guard to appear.

Chapter Sixty-One

4 AM, Friday, February 8, 2019

King had the guard in his sights the second he rounded the cabin. He was about to squeeze the trigger of his M1 sniper rifle when the door to the cottage opened and a second man came out, the light from within illuminating the area for a second causing the IR sight to saturate.

The guard shut the door behind him and stood a moment lighting a cigarette.

"You have him?" King said into his headset.

"I do," Queenie replied coolly, instantly putting the man in her sights.

"Do it!" Maddox said over the Comms link and they both pulled the triggers.

King's man, walking toward the cottage, fell silently, head-first onto the ground but the man Queenie was targeting just happened to drop his lighter and stooped down to fetch it the instant she pulled the trigger. He was hit but not fatally, letting out a loud moan before a second bullet hit him splitting his head apart.

Lieutenant Colonel Norm Guthrie, Lieutenant John "Jack" Ryan, and their SBS unit were about twenty meters north-west of the Cabin, springing into action, running stooped down, weapons at the ready, suddenly had to hit the dirt when a burst of gunfire came at them from a slit in the cabin's door which had opened a fraction.

At the same instant, from the south, Lieutenant Colonel Warren Kidd and his team slipped through the underbrush and were advancing toward the cottage when they hit the ground hearing gunfire.

Colonel Maddox's team, led by Holly Pearson, were advancing swiftly from the east through the trees, behind the cottage. Hearing the gunfire, they stopped getting down on one knee, Holly in front raising her fist.

"All units go!" Maddox called over the communication link, and they rushed toward the cottage. Holly Pearson shot forward reaching the cottage wall, under the window facing back. Four commandos reached that wall with her and took positions under the window while Maddox led the rest around the corner meaning to get to the front door.

Holly hit the window with the butt of her gun, breaking glass, and got ready to jump in when a grenade was lobbed through the window, exploding just a few yards away spraying them with shrapnel. All four of her colleagues were hit. She escaped unscathed being concealed from the blast by her mates who took the brunt of the blow. She looked around seeing a gun barrel peep through the window spraying bullets at her wounded colleagues.

Taking out her revolver from a thigh holster, she raised it to window height and shot blindly through it at whoever was there. The gunfire stopped at once and she, in one swoop jumped through the window and onto the foe she had just shot. He was alive but weak and tried to put up a fight but she shot him again point-blank and looked around, seeing she was in a shower room, the door opened to a large hall.

******

Guthrie looked around at his men, two were hit, lying wounded on the ground. He signaled the medic to stay with them and sprang for the cabin.

Their orders were clear. The Prince must be freed alive. The rest, who were assumed to be the Jemma Stone-Hammond and her family along with Cindy Frost and her kids and possibly the Chisholm couple, could be sacrificed if it meant saving the Prince. It was an extremely unpopular call the PM had to make, but a necessary one for the sake of the kingdom.

It was assumed all hostages would be kept together in the cottage, though they proceeded as though there were people in the cabin as well. They took more fire from the cabin and had to take evasive action. Guthrie signaled three to stay put and provide fire cover while he and six men crawled away from the firing line and sprang forward toward the cabin, reaching the back wall unhurt.

Lieutenant Colonel Kidd, attacking the cottage front door from the south, had to hit the dirt when the fire was opened in their direction, luckily hitting no one. Kidd and his point man, Lieutenant Jim Huxley, watched from behind their cover as Maddox and his men were inching along the side wall toward the front door. Kidd ordered his men to hold their fire, worried they would hit hostages inside, and watched as Maddox rounded the corner.

Inside was total chaos.

Camilla, Cindy, and the rest woke up in fright as the world seemed to explode around them. White came out spattering orders to his men as they put on IR gear and shut the lights, spreading around the cottage and firing through the two windows and door.

White, equipped with IR glasses crouched in the middle of the room, covering the hostages with an M-16. His four men were engaging the enemy from all windows and through a slit in the door.

The fire raged all around and suddenly a blast was heard from the shower in the back, and more bursts of gunfire were released.

Noah and Mary crawled toward where Camilla, Cindy, Jake, and Jemma were cowering and they hugged one another on the floor against the wall covering their heads and emulating Jemma, who had her hands in protective posture over them, looking up from time to time, not seeing much except for flashes of gunfire.

Bond was crouched next to them, ready to spring into action, aware of White's presence, knowing he could see him clearly in the dark. Suddenly a thump was heard from the back and more shots. White aimed his assault rifle at the shower door and fired a burst, apparently seeing something he didn't like. He fired again, then retreated to his office and shut the door, calling for his men, to hold the fort.

Then a shocking explosion rocked the hall, and one of White's men near the window, collapsed back, his assault rifle flying from his hands, when a figure wearing black came in from the shower in the back firing a pistol at the three men left standing, hitting one in the back. A second one turned and returned fire, but the figure was nimble and rolled to the side avoiding the gunfire. At that moment, the front door burst open throwing the man off balance. The figure rolling on the ground, shot again and he fell. The last man was attacked by a large figure wearing black who came through the door. Unable to point his weapon forward, he drew out a knife but was instantly crushed to the ground and held at bay, a pistol pointing to his face.

"The office!" Bond called out, pointing and the figure on the ground leaped up and rushed there, two more figures now through the door following her.

Bond watched as they kicked in the door, two to one side, and one to the other, and stepped through ready to fire. But no shots were heard. The three figures came back out after a few seconds, walking toward them.

"You guys OK?" A female voice addressed them, kneeling by the cowering group.

"No one in the office?" Bond asked, surprised.

"Not a soul," the woman replied.

"Follow me!" Bond said assertively and rushed for the office.

"Stay down," the woman ordered but he ignored her and ran to the door. She took off after him, signaling her mates to stop him.

Bond was caught and brought down hard on the floor.

"White," he said out of breath. "He has an escape route through there."

The large figure that had been first through the door and had subdued the last of the hostiles, approached, having cuffed his man and given him to another to guard.

"Show me," he said, having heard the exchange, and Bond was let go.

"Where's the Prince?" Maddox asked.

"In the Cabin with the children," Bond said. "How many children?"

"Four. Two girls, two boys. Aged ten to fourteen."

"Christ," Maddox muttered.

Bond rushed through the door and looked around the small office that was illuminated by a desk lamp. He went around the table looking at the floor, seeing nothing, then he looked behind the small cupboard White had by the side of his desk, which he now noticed had been moved, and found what he was looking for; A secret passage, the door cut into the wooden floor. He raised it, looking at a dark hollow hole underneath. He slipped in before anyone could object and began crawling, Maddox and Holly Pearson following him.

It took but a minute for Bond to realize the tunnel was leading to the cabin and he stopped, signaling Maddox to take the lead with his IR goggles whispering to him where he thought it was leading. Maddox crawled ahead and reached a spot where he could see the tunnel take an upturned angle and stop, then turned back toward Holly and Bond.

"This is where it goes up to the cabin I assume," he whispered to Bond behind him, handing him his IR goggles for a look.

"Most likely," Bond whispered back, looking through the goggles, seeing the tunnel angle up. "It's about the right distance."

"OK, gals, you stay here and keep an eye," Maddox whispered, taking his goggles back from Bond. "If there are no additional exists," he added, "which there does not seem to be. Stay near the cottage entrance until you hear from me.

White is bound to assume we found the tunnel and could easily blow whoever's in here with a single grenade."

Bond and Holly nodded their heads.

"If you find a closer exit or niche that can provide cover, use it. Otherwise, stay by the cottage side and move in only on my command. Are we clear?"

They both nodded and Maddox crawled back to the cottage, sending in another man with IR goggles to replace bond.

******

"Prince William is in the cabin with four kids aged ten to fourteen," Maddox announced over the net climbing out of the tunnel back into the cottage. "There are at least two hostiles in there with them, armed and desperate."

Lieutenant Colonel Norm Guthrie, glued to the cabin's back wall with five of his men, acknowledged.

"We're at the back wall," he informed his commander.

"Everyone, hold your fire. Do not engage," Maddox said over the net. "Norm, you guys stay there and make sure no one escapes. We need the SWAT team; on the double."

Heads turned toward PM Webster in the crisis room, but he just nodded. "Let them do their job," he said, looking intently at the screens.

Chapter Sixty-Two

5 AM, Friday, February 8, 2019

Dr. Malcolm Joyce received his PhD in Clinical Psychology, from University College London, or UCL, in 1994, graduating with honors. Having enrolled as an undergraduate as a Security and Crime Science major, his doctorate thesis on the psychology of hostage situations and how to deal with them, landed him a position in the London police department as an expert negotiator which he perfected over a 20-year career becoming the lead negotiator for the police force at the age of 45 and it was he who Chief of Police Nelson had insisted on accompanying the SAS force.

Not all of Joyce's outings ended up successful in the extremely complicated art of hostage negotiations, but his record was far better than any negotiator in the UK and his reputation preceded him.

Joyce was rushed into the Dixon cottage with his SWAT team as soon as the SAS commandos completed a thorough search of the premises making sure no hostiles had been left unaccounted for and no booby traps were left behind.

Joyce met the now panicked, Cindy Frost, who could no longer control her emotions and was pleading with him to free hers and Jemma's children at any cost. Jemma, though a trained MI5 operative, was having a hard time keeping her own panic under control and was holding on to an unnerved Jake, crying softly.

Bond had returned from the tunnel and was attending to Camilla and the Chisholm couple, talking to them softly trying to ease their fears.

White's profile was brought up on an iPad and Joyce studied it for a few minutes, looking at his SO1 psychological profile, photos of the man, and his history both as a British embassy employee in Tel Aviv and as a sergeant in the Special Reconnaissance Regiment, and at his record fighting in Iraq and Afghanistan.

The other hostile in the cabin was unknown but it was obvious White was the key.

Satisfied he had what he needed to begin, Joyce nodded his head and followed Maddox accompanied by three of his SWAT team companions, one of them carrying a megaphone.

They exited the cottage and stood by its northern wall. Maddox's men were spread about. Kidd who was the only squad without casualties, had his twelve men covering the south side blocking any escape route toward the lake and the Lea River basin, backing Guthrie's squad who were literally enveloping the cabin at close range but had one dead and a wounded trooper being attended to by a doc and a medic.

Two of Maddox's men were covering a second doctor and two medics attending to the four troopers hit by the grenade behind the cottage. Two were dead and two others were receiving treatment for body and head wounds. Holly Pearson, Maddox's point trooper, along with Sergeant Bill Parsons, were down in the tunnel blocking any escape through the secret passage.

Joe King and Laura Quincy, nicknamed Queenie, the snipers on Maddox's crew, had both their IR sights on the cabin door. The rest had taken positions further away blocking any avenues of escape toward Hollycross Road and east toward where their 212 helicopter had been seized by the two operatives and chopper pilot sent from Kidd's squad. They had moved into position and attacked when Maddox gave the order, surprising a sleeping pilot in the cockpit who surrendered without a fuss.

"You start," Joyce said to Maddox. "Explain the situation and ask them to come out. I'll take it from there."

Maddox, who was six feet three inches tall, looked at the psychologist who was only a few inches shorter than him, with a handsome face, thick graying hair, and a kind smile which Maddox took to. Visualizing the inside of the cabin, as described by Bond, a low bed at the far corner and a small heater spreading dim light, he put the megaphone to his lips and called out:

"I am Colonel Gary Maddox," he began, disrupting the eerie silence of the night. "We need you to lay down your weapons Mr. White and come out with your hands raised. The same goes for your comrade in arms there in the cabin."

Silence.

Then a shot from inside the cabin shattered the silent night.

At the crisis room, Prince Harry jumped from his seat along with Bishop and Nigel Scott.

From inside the cottage, Cindy let out a wild scream and then burst out crying hysterically, Jake and Jemma holding her close, themselves rocked by the blast.

But Maddox held it together.

"Stay calm everyone," he tensely spoke through his headset. "No one does anything rash."

"The next one is for our precious Prince," they heard a voice, White's voice, calling from within the cabin.

Maddox eyed Joyce. "Your show Doc," he said and handed him the megaphone.

"Mr. White, this is Detective Malcolm Joyce from the London PD," Joyce spoke up through the megaphone, once again disrupting the silence, everyone holding their breath. "Please stay calm Andy, and let's talk this over."

"Nothing to talk to me about," was the immediate reply, "you go talk to Dixon."

Joyce eyed Maddox who made a slitting gesture with his hand across his own throat.

"I am sorry Andy, but Dixon is unavailable," Joyce replied carefully.

"Is he in custody or did you kill him already?"

"Sorry, Andy, but he's been badly injured. I am not sure of his condition, but I will check."

"You do that," White called from within the cabin.

"I certainly will but meanwhile I ask you to be reasonable with me…"

"Be reasonable?" White cackled a desperate laugh. "What's to be reasonable about?"

Joyce waited a few seconds before replying.

"I need the people in there with you unharmed," he finally said. More silence.

"Andy, are the kids OK in there?" Joyce called out after almost a minute.

"Jolly good…" White called out. "Having a blast."

"That's good, Andy, now could we discuss their release?"

"They'll go when I go," White called out angrily. "And so will the Prince."

"Where would you like to go?" Joyce asked.

"Anywhere, as long as it's away from this rotten country."

"Is this how you feel about your homeland, Andy?"

There was a pause and some coughing from within the cabin. "You ever been left for dead, detective?" White spoke out again.

Joyce kept quiet, looking at Maddox who made an unwitting gesture. "Anyone know what he's talking about?" Maddox said into his headset.

"Ever been left by your mates to die?" White continued angrily.

Bishop and Ross looked at Harriet who immediately spoke out.

"There was an incident in Afghanistan when he served there as part of the Special Reconnaissance Regiment," she said, looking anxiously at Webster who nodded his head urging her to go on. "He claimed he had been abandoned by his troops after his vehicle was ransacked by an IED and was left by the side of the road unconscious."

"And," Webster demanded, "was he?"

"He made it back to forward command on his own, wounded and claimed the officer in charge left him to die. But a field court ruled against him, siding with the officer who had engaged the enemy in a firefight and had come back to rescue the mutilated bodies from the vehicle. But by that time it had turned dark and White who was thrown into a ditch away from the vehicle, was not found. After that, he was transferred to Kandahar to the NATO Intelligence Corps."

"Well," Webster remarked, "it seems our man has not gotten over that."

"Yes, it does," Harriet said.

Maddox looked at Joyce who nodded his head, indicating he had heard the account.

"Andy, it must have been a traumatic event for you. I understand."

"Why don't you bring Mosby here and let him explain."

Again Joyce looked at Maddox who shook his head.

"Rick Mosby," Harriet said hurriedly over the net, "That's the officer White claims had left him behind."

"We can certainly try to do that Andy if that's your wish but that may take time…"

"It's time you all heard the truth!" White hollered.

Joyce remained silent for several moments, allowing White time to calm down.

Maddox said into the net: "Anyone know where Mosby lives? Can we get him here quick?"

"He has an address in Manchester," Harriet said. "Works for a security firm."

"How long will it take to bring him over?" Maddox asked, never taking his eyes off the cabin door.

"Well, assuming he is there, we can send a jet from Stansted," Minister of Defense Alistair Banks said, "but that would take a couple of hours."

"Or we can get him online," Maggie Fox suggested, "bring him up on Skype and arrange it so White could see him."

"Let's have this as a contingency plan," Joyce spoke into the net. "I doubt it will make much difference to him at this point."

All eyes in the crisis room looked toward Webster who again nodded his head. "Do as the doc said," he acquiesced coolly. "White's got bigger problems than Mosby by now."

Offline, he said: "Maggie get Mosby on the line. Find out what went wrong." Maggie signaled Harriet and they both got up and quickly left the room.

"We'll try to bring him over or put him online," Joyce spoke out again. "But you need to work with me if you want a fair trial…"

"I've been tried once already and was made a fool by Mosby and the got damn Special Forces," White called out. "Why should it be any different this time around?"

"Well, we'll get to hear your side of the story properly…" Joyce was reaching, knowing it was pointless.

"Now that's a damn joke!" White spurned. "You guys will never let me out of here alive."

"That is nonsense Andy and you know it," Joyce said adamantly. "Everyone gets a fair trial."

"I didn't," White countered, "and that was when I was fighting on your side."

"I am really sorry you had to go through that Andy," Joyce assented, "but Prince William and the kids are not at fault here."

"Everyone's at fault!" White bellowed. "Especially the Prince!"

It was one of these moments Joyce knew he needed to take a leap of faith. "Would you allow the kids to go free?"

Once again, a tense silence, and then suddenly the cabin door opened a crack. King and Queenie saw the kids in their sights.

"Hold your fire," Maddox called on the net.

Zoe, aged twelve, and Ian, aged ten, slipped hesitantly through the door wrapped in their parka coats but were not followed by their older siblings. Gabi, fourteen, and Colin, thirteen, remained inside the cabin with their abductors.

"This is a show of good faith," White called from within, as the two children tentatively made their way in the dark toward the cottage. Cindy, Jake, and Jemma stepped out of the cottage, eagerly waiting to meet them behind Maddox who would not let them through to the open ground.

"Let them come to us," Maddox uttered on the net, not wishing to expose his troops' positions and it seemed time had ceased to exist until the two made it behind the cover of the cottage, their parents crying with relief, hugging them tightly.

Chapter Sixty-Three

Maggie Fox and Harriet slipped quietly back into the crisis room.

"Turn off the mics, will you?" Webster addressed the two technicians, sitting in an adjacent room, looking in behind a large glass window.

"Go on, Maggie, what did you find out?" Webster said once the technician signaled the mics in the room were out.

"Retired Major Rick Mosby, then a Lieutenant," Maggie began as she slid back into her seat by the PM, recalls the incident clearly. They were on a seek-and-destroy mission with several Hummers following Taliban rebels south of a village called Mapan when the first vehicle was hit by an IED. There were six troopers in it under White's command.

"The first blast disabled the Hummer, creating a large hole in its side and starting a fire. As the troopers filed out to inspect the damage, a second IED exploded with all of them entirely exposed, then a Taliban force opened up on the rest who had to retreat."

Maggie took a deep breath, looking over at Harriet for support.

"Mosby who was in the last vehicle, retaliated with force, leading his platoon to put up a fight and run the guerrillas off after almost an hour. By the time they had regrouped, it had become dark. Fearing further attacks, being quite vulnerable on that road, they managed to reach the wrecked Hummer finding mutilated body parts such that it was hard to tell who was who."

Maggie took another deep breath, obviously distraught by the account, so Harriet took over.

"They gathered the bodies and pushed the wreckage off the road clearing the route then headed back to forward command."

Harriet looked around in awe at the distinguished crowd, watching her and went on.

"White arrived on foot early the next morning with minor wounds and was taken to the field hospital for treatment. Mosby recalls going to see him there, quite astonished and elated to see him alive. He had escorted the bodies to the hospital's morgue and left a man in charge to account for everyone in the lead Hummer, then drove out to the General's command post to give a report on the incident. As it turned out, it took a while for the doctors to identify the bodies and as soon as it was established White was missing, they sent out a patrol to look for him. White testified that hiking back, he had remained quite a distance off the road for fear of more ambushes and kept to a parallel ravine, which explained why the patrol never found him. But White insisted that no patrol was sent out for him claiming he had the road in sight and never saw it."

"Once out of the Hospital, White filed a complaint with the Recce brigade commander against Mosby who he claimed was negligent leaving him there and that he had to evade more hostiles to make it back."

"The trial went on for several days and finally Mosby was cleared, the court ruling that he had not only done above and beyond, but had saved several lives leading his troops against the ambush and driving them off without any casualties apart from the lead Hummer hit by the two IED's. The court stipulated that because the bodies were in such a state, White being hurled into a ditch in one piece, as a result of the second blast, and on a pitch-dark night, fearing additional attacks, Mosby had acted appropriately and with exceptional courage and could not be blamed for White's misfortune."

"White refused to go on patrols from that day on, Mosby recalls, until finally he was sent to Kandahar in an intelligence support role."

"One might say White was right to be pissed," Webster commented. "This, however, does not justify paralyzing this entire country and killing innocent people. Do we know when he turned?"

"We believe he turned during his term at the British embassy in Tel Aviv," Harriet continued. "But it might have been earlier; maybe even in Kandahar. We're still looking into it."

Webster looked around the room, eyes blazing. He finally focused on Bishop then locked eyes with Ross.

"When this is over, there'll be some explaining to do," he murmured, then looked to the glass window and signaled the technicians to turn on the mics.

******

Prince William sat on the bed by the heater wrapped in the lone blanket together with Gabi and Colin. Both kids had the shakes from time to time, whether from fear or the cold, though wrapped in parka coats and wool hats. His flight suit and flight jacket provided little warmth and felt stuck to his body, having worn them, now the eighth straight day.

Earlier in the night, together with their younger siblings, the kids slept on the floor by the heater, hugging one another, trying to keep warm; the only intrusion was when one of White's armed men, who was later referred to by White as Tracy, came in at midnight and sat himself on the floor by the door, armed with an M-16 and a vest with spare magazines under a long black coat. Tracy was bald but wore no hat and did not seem bothered by the cold. Holding a pistol, his long legs spread forward on the floor, he had his assault rifle lay on his thighs pointing sideways.

When the confrontation erupted, as shots from the direction of the cottage and the mighty grenade blast caused them to rise in terror, Tracy had opened the door a crack and began firing. The only thing William could do was slide off the bed and cover the kids with his body, as luckily no bullets were fired their way.

Tracy let two long bursts through the crack, then turned to watch them, his back to the wall by the door. More shots were heard from the cottage, and then suddenly the cabin floor rose from under the small rug in the corner, and White appeared, his face and red hair covered in dust. For a second William scolded himself for not checking there all this time, but then he noticed the latch White had opened from beneath and realized he could not have opened this door from above.

White stood up brushing his clothes from the dust, his long frame filling the cabin, a gun in one hand and an M16 strapped to his back, same as his colleague. He let the door slam shut and stood behind his subordinate near the door, eyeing the outside through the crack.

Zoe had begun to quietly cry, her older sister trying to comfort her. Both the boys had tears in their eyes and looks of terror on their young faces.

"Hey, Tracy, kill anyone?" White asked, still catching his breath.

"May have," Tracy said. "Can't see a damn thing out there."

"Doubt if they'll be shooting at us," White said, looking over at William, sitting on the floor by the bed in front of the kids.

"You may want to let the kids go," William said to him. "They should not have to suffer through this."

"That'll be my call," White said, turning to look back through the crack in the door. "A call which will not involve you, as surprising as it may seem."

William noticed White kept looking at the door cut in the floor as if he expected someone to rise out of there at any moment, his eyes darting from it back to the front door and back again. He thought of what he could say to White so he would release the kids but realized the man was too far gone in his treachery and would not listen to reason.

A few minutes passed, and the silence was restored. White locked the cabin door and sat on the floor indicating to his man to go sit by the door to the tunnel.

Then a loud voice was heard, calling White to surrender. White cocked his pistol and shot the wall above where William and the kids were huddled.

"The next one is for our precious Prince," he had called back out, fuming with rage, keeping the pistol pointed at him.

The kids would not look up then, keeping their heads down and supporting each other. William looked at white with contempt but said nothing.

Then a second voice, a gentler one began to talk, and White seemed to relax a bit. William recalled his captivity training week, a stint all pilots in training had to go through, MI5 agents keeping him captive for a week, mostly blindfolded, making his existence miserable, depicting how it felt to be held captive and some of the torture he could expect to go through.

He had been consulted whether he wanted to go through it, his instructors claiming he was the one pilot least likely to suffer through it, but he insisted, so they had him locked up in a dark sodden dungeon, with hardly food or drink, and kept bringing him out for interrogations, blindfolded and humiliated. He had nearly broken down, he recalled, wondering all along why he needed to go through that, but made it in the end with the rest of his mates.

Now, he recalled some of the pointers he had been taught, first and foremost, never allow them to spot your fear. He knew from the start that White and the rest of his crew would broadcast any weakness that he showed to the world, knowing people looked up to him and would retain courage if he showed strength. He also knew that no matter how demented his captors were, it would take a colossal mistake to harm him not to mention execute him in front of the entire watching world.

He never really understood why he was being held, other than the threats broadcast by his captors which seemed preposterous, but he figured he was only a pawn in some power game he wasn't aware of.

But the negotiator was good and knew his stuff, and White had relented after less than an hour, allowing Zoe and Ian to leave. In tears, eyes bloodshot and puffed, they were torn away from Gabi and Colin, and allowed out, White making sure he was well out of sight of any snipers whose gun sights he knew would be aimed at the door.

"Andy, that was mighty gallant of you," the negotiator called out after several minutes, "letting Zoe and Ian free."

William watched White, as his face contorted. He was about to shout something back, but then thought better of it, and did not reply. Instead, he looked at William. "Can you guarantee me a safe passage?" he suddenly asked.

"A passage where?" William inquired.

"Oh, I don't know. Venezuela maybe? Russia? Anywhere they hate us and the Americans."

It was the last thing William would have promised these vermin who had just destroyed large parts of London and caused the death of so many, but the two kids were with him and he felt he could not live with himself if he put them in jeopardy.

"I can try," he said, "but you would need to let these kids out first."

White's face contorted again, his hollow eyes looking bizarrely at William.

"I can end it here and now for all of us you know," he said, sounding very tired suddenly.

William shifted his gaze to Tracy who was watching the exchange. He reminded him a bit of the late Telly Savalas, bald with black eyes, a large, crooked nose, and an intense gaze.

"I am not sure there's anywhere on earth you would be able to hide," William pointed out. "You are better off standing trial here and paying for your sins."

White smiled a crooked smile and shifted in his place uncomfortably. "Oh, I am sure there is," he said.

"And what about your sins?" he added. "Ever had to stand in line for food?"

"Do you have family?" William asked, trying to keep away from the pit White was laying for him.

"Yes, I do," White said. "But we haven't been in touch for years."

"I could make sure we take good care of them if you give it up here and stand trial. You too, Tracy."

"I am sure you can," White mocked. "Your family fortune can feed a million families for generations…"

"Now listen, White, I am not to blame for your inferiority complexes. I was born into royalty and there's nothing I can do about it and I have had my share of tragedies…"

"Oh yeah, Lady Di," White mocked. "Now there was a woman worth fucking…"

"She was my mother…" William said with emotion.

"Some mother she was," White said maliciously, "left you and your brother for rich Arab sheiks."

"She…" William started to say but stopped, realizing he was playing into White's hands.

"Andy you there?" The voice from outside boomed once again. White sighed but kept silent.

"Andy," the voice from outside called again. "I need you to talk to me."

"I actually thought you were a decent bloke," White said to William, who was looking at him, not wavering. "Saw you on a visit to Kandahar once. Your brother too. Quite a wild chap."

"I'll make sure you get a fair trial," William said, looking from White to Tracy and back.

"It's Dixon you should fry," White said, "he had you fooled for years."

"He'll be tried as well," William said.

"Nah, he's dead by now," White dismissed.

"Are you sure?" It was Tracy who asked, looking tensely at White.

"Once I stopped getting his signals I knew we were done for," White revealed. "It wasn't by chance I put you and these kids in here. I knew this was coming."

"Andy, please talk to me," the voice from outside called again, beginning to sound desperate.

"You should talk to him," William said.

"I am talking to you," White mocked, "why should I bother with him?"

Chapter Sixty-Four

6 AM, Friday, February 8, 2019

Maddox was beginning to feel extremely uneasy.

White's last communiqué was over half an hour ago, once the two young children were let out, and he hasn't responded since.

"Holly you there?" he called over the net.

"Right here sir," was the reply.

"Norm you there?"

"Yes, sir," came the reply.

"Can you hear anything from inside?"

"Not a thing Gary," Guthrie reported. "Those walls seem pretty thick to me."

"Queenie, King, can you spot anything?"

"Door's been shut since the children were let out sir," Queenie replied.

Maddox thought it over. If White had a silencer, he could kill everyone in there without them hearing a peep. He could also force some cyanide pill down their throats, or simply blow up a grenade to finish them off, he thought, shuddering at the consequences of that happening.

White didn't seem to him the suicidal type, but under the circumstances, anything was possible. White would presume he would carry the blame for everything if Dixon was dead, and decide to abstain from the circus he was going to face.

"Holly, how fast could you get under the cabin?" he asked.

"Three minutes I suppose, with all the gear and if I want to keep quiet."

"You leave the gear and proceed with the goggles and a pistol. How that?"

"That should take about half the time then, I would guess."

"OK, on my signal, you and Parsons, head through the tunnel and get in position under the cabin. Take two more guys as backup. I am assuming there should be a hatch there, but who knows, it may be locked, so be prepared."

"Aye, aye, sir."

"Norm, you get ready to storm the place. The door opens toward the outside, so send someone ahead to blow it open. Holly and Parsons would be coming through an opening in the floor of some kind, so watch for them."

"Got it, sir," Guthrie replied.

"We'll have the doc here talk nonsense to them, making a racket, but you move on my signal only. Is that clear?"

"Clear," he heard both Holly and Guthrie reply.

"King, Queenie, you get these assholes in your sights the second Norm blows up the door but be as careful as possible not to shoot through them and hit any hostages. Can you, do it?"

"Right, sir," he heard both King and Quincy reply, realizing he was putting a heavy responsibility on their shoulders.

"Larry, you there?" Maddox addressed Lieutenant-General Larry Fowler, the SAS chief at SAS headquarters.

"Yes, Gary," Fowler replied. "I think we should wait a bit more. Mike, you with me on this?" He addressed Major-General Michael Bennet, Director of Special Forces sitting with the PM.

"Give him another few minutes and try to coerce him to talk," Bennet said over the net. "If that does not happen, I guess we do not have a choice."

Prime Minister Webster was looking intently at the feed from the various cameras surrounding the cabin. Dawn was just breaking and he could see the cabin through the morning mist, standing innocently as if the turmoil around it never existed.

It was his call to make, most likely the most difficult call of his life. He had no doubt he would have to resign once the crisis was over, acutely aware his party would not survive such a scandal, but the last thing he wanted was for his people to remember him as the one who had given the go-ahead which had killed their beloved William, heir to the throne. But he also knew he would not able to live with himself, if he did not make the call, one that had to be bravely made.

He looked around the room. They were all watching him.

"Bishop, what would you advise?" he asked the MI5 chief, who seemed to him ready to pee in his pants.

"I would not wait, sir," Bishop said bravely. "White's got nothing to lose and the longer we wait; the more time he'll have to come to terms with it…"

"You mean come to terms with killing himself?" Webster asked.

"Himself and everyone else in the cabin, Sir,"

"I disagree," Defense Minister Alistair Banks said. "He will not dare kill the Prince, and the longer we wait, the more fatigued he will be when we finally decide to strike."

Webster looked at Scott. "Where do you stand, Nigel?" he asked the Home Secretary.

Scott who had been wondering that himself looked up at the PM, feeling a tinge of sorrow for letting him down. It was his domain, and he had failed miserably.

"I think William will talk his way out of this," he said, surprising them all. "And we should give him the time."

There were angry murmurs in the room but no one spoke up. "Can you elaborate?" Webster demanded.

"They are both ex-military and have been with one another for a while now so they should have developed a relationship of some kind which will allow William to soften him up."

"We should ask the expert then?" Webster remarked somewhat skeptically, signaling the technicians to turn on the mics.

"Maddox this is Webster," the PM called into the air.

"Yes sir," came the immediate reply.

"Is the doc connected?"

"He is now," Maddox said.

"Doc, this is Webster," the PM said again. "I would like your opinion on a theory developed in my room."

"Go ahead sir," Joyce replied.

"The Home Secretary is claiming William will talk his way out of this on his own."

There was a short silence before Joyce replied. "Never happened on any of my shifts."

"Yes, but there was never a Prince on any of your shifts either."

"True, but it's extremely rare for a hostage to talk his way out of anything, particularly an extremely high-profile one like William."

"So, there you have it," the PM said, turning to Prince Harry once the mics were turned off once more. "Where do you stand on this, Sir?"

"If anyone can talk his way out of a jam, it's William," Harry said. "But my greater concern is White's mental state right now."

"Well, we have to assume he's at his wit's end," Bishop said.

"He seemed quite reasonable talking with the doc, allowing two of the children out." Maggie Fox pitched in, looking hopeful.

"Any thoughts?" Webster addressed DSF Bennet.

"No such miracles where I come from," Bennet said.

"Chief?" Webster addressed the Chief of Police Bradley Nelson.

"Joyce has been through many of these," Bradly said. "I think we should trust his judgment."

Webster became silent for a moment weighing the odds then he signaled the technicians to turn on the mics and spoke: "Maddox, give him ten minutes and have Joyce use his most inspirational arguments to get him to talk. If that does not happen, proceed as planned."

"Aye, aye sir," Maddox confirmed. "Kidd, you make sure the docs and medics are close by once we move in, clear?"

"Got it, sir," Kidd replied and Joyce began a nerve-wracking one-sided dialogue.

******

"Pearson, you there?"

"Just a few more seconds sir," Holly Pearson whispered into her headset, breathing heavy as she scrambled on her hands and knees through the tunnel.

"Norm, you guys ready?"

"We are, Sir," Guthrie replied instantly. "Queenie, King…?"

"I've got the door," Sergeant Quincy replied.

"Me too," King confirmed.

"OK, guys, as soon as Holly is in position…"

Maddox was squatting by the side of the cottage, all his senses alert, ready to lead the assault. Joyce, next to him, was begging White to reply for the fiftieth time without any response.

"Andy, for the love of god, please talk to me." Joyce implored.

"In position!" Holly Pearson declared.

"We're going in!" Maddox announced. "Norm, send your man!"

Norm Guthrie was indicating to his explosive specialist to rush for the door, when it opened a crack, and everyone froze.

"We're coming out! Don't shoot!"

They heard William's voice before they could see him, and then he appeared in the doorway, the two kids at his side, White and his accomplice, weapons drawn, cowering behind, taking cover by the sides of the door.

"Everyone stop!" Maddox called, shoving Joyce behind him and stepping from behind the cottage wall.

"Queenie, do you have him?" He hissed.

"William's is in the way," Queenie replied cooly.

"White throw your weapons where I can see them!" Maddox called out, moving forward carefully, assault rifle drawn.

"They've agreed to surrender," William called out, "tell your snipers to stand down and please don't try to be heroes!"

"Queenie, you hear that?" Maddox hissed into his mic. "You keep him in your sights."

William began inching forward holding on to the children, White and Tracy still hidden behind. Then White appeared, still holding his gun.

"We want him alive!" It was Bennet from the PM's crisis room. "Do not open fire!"

"White, throw your weapons away where I can see them and raise your hands!" Maddox tensely called out, moving forward, watching the foe like a hawk.

White hesitated, then threw his M-16 away and raised his hands, still holding the gun. A shot rang out and White's gun flew out of his hand. William dove to the ground grasping the kids just as Tracy leveled his gun. A second shot rang out and Tracy was hurled back into the cabin, Maddox racing like mad toward the Prince.

Inside the cabin, Holly burst through the tunnel entrance, crashing the door, gun pointed at the hostile who had been blown back by the 7.62 caliber bullet of King's sniper rifle, who hit him at the same instant.

Outside, Guthrie rushed from the back and flung himself at White, throwing him down, grabbing his hands, as Maddox reached William and the children, putting his large body between them and the threat.

More operatives rushed to the scene behind Guthrie helping secure the whimpering White whose arm was bleeding, his face forced down into the dirt.

Holly shouted from inside the cabin: "He's down! He's down!" Then she came out Sergeant Parsons remaining inside to search the body.

"Well I'll be damned," Webster said to himself locking eyes with Ross as everyone in the room rose up in cheer.

Epilogue

The day her dad woke up from his coma was the happiest day in Zoe Frost's young, yet turbulent, life, eclipsed only by the day Prince William and Kate came to their house to visit and she got to play with their kids.

Frosty had been moved from intensive care to the general ward a week after his operation and still, he would not wake up. Then he was moved to a different hospital treating spine injuries but he remained in a coma until they recommended sending him to a home for comatose patients at which point Cindy relented and brought him home with a nurse and the needed accessories provided by a fund for wounded MI5 personnel and a personal grant from the royal family, believing that if there was a chance her husband would make it, it would be only with her and their two loving daughters caring for him at home.

The doctors could not pinpoint the reason for Frosty's cataleptic state, having removed two bullets from his body, one quite close to the lower brainstem but which did not damage it. The cat scans and MRIs of his head and spine all proved negative, yet he remained comatose for almost three months before Zoe found him staring at her one night, while doing her homework next to his bed.

Cindy had researched everything she could on comatose patients and their way to recovery and everything she read pointed to one thing: the patient needs his loved ones close by and talking to him. So she brought him home and made sure her girls talked to their dad nonstop until he awoke.

He wasn't just staring, with that glassy look they had gotten used to, he was actually focusing on her flashing a faint smile. She looked at him for a few seconds, and then said carefully: "Dad?"

He nodded weakly and she knew they had him back.

She ran out of his room and shouted the incredible news from the top of the stairs, then ran back in and hugged him, crying happily.

Cindy was in the kitchen making dinner, and nearly caused a fire as she ran upstairs leaving the gas stove on. Luckily, Viorica, the Romanian nurse, came in minutes later and shut off the gas before she ran upstairs as well, finding Cindy and the two girls in tears, standing around their husband and father, taking turns hugging and kissing him.

It took another week for Frosty to be able to get out of bed, his muscles degenerated from three months of non-use, then another month of intensive physiotherapy to be able to walk at all, and when the announcement came that he was going to be knighted by Charles himself in his own house, together with William, Harry, Kate and the kids, he started taking walks around the block, so when the time came, he would be ready and would not falter.

Meanwhile, he began to receive guests. Everyone wanted a piece of him.

Jemma, Jake and the boys came as soon as the doctors determined his condition was stable, and together with Cindy sat around his bed bringing him up to date. They all described their ordeal in great detail even managing to laugh a bit now that they were in the safety of their own homes. Gabi and Colin had been having some nightmares but to everyone's relief, no one seemed to have been suffering any long-term severe psychological effects though they were all getting treatment from MI5 psychologists.

That was the first Frosty had heard of Reed's and Dylan Oliver's death, which upset him greatly. Everyone from PM Webster, Home Secretary Ross, Bishop, the chief of police, the head of MI6, the defense secretary, the mayor of London, and the entire cabinet had resigned their posts, and elections were set for spring. They told him of Dixon's demise and what little they knew of White's ongoing interrogation, thankfully pointing out his disclosure of three more London sites with explosives ready to detonate which were successfully disarmed by police bomb squads.

Jemma had supplied the list she had kept in her pants pocket throughout their ordeal, of the conspirators recruited to SO1, she had found while researching at the Chisholm house. Simon Lewis and Tompkins were killed because of that list. She then described her current research on the latest background and assessment of which people in the security services, were responsible for the inconceivable fuckup. Jemma had yet to complete her report, but there were many who had failed directly, or indirectly, and it appeared most were recruited from within the UK and had Russian and Muslim backgrounds.

Of the nineteen supposed SO1 conspirators, the fifteen who were on Jemma's list and the four who had been at the Embassy Row site, including Dixon and White, two were killed at the Embassy Row standoff and two disappeared from there, their whereabouts unclear. Seven were killed at the cottage; the two Dixon bodyguards and the 212 pilot were being interrogated at an undisclosed location. Two were killed at the SO1 Comms room takeover led by Olga the late Andy Taylor, but the two bodyguards who were left to watch over Frosty at the hospital had fled and were yet to be located.

Edwards and Harriet came next telling him of Taylor's fate, and of Olga who was paralyzed from the waist down, having been hit by a bullet to her spine. Edwards told of the Flanagan mansion takeover and Harriet described in detail the events at the PM's crisis room during the negotiations for the children and the Prince.

Bishop and Ross came soon after and described the chaos that had been going on since the success of releasing William. A big debate had gone on in Webster's cabinet and in the House of Commons, as to how to retaliate against the Russians, and whether to demand reparations for the damage done both physically and financially to the kingdom, not to mention the great loss of life. It was argued by many that continuing on with the plan for the LNG terminals, supplying Europe with oil and natural gas from America as an alternative to Russian pipelines, and decreasing Russian Gas and Oil supply, was punishment enough.

But many disagreed, claiming good old England was back where it had all begun, only with 489 dead, thousands wounded, great damage to London's infrastructure, Heathrow's terminal 5, and the main tourist attractions, not to mention the long uphill battle to get the pound trading back where it had been.

Webster had argued that although it was the Russians behind the attacks, the masses were not aware of the fact and were still blaming Muslims and the "Sons of Jihad" who had been at the forefront. He claimed the Kremlin would deny any involvement and could get the international community to support their cause to block American oil from reaching Europe. England could end up without any real compensation and would have to defend its LNG program.

Of course, the Russians could and would reduce oil prices to compete, but would not be able to break the pact England had signed with its European allies if England refrained from openly pointing to the Kremlin as responsible for the attacks. He offered to personally meet with each and every European leader and reveal the truth behind the attacks, but publicly he believed they should be careful with accusations of Russian involvement.

Webster thought the place to hurt the Russians was to raise interest on their pending debts and loans to European and American banks, claiming they needed the extra cash to recoup their losses on the Sterling devaluation and to restore London's infrastructure.

"No one in his right mind would criticize England for increasing interests in loans and debt to recoup the damage done," he had said in an emotional plea, knowing he had very little influence left, if any, now that he had resigned.

But his arguments were widely adopted by most MPs and, although there were endless rumors in the press, no official word blaming the Russians had come out of number 10.

Bond came with Camilla. They had become a couple and announced their engagement by Frosty's bed making everyone beam with pleasure. Both had attended Barry's and Blake's funerals in Glasgow where they met Devlin who had described his own brush with the affair, fleeing his house under sniper fire, with his family, and getting word to Webster of Dixon's involvement through the Minister of Education Dr. Abigail Dalton, who was once Ali's college mate.

They also told of Reuben Santana's widely televised honorary funeral with nineteen other London police officers killed in action during the crisis; Camilla described in tears her meeting with Santana's father Jose, and two half-sisters who arrived from Brazil, for the first time. She also testified in front of the investigation committee describing the battle at the MI5 interrogation site at Embassy Row, and her own incarceration there by White and his people.

Privately, she confided in Jemma and Cindy, telling them that though it was quite a short time after losing Santana, she felt a great bond had formed between her and Bond, who being ten years her senior, had not left her side in the three months since their release and that she had fallen for him and felt a great need to formalize their relationship, eager to have children of her own.

The only ones not to arrive were Noah and Mary Chisholm, who Frosty finally met at the ceremony with all the dignitaries and did not have enough time to properly host them. Feeling unfulfilled, they would all travel later to Bath for a visit to the house they had found shelter in. Noah and Mary would be honored as well at the ceremony.

The night before the ceremony, a contingent of MI5 agents and police came by to inspect the street, SO1 being totally dismantled for the time being. They took up positions on both ends of the S-shaped street and along parallel streets and by morning had the entire area sealed off.

The group of inductees which included Bond and Camilla, Noah and Mary Chisholm, the Frost and Hammond families, the Devlin family, AVM Alan

Reed's widow, the late Barry, George and Tim Blake's families, Simon Lewis's parents, and Harry Fleming's widow, had gathered early at the house making final preparations for the momentous day.

The entourage came at noon. Charles and Camilla stepping out of a Rolls Royce limousine, behind them, Prince William who most were seeing for the first time since their release, Kate and the kids, Prince Harry, and the rest of the royal family. Webster, acting as interim PM was there, Nigel Scott, Abigail Dalton, the interim foreign minister, defense minister, and several MPs.

The press was there in hoards, newspaper and television correspondents, TV anchors setting up shop in front of Frosty and Cindy's house, cameras flashing and a general buzz of anticipation sweeping over the crowd, onlookers being kept at bay by a ring of police guard.

A small stage was erected in front of the house and Nigel Scott, acting as master of ceremonies, took center stage recapping what they had all gathered for. Then Prince William stood up in front of the mic to a loud cheer, immaculately dressed in a suit and tie, he looked over at the group who had not three months ago been in the jaws of death and evil and had managed to slip out.

He commended the SAS and SBS teams and the people they had lost without mentioning names, the air force, the military, and the police, omitting mention of the security services, the subject of great public outrage and ongoing investigations, though many of them like Harriet, Edwards, and Bishop had carried the load.

"This was a carefully executed attack on our nation, planned for many years, intending to put fear into our hearts, destroy our prominence, and weaken our resolve. But it failed, and we've come through, gallantly, and in such a way that could make us even stronger."

William looked at the group sitting by his side and smiled.

"But if there is one person who deserves credit above everyone else, it's this man, Adrian Frost, who the conspiracy tried to frame, but who stood his ground and saved the day."

A loud cheer arose as Frosty stood gingerly up, smiling shyly and nodding to the crowd, the cameras catching him from every angle.

"Much will be said and written about what Mr. Frost did, some of it will be true, some of it made-up, and most of it will remain forever classified, but his tenacity and resolve, staying true to his role, is why all of us, including me, are safe here today."

A loud applause rocked the neighborhood as William invited Frosty to stand in front of his dad, and they made him a knight.

Among the crowd of correspondents and media personnel, stood an ordinary-dressed woman with a media badge for the New York Times, a blonde wig covering her short black hair, wearing sunglasses that hid her long taut face, blue eyes, and pug nose, her sculpted lips pressed tight, as she watched the ceremony, videoing its entirety with her mobile phone, zooming in on a few of the faces.

When it was over, she slipped quietly away from the crowd and walked to Edgware station where she took the Northern line south, got off at Tottenham Court Road, and walked toward Oxford Circus, the Central line still under construction on both ends of the station damaged in the attacks.

She reached the roundabout, turned south on Regent Street, then back east on Great Marlborough Street, reached her hotel, overlooking Carnaby Street, scurried up to her room, unlocked her suitcase, took out her computer, downloaded her video to its hard drive, and sent it away, deleting the hard drive when she was done.

THE END